CROSSROADS TO DESTINY

SENTINEL WITCHES BOOK 1

Also By Tora Moon

Legends of Lairheim (Science-Fantasy)

Ancient Enemies
Ancient Allies
The Scourge Incursion
Exile's Vengeance
Redemption

The Sentinel Witches (Urban Fantasy)

Crossroads to Destiny
Descent Into Darkness
Well of Sorrows

Indie Author Guides

Business & Accounting for Authors
Author Business Plan Workbook (forthcoming)

To get an up-to-date listing of all my books or to purchase visit
www.ToraMoon.com

Crossroads to Destiny

Sentinel Witches Book 1

Tora Moon

Lunar Alchemy Publishing

Acknowledgments

An author may sit alone at the computer, but no book is completed without help. A big shout out to my beta reader team: Christa Murry, Kelly Young, LaRinda Lollis, Michele Zaiontz, Paul Richardson, and Shelby Geddings. I appreciate your comments and feedback which made this a much better story.

To my writing buddy and friend, Stephanie Groberg, my deepest gratitude for your support, our long talks deep into the night about story and life, and our writing sprints. You keep me going.

My thanks to my reader, Michelle Vandaley, who named the metaphysical shop Catlyn works at, Mystical Enchantments. Also thanks to Lisa Moon (no relation) for naming Catlyn's crystal jewelry business, Moonstones and Moonbeams. Both had characters named after them for their help.

To my friend, Dana Phillips, without our journey together I wouldn't have rediscovered my love for writing stories and my deep passion for it. You gave me hope and wouldn't let me give up!

And especially to my daughter, Sasha, you have made me become a better person by being your parent. I couldn't have asked for a more amazing daughter.

Thank you to all my readers. Thank you for spending time with my stories and letting me be a part of your life. I hope you love them as much I loved writing them.

*To all those who fight the good fight...
not all demons are monsters.*

 # CHAPTER 1 

Stopped at the red light, Catlyn Hennessey glanced across the street. A mass of bodies stood impatiently waiting for the "walk" signal to begin their day at the amusement park. Movement, weaving through the traffic, and headed toward the crowd, caught her attention. "Not again! I can't be seeing this!" She squeezed her eyes shut and fingered her pendant. *Please don't be there. Please don't be there.* She cracked one eye open.

The ugly creature continued to scurry across the street on its mismatched legs. Fascinated, she tilted her head, puzzled at how it moved with one leg hoofed like a goat and the other a skinny crow's foot. The bells tied around its squat, barrel-shaped body jangled as it ran-hopped to the throng at the crosswalk.

The crowd ignored the creature weaving through them, as if they couldn't see it. Using its sharp two-pronged stick carried in its lobster-claw appendage, it poked a burly man wearing a loud tropical shirt. Catlyn shuddered at its bone-chilling cackle as the man jumped and rubbed his buttocks. He turned to glare at the man in a business suit standing behind him. The creature skittered in front of the businessman, and blue electrical pulses flashed on the end of the creature's other appendage. Electricity arced from it to strike the tourist in the chest. He roared with rage and threw a heavy fist at the businessman, catching him squarely on the jaw and knocking him back.

The businessman tottered backwards from the blow. Using its stick, the creature knocked the man's feet out from under him, making it appear that his foot had slipped off the curb. As he lost his balance, the burly tourist desperately tried to catch him, only to brush the businessman's suit with his fingertips. Aghast, the tourist watched the businessman tumble in front of the semi-truck rumbling up the road. With another cackle, the creature disappeared.

"No!" Catlyn screamed. But unless she had magic—which she devoutly wished she had, and not for the first time—she couldn't stop the accident.

The stoplight changed, and she eased through the intersection. As she passed the incident, the burly tourist stood shaking, his face twisted into horrified incredulity.

By the time Catlyn found a place to turn around and returned to the scene, the police had arrived. She pulled into the nearby lot and parked. Her hands shook as she turned off the ignition and opened the car door. Putting on her big, floppy hat to protect her pale face from the autumn sun—she didn't need any more freckles—she walked to the gathered crowd.

Catlyn passed the burly tourist, who sat on the curb in handcuffs. He muttered repeatedly, "I didn't mean to hurt him. I tried to stop him from falling. What the hell happened?"

A woman stood behind the tourist, sobbing and staring at the sheet covering the man hit by the truck. Two children clung to her legs. Catlyn's heart ached for the family. Their visit to the happiest place on earth had turned into terror and tragedy.

Several people huddled around the police, talking. Catlyn stepped toward them, then halted, touching her gold seven-pointed star pendant with a small diamond in the center like a talisman. She wanted to help, but how could she explain what she'd seen? The police would never believe her if she told them some evil creature had caused the accident. They'd haul her away and test her for drugs, or worse, throw her in a psychiatric ward.

Before she could turn back to her car, a young policeman approached her, notepad in hand. "Did you see it too?"

"Yes, Officer, I saw what happened. I was at the stoplight." Catlyn pointed across the street. "I had a clear view. The tourist thought the businessman struck him with a Taser, and he hit back. When he realized the man was falling into the traffic, he grabbed his shirt and tried to pull him to safety, but he couldn't."

The officer's forehead puckered. "I'm sorry, ma'am. Are you sure? Everyone else says the man just started acting erratically and pushed the victim into the truck."

Catlyn put her hands on her hips. "I know what I saw. That man didn't push the businessman. It was an accident."

The policeman raised an eyebrow, clearly disbelieving her. The quiet muttering of the tourist drew her attention. Sympathy welled in her chest. She couldn't let him go to prison for something he didn't do. Especially when it'd been that evil creature's fault. "A strange creature caused it," she blurted. "It knocked the businessman off his feet and into the truck." The officer rolled his eyes at her, then shooed her off. When she tried to approach the tourist to offer him support, the police blocked her way.

Trembling with frustration and anger, Catlyn tromped back to her old green Honda Civic, climbed into it, and turned it on. Over the last few weeks, she'd started seeing some weird things, but this was the worst.

The first episode had been two weeks ago while she was waiting in line at the coffee shop. The woman in front of her tucked her hair behind her ears, revealing their pointed tips. When Catlyn leaned forward to get a better look, the woman's ears had returned to normal. A few days later, a young man at the grocery store had morphed into a satyr and gave Catlyn a suggestive leer. She'd blushed and averted her gaze when his dark fur didn't hide his erection. When she'd turned back, he'd been nothing more than an attractive young man, grinning at her. When he approached her, she'd been so embarrassed, she'd hurried away.

A few nights ago, when she'd taken her garbage to the dumpster, she noticed her neighbor walking his dog. But the dog had three heads, and her neighbor had long black hair curling around his waist. As he passed her, she swore she'd heard the hissing of snakes. Tossing her trash in the bin, she'd glanced back at her neighbor, who was once again his normal bald self, walking his pit bull.

Catlyn left the parking lot, pulling back onto the busy street, then took the on-ramp to the 5-South freeway. Her hands shook on her steering wheel. Taking deep breaths, she tried to calm down before she reached the metaphysical shop. It would be impossible for her to do any energy healing work or tarot readings as rattled as she was by the accident—and the ugly creature. She fingered her pendant, the only thing she had of her mother's. Touching it eased her nerves as she maneuvered through the heavy Southern California traffic.

Thirty minutes later, Catlyn turned into the parking lot of Mystical Enchantments, the metaphysical bookstore where she rented a room for her healing work. She couldn't have clients visit her in her little one-bedroom apartment located on the edge of a dicey barrio. She also worked the cash register and was one of the tarot readers for the store.

Catlyn parked her car in the rear under the shade of the trees. Even though Costa Mesa was only a few miles from the Pacific Ocean, it was still hot in the middle of September. As she reached to open the shop's back door, she jerked her hand away with a gasp, blinking. A fiery salamander slept curled around the handle.

Feeling silly, Catlyn muttered, "Excuse me, Salamander, I need to get into the shop."

The creature opened its ruby-red eyes and examined her a moment before uncurling from the handle and slithering down the door. With a swish of its long tail, it climbed onto the hood of her boss's car, turned around in a circle like a cat, and laid down. It winked at her, then disappeared.

Catlyn rubbed her eyes, unsure she'd actually seen the magical creature. But when she touched the door handle, she jerked her hand back, hissing at the intense heat left by the mysterious salamander. Wrapping the handle with the fabric of her long skirt, she opened the door.

The welcoming blast of the air conditioner blew into her face. She lifted her damp hair off her neck and turned around, letting the air cool her down. After unlocking her healing room, she tucked her purse into a cubbyhole and wandered into the shop. Shelves filled with books were mixed with glass display cabinets, holding crystals, figurines, candles, and other "witchy" products. The scent of a light incense lingered in the air. Rainbows glinted across the large room from the crystal pendants and wind chimes hanging in the front window.

Michelle Vandaley, the shop's owner, leaned over the glass counter. Her long, light-brown hair falling over her face as she showed a customer some jewelry. A thrill went through Catlyn, when the customer held up the piece. It was one of hers. Crossing her fingers, she hung back. When the woman purchased the wire-wrapped amethyst and matching earrings, Catlyn darted behind a display and did a silent, happy dance. She needed the sale. After the customer left, Catlyn approached the counter.

Michelle smiled at her, the corners of her pale-blue eyes crinkling. "Hey, Catlyn. Is it that late already?"

"Actually, I'm later than I wanted to be." Catlyn walked through the store and leaned against the front counter, fiddling with the pendulums on display. "There was a horrible accident on Harbor Blvd where someone was killed. I saw it happen."

"That's awful! You still look pale, honey. Let's clear off that nasty energy hanging around you."

Michelle picked up a bundle of white sage leaves tied together and a lighter from the counter as she walked around it. She gestured for Catlyn to stand in front of her. Lighting the herb, Michelle blew on it until it smoked. Starting at Catlyn's head and working down her body to her feet, she waved the smoking sage through Catlyn's aura. Catlyn turned around for Michelle to do the same for her back. Lightness filled Catlyn as the smoke cleared the negative energy clinging to her. She breathed in the clean smell, and with a whoosh, exhaled, releasing any lingering distress of what she'd seen.

"There, much better. Go sit down, and I'll fix you a mug of tea." Michelle gestured toward the small table which held an electric teapot, mugs, and an assortment of teas. Customers could pour themselves a cup of tea to sip while they wandered the store. Comfy chairs sat near the table for customers to sit while they waited for their tarot reading or healing session.

Catlyn settled on a chair and a few minutes later sipped from the cup Michelle handed her, savoring the calming chamomile tea. She considered telling Michelle about the creature she'd seen that caused the accident, but hesitated. Michelle was a gifted clairvoyant and claimed to see all manner of strange things. But everything Michelle mentioned were friendly faeries and unicorns, or elementals, or even the Goddess in one of Her many forms. She'd never talked about seeing anything like the evil beast Catlyn had witnessed earlier. When Catlyn told her about the accident, she left out the creature.

The tea and talking about the incident settled her nerves. Catlyn put her empty cup down, then took a deep breath. "Did you know you have a salamander hanging around your shop?"

Michelle whooped. "You saw her! Lorgandy is my friend. She protects the shop." She leaned over the table and hugged Catlyn. "I'm so proud. Your third eye is opening. You've been working on it for a long time."

"She isn't the only thing I've seen recently," Catlyn confessed. "I've also seen someone I'm sure is an elf and another person who is a satyr."

"Have you told Jade yet? She'd be ecstatic."

Catlyn made a face. "No, I haven't."

"You know you're acting like a child, refusing to speak to Jade as long as you have." Michelle placed a hand over Catlyn's. "Jade has always had your best interests at heart. She was only trying to protect you."

"More like put me in a glass bubble and not let me out," Catlyn huffed, jerking her hand back, and crossing her arms over her chest. "I'm twenty-five years old, Michelle, not fifteen. I moved out of my Aunt Lucy and Uncle Robert's house to be on my own and make my own choices. My godmother doesn't need to monitor my every move—or to scare away my boyfriends."

Michelle raised an eyebrow. "Doug used you and treated you like shit. You deserve better. I'm glad Jade scared him off."

"Doug was just the last straw for me! What about Phillip or George or any of my other boyfriends she intimidated? They weren't all assholes."

"None of them were right for you either."

"But I want to make my own mistakes and not have Jade rescue me all the time."

"Remember, no matter what, your godmother loves you and would do anything for you. You're the daughter she never had. You should forgive her."

"Okay, I'll think about it." Catlyn glanced at the clock. "Enough chatting. I have a client coming in for a healing appointment in a few minutes. I need to get ready."

Maybe she should call her godmother and talk to her about the weird things happening to her. Catlyn dug her phone out of her purse, her finger hovering over the call button for Jade's number. But did she want to get into another argument with her? Rolling her eyes at the thought, she tossed the phone onto a small table. Other than the evil creature this morning, none of the things she'd seen appeared harmful. Although the satyr was a bit shocking, the incident was more embarrassing than anything else. If that changed, she'd talk to Jade.

As she prepped her room for her first client, her conversation with Michelle floated through her mind. Was it simply her third-eye opening, allowing her to see the magical in the world? Or was something else going on with her? In the past few weeks she'd had twinges where she felt like something inside her was pushing to be let out.

 # CHAPTER 2 

Detective Sean McLarkin pushed the large file away from him and leaned back in his chair. It didn't matter how many times he perused it, clues of when the damned serial killer would strike next still eluded him. Even after chasing the murderer for nearly three years, Sean wasn't any closer now to stopping the homicides than when he'd caught the first case. He didn't need to pull up the case files to see the gruesome images of that first crime scene. He closed his eyes and was instantly transported back to that awful day.

Strange symbols decorated the floor, and he could glimpse a few from behind the blood-soaked walls. Surprisingly, the floor was only speckled with a few drops of blood. A creak drew his attention from the bloody walls to the middle of the room. Hanging in the exact center of the pentagram drawn on the floor, a large oblong metal box swayed on a chain. It appeared like a coffin. After lowering it, two techs with crowbars pried it open.

It popped apart with a sickening squelch, revealing a mangled body with spikes protruding from it. Sean covered his mouth with the back of his hand, choking on the sudden bile. His partner lost his battle and ran from the room so he wouldn't contaminate the crime scene. Sean stepped closer to the case to inspect the spikes attached to every side. He touched a gloved finger to one of them, jerking his hand from the razor sharp point.

Sean shook his head, dispelling the memory. When he'd been young, his granny had taken him to an exhibit of medieval torture devices. She'd paid special attention to those used during the witch trials. He'd recognized the case as a replica of one of the worst: an iron maiden. The brutal contraption would make anyone, innocent or not, confess to doing anything the interrogators demanded of them.

Later, the autopsy revealed the victim was a woman and had been alive when the metal spikes impaled her. She had been the first of three victims over the course of the next three days, each killed in the same wicked way. The device had earned the killer his name: The Iron Maiden Killer.

The first victim had been a simple hairdresser. There had been no reason to torture her; she didn't have any secrets. Neither did any of the other victims.

At first, the murders were only in Orange County, but then, after a few months, they popped up all over southern California. They occurred in Los Angeles, Orange, and Riverside counties, with Orange County hit with the brunt of the murders. The killings stopped for six months as unexpectedly as they'd begun. Sean had hoped whatever motivated the killer had been satisfied. But then they discovered another victim.

The strange break between the murders raised his suspicions, and he broadened his investigation outside of Southern California, or So Cal as the locals called it. He found murders with the same deranged signature in Las Vegas, San Francisco, Portland, Seattle, Phoenix, and Denver had transpired during the six-month hiatus.

After that first killing spree, the next murders happened once a month, like clockwork, but never on the same day of the month or week. Except eighteen months ago, there'd been another spate of murders over three days. Thirty months and thirty-six victims later, Sean still couldn't figure out the exact timing. As ritualistic as the rest of the killings were, the timing must mean something to the perpetrators. He'd considered everything he could think of, such as tide tables, obscure holidays, and even anniversaries of historical events, to no avail.

Besides the iron maiden, the killer employed other torture devices once used in the inquisitions and witch hunting days. It made Sean wonder if he had a modern-day witch hunt on his hands. But his investigation showed none of the victims had any connection with Wicca or any of the other pagan religions he'd heard about. Although, he'd found most had a collection of crystals, or used herbs, or preferred alternative healing to traditional Western medicine, but that didn't make them witches.

The victims came from all walks of life, races, genders, and ages—thankfully none of them were children—and they didn't seem to have anything connecting them. They weren't acquaintances, nor did they frequent the same places. Most serial killers had a preference, but if this one had one, Sean hadn't discovered it. It seemed like the murderer chose the victims at random. The lack of preference pointed to more than one person committing the crime, and Sean had suspicions of who was the leader. But he lacked any proof. Yet.

"Hey, McLarkin, wake up!" Jerry rapped on Sean's desk. "We've caught a case. Another weird one."

Sean straightened the case folder, then ran a hand through his short, sandy-blond hair. "What is it this time?"

"Some tourist pushed a guy into the street in front of a truck." Lourdes stroked his short brown beard, peppered with gray. "You won't believe what he claims."

"Don't tell me, another 'the devil made me do it,' claim."

"You got it. I don't know where these whack jobs are coming from. It seems like they're oozing out of the woodwork lately."

Sean stood up, buckled on his gun, and grabbed his light jacket. "Let's go."

As they ambled to Sean's black Camaro, Lourdes continued. "The mayor wants this solved pronto. He says it's bad for business when the tourists kill each other in front of the happiest place on earth."

By the time Sean and Jerry arrived at the scene, the patrolmen had sent the gawkers on their way. Sean noticed the police wave away a petite, buxom woman in a floppy hat. When she tried to talk to the handcuffed man, the officer stopped her. Puzzled at the behavior, he watched her stalk to her beat up old Honda and drive away.

"What was that about?" Sean asked the officer.

"Just another nutcase. She claims this guy didn't do it, but a strange monster-like creature caused the accident."

Sean rolled his eyes. "Trust the So Cal crazies to come out. Did you get her name?"

"Of course."

The officer introduced the suspect as Brad Maxwell, a veterinarian on vacation with his family from Montana.

"Tell me what happened," Sean said.

"My family and I were standing at the traffic light waiting to cross the street when it felt like a cattle prod zapped me from behind. I'm ashamed that I instinctively reacted and punched him." Brad lowered his head. "But I didn't think I'd hit him that hard. I couldn't believe it when I saw the man tottering on the curb about to fall off. That truck," —the man gulped and closed his eyes— "it came out of nowhere. I tried grabbing the man, but it felt like his suit was as slick as an oiled hog, and my hand slipped off. I couldn't save him."

The veterinarian whispered the last words. Sean considered his next question.

"I know you're going to think I'm crazy," Brad implored, his eyes haunted. "But I didn't do it. A monster tripped that guy and pushed him into traffic."

"Yeah, you're that monster," Lourdes sneered.

"No. A real monster, like what you see in the movies, only uglier and nastier. I caught a glimpse of him, laughing up a storm as the truck hit that poor man."

Sean scrutinized the parking lot where the Honda had parked. Something strange was going on if two people saw the same thing. But how in the world would he put this in his report? He could imagine the headlines now: Cop claims demon monster killed local businessman. He'd be laughed off the force—and he'd never solve the Iron Maiden Killer case. But he had to wonder. This wasn't the first incident in the past few weeks with violent outbursts by people abruptly killing their families or strangers. None of whom had any criminal behavior or records before the event. Afterward they claimed seeing outlandish creatures, or smelling sulfur, or hearing chilling laughter. Was Orange County possessed by evil creatures?

As he drove back to the station, his thoughts flew to his Granny Eileen and the tales she'd told him when he was little. They featured demons killing humans. A shiver went through him. What if they weren't simply stories? But that was crazy, wasn't it?

Catlyn sank onto the floor of her healing room in front of her small altar in the corner. The massage table dominated the center of the room. Her crystal bowls filled the top of a cabinet. The biggest one, about 30" in diameter, sat next to her altar. Inside the cabinet, dishes of various stones and crystals waited. Candles around the room created a soft ambiance. The clean, fresh scent of white sage smoke lingered in the air.

She had half an hour before her last client of the evening arrived, and after her busy afternoon, Tora used the time to rest and regroup her energy. As her mind quieted, the morning's accident replayed, eating away at what little serenity she'd gained while she'd worked with her clients. *What was that foul creature?* She believed in magical beings and knew if those beings of light and love existed, there had to be those who were evil. Why was she seeing such things?

A short time later, she heard Amelia's high heels clicking on the linoleum floor as she hurried through the store toward Catlyn's healing room. Catlyn stood and waited by the door. Amelia's short skirt showed off her long legs and her silky blouse clung to her generous bosom. The beauty ran a hand through her blond locks that fell to her waist. She hung her designer purse on a hook before slumping into the chair beside the door.

"Sorry I'm late, Catlyn," Amelia said, sliding off her shoes. "Traffic on the 405 was horrendous, even at this time of night. It took me forty-five minutes to drive from Huntington Beach to the 55 interchange. And as I was getting ready to leave, my boss ripped me a new one about the brochures I've been working on for days. He didn't like the graphics, and they were the ones he wanted me to use! I swear, if I could find another job, I would. I'm so stressed and really need this session."

Catlyn smiled at Amelia's non-stop rambling and patted the massage table. "Is there anything else you want to focus on?"

Amelia maneuvered onto the table, tugging at her skirt before laying down. She grinned. "I might have a new boyfriend! He's a gorgeous blond with blue eyes and a body to dream about—and oh, how I've dreamed about it—and rich. I met him at the Red Orchid the other night. Damn, he's a good kisser."

An unsettling chill skittered down Catlyn's spine as Amelia spoke about the new guy. Catlyn's pendant from her mother warmed against her skin. She rubbed the gooseflesh on her arms, troubled by the clanging warning bells of her intuition. "Don't tell me you slept with him."

"No, I didn't," Amelia huffed, sounding affronted. "I don't sleep with every man I meet."

Catlyn refrained from rolling her eyes. Amelia had a free spirit and a bubbly, out-going nature. Her blond hair, blue eyes, and curvaceous body attracted men like bees to a flower. Amelia drank it in and didn't say no often.

"At least not yet. He has to take me out on a proper date before he gets any of my honey." Amelia's wink held mischievous delight. "I'm so excited. I ran into him again this morning while grabbing coffee before work. He wants to see me tonight."

"Be careful, Amelia. I have a bad feeling about him." Catlyn's earlier conversation with Michelle played in her mind. Was she being a hypocrite? Should she try keeping her client and friend from getting hurt by a jerk while she was angry at Jade for doing the same thing to her? She set the thought aside as she lit a sage bundle and smudged Amelia's aura. Before she put it out, Catlyn paused and ran the smoke through her own.

Catlyn spread a soft, multi-colored blanket over Amelia's prone body. She moved to stand at Amelia's head and closed her eyes, focusing on attuning with her client's energy. Letting her intuition guide her, she selected various crystals from the trays sitting inside the cabinet. She laid the ruby-zoisite wand on the table beside Amelia's left arm. Catlyn next placed a brown marble wand along with a piece of raw kyanite at Amelia's feet. She gently laid a rose quartz heart on Amelia's chest and a chunk of citrine went on her solar plexus. Catlyn continued to place the stones she felt called to use on or around Amelia. Catlyn turned back to the table and picked up the suede-wrapped striker. She ran it around the lip of her largest crystal bowl, drawing out its deep tones. As she worked, she chanted softly, singing words from an unknown language that flowed from the Goddess.

An hour later, the ringing tones of the crystal bowls reverberated in the small room. Amelia's breath flowed in a deep, even pace. Now relaxed, the lines of tension and stress eased from her face.

Catlyn narrowed her eyes and examined Amelia's aura. Normally, she simply felt the energy and took it on faith what she was sensing. But all day, she'd been seeing colors and patterns in her client's auras. Frowning at the dense, charcoal-gray energy swirling sluggishly above Amelia's pancreas, Catlyn did more energy work on the area until it moved more freely. Sensing she'd done all she could for the day, she gently removed the stones, then combed and patted Amelia's aura back in place. She settled quietly on a stool in the corner, closing her eyes while she waited for Amelia to stir.

After a few minutes, Amelia blinked her eyes and stretched. "It was wonderful, Catlyn." She stretched again and yawned. "I always feel so much better when you're done."

Pleased with the compliment, Catlyn smiled, then pursed her lips as she debated telling Amelia what she'd seen. Finally, concern for her friend and client won out. "I sensed something off with your pancreas, Amelia. You might want to make changes to your lifestyle and eating habits."

Amelia sat up and swung her legs over the side of the table. "I eat when I'm stressed out at work, which is all the time. My boss is always on my case. I can't seem to do anything right."

"It sounds like you need to find a different job."

"I've been looking. The job market sucks right now. At least the one I have pays well." Amelia hopped off the table. "Hey, I'm going to the Red Orchid tonight. Do you want to come with me?" Amelia smiled. "Come on, it will be fun. Have a few drinks, dance with hunky men, maybe even see the guy I told you about. My treat—well, my boss's treat. He owns the club, so we get discounts on the drinks."

Catlyn shook her head. "Thanks, but not tonight. It's been a long, tiring day. I'm not up to going out. Another time?"

"Sure, sure."

Catlyn hugged Amelia, then escorted her through the darkened store, unlocking the door to let her out. She returned to her healing room and cleared the crystals she'd used with sage smoke. Still feeling unsettled, she sank onto the floor before her small altar, staring at the candle flame and rubbing her arms. She jumped when the window rattled from the Santa Ana winds blowing off the San Bernardino desert. Shivers raced down her spine. *What can I do to calm my spirit?* As she took a deep, cleansing breath, she caught the unmistakable scent of salt and seaweed. The ocean called to her.

Smiling at the omen, Catlyn packed her smaller frame drum into a bag, blew out the candles, and locked up the shop. She'd have enough light with the nearly full moon for a night visit to the beach. Before climbing into her car, she picked a rose from the bushes growing by the shop. It only took her a few minutes to drive the short distance from Costa Mesa to the Pacific Coast Highway and her favorite beach.

CHAPTER 3

The moon glinted on the ocean waves and lit Catlyn's path down the high bluffs to the beach. As she settled her bag more securely over her shoulder, a dull *whomp* sounded as the drum inside bumped against her leg. The air smelled fresh and clean, with the sharp notes of the desert plants on the bluff. She paused in her walk down the steep incline to rest her burning thighs and watched a rabbit hop from the underbrush. A night bird trilled. Taking a deep breath revived her soul.

She stepped off the path and onto soft sand. Before going further, she took off her shoes and tucked them into her bag. The ocean breeze snatched at her long skirt, whipping it around her legs. Catlyn grabbed it and strode to the water's edge. Only the waves greeted her on the empty beach. The cold water kissed her toes, and she bent, placing a loving hand on a wavelet.

"Greetings, Yemaya," she whispered. An unexpected wave crashed over her feet and reached for her skirt's hem. Laughing, she danced away, barely avoiding getting wet. The ocean's serenity drew a song from her, and she sang as she walked along the edge of the waves. Her spirit more at ease, she stopped walking. Putting her bag on the sand—well above the waterline—she took out the rose. After plucking the petals from the stem, she picked up her frame drum and went back to the water.

"Yemaya, guide me on my path," she prayed. "Show me what I need to know. Help me understand what is happening to me."

Reverently, she offered the rose petals to the goddess, scattering them on the waves. As she watched the ocean, she played her drum. Soon a dark shape cut through the water near the break in the waves. Dolphins always came when she drummed to the ocean.

A low moan coming from the ocean underscored her drumbeat. Her fingers stumbled at the sound, breaking her rhythm. When a long, sinewy neck rose from beyond the breakwaters, she gasped, the drum slipping from her hands. She caught it mere inches from plunging into the wet sand. When she looked back at the water, the creature had disappeared. *Now I'm seeing water monsters! What's next? Dragons?*

Catlyn resumed drumming, attempting to restore the sense of peace the beautiful night had brought her. A short time later, the sensation of someone watching pricked her senses, interrupting her reverie. Her pendant laying between her breasts burned. It did that sometimes when she was in danger. She believed her departed mother watched over her and sent her messages through the amulet. She stopped playing, lowered her drum to her side, and looked up and down the beach, confirming she was alone. The feeling continued.

A man stood on the bluff above her, the breeze billowing his long-sleeved shirt. Darkness hid his features, but not the intense scrutiny he gave her. Her body shuddered, completely creeped out by the man.

Afraid and uncomfortable, she hurried to stuff her drum into her bag. When she looked back up, the man had vanished. Remembering Jade's self-defense lessons, she dug her keys out of her bag. Jade had insisted on teaching her some martial arts moves, even though Catlyn didn't want to learn it. She gripped her keys in her hand with the pointy edges out.

Sweat trickled down her back and her legs trembled as she crossed the sand to the path leading up the bluff and to the parking lot. She trudged up the steep hill, wishing she had a walking staff with her. It would help her up the slope, and she could use it for protection if she needed it.

Catlyn's eyes darted from side to side, searching for any sign of the strange man. She tensed when she heard a rustle in the bushes and nearly jumped out of her skin when a rabbit hopped out.

By the time she reached her car, she was shaking, her shoulder blades hurt from scrunching them, and she was panting hard. Her little Honda Civic waited for her alone in the parking lot. Her heart hammered in her chest. She hadn't seen any car lights nor heard an engine.

Catlyn tossed her bag into the trunk, whispering a quick apology when her drum thumped. As she closed the lid, a shadow passed over the moon. A shiver of fear snaked down her spine. Above her, a dark shape floated past. *I must be imagining things. There's no way that was a dragon!* Nervous laughter burst from her. The strange man was merely one more on the long list of weird stuff her mind was conjuring up for her. She warily watched the road behind her, glad when nothing more happened on her drive home.

The next afternoon, Catlyn rushed from her apartment, flinging her damp hair over her shoulder. She clicked her tongue, frustrated about spending too much time working on the necklace and earring set she was making for a customer. If she didn't hurry, she'd be late meeting her best friends, Bri Nelson and Lisa Moon, for lunch at their favorite Mexican restaurant.

Catlyn jumped into her car, pulling her long skirt in after her before slamming the door shut. Turning her head over her shoulder to back out of her parking space, she froze. A naked pumpkin-orange man, clutching an old-fashioned bellows under his arm, ran behind her car, then vanished.

A few miles later, she drove past the park. Her jaw dropped open when a woman with long, honey-blond hair running with her Doberman shifted into a golden unicorn. Sparks flew from her hooves as they struck the concrete. She glanced in her rearview mirror, and the unicorn was again a normal woman.

Cursing the red light at the next intersection, Catlyn's fingers tapped the steering wheel as she anxiously noted the time. *At least a unicorn is better than those strange, ugly beasts I've been seeing.*

No sooner than she had the thought, a large creature bolted onto the trunk of the car in front of her. It rotated its owl-like head toward her and hissed, revealing a beak filled with needle-sharp fangs. It gathered its long greyhound legs beneath it and, with a last slap of its crocodile tail, bounded away. The driver flung open his door and stomped to the rear of his car, glaring at her. Catlyn raised her hands, mouthing, "It wasn't me!" The driver looked between his car, now with a sizable dent in the top of its trunk, and Catlyn's unmarred bumper. The light changed and Catlyn turned into the next lane and gunned past the perplexed—and angry—man.

What is going on with me? The many sightings of all sorts of mythical creatures had to mean something. She rubbed the center of her forehead, trying to relieve the throbbing there. If anyone could tell her what was happening to her, it would be Jade. For once, Catlyn wanted her godmother's over-protectiveness. She was the most powerful and knowledgeable witch Catlyn knew. For the first time in weeks, she looked forward to seeing and talking to her godmother at the full moon ceremony that evening.

Sean leaned back in his chair, staring at his computer screen, unsure how to write up his report on the strange incident in front of the amusement park. No matter how he worded his questions to Brad Maxwell, the person others claimed to have pushed the victim into the oncoming truck, Brad never changed his story.

Sean called the Montana county sheriff, the only police in the area, to gather more information on the suspect.

"There isn't a gentler man," Sheriff Neilly said, "than Brad, no matter that he still looks like a football linebacker. The Maxwell family are upstanding citizens. Such a tragedy." The sheriff clicked his tongue. "I can't believe Brad would kill someone over a simple thing like a jolt from a cattle prod. He experiences worse injuries tending the local rodeo stock. It's a shame he's been accused of such a horrendous crime. He's running for county commissioner. This accusation will ruin his chances, and he was the front leader. Brad's a close friend. Can you keep me informed about his case?"

"Sure thing," Sean agreed. "Thank you, Sheriff, for the information."

Sean hung up the phone. Nothing about this case made any sense to him, and his gut instincts told him something more was occurring. He scrolled through the file until he found the responding officer's report of the interview with the young woman. Catlyn Hennessey claimed to have seen a strange creature knock the victim into the truck. The officer commented he thought she was whacked out on drugs and seeing things, and her report wasn't believable. Sean wasn't ready to dismiss it so out of hand, but he didn't have any basis or proof.

"Hey McLarkin, Lourdes!" Captain Alex Green shouted as he stomped to his office door, scowling at Sean and his partner. "There's been a riot at The Block, shots fired, multiple people down, including some kids. The press is calling it a terrorist attack. God, I hope it isn't another one of those peculiar cases. Get your asses out there!"

"Yes, sir!" Sean answered, scooting away from his desk. Lourdes scrambled from his chair, and the two men hurried to Sean's car.

"What on earth is going on?" Jerry scrolled through the initial reports coming through on his tablet. "There are multiple accounts of strange green creatures fleeing the scene, cackling ... cackling! Who cackles except witches in movies?"

Sean's stomach clenched as it dropped to his toes. He vaguely remembered a story his Granny Eileen told him about a green demon that delighted in causing mayhem, riots, and chaos. Its whip caused hallucinations. But that cwas only a fairytale to scare children, wasn't it? Demons couldn't be real.

Pure disarray ruled the scene at the shopping mall when they arrived. People lay or sat on the sidewalk, blood pouring from various wounds. Paramedics moved through the crowd, separating the seriously injured from the slightly wounded. There had been an art fair in the center plaza. Oil paintings lay scattered haphazardly, frames broken, canvases ripped, and blood adding a bizarre effect on serene landscapes and idyllic street scenes.

Sean paused at the sight of five corpses covered with white sheets. His heart sank as he observed two were children. There had never been a riot at a peaceful art gathering or shopping mall before. He crouched down by one of the small bodies and lifted the sheet. The boy's face was frozen in a scream of terror. Sean resisted the urge to smooth the boy's features into something more serene. The coroner needed to examine the body as it appeared when the boy died. The second child was a three-year-old little girl, still gripping her stuffed blue bunny tight to her chest. Horror filled her dead, empty eyes. He couldn't see any obvious wounds on the children. Sean dropped the cloth, turning his face away, and rubbed surreptitiously at his eyes.

"What could terrify a child so much?" he mused out loud.

Jerry shook his head. "I don't know. Two of the adults also look like something scared them to death, but the other one, a man, died from a beating." He pointed to the handcuffed people lined up against a store wall. "Those are the culprits."

Sean scowled at the men and raised his eyebrows at the sight of a few women in handcuffs. None of them wore the colors or other obvious gang affiliations. They appeared to be average, everyday citizens. He'd never suspect them capable of flying into such a rage as to pummel a man to death. Their faces all held shocked expressions, similar to what he usually saw on victims.

One woman leaned her head on a man's chest, sobbing. The man attempted to put his arms around her, groaning in frustration when he couldn't because of his handcuffs. Sean studied the group as he approached and shook his head at the image of a dark gray cloud surrounding them. Each person had a long red, swollen mark on them.

"Hey, Lourdes, what do you make of those marks?"

Jerry narrowed his eyes. "From here, if I didn't know any better, I'd say they were welts caused by a whip."

"Brian!" Sean called out. A young man with brown hair, brown eyes, and glasses looked up. Sean motioned to him. He finished placing an evidence marker, then strode over to Sean and Jerry.

"Take pictures of those wounds and have the medical team examine them. It's strange that all the suspects have them."

"Sure thing, boss!" the crime scene analyst said.

"I'll start interviewing on that end." Jerry pointed to the farther group of handcuffed people. "You can talk to the others."

Sean touched his fingers to his forehead in a casual salute. Sometimes the older man forgot they were equals. He strolled to where the obvious couple sat.

"I can't believe we did what they're saying we did, Harold," Sean heard the woman say. "I don't remember anything."

"Neither do I, Lana, neither do I." Harold looked up at Sean's approach. "Are you in charge? We need to call our parents to arrange for them to go care for our children. A babysitter is watching them, but she's just a kid."

"Please, Officer," Lana pleaded. "They're only two and four." She snorted and tried to wipe the snot running from her nose on her shoulder.

"Detective McLarkin." Sean took pity on her, found a tissue, and helped her blow her nose and clean off her face. "Tell me what happened here."

"We were enjoying an afternoon date," Harold said, "admiring the artwork before going to a movie. I saw several strange green creatures scamper through the crowd. I felt a searing pain on my arm. A few moments later, a red welt appeared on it. My eyesight blurred, and the world spun. I remember being terrified of something, something horrible. Then I woke up with screaming in my ears, my fists bloody, and a dead man staring up at me." Tears streamed down Harold's face. "I'm not a violent man, Detective. I've never hit anyone before. I ... I don't know what would have caused me to beat up someone."

His wife and the other suspects told similar stories. Lourdes finished talking with his group. When they compared notes, every person involved had felt a searing pain, then blinding terror before blacking out. The two detectives exchanged a worried look.

"I'll call Captain Greene and give him our initial report." Lourdes stalked away from the noise, his cell phone at his ear.

Sean glanced at the couple, Harold and Lana. He sighed heavily. Another family destroyed by whatever was causing this insanity. He waved at an officer and instructed him to allow Lana to call her parents to care for her children. He gazed around the scene, and the back of his neck tingled. It seemed like someone had drugged the suspects. Following that train of thought, Sean beckoned Brian to him.

"Take blood samples from everyone," Sean said, "including the victims. Have the lab test if there are any toxins in their system that could account for hallucinations and them passing out."

"What about the people who were part of the mob that damaged all the artwork? Do you want their blood tested too?"

Sean nodded. "Something stinks about this whole thing and makes my hackles rise. Something ... or someone ... caused this."

"I'll get on it. Your instincts are usually right on."

Sean spent the rest of the afternoon and evening interviewing the people who had witnessed the riot or had been part of it. No one could pinpoint what or who had instigated the trouble. Except, everyone who had committed some form of violence had seen green creatures out of their nightmares or some alien sci-fi flick. When they brought in a sketch artist, none of the people could describe the creature well enough for the artist to draw it.

As he drove home that night, Sean picked up his cell phone and debated calling his grandmother. The creatures sounded like those from her stories. He glanced at the clock and put the phone down. She'd wring his neck if he called at this late—or early morning.

 # CHAPTER 4 

Catlyn found a parking spot in the strip mall close to the little Mexican eatery. The hole-in-the-wall place served the best fresh fish tacos, and their smoky black beans were to die for. A breeze tugged on her floppy hat, and she threw a hand up to keep it from blowing away. As she hurried into the restaurant to escape the sudden wind, she noticed a man standing by the door. She took off her hat and scanned the room for Bri and Lisa. As she did, she turned her head toward the door. Something about the man's shadow against the frosted glass caught her attention. For an instant, she thought he snapped a tail once in irritation before curling it around his feet.

Bri half-stood and waved her hand. Catlyn weaved around the tables to join her friends sitting next to the window. Sunlight warmed Bri's brunette hair, and her blue eyes sparkled with pleasure. Her spaghetti-strap top revealed toned and tanned arms from playing tennis. Lisa's long hair shimmered down her back in ebony waves. Her smile lit her hazel eyes as Catlyn slid into the booth across from her two friends. Like Catlyn, Lisa's curvy shape held a few extra pounds.

The waitress came to take their order.

"I'll take two cheese enchiladas with rice and beans," Lisa told the waitress.

Catlyn didn't even glance at the menu. "I'll have the number thirteen."

Bri placed her order. "You always get that."

Catlyn shrugged. "What can I say? I like their fish tacos and chicken enchiladas."

They chatted, munching on chips and salsa while waiting for their food.

Catlyn took a sip of her Dr. Pepper, then glanced at her friend's faces. "How do you think you'd react if you started seeing weird shit?"

"Define weird." Bri crunched on a chip. "We're in Southern California after all. We see weird shit all the time."

"No, I mean mythological creatures or magic weird ... like unicorns or harpies or satyrs."

"Oh, that changes things a bit. I'm not sure if I'd be freaked out as hell or jubilant. Probably both."

"I think I'd be scared shitless," Lisa's eyes widened, "and afraid I'd be thrown into the psychiatric ward. Why? Are you seeing strange stuff?"

Catlyn nodded, then waited for the waitress to place their hot plates onto the red-checkered vinyl tablecloth and leave.

"Yeah, just now, on my way here, I swore I saw a woman shift into a unicorn. And last week at the grocery store, there was a satyr—in all his glory. Whew, let me tell you, he had some glory to show off."

Bri leaned forward, her elbows on the table and her eyes alight. "Really? That is so cool!"

"It is, isn't it?" Catlyn grinned.

Lisa shivered. "With my luck, I'd probably see evil crap."

Catlyn's smile fell, reminded about the car accident. "You aren't the only one. I've seen some seriously creepy things too." She told Bri and Lisa about the incident and the various evil creatures she'd seen.

"Holy shit, that's messed up." Bri slumped back against the padded seat of their booth, fiddling with her fork. "Have you talked to Jade about it? She'd know what those creatures were and what's going on with you."

"Not yet. I plan on it tonight after the full moon ceremony. You're coming, aren't you?"

"Of course, I love the ceremonies," Bri said.

"If I can get off in time, I'll come and help set up," Lisa added.

"Too bad we can't find a real coven to work in," Bri sighed. "I like my solitary Wicca studies and doing ritual with you two. But it would be so much more fun to celebrate the holy days of the wheel of the year in a group, not only at the community gatherings at the store."

"I know what you mean." Catlyn pushed her plate away and rubbed her tummy. She shouldn't have eaten that last tortilla chip loaded with beans and rice. "I wish Karl was more open to doing magic with me. I assumed he would after meeting him at the psychic faire. He'll only grudgingly come to the full moon ceremonies with me."

Bri made a face. She didn't like Catlyn's current boyfriend. "I told you from the beginning. All he was there for was picking up women."

They finished lunch, and Bri headed to her retail job, while Lisa returned to her office. Catlyn drove to the Mystical Enchantments for her afternoon shift as the store's cashier. When she arrived, she let out a breath of relief when the salamander wasn't curled around the door handle.

As evening drew near, Michelle bustled around the large room at the back of the shop used for ceremonies, rituals, and other gatherings, readying it for the full moon ceremony. Since autumn equinox was in a few days, they'd be combining the Sabbat celebration with the full moon medtiation. Catlyn helped set the candles around the room, scatter pillows on the floor, and place chairs in a circle. She frowned when Michelle spread a beautiful orange autumn print cloth in the center of the room for their altar and laid crystals, flowers, and pictures on it.

"Isn't Jade leading the ceremony tonight?" Catlyn asked.

Michelle shook her head as she adjusted the position of the large piece of quartz in the center of the cloth. "No, she called me this morning. She's still out of town on business. She'd hoped her current job would be finished by now. There were some complications that forced her to stay in San Francisco longer."

"Darn, I wanted to talk to her."

"That makes me very happy to hear." Michelle beamed at her. "She mentioned she'd be home on Friday."

"Thanks, I'll call her then." Catlyn chewed on her lower lip. She didn't like to call Jade while she was investigating for someone or on bodyguard duty. It could endanger her. Living this close to Hollywood, some of Jade's clients were famous movie stars. Her newfound ability to see peculiar creatures wasn't an emergency. She could wait for the weekend to talk to her.

A half hour before the ceremony, Lisa came into the store. "Hey, Catlyn, Michelle." Lisa set down her purse.

Catlyn waved at her. "Looks like you were able to get away early."

"Yeah. I finished the report I was working on and traffic was surprisingly good. Is there anything I can help you with to set up for tonight?"

"We're pretty much done." Michelle glanced around. "You could clean up the tea service area and put on a fresh pot of water."

"Sure, I can do that." Lisa picked up the electric kettle and took it to the small kitchen.

A few minutes later, a tall man with close-cropped blond hair entered the store. He seemed familiar and the hair on Catlyn's neck rose. Her stomach clenched as he walked past her, and she caught the faint smell of an obnoxious incense. He wandered around the shop, not picking anything up to examine. When Lisa carried the pot back in and set up the tea service table, his eyes followed her every move.

There was something off about him. Catlyn narrowed her eyes and opened her third eye to see his aura. She blinked her eyes when his face blurred out.

He doesn't have an aura!

Everyone had an aura. She rubbed her eyes and forehead and tried again. He whirled around to face her and snarled. Catlyn stepped back, her hand flying to her chest. Her breath caught in her throat as she glimpsed red skin, knobby horns on his head, and a tail.

He was the man standing outside the Mexican restaurant at lunch!

He glanced at Lisa again, licking his lips, then exited.

"Catlyn, are you okay?" Michelle asked.

"Didn't you notice that strange man ogling Lisa?"

Michelle shook her head. "There hasn't been anyone in the store except the three of us for the last fifteen minutes."

"That can't be right. A tall, blond man entered the store right after Lisa. He just left."

Lisa heard them and glanced all around her. "I didn't see anyone, but I felt the creeps a few minutes ago. It's gone now."

"I wish Jade were here. She'd know what's going on," Catlyn mumbled. Jitters still tightened Catlyn's stomach when she closed the shop for the ceremony.

Michelle opened the ceremony, then led the group in a guided meditation. It took some time for Catlyn to relax. When she finally went deeper into the mediation, all sense of the room disappeared. Michelle's voice faded away.

A pair of brilliant cerulean-blue eyes, surrounded by white, emerged from the darkness. They bored into Catlyn. Fear swept through her after everything she'd seen lately. A sense of calm immediately replaced it. The being projected love and curiosity. The striking eyes dissolved, leaving her bereft of the entity's warmth. She sucked in a breath as loneliness swamped her. Tears leaked from her closed eyes.

The sensation gradually passed.

Gray filled her vision. The Goddess Hecate strode from the mist and approached Catlyn. She searched the Goddess's face, expecting cerulean-blue eyes. Disappointment flared when Hecate's hazel eyes bored into hers.

"Daughter of my line. It is time."

"Time for what?" Catlyn asked, but the Goddess had vanished.

Michelle's voice returned, calling the people back from their meditation and into their bodies. As Catlyn stretched, she wondered what the Goddess had meant. *Time for what? Why is all this bizarre stuff happening to me?* The weekend couldn't arrive quick enough so she could talk to Jade about it.

The morning after the riot at the Block, Sean combed through the reports, hoping to glean a composite of the creature from the various descriptions.

Captain Green crossed the floor and loomed over Sean and Jerry. "Well, what have you learned? Was it a terrorist attack?"

"No, Sir." Jerry shook his head. "We don't know what caused that riot yet. We're still shifting through the statements."

Sean leaned back in his chair, looking up at his boss. "Something terrified all those people and turned them violent. But damned if we can determine what caused it. I have the lab checking their blood for anything, a drug or some substance, that could explain their actions—"

"—or their mass hallucinations and hysteria," Lourdes added.

"Keep me informed." Captain Green tromped back to his office.

Jerry headed to the coffeepot. Sean leaned forward, tapping on his computer. He opened a new file to compile the description, only to be interrupted by Captain Green returning, shaking his head.

"Another crazy incident has been reported," Green said. "Go check it out."

Sean saluted, then pulled Jerry from fixing his coffee. "We've caught a new case."

Jerry rolled his eyes. "Not another weird one."

"Yep."

"This is getting ridiculous."

They drove into an expensive gated neighborhood. The ashen-faced guard directed them to the crime scene. The two-story beige house had a Mercedes Benz and BMW parked in the garage. Palm trees edged the immaculate yard.

Sean stepped inside and paused.

Blood covered the white marble floors and cream walls of the open concept living space. A man lay sprawled face down on the living room floor. The back of his head bashed in, presumably by the large geode bookend covered in blood laying next to him. Strands of dirty blond hair stuck out in weird angles to the dark purple agate. A semi-automatic gun lay abandoned a few feet away. He'd also taken a shot in the leg and chest. Sean's eyebrows crunched in confusion. Why had the woman resorted to using the bookend when she'd had a gun? The trail of blood showed the confrontation had started in the kitchen before ending in the living room.

Lourdes approached the officer standing next to the body, then drew him aside. They talked quietly for a moment before Lourdes followed the officer and the blood trail into the kitchen.

Sean's attention was on the woman in her early thirties, who sat on the floral couch across the coffee table from the body. She held her infant close and rocked back and forth, whispering over and over, "Don't worry, little one, he isn't going to hurt you ever again."

Sean talked to the responding officer to get the details, then carefully stepped over the blood and approached the woman. He crouched in front of her.

"Mrs. Holcomb, I'm Detective McLarkin. Can I call you Carol?"

She nodded, dazed.

"What happened here?"

"He tried to eat my baby!" Carol cried, hugging her child closer to her chest. The baby cried weakly. "I stopped him. I wasn't about to let that ... that thing hurt my baby. I don't know what it did to my husband, David." She pointed a shaky finger at the body. "Whoever ... whatever that is, it isn't my husband. I've known David for ten years, and I can assure you, he wasn't a fucking demon!"

Sean pulled back, blinking in surprise. He turned his head to glance at the body, which seemed human enough to him. He turned back to Carol, noticing for the first time the blood dripping onto the couch.

"Um... ma'am, are you hurt?"

"What? No, I don't think so." Carol glanced down and saw the blood, her eyes going wide.

She hurriedly laid the baby on her lap. As she leaned forward, Sean's jaw tightened. Something had ripped the back of her blouse to shreds, and great bloody gouges covered her upper back. A bite on her upper trapezius oozed blood. Before Sean could comment on her injuries, Carol finished unwrapping the blankets around her baby. He gaped at the blood seeping from the soaked bandage placed on the infant's arm. The baby whimpered through his blue lips.

"Oh, my God!" Carol cried. "He's still bleeding. Call an ambulance!"

"Hardy!" Sean yelled at the young patrolman guarding the door. "Grab a first-aid kit and call a bus! Tell them we have an injured baby and woman."

"Yes, Sir!" the young man called. His face blanched as he took in the blood dripping from the baby's arm. "I'll tell them to hurry." He ran outside and returned a few moments later to Sean's side, handing him the white first-aid box.

Carol tried to remove the child's bandage but cried out as the movement caused fresh blood to gush from her own wounds. Sean took over for her and grimaced at the large wound revealed underneath the baby's bandage. Hardy gasped, then ran for the kitchen, returning with a wet cloth. Sean gently cleaned off the blood, only to have it well back up as soon as he'd wiped it away. The jagged bite nearly encompassed the boy's entire arm. The teeth marks didn't appear human. He hadn't seen any sign of dogs in the house.

"Where is that ambulance, Hardy?" Sean growled.

"It's on its way. It should be here in a few minutes."

"We might not have a few minutes," Sean muttered.

The baby quit whimpering and lay still. The only signs of life were his rapidly rising and falling chest.

Damn it! Damn it! I won't let this child bleed out! Sean cast about the room. He grabbed a bib sticking from the diaper bag. Luckily, it was an old-fashioned type with ties instead of snaps or Velcro. He used the ends to tie a tourniquet around the baby's arm. Carol snatched up the baby, holding him close to her chest.

Sirens blared, announcing the ambulance's arrival. The paramedics raced inside, stepping over the body and blood, then crouched down in front of Carol. The female paramedic tried to pry the baby from Carol's tight grip. "We have him now..."

"Carol," Sean supplied.

"Carol, let us take him. We can't help him if you don't let go."

With a sob, Carol released her hold on the infant, and the paramedic gently placed him on the gurney. The child looked so tiny as they fit a respirator over his face.

"What hospital are you taking him to?" Sean asked the lead paramedic.

"CHOC, in Orange." She continued to work on the child.

"You need to examine the mother. She's hurt too."

The second paramedic hurried to her, his lips thinning at the sight of her bleeding back. He worked feverishly to staunch Carol's wounds. Her eyes stayed glued to her baby, wincing when the paramedic touched her back. She passed out. The paramedics made room for her on the gurney with her infant.

"We'll take the woman to St. Joseph's, since it's close to CHOC," the lead paramedic told Sean.

Lourdes scowled at the retreating paramedics. "You're not buying her claim of self defense, are you? She shot her husband two times before braining him."

"I am. She may have shot him, but it was after she and the baby were viciously attacked. She might be confused from the blood loss about what she saw, but nonetheless, something horrible happened here. You didn't see the baby's wound. I did. It wasn't like any human bite I've ever seen. And her back looks like claws raked her. I don't know what's going on in this city, but something isn't right."

Anger gripped Sean, and he turned away from his partner. The older man should retire soon if he was getting so jaded. Sean slipped on a pair of latex gloves and walked the crime scene, beginning in the kitchen. A small spray of blood marred the gray painted cabinets and drops spattered the pale granite countertop. Shards from a shattered mug covered the floor, and the dark scent of coffee rose from the puddle. For a moment, he saw a ghostly Carol wander into the kitchen. He shook his head to clear his fantasies.

As he surveyed the scene, he let it tell him the story. He imagined Carol getting a cup of coffee while her husband held the baby, and her horror at finding him taking a bite from the infant's arm. Sean stepped to where another spatter of blood covered the kitchen doorway leading into the living room. *This must be where she was slashed with the unknown weapon.* The trail led him next to the buffet cabinet, where a drawer gaped open. Bloody fingerprints marred the handle and inside of it. *She ran here to find the hidden gun.*

"Lourdes," he called out, "how many shots were fired?"

Jerry examined the gun. "Just the two. She knew how to shoot. My guess is she shot him in the leg first, then the chest, before finally smashing his head with that bookend. The coroner can confirm it." He shook his head. "Why would she need to shoot him so many times?"

Sean pointed to the bloody footprints, marking where the man had continued to follow Carol, even after being wounded. "From the evidence, he wouldn't stop." As Sean studied the footprints, a foul, rotten smell drifted up. He knelt to take a better whiff, gagging at the stench. It wasn't the normal coppery scent of blood. He followed the trail to the living room. Shards of glass from broken knick-knacks littered the floor, smears of blood marred the tile, and bloody fingertips clawed the coffee table. A smaller puddle of blood on the coffee table showed where the infant had lain while his parents fought. In Sean's mind's eye, the man held Carol down, even as she fought him, until finally her questing fingers snatched the heavy bookend. A mother terrified for her baby would have the strength to bash in a man's head.

Brian, the crime technician, came in carrying his bag. He glanced around and wrinkled his nose. "This is a bad one. Although, thankfully, not as bad as the Iron Maiden murder scenes."

"Don't remind me," Sean grumbled. "We're due for another one of those within the next two weeks." He took Brian into the kitchen. "This is where it started. We should have three sets of blood and DNA: the deceased, the mother, and an infant."

Brian set up, then moved around the house, marking the crime scene, taking pictures, and collecting evidence.

Everything about this case made Sean's hackles rise and his instincts burn. He couldn't shake the feeling something supernatural had occurred here.

He hunkered down next to Brian, who was collecting evidence near the body, and murmured, "Check his blood and DNA against David Holcomb's, will you? There's some question of his identity. I'm not sure this is David Holcomb. His wife claims it isn't."

Brian raised his eyebrows. "Anything else?"

"If you find any strange blood samples, see if they match anything we've found at the Iron Maiden killings. There may be a link, but damned if I know what it is, I just feel it in my bones."

Finished with what they could do, Sean and Jerry left the scene in the care of the crime scene investigation team. Later in the evening, Sean checked with the hospital. The infant was in intensive care, and they weren't sure yet if they'd have to amputate his arm or if he'd survive. The receptionist transferred him to the hospital where Carol had been admitted. Her injuries had become severely infected. *What had happened to that poor family?*

 # CHAPTER 5 

Catlyn tossed and turned, finally dropping into sleep. Someone approached her. Darkness shrouded his face, leaving only his chilling pale-blue eyes visible. Even though she hadn't seen him clearly, she knew it was the same man from the incident at the beach. Evil cloaked him, filling his breath with a miasma of foul deeds. "You are mine," he said. She whirled around and ran in terror, slipping on gravel. Skeletal limbs grasped at her. A deep bray, unlike any she'd heard before, sounded at her heels. She quickened her pace. Her breaths came in hard gasps. A light shone ahead of her—safety. Before she reached it, the man loomed on the path, blocking her way.

"Help me," she cried into the dark. Cerulean-blue eyes in a white face materialized behind the man. The same eyes as from her full moon meditation.

"I am coming." The voice rang with otherworldliness. Catlyn couldn't see anything of the being beyond its eyes. It attacked her pursuer, driving him away from the path.

Catlyn dashed for the light, and as she passed through it, a sense of safety enveloped her. She sighed deeply, turned over, and snuggled with the cat sleeping next to her. The cat's soft purrs eased her into a deep, dreamless sleep.

Catlyn woke up with Mittens, her long-haired, gray cat, sitting on her chest and patting her face. A rough tongue scraped across her chin, and she opened her eyes to see Mittens' blue eyes boring into her. She didn't need an alarm clock. Mittens always demanded her breakfast at the same time every morning and wouldn't leave Catlyn alone until Catlyn fed her. The weight of Boots, her male orange tabby, on her feet comforted her. After petting Mittens, she sat up and reached down to pet Boots. His rumbling purr vibrated her hands.

The dream came back at her full-force. She lay trembling until Mittens butted her head hard against Catlyn's chin, meowing a loud complaint. Shaking off the dream's sense of dread, Catlyn climbed out of bed.

After feeding her pets, she hurried to start her yoga routine. She managed to do a few poses before her cats joined her. Soon, it became an exercise in keeping her focus when one cat rubbed against her face while the other tried to bite her toes. She could go to a yoga studio—if she had the money—but then she'd miss out on all the fun of doing yoga with cats.

Finished with her routine, she sat in front of her altar, lit a candle and a stick of incense, and began her morning meditation and prayers. Mittens curled up in her lap. During her meditation, she again saw the deep, cerulean-blue eyes in a white face. *"I am coming!"* The otherworldly voice echoed her dream, then added, *"Soon."* The eyes zoomed straight at her and passed through her.

Startled, Catlyn gasped, her eyes flying open. She'd never had such vivid visions before. Clairvoyance wasn't her strong gift. She had always been more clairsentient—clear knowing.

The dream and the vision stayed with her as she showered, dressed, and ate her usual breakfast of a bowl of cereal and a glass of orange juice. After tucking her dishes into the dishwasher, she sat at her kitchen table/office desk, opened her laptop, and checked her Etsy account.

"Whoo-hoo, two orders!" she told the cats. She packaged the jewelry for her customers. Since she didn't have any appointments at the store until later in the afternoon, she worked on a new piece. Perusing her collection of stones, she selected an oval cabochon of blue beryl. She decided on a herringbone pattern to create a setting for it with thin, flexible sterling silver wire. It soon reminded her of a cat's eye.

Her thoughts wandered to the entity, who contacted her in her meditations—and saved her in her dreams.

Although she was psychic and did tarot readings, she wasn't a medium. She didn't contact the dead; she left them alone, and they returned the favor. This seemed something entirely different.

Could it be a spirit animal or my new totem animal?

The eyes didn't give her a clue of what animal species it was. Catlyn picked up her phone, staring at it while she debated about calling Jade again. Her godmother could help her decipher what the entity was, and what it wanted from her. But she'd already left several messages on Jade's voice mail. Jade would call when she could.

An hour later, Catlyn tucked the last tail of wire behind the others, cutting it flush so it wouldn't snag the wearer's clothes. She dug in her supplies and found an appropriate chain. After adding a lobster claw hook and jump ring to it, she threaded the chain through the bail she'd fashioned on the wire-worked crystal pendant. Finished, she glanced at the clock. She had time to stop at the post office to mail the Etsy orders before her first healing session.

Flinging a large scarf, big enough for a shawl, printed with a peacock over her shoulders, she slipped on sandals and rushed out of the house.

Her eyes darted around the parking lot, checking for any strange creatures lurking. As she approached her car, a green rat-like creature with big ears, sharp claws, and a long tail skittered from under her neighbor's truck. It saw her. It hissed at her, raising its bushy tail. A whirring noise made her jump. Several spines zoomed toward her. The creature chittered as it dashed into the nearby bushes.

Catlyn hurried to her car, but as she stepped into it, something sharp dug into her leg. She examined her skirt and discovered one of the creature's spines tangled in it. She extricated it, grimacing at the barbed spine. It reminded her of a porcupine quill, but much larger. It would have hurt had it hit her.

Catlyn sucked in a breath as terror swept over her. The scar on her palm throbbed painfully. She had a quick vision of herself as a small child with spines, like those the creature had, embedded in her hand. Rubbing her palm on her thigh, she tried to wipe away the flash of memory. Her forehead crinkled in confusion. She'd never seen such a creature before—not that she remembered. She stared at her palm. Jade had told her she'd received the scar from falling off her bike as a child. Now, she wondered what else Jade hadn't told her the truth about.

She walked over to the big dumpsters and tossed the quill in, wishing she could rid herself of the unease that settled in her gut as easily.

As she backed out of her parking space, she noticed a black sedan parked along the curb. It rumbled to life when she drove past. During the short drive to the post office, she glanced in the rearview mirror to find it trailing behind her. She hurried into the post office. No one came in after her, but the sedan waited in the parking lot. As she headed to the freeway, the black sedan wove through the traffic, keeping her in sight.

It might be a coincidence that the driver lived in the same apartment complex as Catlyn. And an even bigger one if he needed to go to the post office at the same time she did. But she'd never seen that particular car at the complex before. It was too expensive.

She lost him in the heavy traffic on the 5-south to Costa Mesa. But her heart dropped when it pulled into the Mystical Enchantments' parking lot as she opened the store's door. She hurried inside.

"Hey, Catlyn!"

Her boss's cheerfulness eased some of Catlyn's fear.

Michelle's smile faded. "What's wrong? You look upset."

Catlyn stood by the glass door, scanning the parking lot. The man had parked his car where he had a good view of the store's entrance.

"Come and look outside. Do you see that black sedan?"

Michelle moved so she could peer through the windows. "What black car? There isn't one out there."

Catlyn narrowed her eyes. She could clearly see a black Mercedes facing the store. She shook her head to clear it and rubbed her eyes. The car was still there. *Why can't Michelle see it? What's going on?* Her nightmare intruded in her mind.

"I thought someone followed me," she said nonchalantly, but she heard the fear in her voice. "I guess I just spooked myself."

Michelle picked up a wand made from white sage leaves and stood in front of Catlyn. "Here, let's clear the negative energy from you. You don't want to share it with your clients."

Catlyn put her purse on the counter and stood with her arms outstretched while Michelle lit the smudge stick. When the leaves smoldered, Michelle wafted the smoke through Catlyn's aura. Catlyn breathed in the sacred smoke, letting it banish any negative energy attached to her aura.

When Michelle finished, she rummaged through the baskets of stones on a display, then pressed a piece of black tourmaline into Catlyn's hand. "Here, keep this with you for protection."

Feeling better, Catlyn tucked the crystal into her skirt pocket, then prepped her room for her first client. Even though she exclusively used the room, she cleansed it anyway. She did a quick smudge outside the door with a few white sage leaves, enough to clear it but not make it too smoky. The smoke bothered some of her clients. Inside, she spritzed the air with an aromatherapy spray she'd made. The fragrance of the essential oils diffused through the room.

Still feeling spooked and on edge, she drew sigils in the air with her hands in front of the door, window, and each wall. Using her crystal singing bowls, she performed a short ritual to bless the room and guard it from any who had malevolent intentions. Now, only those with energies of the light could enter her space.

A few moments later, her first client for the day walked in.

The day passed pleasantly for Catlyn until early evening. During a break between clients, she passed through the main store on her way to the small kitchen. Her breath hitched, and she paused at the doorway. A broad-shouldered man with longish blond hair wandered the shop. He looked up at her entrance, and cold, pale-blue eyes bored into her, the same ones from her dream. A slow leer crossed his face.

Nausea gripped Catlyn's stomach from the nasty, slimy energy snaking from him toward her. Without thinking, she jerked her arm into a cutting motion, and the energy subsided. She hurried into the kitchen and shut the door, leaning against it, breathing hard. Certainty filled her that the man prowling the store was the same one who'd watched her at the beach. They had the same evil energy about them.

Her hand slid into her pocket, and she fingered the piece of black tourmaline Michelle had given her. She waited in the kitchen until she sensed the disgusting presence leave the shop before scurrying back to her room. The strange sightings and this creep weren't normal events. She needed some magical, energy protection.

Her mother's pendant warmed against her skin. Taking it as confirmation, Catlyn opened her book on crystal properties and researched those good for protection. Three stood out: black tourmaline, amber, and fire-opal. Last week, a client had given her a small, polished fire-opal as payment—otherwise she'd never be able to afford one of the expensive stones. In her mind, she considered her stash of crystals she'd collected, like some women collected shoes. Catlyn thought her hoard included a nice piece of amber. Along with the fire-opal and the new tourmaline, she had all the crystals she needed to make a protective necklace.

The man's cold eyes popped into her memory, and her breath came in quick pants. Dropping her head between her knees, she forced herself to take long, slow breaths until the panic attack receded. She vowed she'd resume practicing the self-defense moves Jade had taught her—if she could still remember them. She didn't believe in violence and had only learned them to appease her godmother. It had been one of the many things she and Jade had argued about. She knew her godmother would insist she pick up her training again once she heard about the car following her—and the man.

Catlyn peered out the shop window. The parking lot lights shone on another black sedan. This one an Audi rather than the Mercedes that followed her earlier. A man with short brown hair, a square jaw, and pale-blue eyes leaned against it, smoking. His eyes flickered orange as he stamped out his cigarette. As he climbed into his sedan, Catlyn thought she saw the twitch of a red tail. He waited until she passed by before pulling out to trail her. Even in the heavy freeway traffic, he somehow stayed a car length or two behind her all the way home.

She parked, ran into the house, and locked the door, panting as she leaned against it. *Why is someone following me? I'm nothing special. My only claims to specialness is I'm an orphan with a knack for reading tarot cards and energy healing.*

Her worry and fear faded in her cat's exuberant head-butting and rubbing against her as they requested attention from her being absent all day. After feeding them and herself, she pulled out the wooden box that held the crystals she used for spell work. On top of the jumble of stones sat the piece of amber and the fire-opal. She swallowed hard, freaked out over how everything she needed was coming to hand so easily.

She spent the next few hours creating bezels from thin, sterling silver wire for the crystals, turning them into a beautiful necklace. To make it more than simply decorative, Catlyn used a drop of frankincense essential oil to draw a protection sigil on the stones, singing as she did.

She carried the necklace into her bedroom. Holding it in her palms, she lifted it in front of her. "Goddess Hecate, bless these crystals to protect me," she prayed. "Fill them with your power to keep my enemies from hurting me."

Catlyn placed the necklace on a silk scarf, then put it on her bedroom's southern-facing window sill. A beam of moonlight fell on it. Light danced around the stones. Unexpectedly, they seemed to suck in the moonlight. The fire-opal glowed with deep-orange light, while the amber shone more golden. Even the tourmaline pulsed a darker black. Catlyn blinked, and the crystals no longer appeared to hold any supernatural light.

Catlyn gaped. "That didn't, couldn't, happen. I'm just imagining things."

While shutting off the lights before she headed to bed, she peeked out the window. The driver had parked the black sedan where he had a clear view of her apartment. The glow of a cigarette butt briefly lit her watcher. Trembling, she called the police.

When the cruiser arrived an hour later, an officer knocked on her door.

"Sorry, ma'am," the young man said, "we couldn't find any sign of the car you reported."

Catlyn stepped around him and pointed. "But it's right there!"

"Ma'am, nothing is there. It's empty."

Out of the corner of her eye, his partner shook his head and rolled his eyes. They thought she was crazy.

"I'm sorry to have bothered you, Officers. I must have frightened myself."

As the cruiser drove away, her watcher lit another cigarette. A dark chuckle chased her back inside.

After a sleepless night filled with nightmares of the man with cold, blue eyes, Catlyn woke groggy. Unwilling to be scared so early in the day, she refrained from looking out her window as she opened the curtains to let in the morning sunshine.

After flowing through her yoga stretches, she slid her feet apart to double her hip width and sank down into horse-stance. It looked like a ballet plié, but with her toes pointing forward rather than out. Slowly she punched chest level, head level, then groin and back again, adding more speed to her strikes. Moving forward and back, the sequence of upper block, side block, and lower block flowed as her body remembered the martial arts movements Jade had taught her. Catlyn kicked front, side, back, then threw a few roundhouse kicks.

She pulled her coffee table into the kitchen to give her room to do the katas, or forms exercises, that combined the movements as if she were fighting an opponent. After so long of a hiatus, her memory only dredged out the basic ones—that thousands of repetitions had ingrained into her body. Catlyn had always questioned whether she'd actually be able to fight someone; however, that question might soon be answered. The thought depressed her. The sight of a black sedan, a twin to her late-night watcher, sank her spirits even lower.

Catlyn showered and dressed. She'd grab some tea and a croissant at the Jupiter Moon Coffee and Café on her way to the shop. The popular place had fabulous coffee and food. She wandered into her bedroom, and the sun glinted off the necklace sitting on her window sill. The fire-opal gleamed with a red light reflecting deep in its center. Catlyn fastened the necklace over her throat, covering the chain that held her mother's pendant. Immediately, heavy gates slamming closed rang in her head, and the snapping of armor plates echoed as they wrapped around her. They'd protect her against any psychic or spiritual attack. Now if only her martial arts training would keep her safe from the scary man.

She hurried down the stairs. Her watcher gazed over the rim of his dark sunglasses before climbing into his vehicle. Streamers of slime that made her flesh crawl oozed from him, reaching for her. Catlyn jumped into her car, slammed the door shut, and started the engine. As soon as it chugged to life, she peeled out of her parking spot. The sedan roared and leaped to follow her. Catlyn needed help, but the only one she knew who could help her was Jade, and she wasn't returning her phone calls.

# CHAPTER 6 

Sean stood in line, waiting to order his morning coffee and snack. Jupiter Moon Coffee and Café shops had been popping up all over the county. He preferred this one, the original one in Tustin, right off the 55 Freeway. A quick scan took in all the people in the coffee shop as he searched for threats—and unusual creatures.

He rubbed his temples, trying to soothe his headache. The last few days had been brutal. The riot at The Block had been the first in a long string of bizarre incidents. Stories of similar cases from all over Orange County floated through the station. Upstanding citizens were committing random acts of violence, many ending in death. The suspects all claimed to see something peculiar, lost time, then woke up in handcuffs with blood on their hands and loved one's dead.

This morning, two traffic cops were killed during a routine traffic stop in Cypress, a normally quiet, peaceful city. It made all the police officers jumpy, even those like himself, who worked in plain clothes.

If he didn't know any better, he'd swear the county was under supernatural attack. But he'd die before he'd say that out loud. It would cost him his career.

He noticed the pretty, petite, curvy woman behind him. She looked familiar, but he couldn't place where he'd seen her. She had thick, medium reddish-brown hair that curled in waves to her shoulders. Her clear green eyes gleamed with intelligence. Freckles dusted the pale, creamy skin of her nose and cheeks. She wore a long dress, and a bright-colored shawl draped over her shoulders. An amethyst pendant encased in decorative wire hung from a purple and white beaded chain. Matching amethyst earrings dangled from her ears. She reminded him of a gypsy.

His Granny Eileen loved amethysts. He'd thought about his grandmother yesterday, and now someone reminded him of her. He snorted softly. When his granny wanted to talk to him, he'd get little messages similar to this. She'd never just pick up the phone and call him. She always said it was more fun this way.

The woman noticed him smile at her, and she gave him a shy grin. It lit up her heart-shaped face.

"Hi," he said. "That's a lovely necklace. My grandmother would love something like that. Where did you get it?"

She smiled wider, and her hand fluttered to touch the necklace. "Oh, it's one of my designs. I make jewelry."

"Do you have a website?" They shuffled a few steps closer to the register.

"Yes, I do." She dug into her purse and handed him a card.

He read: *Moonstones and Moonbeams, crystal jewelry by Catlyn Hennessey.*

"I do special orders besides what's listed on the site. If your grandmother has some favorite stones, or if you want something that fits her astrology sign, I can design a piece for you."

Her gaze shifted behind him, her eyes widened, and she inhaled sharply. Her already pale skin lost even more color. He twisted around and glimpsed one of Michael's—his lead suspect in the Iron Maiden Killer case—buddies standing near the door. Sean surveyed the shop, but he couldn't see Michael Drogger.

"Are you okay—" he glanced down at the card for her name "—Catlyn?"

She gave a shaky laugh. "Fine. Just seeing ghosts. Thanks for asking..."

"Detective McLarkin. Sean." He held out his hand. Her firm handshake pleased him, and he liked how warm her skin was against his own. Small electrical pulses buzzed between their palms. Her eyes widened as she dropped her hand.

He reached the register and gave his order. "And the lady will have ..."

"Oh, you don't need to buy my drink."

"Please, let me." He wanted to spend more time with her.

"A hot chai latte, please."

He paid, and they moved to a table to wait for their drinks. "How did you get into making crystal jewelry?"

One side of her mouth slid into a smile. "I love working with crystals. They help me in my healing work too."

He raised his eyebrows.

"I'm an energy healer. I use crystal singing bowls, essential oils, and, of course, stones in my practice. Making jewelry is a natural extension of that work. I like to think my jewelry is more than just pretty, but that it also helps people in their spiritual journey." She glanced away and pulled her shawl tighter around her shoulders.

"That's cool."

She looked back at him sharply, as if she hadn't expected him to still want to talk to her. He smiled at her. "My grandmother loves crystals, too. She'd probably dig getting a healing using them. Where's your office?"

"The Mystical Enchantments metaphysical store. Ah, there are our drinks." She took her cup and smiled shyly at him. "Thanks for the tea. I need to go, or I'll be late."

She plopped a big, floppy hat on her head, and he walked out of the shop with her. She stopped and stared at an empty parking space before grimacing, then hurried to her little Honda Civic.

It finally clicked why she looked familiar. She'd been at the incident by the tourist attraction. He narrowed his eyes as he studied the spot. It wavered, like the shimmer of heat rising off the blacktop. He glimpsed a black sedan before it disappeared. He shook his head to clear it, wishing he could blame a heat wave on the recent craziness. But he doubted it had anything to do with the rash of evil.

Sean sipped his coffee as he watched her leave, frowning at her fearful gaze into her rearview mirror. He'd rather see her smile shyly at him than have that terrified expression on her face. A slow smile lifted his lips. It would be easy to convince his grandmother she wanted to have one of Catlyn's healing sessions. He was sure his granny would love it. Driving his grandmother from Temecula to Costa Mesa would give him a good excuse to talk to Catlyn again.

He climbed into his car and turned it on; the engine purring to life. He eased through traffic and drove to the station. His thoughts kept straying to images of green eyes and a heart-shaped face. Others might consider Catlyn odd, but Sean had grown up around his Granny Eileen. Compared to her, Catlyn was downright normal.

He'd been close to his granny while growing up, but then his grandfather had been killed. For some reason, his dad blamed Eileen for his father's death and had forbidden Sean and his sister Rachel to see her. But when he turned sixteen a few years later, he'd rebelled and secretly drove to his grandmother's place to visit with her. Now, he made a point of visiting her every couple of months.

Granny Eileen had changed since her husband's death. She'd refused to tell Sean stories of strange people and fearsome monsters and demons. As a child, he'd loved the thrill of fear those stories had sent up his spine. He hadn't lied to Catlyn. Crystals still decorated his grandmother's house, and she wore jewelry similar to what Catlyn made. He smiled at the thought of those two meeting. If they did, he'd better brush up on the metaphysical meaning of crystals.

At the office, he pulled open the file on the amusement park incident, and sure enough, Catlyn Hennessey's name was on the report. She claimed the tourist had attempted to save the businessman and hadn't pushed him into the truck. Sean considered if an interview with Catlyn would help the tourist. It might sway the District Attorney's office into not charging the tourist, especially with so many other strange incidents lately. But before he could pick up the phone, the captain sent Sean and Jerry to investigate another violent murder by a loved one.

Maybe he'd see her at the Jupiter Moon the next morning.

Sean swiped a hand through his hair. He needed a haircut, but he hadn't had time to even call for an appointment. He'd been slammed all week with case after case of strange, violent events. The Anaheim department wasn't alone. The same weird calls swamped every police force in Orange County.

Sean sat in the office on Saturday afternoon rather than watching football on television, clearing the piled up paperwork. His heart flip-flopped as he worked on the Holcomb case. He gazed at the picture of the baby's bite wound. The lab hadn't sent over the results yet, but Sean bet the teeth marks wouldn't be human. The poor mother and child were still hospitalized. Each file he examined added to his growing certainty something supernatural was behind the attacks.

Sean leaned back in his chair and stretched. He winced at the loud popping in his neck. Darkness had fallen while he'd worked on the reports. He stood with a groan, dropped the stack of folders on Jerry's desk for his review, and grabbed his jacket. He needed to unwind. Sitting in his car, he called his buddy and childhood friend Charlie MacNamara.

"Hey, you in town?"

"Yeah, I arrived back this afternoon."

"I need a drink. It's been a hell of a week. Meet me at the Red Orchid?"

"Ugh!" Charlie's voice dripped with distaste. "You always want to go to that place. I hate it there. Why not someplace else?"

"You know why."

"Fine." Charlie hung up on Sean.

Forty-five minutes later, Sean pulled into the packed parking lot of the Red Orchid. The club was one of the hot spots in the county, boasting elaborate cocktails, trendy micro brews, and great food. Too bad Michael Drogger owned it.

Sean threaded his way through the crowded bar area, homing in on an empty table where he had a good view of his target. He plopped onto the high stool and sipped on his scotch while gazing around the room. After several minutes, he spotted Charlie meandering toward him. He wore his black hair slicked-back and a dark green button-down shirt highlighted his green eyes. Charlie slid onto the chair opposite him and took a deep draught from his foamy mug of beer before greeting his friend.

"Gods, I hate this place," Charlie grumbled, then wiped the foam from his upper lip. "The only saving grace is they have great micro brews. You mentioned it's been a rough week. What's going on?"

Sean filled him in on the odd cases he'd investigated. "The worst one by far is where a wife and mother shot her husband because he tried eating their baby. You wouldn't believe the bite mark on the baby's arm. I've never seen anything like it. The baby is still in critical condition." Sean leaned in and lowered his voice. "Something with a claw raked the wife's back. The doctors can't determine what's causing her strange, life-threatening infection."

Charlie's eyes widened. "That's awful!"

A bray of loud laughter rang through the crowd, and Sean swiveled in his chair toward the sound. Michael Drogger stood at a nearby table, his head thrown back as he laughed. He shuffled the deck of cards he held with a flourish before tucking them in his trouser's pocket. Still laughing, he slid his arm around a pretty blond and ran his hand down her back to squeeze her buttocks. The woman's cheeks flushed pink. Michael bent down and kissed her, causing her blush to deepen.

Sean rolled his eyes at Michael's unbuttoned silk shirt, revealing a tanned chest that the girl couldn't keep her eyes—or hands—off. Michael laughed again as he brushed his longish hair back from his face. He turned and caught Sean staring at him. Michael's lips thinned. A predatory gleam filled his blue eyes as he stalked toward Sean and Charlie.

"Detective McLarkin," Michael sneered, "you can't seem to stay away. What is it this time?"

Sean held up his glass of scotch. "I'm only grabbing a drink with my buddy. But if you want to confess, I'll gladly be your confessor."

"I have my own priest. Besides, I've done nothing wrong."

"Just because I can't pin anything on you, doesn't mean squat. Who's the girl?" Sean indicated the blond with his chin.

Michael twisted around and leered at her. "A nice piece of ass. You should get one of your own. It might loosen you up a bit. How long has it been? A year?"

Under the table, Sean's hand fisted, and he itched to slam his fist into Michael's face. Instead, he gripped his glass, letting the cold smoothness cool his anger.

"Let it go, Sean," Charlie warned in a low voice.

"Yeah, let it go, Sean," Michael drawled. "Ginny was a spectacular piece of ass. Too bad you couldn't keep her satisfied, and she turned to me. We had such fun."

"Where is she now?"

Michael rolled his eyes. "Don't know. Don't care. She served her purpose."

"You're such a bastard," Sean hissed.

"Tut, tut." Michael made a negating gesture with his finger. "My parents were married. But yes, I can get what I want, when I want. Money and good-looks will do that. Too bad you don't have either."

Sean glared at his adversary. "I do just fine. Money can't buy class, which you'll never have."

Michael snorted. "Is that the best you can do?"

"For now, I haven't had enough to drink yet. I know you're involved in the killings, if not the murderer. You'll make a mistake someday, and I'll be there when you do."

"It will be a cold day in hell, Detective, when you can get the better of me." Michael sauntered to the blond woman, bent over her and kissed her deeply, running his hands over her body.

Sean growled at the display, tossed back his scotch, and motioned to a server for another one. He and Ginny had been together for six years, and he'd even bought her an engagement ring. Before he could give it to her, he'd come home early from work to a nasty surprise. He'd caught her with another man—his nemesis, Michael Drogger, no less—in their bed.

They'd laid there and laughed at him as he stood sputtering, trying to push the words from his mouth. He'd packed her things the next day. The bed, he burned. Afterward, he'd sworn off relationships. Her betrayal had thrown him into a nine-month funk. Even after nearly a year, it still hurt that she threw away their relationship for a roll with the rich playboy.

While waiting for his drink, Sean scanned the crowd. His eyes stopping on several groups that made the hairs on the back of his neck rise in warning. When he turned around, Charlie was peering at his phone, busily texting.

The server slid a fresh glass filled with dark amber liquid in front of him, the ice cubes clinking. For a moment, he thought her long red nails were tips of claws. He blinked, and her hands returned to normal.

"I don't know why you put yourself through this." Charlie drained his mug and ordered another beer. "We go through this at least once a month."

"Yeah, but it gives me an excuse to watch the bastard. I tell you there's something off about that man. He's as slimy and vile as they come."

"So you say. But if you haven't linked him to the murders yet, what makes you think he's involved?"

Sean tapped the side of his head. "Granny vibes. You remember when we were kids and Granny Eileen would give us games to test our intuition? Well, every warning bell she ever instilled in me goes off around Michael."

"Some of those were gnarly." Charlie grinned. "Although, I've been mighty grateful for them more times than I can count. My Granny vibes have saved my life and my client's. Have you talked to her recently?"

"Not as much as I'd like. It's hard to drive out to Temecula with my busy schedule." Sean ran his finger around the rim of his glass. "Hey, Charlie, do you remember the old stories Granny would tell us?"

"Which ones? She loved to tell stories."

"The ones about demons and other evil creatures."

A guarded expression crossed Charlie's face before he quirked an eyebrow. "Yeah, those used to scare the piss out of you. Why are you bringing it up now?"

"Do you think there might have been some truth in them?" Sean pinched the bridge of his nose. "We're being inundated with strange calls lately. People with no previous history of violence are killing their loved ones and claiming to have seen evil creatures immediately before it happened."

"That is weird. But then, this is Orange County, it's known for being a bit odd."

"This goes beyond the odd. If I didn't know any better, I'd swear we're under some sort of supernatural attack."

Charlie coughed, then took a long swig of his beer. "You've been watching 'Supernatural' too much, Sean. Nothing like that is real."

"Are you sure, Charlie? Something weird is happening."

Sean peered over Charlie's shoulder. Two of Michael's goons stood at either side of his table, arms crossed in front of them, identical shaved heads of dark hair, square jaws, and cold blue eyes. As the man on the left blinked, the pupils of his eyes changed to the oblong orbs of a reptile, then back to human-round. Sean shuddered as a feeling of evil crept up his spine.

 # CHAPTER 7 

Catlyn glanced in her rearview mirror. A frisson of fear punched her. The black sedan continued to follow her. It unnerved her that only she could see it. Even though she'd called several times over the past few days, she still hadn't reached Jade. When Jade worked a high-profile bodyguard job, she'd be out of contact for weeks. Catlyn hoped Jade would hurry home. She needed her godmother's help.

Catlyn's thoughts flew back to the man with sandy-blond hair, goatee, and dark blue eyes she'd met Saturday morning at the Jupiter Moon. He seemed nice, and her unusual line of work hadn't turned him off. As a police detective, Sean McLarkin probably dealt with all kinds of weird stuff. Maybe he'd be able to help her. Although she'd kept an eye out for him, she hadn't seen him in the coffee shop again. She wished now she'd asked for his card.

Catlyn pulled into the Mystical Enchantments' parking lot, parked, and rushed inside the store. Michelle quirked an eyebrow and frowned at her before returning her attention to her customer.

Instead of working on her own clients, Catlyn was scheduled as the store's on-call tarot reader. She set up the room, covering the table with her own cloth. By her left elbow, she placed a clear selenite tower to absorb any negative energy from her clients. Next to it she laid a pale green prehnite to connect with her and her client's spiritual helpers. The last stone she placed was the small pale yellow apophyllite cluster that helped open her psychic abilities.

Besides her usual Gilded Tarot deck, she pulled out her Lakota Sweat Lodge cards and her Medicine Animal deck. Sometimes a reading called for using oracle cards instead of the normal tarot. After spritzing the room with her aromatherapy spray, she sat behind the table and closed her eyes. Breathing slowly and deeply, she cleared her mind of the worry and fear that now clouded it almost constantly.

Cerulean-blue eyes in a white face appeared, and along with them came a sense of peace. Ever since the full moon ceremony, every time she'd medtiated, they showed up. Instead of frightening her, they comforted her. She sensed someone in the doorway and opened her eyes.

Amelia stood on the threshold and beamed at her. "Oh, good. I'd hoped you were the reader today. Something exciting has happened and I need some insight."

Catlyn smiled at Amelia's exuberance. She gestured to the chair opposite her. "Come in. Sit. Tell me about it."

Amelia closed the door and took a seat. She leaned forward. A lock of long, blond hair fell onto the table. "You know the guy I met at the club I told you about? Well, it turns out he's my jerk boss's son. I'm not sure how I feel about that. We've been on several dates now. Damn, his body is fine!" She sighed, a dreamy look crossing her face.

"Anyway," Amelia continued, "what I want to know, is he the one?"

Amelia desperately wanted to find 'the one' to be her soul-mate and to complete her. Catlyn didn't believe in such things. She thought you gave up your own power when you depended on someone else for your happiness or completeness. Drawing in a breath, she tapped into Amelia's energy while she picked up the tarot deck and shuffled them once. She handed them to Amelia, who shuffled them a few times, then passed the cards back to Catlyn. Catlyn cut the deck into three piles and picked up the middle one.

The first card she laid down was the Devil. "This makes sense since you're focusing on lust."

A gleam lit Amelia's eyes. "Yeah, the sex with this guy is fantastic. Just thinking about him makes me squirm."

The next card was the Magician, and she sensed a man who easily manipulated people and his surroundings. The eight of Swords followed. A stab of pain pierced Catlyn's ribcage as she gazed at the picture of a woman, blindfolded, bound, and surrounded by swords. An image of Amelia bound and gagged, a sword swinging toward her, flashed in Catlyn's mind. She shook her head; she'd never before received such clear images.

"This signifies you're feeling helpless and unable to see what is in front of you," she said, telling Amelia the usual meaning of the card. She'd wait until the rest of the cards were down before deciding what the image she'd seen truly meant. "There's more going on than what you're willing to admit."

As she continued to put down the other cards, each one added to Catlyn's sense of unease. The last card she turned over filled her with dread. In most instances, the Death card signified only a metaphorical death or a situation ending. In Catlyn's minds-eye, Amelia sprawled on the ground in a pool of blood.

She reached across the table and grabbed Amelia's hands. "Please, Amelia, don't go out with this guy. He isn't what he seems. All the cards point to him hurting you."

She bit her tongue to keep from adding she'd seen Amelia's death. Ethical practitioners didn't scare their clients with portents of death. The cards only showed the possibilities of what might occur under the current circumstances. Events changed as people made different choices, and this outcome may never occur. However, the cards clearly showed Catlyn that if Amelia continued dating this guy, something terrible would happen to her.

"But ... but he's so handsome—and rich. The cards even say so." Amelia pulled her hands away and jabbed a finger at the six of Pentacles.

"Everything else points to him being greedy and cruel. It won't end well." Catlyn pointed to the devil card, then the death card.

Amelia slumped back in her chair and crossed her arms. "Don't you want me to be happy?"

"Oh, Amelia, I do. I want you to find a man who will love you and treat you like a queen. This guy isn't it. Let him go. Find someone else."

Amelia glared at the cards for a long time, before finally huffing out a breath of air. "Okay, fine. I won't go out with him again. You've never steered me wrong before."

Catlyn sighed with relief. She glanced down at the cards, again seeing Amelia in a pool of blood. She gathered the cards together and shuffled them in with the rest of the deck.

"Are you still coming for your healing appointment on Monday?"

"Yeah, sure. I'll be here." Amelia walked out.

Catlyn stood in the doorway, watching Amelia leave the store. She couldn't shake the image of Amelia's dead body. "Please, Hecate," she prayed, "watch over her." Catlyn could only warn her clients, not make them follow the guidance she gave them. Her unease about Amelia's reading stayed with her throughout the day, intruding into her quiet moments between a steady stream of tarot readings.

As soon as he arrived at work, Sean called the hospital to check on Carol Holcomb and her baby, like he had every day for the past week. Each time, he hoped for good news. Instead, Carol's infection was worsening and hadn't responded to any antibiotics. They'd rushed the baby into emergency surgery during the night to amputate his arm, and he was still in critical condition. Sean hung up and cradled his head in his hands.

Sean and the other detectives worked overtime on dealing with the rash of bizarre crimes. But the Holcomb's tragedy weighed heavily on Sean's mind. He kept seeing that poor baby's arm nearly bitten off and his mother's raked back. He doubted a human had caused the injuries, but then what had? Memories of his Granny's stories continued cropping up. Could one of the monsters in them be responsible for the Holcomb's injuries? He'd been too busy to drive to Temecula to visit his grandmother, and this wasn't something he wanted to talk about on the phone.

His phone rang and the crime tech, Brian, was on the other end.

"I received the coroner's report on the Holcomb case this morning," Brian said. "You're not driving, are you?"

"No, I'm in the office. It's that bad?"

"That weird. Whatever Mrs. Holcomb killed, it wasn't human, or at least it's nothing the coroner's seen before. The guy had an extra set of teeth."

"What?" Sean rubbed a finger in his ear, unsure he'd heard Brian correctly. But it confirmed his suspicions that the person Carol had killed wasn't her husband. He'd have to make time to go visit his grandmother soon.

"It's nothing like what you see in vampire or werewolf movies," Brian added, "more like how sharks have an extra set. We located David Holcomb's dental records, and they don't show anything like what they found in the dead guy. We tested his DNA from hair samples against the blood we recovered from the crime scene. They didn't match, and the unknown sample wasn't normal DNA. As if it couldn't get any stranger, the blood samples I collected show odd microbes. The computer can't match them to anything in the system."

"Send a sample of that to the hospital, will you? Mrs. Holcomb and the baby both have an infection the doctors can't make any sense of. They're fighting for their lives. Perhaps it's caused by those microbes."

"Sure thing."

Sean hung up and told Jerry what the lab had found. "We have another murder on our hands—David Holcomb's."

"You're not buying it, are you?" Jerry snarled. "The wife confessed to killing her husband."

"The body on the coroner's slab isn't David Holcomb, so she didn't kill him. I've already recommended that the DA's office not file any charges against Carol. Her and her baby's injuries prove it was self-defense. With this evidence from the lab, we don't know what she had tried to defend themselves against."

"The lab made a mistake." Jerry didn't sound certain. He ran a hand through his hair.

Sean leaned forward. "We need to find out what happened to David Holcomb."

"As if we don't have enough strange shit going on. At least most of the cases are open and shut. The perps are being caught red-handed."

"Or they're being framed, or someone is drugging them."

"Really?" Jerry raised his eyebrows. "You're going to go with that excuse. I like the one most are claiming—the devil made them do it."

"You have to admit, something is turning our law-abiding citizens into maddened killers and making our streets a war zone."

"Maybe there is a new drug out there," Jerry conceded. "I'll check with my buddies in the narc division, see if they've heard of any new drugs hitting the streets."

In the meantime, Sean would investigate what happened to David Holcomb. He wished he could ask Carol more questions, but she wasn't coherent. He did a background search on her husband. It was nice to be working a normal homicide after all the craziness of the past two weeks. A familiar name popped up: Michael Drogger. The Red Orchid had hired Holcomb a few months ago as a bouncer. Sean didn't like the coincidence of the connection. Sean studied Holcomb's picture, frowning. He didn't recall seeing Holcomb at the club.

"I'm checking on a lead," Sean informed Jerry as he slid his chair from his deck and stood up.

The late fall sun warmed his face. Enjoying the nice weather, he rolled up his shirt sleeves and popped the top off his convertible Camaro. The breeze ruffled his hair as he drove down the freeway to the Red Orchid club. He'd caught the traffic at a lull between the morning going to work and lunch traffic, and he reached the club in a short time.

Joshua Wyndmeyer, the acting manager of the Red Orchid, met him at the door and took him up to his office. Michael held the title of manager, but Joshua did all the work. Over the past two years, while Sean chased the Iron Maiden killer, he'd come to like Joshua and appreciated his candid dislike of his boss.

"Where's your boss?" Sean asked after he'd sat on the plush leather seat facing Joshua's desk. He accepted the bottle of water Joshua handed him and sipped on it.

Joshua examined his cuticles. "Probably fucking his new lady friend. I don't know how that asshole gets such lovely women. This one doesn't fit his usual tastes. She's too sweet and innocent."

Sean absorbed this information. Michael tended to prefer the slutty type, but would charm any woman. He made it as a personal challenge to sleep with every woman who crossed his path, then throw them away—like Ginny. Heat suffused Sean's face. Even after a year, the thought of his ex-girlfriend and Michael together made him furious. He took a drink of water, letting it cool his anger.

"Is David Holcomb your employee?"

"Yes, he was. What's this about, Detective?" Joshua leaned forward, his elbows on the desk. "You usually ask that type of question when there's been another murder. But it's too early for the Iron Maiden killer to strike, isn't it?"

"It is. David's dead, at least we think he is. We haven't found the body yet. I don't know if it's connected or not. You said he was an employee. What happened?"

"Last week he got stoned and drunk on the job, which was surprising because he was proud of being five years sober. I don't allow that behavior in my bouncers."

"What day was that?"

Joshua crinkled his nose, looking to the side. "Wednesday."

Sean jotted it down in his notes. That was three days before the attack on Carol.

"I had to fire him. Michael was pretty upset. Turns out David was a college buddy. He forced me to rehire David. He worked Thursday, still acting hungover, but hasn't shown up for work since, so I let him go—again. Michael can bite me. I'm in charge of personnel. I thought David was on a bender. When people fall off the wagon, they usually fall hard. It's a shame. He was extremely proud of his new baby and being a father. How's Carol taking this?"

"His wife and baby are in the hospital with a serious infection." Sean didn't elaborate on how they'd become infected. He told Joshua which hospital they were in. "Is Michael going to be in tonight? I'd like to ask him about David."

Joshua shook his head. "No. He mentioned taking his new fling out to La Boucherie in LA. They might swing by after dinner, but I doubt it."

Sean thanked Joshua and drove back to the police station. Something about David had his instincts pinging. He thought about the Holcomb's house and couldn't imagine David being able to afford it on a bouncer's salary. Perhaps he was one of those losers who lived off his wife's income.

Like he told Joshua, David's death was too early for the Iron Maiden killer, but the time was close. He expected to find a gruesome body in the next week or so. He couldn't help wondering if this latest spree of violence and the Iron Maiden case were somehow related. There had always been an increase in violent crimes at the same time as the Iron

Maiden killings. But it hadn't ever been as bad as the past two weeks had been.

Sean worried Michael's new playmate was another Ginny. As soon as things calmed down, he'd check on Ginny and make sure she was okay. In the meantime, he'd trail Michael and get a good look at his girlfriend. He'd never forgive himself if he didn't, and something happened to her. A call to the restaurant, and a few choice words about obstructing justice, and he learned Michael's reservation was at eight. Before Sean left the office to head to LA, he grabbed a surveillance camera.

 # CHAPTER 8 

Throughout the next day, Catlyn couldn't shake the final image of Amelia lying dead out of her mind. Catlyn rarely recalled the readings she did. They weren't for her, but for her clients. She didn't need to remember the message the cards and Spirit had for them after she'd shared it. The unusually vivid vision of impending doom bothered her.

Her phone's ring tone for her boyfriend, Karl, startled her into dropping the jump ring she was attempting to affix to a new necklace for the third time. She hadn't seen him since all the craziness in her life started. His sales job took him out of town frequently.

"Hi, Sweetie," Karl said, trying to make his voice sound sexy. She rolled her eyes. "I'm back in town, and I closed that big deal."

"That's fabulous, Karl. I know how much it meant to you."

"It isn't every day you can negotiate a deal with the great Thomas Drogger."

A shiver shot up Catlyn's spine. She didn't know why the name of the wealthiest businessman in Orange County would cause such a reaction. An image of Amelia popped into her mind, and she recalled Amelia now worked for Mr. Drogger.

"I made reservations at the exclusive La Boucherie in Los Angeles for tomorrow night," Karl continued. "Be sure to wear something nice and not your usual witchy garb. It isn't appropriate for such an upscale place. I'll pick you up at six."

Tears pricked Catlyn's eyes at his hurtful tone and comment. He often chided her on the way she dressed, or wore her hair, or the extra weight around her hips. Before she could formulate a response, he hung up.

She fumed, wondering why she still dated him. He hadn't even asked if the time would work for her. He'd assumed she'd rearrange her schedule if it wasn't. Their sex was good—well, better than good—but that didn't build a lasting relationship. She wanted someone she could trust and who treated her with respect.

The kind eyes of Detective McLarkin flashed in front of her. She snorted at her foolishness. She'd only met the guy once, and it was unlikely she'd run into him again. Although she kept hoping he'd show up at the Jupiter Moon.

She went online and Googled the restaurant, whistling when she found it. The swanky French steakhouse appeared to be fabulous. She'd wait to see how this date with Karl turned out before she made any rash decisions about them.

She called her friend Lisa. "Hey Lisa, do you think I can borrow your cute black dress? Karl's taking me to a ritzy restaurant, and I need a chic dress appropriate for it. You know I don't own anything like that."

Lisa laughed. "Yeah, your style is more shabby chic or Gothic goddess. Where is he taking you?"

"La Boucherie."

"Ooh, I've heard about it. It's about time he took you some place fabulous. Come on over. I have a few dresses that would work."

Catlyn spent the evening having fun with Lisa, trying on dresses. The designer dresses were way out of Catlyn's price range. For a moment, she allowed herself to wish she had extra money to buy fabulous clothes—or not worry if she could make her rent.

Her Friday schedule was light, and Catlyn had the afternoon free to get ready for her date. Catlyn pulled the short, lacy black dress she'd borrowed from Lisa over her hips. She tried to tug it down farther, uncomfortable with the short length. She normally wore maxi skirts. Pulling her red-gold hair into an up-do, she let a few strands fall into loose curls around her face. Her two cats, Mittens and Boots, watched her. She crouched down, carefully petting them to keep cat hair off her black dress, especially Mitten's long gray fur.

Catlyn finished putting on her makeup at the same time Karl knocked on her door. She pulled it open and took in Karl's expensive dark gray suit with subtle pinstripes. His emerald green silk shirt brought out the green in his hazel eyes.

"Wow!" Karl whistled as he brushed a hand through his short, brown hair. "I didn't know you could look so fabulous. You should wear miniskirts more often. You have the legs for them." He pulled her close and kissed her deeply, running his hands over the curve of her butt. "If it hadn't taken days to get reservations at the restaurant, I'd suggest we stay here."

His voice was husky, and she felt his desire press against her. Her stomach growled, reminding her she hadn't eaten since breakfast that morning.

"I'm starving." She pulled away from him, then picked up the small clutch she'd also borrowed from Lisa rather than carry her oversized purse. The shimmery black shawl she swung over her shoulders was her defiant touch of "witchy" clothes. She enjoyed wearing feminine clothing.

As they drove into LA, their conversation stalled, almost as much as the northbound traffic on the 405. Catlyn wanted to tell Karl about the bizarre things she'd seen, but doubted he'd react well. Especially after his snide comments about her wardrobe choices.

They finally arrived at the hotel that housed the restaurant, and the valet helped Catlyn from the car. Huffing, she hurried to catch up to Karl, who hadn't waited for her. Her heels clicked on the hotel's marble floors as they made their way to the elevators that would take them to the 70th floor.

As they walked into the restaurant, the sweeping views of Los Angeles caught her breath. The traffic lights flickered far below them like fairy lights. She hated going into LA, but for this view, she'd make an exception. A spectacular bar, with modern sculpted lights highlighting the top-shelf alcohol, dominated the entryway. Couples sat on plush teal velvet lounge chairs, chatting and sipping on their drinks while they waited for their table. The booths featured tufted velvet backs and leather seats. Soft jazz music played in the background. The whole vibe was modern, elegant, and chic. After seeing the other women in expensive cocktail dresses, Catlyn was grateful she'd borrowed a stylish, designer dress from Lisa.

The maitre d'hotel led them to a small golden table, pulling out a sleek modern chair for Catlyn. Every table had a good view of the LA skyline. A tiny gasp escaped her when she opened the menu. Karl glanced up at her and glared.

"Order whatever you want," he snapped. "I can afford it. This is a celebration. I'm getting a hefty commission on the deal I closed with Drogger."

If Karl had closed the sales deal he'd been talking about for weeks, then he did have some extra cash. Sometimes the disparity in their incomes bothered her, and she wondered why he dated someone so far beneath him. Even with her multiple jobs, she barely made her rent, and that was in a seedy part of Anaheim.

Catlyn took a deep breath, opened the menu again, and choked at the $55 price for a pork chop. When Karl ordered the most expensive item on the menu and the costliest bottle of wine, Catlyn narrowed her eyes. He didn't normally flout his money at her so openly. She decided to enjoy the rare luxury and ordered the filet mignon.

The waiter brought over a tray filled with salts and mustards from around the world. As Catlyn was making her selection, trying to seem worldly, a commotion at the front caught her attention. A man with longish blond hair walked in with a willowy blond on his arm. Catlyn's mouth dropped open at the sight of Amelia decked out in a gorgeous red gown and diamonds glittering at her throat. No wonder she'd been in a tizzy about her boss's son if he gave her such an expensive necklace. Two guards walked ahead of the couple, with two more behind them.

They crossed a few feet from Catlyn and Karl's table, and Catlyn sucked in a breath. The blond guard trailing the man was one of her stalkers. A slimy, evil energy wafted off the group. Catlyn's heart faltered when Amelia's date stepped into view. He was the man from the beach. He'd turned up at the shop the other day, and every time she saw him, he gave her the heebie-jeebies.

Catlyn sat back, stunned, when Amelia walked past her and pretended she didn't know her. She wrinkled her nose at the unfettered lust and greed on Karl's face as he watched Amelia and her date walk to their table. Rather than being seated at one of the private booths, Amelia and her date sat at a central table where everyone in the restaurant could see them.

"Someday, I'll be able to dress my date like that," Karl breathed. "Did you see the watch he's wearing? I swear it's an *Audemars Piguet*. It costs at least $160 thousand. Can you imagine wearing a watch like that? Someday, Catlyn, someday, that will be me."

Catlyn gaped at Karl. She hadn't seen such lust and greed in him before. She only wanted to be able to pay her bills and keep the lights on. Her godmother Jade did well in her business and lived in a gated community in Newport Beach right on the beach. But it was nothing like what Karl now gushed about.

Amelia's date glanced up and saw them staring at him. He gave Catlyn a slow wink and Karl a sly grin. Catlyn's skin crawled.

The rest of the night, Karl couldn't stop talking about the rich man and his beautiful date. He seemed oblivious—or didn't care—that the way he talked made Catlyn feel ugly and unwanted. By the time they returned home, she claimed a headache and turned him away. She wasn't sure she ever wanted to see him again, let alone sleep with him. Her abused and battered heart ached as she dropped into bed with her cats snuggling next to her.

Sean wove through the heavy northbound 405 traffic, arriving at the InterContinental Hotel, which housed the restaurant with half an hour to set up before Michael's reservation. He parked his car with a good view of the entrance and balanced the long lens of his camera on the steering wheel. Several luxury cars pulled up to the valet stand while he waited. He whistled appreciatively at a red Lexus RC sports car. A beautiful, curvy woman with auburn hair stepped from the car, uncomfortably tugging down her short skirt.

She turned, and he glimpsed her face. His gut wrenched as he recognized her as the cute woman from the Jupiter Moon coffee shop, Catlyn. He hadn't even considered she might be dating someone—someone with more money than he made as a police detective. The guy had to make good money to drive the Lexus sports car he did and take his girl to such a ritzy restaurant. Sean's heart squeezed, doubtful he'd have a chance with her now. He snapped several photos of her, anyway. She was just too beautiful.

The man with her wore an expensive gray suit. Sean's hackles rose as the guy possessively grabbed Catlyn's arm and pulled her next to him. "You jerk," he muttered.

The guy's long strides made it difficult for Catlyn to keep up in her heels, which from the way she walked, she didn't wear often. Before they disappeared into the hotel, Sean snapped a photo of them. He wanted to do a background check on the creep.

A little later, a big black limousine eased into the valet station. Sean sat up straighter and readied his camera. He took photos of Michael's bodyguards as the four big men piled out and waited. Michael exited the car, wearing a black and white tuxedo. He tugged the sleeves over the diamond cuff links Sean could make out even from the distance. Sean snapped several photos.

Michael swaggered to the passenger side and held out his hand. A long, pale leg emerged, followed by a beautiful blond wearing a red gown with diamonds glittering at her throat. Even as he furiously took pictures, Sean appreciated her beauty. She turned her back to him, and his breath caught at her dress's open back, plunging past her waist. He compared the tall blond with Catlyn, and he'd take Catlyn over the blond any day. She had an earthy warmness about her that drew him to her.

He slapped his cheek. "Focus, man! You can't let her distract you from your job. You're here for Michael, not to ogle the pretty psychic."

He waited several minutes, giving Michael and his entourage time to take the elevators to the restaurant on the 70th floor. He ran into the hotel and jumped into the elevator. As it made its slow way up, Sean leaned against the far wall, away from the glass that showed the lights of

LA growing further distant. He took deep breaths to calm his fluttering stomach. Heights always bothered him. The elevator finally opened and spilled him out in the fancy steakhouse's lobby.

The maitre d'hotel sniffed at his lack of jacket and tie but left him alone when Sean flashed his badge. Sean peered around the man, noticing Michael and his date walking to their table. They passed Catlyn and her date. Catlyn glanced up. Her jaw dropped, and her eyes widened. "Amelia?"

The blond woman glanced at her, but instead of smiling, turned her face away. With her nose in the air, she stalked to the table the server indicated.

The odd exchange set off Sean's cop radar. Then it hit him. The incident gave him a perfect excuse to talk to Catlyn again. She had information about Michael's girlfriend. It may be the break Sean needed to catch Michael.

His quarry ordered a bottle of wine. Sean sighed. They'd be here a while.

"Can I see a menu?" he asked the maitre d'.

His nose up in the air, the man gingerly handed it to him. Sean glanced at the menu, gulping at the prices. *$55 for a pork chop! That's insane.* Give him an Outback ribeye, or even better, a T-bone tossed on the backyard barbecue, and he'd be in heaven. He gave the menu back to the waiter without ordering any of the outrageously priced food.

Sean found a plush chair that gave him a good view of Michael's table, and which also conveniently had a large potted plant he could hide behind. He settled in to wait, ignoring his growling stomach as the tantalizing smells wafted from the plates the waiters carried by him.

Finally, the maitre d' handed him a plate of fries. "If you insist on sulking here, Officer, at least do so quietly."

Sean bit into a fry, the rich flavor melting in his mouth, unlike anything he'd had before. Then he remembered seeing duck fat fries on the menu. He savored every last delicious morsel of them.

Catlyn and her date stood to leave. She didn't appear happy. Sean turned so she couldn't see him. He didn't want her to think he was stalking her. As they walked to the elevator, Sean heard the guy gushing about Michael's wealth and his knockout date. *He's a complete jerk! I might have a shot at dating Catlyn, after all.* His nose wrinkled as he remembered she was a witness in one of the weird incidents. He'd have to close that case so there wouldn't be any issues of impropriety.

He yawned, then grimaced when the waiter brought Michael another bottle of wine.

Two hours later, Sean scrambled from his hiding place as Michael and his gang pushed their chairs back. He rushed to his car, slamming the door and turning on the engine in time to follow Michael's limousine onto the freeway. At 11 o'clock, the Friday night traffic thinned enough that Sean easily kept the car in view. "Oh, shit!" he swore when they took the Long Beach exit and drove to the marina.

Sean slammed his hand on his steering wheel as Michael escorted his date onto his yacht. It pulled away from the dock. "Dammit all to hell! Can't I catch a break on this case?"

Unable to follow, he turned the camera on to look through the pictures he'd taken. The ones of Catlyn and her date were clear and sharp. But any pictures of Michael or his group were blurred—again. Every time Sean tried to take photos of his suspect, any that had Michael or his goons in them never turned out. The camera worked fine when Michael wasn't in the shot.

"Damn, damn, damn!" Sean tossed the camera onto the passenger seat. He'd hoped he'd finally get some evidence against Michael.

Calmed down, he flipped through the photos again. All he had to show for his night of loitering was the picture he'd taken of Michael's date as she exited the car.

 # Chapter 9 

Over the next several days, one of the two men stalking Catlyn followed her whenever she left her home. Both were big bruisers whose wide shoulders stretched their thin T-shirts. They wore their hair buzzed close to their heads and dark glasses hid their eyes, making them look similar. One had dull blond hair and the other brown. Their only other distinguishing trait was the brown-haired man smoked, and the blond didn't. They sat in expensive black sedans and watched her every move. After the first time, when the cops couldn't see them, she didn't bother calling the police again.

Catlyn tried convincing herself her stalkers were figments of her imagination, but then the stench of Smoker Dude's cigarette would waft to her. Its unique odor was unlike any other tobacco she'd smelled before. Blond Guy had the habit of whistling an eerie sound and tune whenever she stepped outside. He'd only stop when she raced into the house and slammed the door behind her or jerked her car door shut.

She worried about paying her skyrocketing electrical bill from using her air conditioner so much. Every time she opened a window to let a little air into her tiny apartment, either the cigarette stink or the awful tune filtered inside.

Her cats, Mittens and Boots, had taken to pushing their way behind the living room blinds. They pressed their noses against the glass with their tails swishing in anger. Every few minutes, one or the other would let out a low, hissing growl.

The Sunday after her disastrous date with Karl, Catlyn had a rare free day from the store. She spent the time working on several new jewelry pieces for her Etsy shop. After hours of listening to her cats, she flung down the crystal she'd been trying to create a wire bezel for in irritation.

"Come on, kitties, give me a break." She crossed to the window. With one knee on the couch, she leaned over and raised the blinds. Smoker Dude leaned against his car, smoking. He glanced up, giving her an evil grin.

A thrill of fear washed through her, sure she'd seen a glimpse of fangs. Gulping, she looked away and stroked Mittens, unsure if she was soothing the cat or herself. The cat continued to glare furiously at Smoker Dude, her tail thumping on the back of the couch. On the other side of Catlyn, her orange tabby, Boots, hissed, then bumped his head against Catlyn's arm. "At least you two can see them. Why can't anyone else?"

An idea sparked, and she grabbed her phone, snapping several pictures of Smoker Dude. She'd show them to the police, then they'd do something about her stalkers! But when she scrolled through her camera roll, the only thing on them was the apartment building across the way. She looked out the window again. Smoker Dude threw his head back and evil laughter wrapped around her. Tears of frustration—and fear—coursed down Catlyn's cheeks as she sank onto the couch. Mittens leaped down and curled up in Catlyn's lap.

After a while, Catlyn called Jade again. This time, she received a message telling her Jade's voicemail was full. Still shaken, Catlyn sent a text: *Help! I'm scared. Call me, please.* She gripped her phone with white knuckles, willing it to ring until the dark shadows of evening blurred the room. Finally, she wandered into the kitchen where she heated a can of spaghetti and meatballs in the microwave—all she had the energy to do for dinner. She tried watching a movie, but the fear that had taken up residence inside of her stayed entrenched.

Before she went to bed, she checked her lunar calendar. The moon was in its final waning stage, only a few days before the dark moon, making it a perfect time for a protection ritual. She lit candles around her bedroom and in the bathroom, then ran hot water into the tub, dumping a handful of bath salts for purification.

After her bath, she pulled on the black dress she reserved for ritual wear. Carefully choosing the symbolic items to represent the elements of earth, air, water, and fire, Catlyn set up her altar. Taking a deep breath, she thought about her intention for the ritual: to be safe and protected.

She cast a circle and called in the directions of east, south, west, north, above, below, and center. Then she stood before her altar. In the center lay a drawing she'd made of a heptacle—a seven-pointed star in a circle. She pointed her crystal wand at the heptacle to call in the seven elements. In addition to the four elements of air, water, fire, and earth, she added the elements of light, shadow, and dark to join her circle. She took it on faith that the energies came to her bidding.

As she called in the air element, a pale-yellow wisp of light floated above the point of her heptacle dedicated to air. Her heart fluttered with excitement. Perhaps she was becoming a real witch and doing actual magic after years of wishing. Awed, she continued calling in the remaining elements of water, fire, and earth. She tamped down her disappointment when nothing else supernatural occurred.

Sitting down, she began the work of her ritual. She prayed to the Goddess Hecate to protect her, telling the Goddess of her need and fear. She concentrated on her faith and her trust in the power of the Goddess. In her mind's eye, she imagined her home, her car, and herself encased in a magical bubble where nothing could harm her.

Peace wrapped around her. Cerulean-blue eyes in a white face floated before her mind's eye. *"Soon, little one,"* she heard the etheric voice say. *"I'll be there soon. You are safe. I'm guarding you."*

Catlyn decided the voice sounded feminine. As the eyes and voice faded away, Catlyn's loneliness and fear evaporated.

The next day, as Catlyn climbed out of her car, the familiar black Mercedes drove into the Mystical Enchantments' parking lot. As he passed her, Smoker Dude rolled down his darkened window, lowered his dark glasses, and leered at her.

Catlyn's heart skipped a beat at his glowing yellow-orange eyes.

"Soon, priestess, it will be your time." He licked his lips with a forked tongue. He'd never spoken to her before.

His laughter chased her as she ran into the store. Inside, she leaned against the door, panting.

Michelle looked up from where she sat on the floor stocking a shelf with a new shipment of books. "Honey, what's wrong?"

"Michelle, I'm so scared. Strange men have been following me for over a week."

"What men?"

"Haven't you noticed the black sedan sitting outside all day?"

Michelle frowned and shook her head. She stood, walked to the window, and peered out. "There isn't a black sedan out there now, just a blue pickup truck."

Catlyn whirled around. Her stalker's car crouched next to the truck. "It's the Mercedes with tinted windows."

"There isn't anything there, honey. Are you sure you're okay? I didn't think you saw ghosts."

"I don't," Catlyn huffed. "That car and the men in it are as real as you or me. They aren't ghosts."

Michelle looked out again, squinting her eyes. "I still don't see anything other than the blue truck. But if you say someone is following you, then I believe it. Have you talked to the police?"

Catlyn snorted. "I did the first night they followed me. The police couldn't see anything and thought I was crazy."

Later that afternoon, Catlyn waited for Amelia to arrive for her healing appointment. The time passed and still Amelia didn't show up. The heavy Southern California traffic sometimes caused her to be late, but she always let Catlyn know she was on the way. After waiting half an hour, Catlyn called her friend. When Amelia's perky voice told Catlyn to leave a message, her heart plummeted to her toes, and painful heat washed over her. An image flooded Catlyn's mind of Amelia blindfolded, bound, and sliced open with a sword, her blood pooling beneath her. She knew with a cold, clear certainty something bad had happened to Amelia.

Maybe I'm being paranoid and Amelia is off somewhere with her rich boyfriend. Catlyn couldn't shake the awful feeling she had about Amelia or the frightening image. After trying to reach Amelia throughout the evening and the next morning, Catlyn called the police, only telling them that her friend was missing. She didn't dare tell them anything else. They wouldn't believe her if she told them she'd seen Amelia's death in a tarot reading and now saw it as a psychic vision. Her thoughts flew to the cute detective, Sean McLarkin. Would he believe her? Would he help her find her friend? Her hopes sank. She didn't know what precinct he worked in.

Sean held the photo of Michael's date by the corner, tapping it on the folder. His job would be much easier if his department had access to the facial recognition software shown so often on television cop shows. He couldn't use any official resources to research the blond woman, otherwise, his captain would find out he was investigating Michael.

The playboy's father, Thomas Drogger, had made it clear Sean was to leave his son alone. The billionaire had enough clout to destroy Sean's career. Sean's "Granny Vibes" pinged every time he encountered Michael Drogger. Something was off about the guy. He refused to dismiss his intuition's warning bells simply because Michael had ruined Sean's relationship with Ginny. He'd tried calling her over the weekend, but someone else had her cellphone number. When he arrived at the office, he searched her name in the missing persons database. Thankfully, it hadn't appeared. A search of her driver's license revealed she no longer lived in California.

On Saturday, Sean had driven to the Long Beach marina, the usual berth for Michael's yacht to find it empty. He spent Sunday afternoon driving down to Newport Beach on the off-chance it was there. No luck. He'd driven to Oceanside to check the San Diego county marinas when his better sense finally grabbed hold of him and shook him back to reality. He could hit every marina between Santa Barbara and Los Cabos at the tip of Baja California and could still miss whatever port Michael had pulled into. Sean didn't have any cause to call the Coast Guard and ask them to search for the boat.

Sean slid the photo back into the file folder. Pursing his lips, he tapped Catlyn's business card as he contemplated calling her.

"Hey, Sean! Earth to Sean," Lourdes called, banging on a clear spot where their desks met. "We have another call. Quit daydreaming about that blond beauty. She's out of your league."

Sean scowled in confusion.

"I saw you gazing adoringly at that bombshell's photo you slipped into your folder."

"She isn't my type."

"Come on, she's every man's type."

"I don't even know her. She was Michael's date Friday night." Sean groaned. He hadn't meant to let that tidbit slip.

"McLarkin!" Lourdes hissed, then pulled Sean from his chair and dragged him by his elbow down the hall to the elevator. "Are you trying to get fired? What are you doing chasing Drogger? The captain read you the riot act when you accosted Drogger after the last Iron Maiden killing."

"I keep telling you, Jerry, Drogger is involved." Sean entered the elevator and leaned his back against the wall, his arms folded across his chest. "I can't prove it, but I know it in my gut."

"Guts don't convict people, evidence does. You find the evidence, and I'll help you nail that bastard."

Sean relaxed his stance. His partner was a good guy with double the years of Sean's experience chasing murderers under his belt.

"What's it this time?"

"Another murder." Jerry opened the driver's side door and slid into the car.

Sean grimaced. He preferred to drive. Jerry drove like an old man.

"Thankfully," Jerry continued, pulling away from the police station, "this one is a straight-up murder, unlike the last dozen cases we've dealt with. Someone found a mutilated body by the Double Tree Hotel's dumpsters."

Sean whistled. "It's rare for a homicide to be committed at the upscale hotel."

"The initial forensics indicate it's the dump site, not the murder scene."

Twenty minutes later, they pulled into the hotel's parking lot and around the back where a slew of police cars, their lights flashing, had taken up temporary residence. They would have arrived ten minutes faster if Sean had been driving. After the first red light, Jerry had hit every one between the station and the hotel.

Sean spotted his forensic buddy, Brian, and made a beeline for him. "What do we have, Brian?" he asked as he surveyed the scene. Body parts lay strewn on the ground, or what remained of them. Something large had chewed on them and ripped huge chunks of flesh from the bones.

"We think the vic was male, based on the shreds of clothing we found."

"Hey!" a crime tech called from the depths of the dumpster. "I found the head." The tech emerged from the dumpster, holding aloft a man's head by his short, dirty blond hair.

"I know that man," Sean said. He opened his photo app and scrolled through it. He examined the picture and the man's face, frozen in a terrified scream.

While the crime tech put the severed head in a bag, Lourdes strolled up. His face scrunched. "Isn't that ..."

"David Holcomb. The real David."

"You were right," Jerry muttered. "Mrs. Holcomb didn't kill her husband."

Sean straightened his back, pleased with the acknowledgment. He turned to Brian. "Is there any way to tell how long he's been dead?"

"Not here. The coroner will have to do tests to determine that." Brian examined Sean's face. "But from the putrefaction, I'd guess it's been at least two weeks."

"Thanks, Brian."

If Brian was right, that meant David Holcomb had been dead before the attack on Carol and her baby. Deep in thought, Sean shuffled back to Lourdes' car and leaned against it as he flipped through his notes. He found his interview with Joshua, the manager of the Red Orchid. David had acted strange a few days before Carol's assault. It must have been the impostor.

But who could duplicate another person so well that those that knew him intimately couldn't tell the difference? Carol hadn't suspected the man living with her wasn't her husband until he tried eating their child. Sean flicked to the picture Brian had sent him of the creature's teeth. There was no denying the creature emulating David Holcomb wasn't human. Was it an alien? What had it wanted with David or Carol?

Sean knew Michael Drogger was mixed up in this somehow. He needed to find the evidence to prove it. The link between David and Michael may be the missing piece to tie Michael to the Iron Maiden Killer. If Sean could just figure out how it all fit together.

 # CHAPTER 10 

Catlyn called Amelia frequently over the next three days, but all her calls went directly to voicemail. The police hadn't contacted her yet with any information. Her fear for her friend raged, no matter how many times she told herself Amelia was having a great time with her new boyfriend and she was being paranoid. At odd moments, the image of Amelia in a pool of blood would rise in her mind to haunt Catlyn.

Trying to get her mind off her friend's plight, Catlyn bustled around her tiny apartment, cleaning. Laughter bubbled up as Mittens skittered across the living room floor, barreling into the bedroom when Catlyn turned on the vacuum cleaner. Boots casually jumped onto the breakfast bar in the kitchen, where he warily watched the mechanical monster making all the noise.

Her timer pinged, reminding her to take her last batch of laundry out of the dryer. She flipped off the vacuum and slid the machine into the small utility closet in the hallway between her living area and the bedroom. Grabbing an empty basket, she skipped down the stairs to the apartment complex's laundry room.

When she returned, a tough-looking woman in her late forties sat on the top stair, waiting. Her pixie cut brown hair accentuated her triangular chin. At the moment, tufts stuck out at odd angles. She wore dark jeans, black ankle boots, and a dark t-shirt, showing off her toned, muscular arms. The woman's cinnamon-brown eyes held the promise of lethal menace, but Catlyn knew it was a facade. Jade had a heart of gold.

Catlyn paused at the bottom of the stairs, studying her godmother. A black eye swelled her right eye shut, and a butterfly bandage sealed a cut over her left eyebrow. Mottled purple and green bruises covered both arms, and her left arm hung in a sling.

"Damn, Jade, you look awful," Catlyn said. "That must have been one hell of an assignment. No wonder you haven't called me back."

"Thanks, kid." Sarcasm dripped from Jade's voice. She grimaced as she pushed to her feet. She usually moved with lithe grace. "I've been down for the past week. My staff didn't think to check my personal phone for messages."

"But what about the week before that? I've been trying to reach you for two weeks now, Jade."

"I was out of town. There wasn't any cell reception where I was. Can we go inside where it's more comfortable?"

Catlyn climbed the stairs, joining Jade on the landing, who at five-ten, towered over Catlyn. "Sure, the door's open. Why didn't you go in? You have a key."

"It didn't seem right to invade your space after the way we last parted company. I am trying not to be so overprotective of you."

Jade preceded Catlyn into the apartment, her eyes skimming over the area. Catlyn rolled her eyes. Jade always searched for threats, even in a safe place. Catlyn dumped her clean clothes out of the basket and onto her bed so they wouldn't be as wrinkly when she folded them later. A smile played on Catlyn's lips at the sight of Boots in Jade's lap, rubbing against her hand and demanding attention. He'd love anyone who would pet him.

Catlyn opened the fridge and filled two glasses with ice water. She held out one to Jade, debating if she should also offer a couple of aspirin.

Jade murmured her thanks and took a deep drink. "So, sweet girl, tell me what has you so frightened and worked up about."

Catlyn slumped onto the other end of the couch. "It's so scary, Jade, and it's totally freaking me out." She told Jade about the two men following her. As she did, she nonchalantly pushed the blind up. Smoker Dude leaned against his car, smoking. "One of my stalkers is out there now."

Jade swiftly twisted to peer out the window. "That guy smoking?"

Catlyn's jaw dropped. "How can you see them when no one else has been able to?"

Jade made a face, then winced as it tugged on her healing cut. "You don't think all the magic I've taught you is just imaginary or pretend, do you? The asshole is using a cloaking spell." Her lips pulled into a thin line, and her uninjured hand balled into a fist.

Catlyn's eyebrows squished together, confused why it made her godmother so angry.

"I'm putting a protective detail on you," Jade announced in a tight voice, "and tomorrow morning you're going to start training with me again." She scowled down at her arm in the sling. "I'll arrange for someone to spar with you."

Catlyn had anticipated the training, but not the bodyguards. "No, Jade. I don't need to be babysat by your people. I don't want them hanging around. It's bad enough to have my every move watched by those guys."

"My men will be monitoring those idiots, not you."

"But they'll still be getting in my way."

"Posh." Jade waved her hand in a negating motion. "You won't even know they're around. You haven't before."

"What?" Catlyn shifted on the couch to face Jade, glowering at her. "You've had people watching me?"

Jade held up her hand defensively. "Only in times of danger, honey. They've never been there to intrude or interfere with your personal life. I just want to make sure you're safe. Do you remember Robbie?"

Catlyn inclined her head. Robbie was one of her boyfriends Jade had run off.

"He wasn't who or what you thought he was, Catlyn. He was dealing drugs and ran into trouble with his supplier. They threatened to hurt you if he didn't pay up. Remember the car accident you two were in? That wasn't an accident. If my guys hadn't been protecting you, you'd be dead right now."

Catlyn's hand flew up to cover her open mouth. "Oh! I didn't know."

"Your safety is important to me. I'd much rather have you alive to be angry at me, then to bury you like your parents."

Jade's eyes misted over, and she looked away. Jade had been good friends with both of Catlyn's parents before they were killed. Even after Catlyn had moved in with her mother's sister, Aunt Lucy, Jade had stayed close with Catlyn.

Catlyn's hurt and anger slid away like water down the drain. Jade always had Catlyn's best interests at heart. Jade didn't have any children of her own and treated Catlyn like the daughter she wished she'd had. The awkwardness between them lifted like a broken creek dam, and their conversation flowed again as easily as it had when she was younger.

Catlyn reached up to switch on a lamp as twilight deepened the shadows in the living room. A contented smile lifted her lips. It had been a long time since she and Jade had talked the afternoon away.

"Leave it off," Jade said. "Grab your purse. Let's go get dinner. My treat."

"Mexican?" Catlyn jumped off the couch.

Jade's eyes glittered with amusement. "Of course."

Catlyn's Aunt Lucy and Uncle Robert hated Mexican food, which was unusual for people living in Southern California where the cuisine was so prevalent. Whenever Catlyn had spent time with Jade growing up, she'd beg to go out for her favorite food. It had become their "thing."

When Catlyn returned from her bedroom, bag in hand, Jade was tucking her cell phone into her jeans pocket. Catlyn assumed she'd been calling in reinforcements to watch Catlyn. Jade made a point of walking in front of Smoker Dude and glare at him. His face paled, and he slithered into his car, talking frantically with someone on his cell phone.

Catlyn's respect for Jade grew to new heights with her ability to frighten the tough guy with simply her presence. It didn't stop Smoker Dude from following them from the parking lot. Jade zipped through a yellow light as it turned red, leaving him behind. Catlyn twisted around and saw him hitting his steering wheel in frustration.

Jade took several turns on small side streets and through the neighborhood. When Catlyn looked back again, there wasn't any sign of the black sedan that had been her constant companion for the last two weeks. She pressed a palm to her chest. Maybe it wouldn't be so bad to have Jade's people protecting her.

Her feeling of safety fled when she glanced up from her food. Amelia's date from the other night and Blond Guy sauntered past her. *How in the hell did he find me? Where's Amelia?*

Amelia's boyfriend insisted on taking a table where he had a clear view of Catlyn. He gave Jade a disdainful flick of his eyes, dismissing her while he leered at Catlyn and seductively licked his lips. Catlyn's skin crawled, and her fork clattered to her plate.

"Catlyn, what's wrong?" Jade turned her head, her body going rigid. Her voice sounded strained when she asked, "Do you know that man? The one with the long hair?"

"No, but his friend is one of the men stalking me. For some odd reason, they've taken an interest in me. I saw the man when I went down to the beach at the last full moon. He didn't say anything, but he freaked the hell out of me. The next day, the short-haired guy and that other goon started following me. It's why I've called you so many times."

"This isn't good." Concern filled Jade's eyes.

"And to top it off, he's dating one of my clients, who is also a friend."

"Tell her to stay away from Michael Drogger. He's as dangerous an asshole as they come."

Catlyn squeezed her hands together in her lap, staring down at them. "I think it's too late. She didn't show up for her healing appointment, nor is she answering her phone."

She told Jade about seeing Amelia and Michael on her date and her reading for Amelia.

The muscles in Jade's jaw tightened, and anger filled her eyes as Catlyn talked.

"How do you know him?" Catlyn asked.

Jade closed her eyes and took a deep breath. "Long story, and it isn't important right now. You *will* accept the protection detail I put on you and you *will* train with me, not just the martial arts, but the magic as well." Jade motioned to the waitress for their check.

Catlyn kept an eye on Michael and his bodyguard, her breaths coming in quick pants. When they were back in the car, her breathing eased.

"Do you remember the protection ritual against psychic attack I taught you?" Jade asked as they left the restaurant parking lot.

"Yes..." Catlyn stuttered, fear blooming in her chest, cutting off her breath.

"Then do it. Tonight. It's dark moon, a perfect time for it. It will protect you in the spiritual realm while my guys will guard you in the physical world. Michael is capable of hurting you in either place, or both."

Catlyn moaned and ducked her head between her legs. A crippling, knotting terror took residence in her belly.

"What ... what does he want with me?"

"I don't know. Nothing good, I can assure you." Jade rubbed her back. "I'll keep you safe, sweet girl. Just as I always have."

They rode in silence the rest of the way to Catlyn's place. As Jade pulled into the parking lot, they passed a car parked with a view of both Catlyn's apartment and Smoker Dude's sedan. The man inside saluted them. Catlyn's breathing eased, knowing someone stood between her and her stalkers.

After Jade left, Catlyn cleared her altar and called in the elements and directions. Then she created a crystal grid on it to neutralize and protect her from psychic attack. She formed a circle of tumbled black sardonyx stones. To create the main spokes of a wheel, she used wands made from rose quartz, amethyst, citrine, and rutilated quartz. In the center, she put a large chunk of clear quartz.

Catlyn laid down twelve pieces of deep-blue lapis lazuli to create an equal-armed cross, pointing to the four cardinal compass points. She set a piece of tourmalinated quartz in the northeast quadrant, and across from it, a piece of raw amertine. In the southwest quarter rested a large raw ruby with a rod of black tourmaline in the opposite quarter.

She called on the Goddess Hecate to guard and protect her. She picked up a small crystal singing bowl and tapped the leather encased mallet against the bowl. The pure, high-pitched tone echoed in her bedroom. As she ran the mallet around the rim, the sound grew. From somewhere deep within her, she sang a chant in an unknown, sacred language. Catlyn could feel the central clear quartz gather in the energy from the other crystals, the crystal bowl vibrations, and her chant.

Opening her eyes, she sat with her mouth agape. A powerful, dark energy swirled faster and faster within her magic circle. She knew that not everything dark was evil, nor was all that appeared light, good. When the energy peaked, the clear quartz absorbed it. Catlyn stopped chanting and playing the crystal bowl.

As the vibrations of the bowl faded, she held her breath. Before she ran out of air, a beam of dark light shot out of the tip of the crystal, through the ceiling, and burst from the room. The crystal pulsed once more, and the dark light zoomed toward her, surrounding her in a protective shield. She knew and trusted that nothing evil could penetrate it.

That night, she slept better than she had since sensing Michael watching her from the bluffs at full moon.

CHAPTER 11

When Catlyn left her apartment for work the next afternoon, she stopped in her tracks. The pernicious black sedan wasn't loitering in its usual spot. Swiveling her head around, she searched the parking lot for it. A tall man with short black hair, wearing jeans and a polo shirt with Jade's company logo embroidered on it, stepped from the side of the building. Catlyn recognized him as one of Jade's top specialists, Charlie MacNamara. Jade was serious about protecting Catlyn if she assigned him as part of her protection detail.

Charlie gave her a nod of acknowledgment, then headed to a silver beast of a truck. The outline of a weapon bulged from under the back of his shirt. The diesel engine roared to life before he even opened the door. He waited to get in until her puny Honda puttered awake. By the time she'd backed from her space, he had his truck in gear and ready to prowl behind her.

She wondered what happened to her stalkers, but not seeing them released the knot of fear in her stomach. She sang with the radio as she drove to work. Something she hadn't done since the sedans had first appeared in her rearview mirror.

Her protector's truck easily kept up with her through the afternoon freeway traffic. He pulled ahead of her before she reached Mystical Enchantments, peeling into the parking lot. When she pulled in, she glimpsed Charlie's empty truck. By the time she parked, he stood at the front door, opening it for her.

"All's clear, ma'am." He handed her a simple business card with Jade's logo and a phone number on it. "I'll be out here if you need me. Call that number. We've programmed it into the favorites on your phone. Your call will be routed to me or whoever is on duty."

A wisp of anger snagged her at the thought her godmother had already messed with her phone. But then she remembered Jade's reaction to Michael. If he was as dangerous as Jade believed, Catlyn had better follow Jade's guidance. Her godmother didn't scare easily.

"Thanks, Charlie. I will. I already feel safer with you around."

Charlie's green eyes lit up as he grinned.

The afternoon flowed from one client to the next without the problems or tension she'd been experiencing lately. Catlyn finished her last appointment with only a few minutes to spare before the weekly Shamanism class held at the store. She gathered her notebook and pen, then wandered to the small kitchen. Opening the fridge, she snatched a bottle of cold water. Her mouth watered at the sight of the homemade chocolate chip cookies someone had brought in. After eating the cookie and drinking most of the water, she stretched, refilled the bottle, and walked to the store's classroom.

Jade saw her enter and smiled. Where Catlyn looked the part of a psychic and weirdo, Jade was the antithesis of that persona. Dressed in her normal black t-shirt and black jeans, Jade sat cross-legged on a pillow. Her black leather jacket, boots, and motorcycle helmet were piled by the wall next to the door. She'd removed the bandage over her left eye, and her black eye had turned a lovely green. A sling still held her left arm.

Catlyn ambled over to Jade and leaned over, brushing a light kiss on her cheek, and whispered, "Thanks for the detail. I appreciate it. I do love you."

Jade grinned, her eyes bright with gathering tears. She awkwardly patted Catlyn's back with her uninjured hand.

Catlyn glanced around the room at the ten other women sprawled on the floor. She grabbed a pillow and a yoga mat from the waiting pile, putting them down between her friends Bri Nelson and Lisa Moon.

Once everyone had settled into their places and the door closed, Jade began the class. "Shamanic journeys are the mainstay of shamanic healing. We've taken journeys to the upper and lower worlds as visitors. Today, we'll travel to the lower world with the purpose of meeting our animal helper. These are spiritual beings who, by their choice, have decided to assist you in your journey. Some only appear once to give you a message, while others stay with you for days, sometimes for the rest of your life. The former are guides; the latter are totems."

She caught the gazes of the participants and leaned forward, resting her injured arm on her knees. "Place no judgment on the animal that comes to you. A mouse or a fly are as worthy as a wolf or jaguar, and all have lessons to teach you or wisdom to share. Did you bring your journals?"

Jade looked around the circle at all the women nodding. "Good. It's always an excellent idea to write about what you've seen or heard after a journey. For some, this will make the experience more real. For others, the act of writing continues the journey and allows more information to flow to them. There is no right or wrong way. Whatever works for you is the right way for you."

Catlyn glanced down at her journal and pen, waiting by her water bottle. For her, she usually received more insights as she wrote down her experience. She enjoyed reading her entries later to remember the amazing experiences she'd had, especially when life became a struggle.

"Let us begin." Jade stood up, lit a sage bundle, and walked around the outside of the circle, stopping at each person and smudging them. Then she faced east and called in the directions, one by one.

The familiar ritual calmed Catlyn's mind and spirit. The worry and stress of the week slid away. By the time Jade picked up her Native American-style drum and began beating a heartbeat rhythm, Catlyn had already fallen into a trance state. She listened as Jade led them on a Shamanic journey. Once Catlyn entered the lower world, Jade's voice and the drum faded into the background.

> *Catlyn stepped from the cave into a thick mist. The humidity soaked into her skin. Bright-colored birds squawked in the tall trees above her. The tree's bluish leaves and smooth gray bark were unlike anything she'd ever seen, even in pictures. She noticed a path between the trees and followed it. Ferns, glowing with lavender light, lined the path. The tiny heart-shaped leaves reached out toward her. Wherever they touched her, her skin glowed with the same pale light. Her heart rate slowed, and she grew calmer. The soft moss on the ground looked inviting, and after the last few stressful weeks, she yearned for a quiet, peaceful moment. She sank down on it and curled up, her eyes closing.*

No, I can't sleep. I'm here to meet my animal guide.

The insistent drumbeat become louder and faster, calling the journeyers to return to their own world. Catlyn tried not to feel disappointed because she hadn't met any animals. The hard floor pressed against her back as she returned from the trance.

A puff of air blew on her face as something snorted. Catlyn's eyes jerked open. A large white tigress stood over her. Catlyn's breath caught in her throat as she recognized the familiar deep cerulean-blue eyes. She blinked, unsure if she was awake or still in meditation.

The cat shimmered. In the graceful way all felines have, she settled down. Her body melted into Catlyn's until only her head remained hovering over Catlyn. The tip of her tongue flicked out and touched Catlyn's nose.

The tiger disappeared.

Catlyn jerked up and looked at Jade, but Jade didn't act like she had seen anything supernatural happen. She blithely continued to call the remaining travelers to return to their bodies. Catlyn brushed it off as part of her trance until she rubbed her nose and found it wet. *Oh my Goddess! It was real.*

Catlyn gaped, trying to understand what had happened to her. She'd never read of a totem merging with a human. When she tried to tell Jade about it after class, her tongue stuck to the roof of her mouth, and she couldn't get any words out.

The same otherworldly voice as in her visions whispered into her mind. "*Shh ... I am here. All is as it should be.*"

A feeling of rightness and purpose washed over Catlyn. Whoever—whatever—the tiger was, she wasn't evil. Catlyn thought of the protection spell she'd done last night. *Perhaps the spiritual tiger is how it manifested. Strange, but cool.*

Catlyn left the store and searched the parking lot for Charlie's truck. Her heart dropped when she spotted Blond Guy's familiar sedan. She glared at Blond Guy, worried something had happened to Charlie. A low growl escaped her throat. She clapped a hand over her mouth, astonished.

A moment later, a well-built man with a long, brunette ponytail stepped from the shadows by the door. "No worries, ma'am," he said with an Australian accent. She noted Jade's logo on the shirt stretched across his chest. "I'm Todd Fleming, one of your guards. I'll escort you to your car and follow you home."

"Okay." When she was safely in her car, she worried he'd heard her growl. *What the hell was that?*

On the way home, Catlyn's eyelids drooped lower and lower. The second time she jerked awake, she took the next exit off the freeway. She glanced in the rearview mirror at the truck following her and wondered if the bodyguard would think it odd if she asked him to drive her home. Lethargy filled her, making even the thought of picking up her cell phone and dialing the number a chore. Driving slowly on the familiar surface streets of her neighborhood, Catlyn finally made it home.

After parking in her assigned spot, she struggled to lift first one foot, then the other, from the car and to pull herself from its confines. She stood for several minutes, panting and hanging onto the door.

Her pony-tailed bodyguard slipped his arm around her waist. "Are you okay, ma'am?"

"I don't know what's wrong with me, but I'm suddenly so tired. Can you help me?"

Todd gently gripped her elbow, and with his help, she made the arduous climb up the stairs to her apartment. Each movement she took was a challenge with what felt like an extra five-hundred pounds added to her body.

"Do you need help to get inside?" he asked.

Catlyn shook her head. He stepped away from her, and his heavy steps plodded down the stairs as she pulled her keys from her purse. They jingled as she inserted the correct key. Soft meows filtered out—her welcoming committee getting into position. When she opened the door, her cats sat on the edge of the carpet where it met the tile entry. Both her cat's eyes widened and laid their ears back. They hissed at her and turned tail, running into the bedroom.

"Boots. Mittens," she called out. "What's wrong, babies?" She tracked them down to their hiding spot under her bed. They wouldn't come out, no matter how much she coaxed and cajoled. She raised an arm to her nose and sniffed. Nothing. *Can they see or smell the spirit tiger?*

Starving, Catlyn padded into the kitchen, opened the fridge, and stared, frowning. Nothing in it looked appetizing. She rummaged in her cupboards and took out a can of tuna. Scooping the fish out with her fingers, she stuffed it in her mouth, barely chewing. She wiped off the juices dribbling down her chin with the back of her hand. Her stomach still ached with hunger. Opening the freezer, she found a small steak and tossed it in the microwave to thaw. She threw it on a hot skillet, seared one side, then the other, just enough to warm the meat, and slid it onto a plate. Not bothering with a fork and knife, she picked up the steak and devoured it.

Stunned, Catlyn scrutinized her bloody hands. *This isn't like me. I don't eat raw meat. What's happening to me?*

She felt less heavy after eating. She cleaned up her dishes, put food down for the cats—who were still hiding—and prepared for bed. Lighting a candle and some incense, she sat at her altar, took several deep breaths, and relaxed into meditation.

Warm breath fluttered over her face. Catlyn's eyes flew open. Cerulean-blue eyes bored into hers. The white tiger crouched in front of her, their eyes now on the same level.

"*I have come,*" the tiger said in Catlyn's mind. Her voice familiar from Catlyn's visions. "*I am here to help you.*"

"Are you my totem helper?" Catlyn asked out loud.

"*No. Something more. You may think your words and I will hear them. After all, we now share the same body.*"

"What?" Catlyn exclaimed, scrambling backwards until her back hit her bed. "You possessed me?"

The tiger lifted her lip and gave a low growl. "*Nothing so crass. That is what demons do, and I am no demon.*"

"Then what are you? Who are you?"

"*I am Maak.*" The tiger pronounced it with two syllables. She dipped her head. "*I come from another world, another dimension. I can only exist in this dimension if I am connected to someone like you. You are still you, as I am still me. You are not possessed; we are merely tethered. We have great work to do together.*"

Catlyn frowned. "What work? Are you here to help me with the healing work I do?"

"*Nothing so simple. All will be revealed at the proper time.*" Her tongue flicked out to touch Catlyn's nose, then she disappeared again.

Catlyn rubbed her eyes. *It's just a vision. It isn't real.* She lifted a hand to her nose to find it wet. *Oh, sweet Goddess! It's real. Maak's real! What am I supposed to do?*

 # CHAPTER 12 

Sean McLarkin pulled up to the abandoned warehouse. His partner, Jerry, had a court appearance. Sean's stomach clenched with dread. The Iron Maiden serial killer had struck again. He'd been anticipating the call, but with all the other crazy murders, he'd hoped the Iron Maiden killer would take a vacation.

He followed the signs from the crime techs through the warehouse. The smell of blood and entrails blasted him as he made his way deeper into the warehouse's depths. Before he reached the actual crime scene, Brian, the crime tech he regularly worked with, stopped him and handed him a mask and plastic booties.

"Here," Brian said, "you'll want these if you don't want to ruin your shoes."

"That bad?" Sean grimaced.

Brian nodded, then went back to work collecting evidence and samples.

Sean had been a police officer in Anaheim for ten years and a homicide detective for the past four. He'd thought he'd become inured to death and murder until he'd caught this case. Normal people shot or stabbed their victims for the usual motives of money or passion—or both. Even psychopaths killed for sexual release or from some twisted form of love. Sean still couldn't figure out what triggered this killer, and neither could the FBI profiler who had shown up last year. The profiler had been smug and superior, showing his disdain for local cops at every opportunity. He'd bragged that he'd catch the guy before he struck again. The next victim had been the profiler.

All the scenes related to this crime were gruesome. Sean steeled himself as he put on the booties and mask. He walked through the door with a snap of his gloves. And immediately pressed the back of his hand to his mouth to quell a gag. A nasty and potent incense hovered underneath the sweet, iron scent of blood and the foul stench of punctured intestines.

A body hung from a hook by its wrists on a heavy chain descending from the ceiling. The perp had made thousands of deep cuts, nearly skinning the victim. Only the hands, chained to the hook, were left unscathed. He knew from experience the cuts were antemortem. He wondered briefly which ghastly medieval torture device the sick bastards had used this time. No matter which one, he was sure the coroner would find the poor person had suffered immensely over several days before finally being allowed to die.

Sean inspected the mutilated corpse. Like the others, the final killing blow had been a horizontal sword-cut to the abdomen, opening the intestines, then a vertical slice split open the chest cavity. If this one followed the pattern of the others, the heart and liver would be gone, as would a chunk of intestines.

The victim's hair had been shorn close to its head. The color undetectable under the coating of gore. Sean's gaze traveled up to the hands. They were small and delicate, with chips of bright red winking from under all the blood. A woman. His hands clenched into fists, and his teeth ground together. There would be evidence of rape, no matter the gender. The sick bastard, or bastards, who did this didn't have a sexual preference of who they violated. They had to be evil sons of bitches to do this to a woman—to anyone.

The culprits had painted a large, eight-foot pentagram—a five-pointed star within a circle—in blood on the floor. The blood would be mixed; some would be from his current victim, some from prior victims, and a small portion from an unknown source. The lab still couldn't determine what it came from, but it wasn't human—or any known animal. Sean's thoughts traveled back to the Holcomb Case, his heart squeezing. The baby had died yesterday. How he'd hung on for two weeks baffled the doctors. His mother, Carol, continued to languish in a coma from her injuries.

"Hey Brian, when you run the tests on the blood, check them against the Holcomb file, will you? See if there's a match or if those microbes you found are present here too."

Brian glanced up from where he crouched on the floor and gave Sean a brisk salute before turning back to work.

Sean turned his attention to the pentacle. Gore spattered the occult symbols drawn inside it. The body hung over the pentacle's precise center. A surprisingly small amount of blood covered the floor beneath it. Blood must have flown everywhere when the perp slashed the victim, but not a drop marred the floor or walls beyond the circle. The blood stopped at the circle's edges and pooled around it, almost as if a wall blocked it.

Sean was beginning to take it personally that he couldn't solve the case. The unsubs were always careful not to leave any DNA or other forensic evidence, making it nearly impossible to discover the culprits.

His superiors were making noise about reassigning the case. He sometimes thought someone new might see something Sean couldn't, but he didn't want to be kicked off the case. He'd spent too much time and been submitted to too much horror to let it go easily. The killer would have to make a mistake sometime, and Sean wanted to be the one to bring him in.

He paced to the side out of the way and stood with his arms crossed, watching Brian and the crime techs scour the scene. Sean glared at the tableau, as if it could tell him something more. For a moment, he saw ghostly figures of men dressed in hooded robes parading around the circle, swinging incense censors, and chanting. He blinked, and the vision vanished. Walking in the same pattern as the spectral images, Sean kept his eyes trained on the ground. A scuff mark on the otherwise clean floor caught his attention. He bent over and placed an evidence marker by it.

"Hey, Brian," he called out, "there's a scuff mark here. Also, check outside the perimeter of the circle, about a foot away."

"What am I looking for?"

Sean shrugged. "Not sure. Just a hunch. Let me know if you find anything or if something is different about this one."

Brian carried his forensic tool bag to the marker. After snapping a photo of the scuff mark, he eased onto all fours, and with distaste, crawled, his nose close to the ground. He stopped and scraped a minute bit of dirt into a plastic baggie.

As he did, Sean heard a deep, evil laugh echo in the large space. Sean searched the area but couldn't see anyone except the crime tech people. Brian continued searching for evidence and acted like he hadn't heard anything.

All the craziness of the past few weeks was catching up with Sean. He was now hearing things. With a shake of his head, he decided to talk to his favorite suspect.

Sean pulled his black Camaro into the popular gym's parking lot and had to drive around it a few times before he could park. He flashed his badge at the receptionist and surveyed the workout area. His suspect had a home gym, but Michael liked to work-out during the busiest times at a public gym. He enjoyed flexing his muscles at the girls and intimidating the men.

Several girls who frequented this facility had turned up dead after Michael joined it. Even though they weren't part of the Iron Maiden killings, Sean suspected Michael's involvement. Sean hadn't found enough hard evidence yet to pin those murders on his suspect, who always had friends to corroborate his story. When you were as rich as Michael Drogger—or at least have an insanely wealthy father—you could buy all the alibis you needed. For all of his money, the guy was a sleazebag and tripped every one of Sean's alarms.

Sean spotted Michael by the free weights, doing bicep curls. Michael finished his set, dropped his weights to the floor with a bang, and brushed back his longish blond hair from his face. Surveying the room, his smile settled on the pretty girl watching him. He flexed his muscled pectorals at her, and she giggled. A predatory gleam lit his eyes as he glided over to her.

Before he could reach her, Sean stepped into his path.

"Michael," he said through a false smile, "it's been a long time."

"Not long enough, Detective." Michael's eyes flicked to the side where his ever-present bodyguards loitered.

"I heard rumors you had a girlfriend. Isn't one enough for you?" Sean glanced at the girl still ogling Michael. He lifted the hem of his shirt, letting his badge show. She gulped and hurried into the locker room.

Michael bared his teeth and growled. "Now, that wasn't nice, McLarkin. As for my girlfriend, I broke up with her over the weekend. What are you harassing me about now?"

"Where were you the last three nights?"

"Let me guess, there's been another murder."

Sean nodded.

"And I'm the first person you thought about. How many times do I have to tell you, Detective? I didn't kill them."

"So, what's your alibi this time?"

Michael crossed his arms, his muscles bulging. "The boys and I sailed the yacht down the coast to Mexico. We did a little gambling and fishing."

"Is that before or after you took your girlfriend out on the yacht?"

Michael's eyes narrowed. "You've been following me again. I thought your captain made it clear to you to stay away from me."

Sean shook his head. "Nah, I happened to be down at the marina Friday night and saw your boat pull out of its slip. Answer the question."

"After, of course. She turned out to be a whiny bitch. I dropped her off Saturday morning. Then I took the boys fishing."

"What did you catch?"

"Nothing serious, oh, you mean fish." Michael laughed. "A red snapper. Man, that bugger was tasty. Ate it right there on the boat."

"I need the usual—names and contact info—to verify your alibi." Sean held out his notebook and pen.

Michael grimaced. "So old school. Can't the police force afford to get you a tablet?" He snatched the notebook from Sean's hand and wrote down several names.

With as much distaste, Sean took back his notebook and pen. It felt slimy and nasty energy crawled up his hand. He flicked his hand to shake it off. Frowning, he narrowed his eyes. A black mist surrounded Michael, oozing evil, and his eyes glowed red. The same haunting, deep laugh from the crime scene echoed in Sean's mind. He blinked, and his vision returned to normal.

"If that is all, Detective," Michael sneered, "I'm going back to my workout. And yeah, yeah, I know, don't leave the country, although I don't think Baja California counts." He turned on his heel and resumed lifting weights.

Sean watched him for a moment as he tried to make sense of what he'd seen. Shaking his head, he returned to his car. As he pulled out of the parking lot, his cell phone rang. He glanced down to see it was the crime tech. "Hey, Brian, did you find anything?"

"I don't know how you do it, man, but we found some trace evidence on the outside of the circle, right where you suggested. It's at the lab, and I put a rush on it."

"What kind of trace?" Sean switched lanes, although it didn't do much good in the heavy going-home traffic.

"Dirt. Ash. Where you discovered the scuff mark, there was a footprint of a man's boot. The coroner says this victim was a woman by the shape of the pelvic bones. Young, in her twenties. We're checking the missing persons reports."

"Did she have blond hair?" Dread twisted Sean's stomach.

"I'll have to ask. The coroner didn't say, and I haven't looked at the body after it was cleaned up yet. I can handle most other cadavers, but this killer mutilates them so badly I have a tough time stomaching it. I'll call you when I know more."

"Thanks, Brian."

Sean called his partner to update him. "The Iron Maiden killer has struck again."

Jerry groaned. "As if we don't have enough work to do with this damned crime spree."

"Are you back in the office?"

"I am. What do you need?"

A year ago, Sean had been reassigned as Jerry's partner. The brass had hoped the fresh eyes would solve the case faster. Jerry wanted to catch the killer as much as Sean did. Both their careers depended on it.

"I talked to Michael Drogger. Can you check out his alibi? We know his buddies are going to back him up, but we need to make the calls. Maybe one of them will slip up." He read off the list of names, not bothering with the phone numbers. He'd recognized the names from Michael's other alibis. Jerry probably had them on speed dial; Sean certainly did.

"Will do."

Sean tapped the steering wheel as he inched forward, thinking about the murders. His "Granny Vibes" screamed the murderers were more than a group of psychos getting off on the killing or some kids playing at being a satanic cult. He felt it in his bones that there was some purpose to the killings and whatever it was, it wasn't good.

 # CHAPTER 13 

After eating dinner, Sean slumped on his couch, put his feet up on the coffee table, and flicked through the channels. Nothing struck him as interesting. Another young woman had died horribly on his watch. He couldn't sit here as if nothing had happened. He picked up his phone and dialed his friend, Charlie MacNamara.

"Hey, Charlie," he said, "how about going out for a drink with me?"

"There's been another murder, hasn't there?"

"Yeah. How did you know?"

"You always want to drink after finding a body. Bro, after what you've told me, I can't blame you. Are we going to the same place, so you can stalk your favorite suspect?"

"Oh course."

"See you in thirty."

Sean changed into a fresh shirt and jeans and then headed out.

When he pulled up to the Red Orchid, a sign blocked off the full parking lot. Sean hadn't expected it to be so busy on a Monday night. He rolled down his window and shivered in the chilly October evening. Wrinkling his nose, he rolled the window back up, pulled into line, and grudgingly paid for valet parking. The club, owned by Michael's father, received rave reviews for its good food and great music. But for Sean, its allure was that Michael usually showed up at some point during the night. Sometimes he did magic tricks and illusions for patrons.

The music blared, just shy of deafening, and a crowd writhed on the dance floor. Sean scanned the people at the bar, saw Charlie, and made his way over.

"Here, my friend." Charlie grinned, his green eyes crinkling at the corners, as he handed Sean a foamy glass of beer. The club specialized in hand-crafted beers and funky cocktails. "Let's go find a seat. I ordered snacks."

Weaving through the throng, they found an empty table. Sean sipped on his brew as he surveyed the crowd.

"How bad was it this time?" Charlie put down his drink and leaned over the table to be heard.

"Bad." Sean took another swig. "A young woman, not even out of her twenties yet. God, I hope we catch a break on this case soon! I don't know how many more mutilated bodies I can see."

"Detective!" Michael stepped up to their table and leaned on Sean's chair, a grin plastered on his face. "As if I hadn't seen enough of you today."

Sean glared at the man's arm. Something seemed to writhe beneath the skin. Sean put a hand to his mouth to hide his gagging. As soon as he'd regained his composure, he turned back to Michael. "Just having a brew with my buddy. This place sells nice craft brews." He lifted his beer glass.

"What do we have here?" Michael reached a hand to the back of Sean's head and brought it around to his face, a coin held between his fingers. "Careful, Detective, you need to take better care of your money. I've seen your suits. The city certainly doesn't pay you much." He put the coin on the table, then with a laugh, walked away.

Two beautiful women joined him and hung on either arm. Sean dug his phone from his pocket and snapped a photo of the women. He doubted Michael would be stupid enough to do anything to them after Sean had seen them.

As he placed his cellphone on the table, the light caught on the coin. A serpent, its mouth gaping wide, showing long fangs, rose from the coin's surface, poised to strike Charlie. Sean batted Charlie's hand out of the way and flicked the coin into his empty glass.

"Hey, what's going on, Sean?" Charlie shook his hand, nursing it. Sean might have hit it harder than he intended.

"Sorry, bro. I didn't want you to touch that foul thing. Who knows where it's been."

Charlie glared at him, his mouth in a tight line, and tilted his head. His eyes flicked back and forth between Sean and the coin. "What did you see?"

"Nothing."

Charlie continued to stare at him.

"I didn't see anything! You know I don't believe in all that psychic crap."

"Ha!" Charlie laughed. "I remember the freaky things your Granny Eileen did and the stories she told us."

"That's all they were, stories. None of them could be real. I need another beer." Sean wended his way back to the bar, his thoughts on the strange tales his Granny had told him and Charlie when they were kids. After the crazy few weeks he'd had, he wasn't so sure they were only stories. He hadn't had a day off where he could go visit her. A faint memory floated to mind of the three of them doing magic together. "Sean, boy, get a grip," he mumbled as he waited for his beer. "Magic isn't real."

The lethargy stayed with Catlyn throughout the day on Sunday. Every muscle hurt. She could barely shuffle from her bed to the bathroom from the sensation of experiencing an enormous weight gain. She gulped three aspirin to quell her headache, then trudged back to bed, pulling the covers over her head. Thankfully, she didn't have to go into the store for work. Late in the afternoon, hunger—and the insistent meowing of her cats—spurred her from bed. She fed her fur-babies, then slurped down two cans of tuna. Her bed called her back to its sweet, dark confines.

Catlyn awoke the next morning, the sunlight sneaking under her blinds. The heaviness in her body had lifted some, she could now move without pain. Mittens sat on Catlyn's chest and batted her nose to wake her. Boots purred at her feet. Catlyn sighed with happiness; her beloved fur-babies were acting normal again. The previous day blurred in her memory. "I can't believe I slept all day and ignored you." She stroked Mitten's soft fur. The cat bumped her hand, purring louder. "I'm so sorry, kitty." Boots heard her and slunk to her side to receive his share of loving.

After feeding her cats, Catlyn fixed her own breakfast, humming as she cooked. She sat at the snack bar to eat. "What the hell?" A full pound of bacon and half-a-dozen eggs filled her plate. She only remembered pulling a couple of slices of bacon from the package and cracking a single egg. Her hollow stomach cramped, and she wolfed down the food. Finished in record time, Catlyn did the dishes and cleaned up the kitchen.

She leaned against the sink, considering. The only explanation for her unprecedented appetite was her new spirit guide. Her cats sat on the back of the couch, staring at her, their tails swishing in agitation.

"Hello?" she said out loud and in her thoughts. "Are you here? Maak? Maak?"

Contentment flooded her. She waited, but no other response came from the spirit tiger.

Throughout the morning, Catlyn tried to talk to Maak and to ask her questions. The only communications she received were emotions, feelings, and an occasional visual image. Everything Catlyn had studied said totems and spirit guides appeared to their chosen people. They actively worked with them, aided them in decisions, told them where to go or what to do, and answered questions. Some even shared great wisdom. But her guide did none of these things. After their first conversation, Maak hadn't spoken a word.

"It'd be nice if I knew what was going on," she finally said to the cats sitting across the room from her. "Why is she here? Why me? What work do we have to do? Where did she come from? Something, anything, would be helpful!"

An image of the strange trees and ferns she'd seen in her shaman journey floated into her mind.

"Is that where you're from? Is that your world?"

A tidal wave of homesickness swamped her.

Along with immense hunger. Catlyn flung open her fridge, grimacing at the bare pickings. The freezer held even less. Her insides cramped painfully. Not three hours ago, she'd eaten a huge breakfast. She shouldn't feel this starved. Another hunger pang gripped her. "All right, all right! I'll feed you."

Catlyn snatched up her purse. As she descended the stairs, an acrid scent tickled her nose. At first, she thought it was Smoker Dude's awful cigarettes. She sniffed, turning her head to locate the source. Her watcher for the day, Blond Guy, sat in his car with the window down. Disappointment engulfed her, and a snarl lifted her lips. She'd hoped her new bodyguards would scare away her hated stalkers. The slight breeze brought the strange aroma again. Her mouth dropped open as she breathed in deeply, then coughed on Blond Guy's contempt for her, heavily laced with impatience.

Emotions don't have a smell, she chided herself as she hurried to her car. A black truck with Jade's company emblem on its window was parked along the curb. A tall, lean man with short red hair stood next to it. The sunlight brought out the red-gold highlights in his scruffy beard. His hands fisted as he scowled at Blond Guy. Her guard abandoned his staring contest with Blond Guy when she appeared, and he sauntered toward her.

The scent of concern and confidence wafted to her.

"Good afternoon, Catlyn." His friendly smile lit his light-green eyes.

A blush crept over her face as he assessed her from head to toe.

"I'm Dilan McGowan. Are you feeling better today? Todd mentioned you were ill Saturday night, and you didn't leave your apartment at all yesterday."

"Yeah, I'm okay, just exhausted. All the stress from the last few weeks caught up with me, and I crashed all day. I'm headed to grab some lunch at the Bamboo Grill." She salivated at the thought of fresh sushi.

"Thanks for letting me know. I'll make sure you're safe." He glared back at Blond Guy's black sedan. Dilan opened her car door for her, before stalking to his truck.

Her belly stuffed with sushi and a shopping bag loaded with more steak than she could afford, Catlyn returned to her apartment. After putting the food away, she debated on what to do for the rest of the day.

Stacks of jewelry supplies filled the third-hand bookcases lining her living room walls. A half-finished project lay on the table, covered to keep her curious kitties away from it. She wandered to stand over the table. She reached for the covering, only to drop her hand as a deep lassitude swept over her. Instead of working, she picked up a novel and stretched out on the couch. Mittens and Boots curled next to her, and she absently petted them as she read until hunger drove her to the kitchen.

This time, she made sure she seared the steak before slapping it on a plate. A growl escaped her as she reached for it. Mittens' scrambling claws as she pelted out of the kitchen startled Catlyn. She shook her head and meticulously placed her dish on the breakfast bar and gathered utensils. "No," she said sternly to her new body mate. "We'll eat civilized."

With great care, Catlyn cut the steak into small pieces and chewed slowly. No matter how "evolved" her new spirit totem was—who seemed awfully corporeal to want food—it was her body, and she'd control it.

Sean rubbed his gritty eyes. After leaving the club last night, he'd stayed awake until the wee hours of the morning. He'd studied the new crime scene data, comparing it to his files on the killer, searching for something—anything—he'd missed. He hadn't found anything. This new one was even more gruesome and awful than the others. He needed to clear his mind.

On his way in to work, he stopped at the Jupiter Moon coffee shop where he'd first met Catlyn. He knew her schedule at the metaphysical store varied. It was a crap-shoot if he'd see her again or not. He'd started getting his coffee here on the off-chance he'd meet her here again. Even after seeing her with her boyfriend, he couldn't stop thinking about her. She played a prominent role in his dreams. Warmth crept over his face as he recalled a particularly steamy one. He'd never fallen for someone after meeting them once. Remembering their first meeting in this same spot made him smile. His lips thinned into a frown as he remembered the frightened look in her eyes when she'd walked to her car like someone trudging to the gallows. It had triggered his protective instincts. At least, that's what he tried telling himself. But the bigger part of him believed she was something special. Someone worth getting to know.

"Detective McLarkin?" a quiet voice asked from behind him. He whirled around to see the woman who'd been in the forefront of his thoughts. He admonished himself for daydreaming when he needed to stay alert. Things may have quieted down now the Iron Maiden Killer had struck again, but Sean doubted the other strange crimes, connected or not, had disappeared.

"Hi, Catlyn, isn't it?" He grinned at her, hoping his smile was charming and not a leer.

Her smile lit her face. "Do you live around here?"

"Just stopped here on my way to work. What about you?"

"The same."

"They have great coffee." Couldn't he think of something less inane to say to her? He was an experienced interviewer and could get criminals to tell him their life stories. Yet when faced with talking to a beautiful woman, he felt tongue-tied. They shuffled forward a few steps.

"So, Detective McLarkin, do you work on missing person's cases?"

He shook his head, rubbing his hand against his thigh. "No, only when they become murder victims."

"Then, I hope we don't meet under official circumstances. My friend is missing."

"How long?"

"A week now."

"Is it common for her to disappear for a few days?"

Catlyn shook her head. "No, she's conscientious. She left me hanging without canceling her appointment, which she's never done before. It isn't like her to take off, even with a new boyfriend, without letting anyone know where she's going."

"I hope you find her alive and well." After that long, Sean doubted her friend was still alive. He hoped the body they'd found yesterday wasn't her friend's. As mutilated as it was, it may take days for them to identify the victim.

His heart plummeted when she ordered an iced chai latte and a mocha frappuccino. He surveyed the shop but didn't see her boyfriend. They chatted while waiting for their drinks, and he redeemed himself with the small talk. He walked outside with her and noticed her glare at an empty parking space. Her face lit up with a smile, and she handed the mocha to a red-headed man with a wide, muscle-bound chest. Jealousy ripped through him. He'd lost out again. Then he noticed the logo on the man's shirt. He worked for the same company as Charlie did. *Why does Catlyn, a psychic, need a bodyguard? They only take on high-profile clients. Who is this woman?*

 CHAPTER 14 

The next morning, when Catlyn woke up, the strange lethargy and heaviness had completely left her body. After another huge breakfast, she hurried down the stairs from her apartment.

The stench of Smoker Dude's cigarettes smothered any emotions she might have picked up from him. That was fine; she didn't want to be subjected to his evil anymore than she had to. Her unease vanished when Dilan stepped to the stairs.

"Hey, Dilan. Are you my bodyguard again today?"

"Yes, ma'am," he tipped an imaginary hat at her.

Catlyn laid a hand on Dilan's arm. "Thanks for watching out for me. I can't tell you how much it means to me." They both turned to glare at the black sedan holding Smoker Dude.

"It's my pleasure to thwart evil." Dilan tucked her hand over the crook of his elbow and escorted her to her car.

Catlyn's mood lifted. She'd initially hated the idea of having Jade's bodyguards tailing her. Her irritation had died the first time she glanced in her rearview mirror and saw the big silver truck rather than the snarling black sedan. On a whim, she took the exit that would take her to the Jupiter Moon on the way to work. Maybe that cute police detective would be there.

She hurried to Dilan's truck before he could get out. "I'm grabbing an iced chai. Do you want anything?" She didn't want him to ruin any chances she might have with the guy if he were in the coffee shop.

He eyed her, then the trendy shop. "Sure, a mocha frappuccino."

Later, Catlyn strolled out of the coffee shop, although she wanted to skip. The dreamy police detective, Sean McLarkin, had been in line and they'd talked. Even the sight of the hateful Smoker Dude's sedan couldn't put a damper on her spirits. After handing Dilan his drink, she slipped into her car and turned the music up. Dancing in her seat, she drove the few miles to Mystical Enchantments.

When she arrived at the store, she lifted an eyebrow in surprise to see the parking lot of the strip mall nearly full on a Monday afternoon.

Catlyn hoped the store would be busy. She was scheduled to be the on-call tarot reader and could use the extra money from the readings. October and the hype about Halloween always increased the number of people coming to the metaphysical store for a tarot reading.

She found a spot in the rear corner of the parking lot. If Dilan hadn't parked beside her, she'd have felt vulnerable having to walk so far to the shop. Somehow, her stalker had arrived before them and snagged a parking spot where he could watch the store.

Catlyn pulled on her floppy hat to shade her fair skin from the warm sunny day and strolled to the back door of the store. A breeze twisted her skirt around her ankles, bringing with it the salty-fishy aroma of the ocean. Breathing deeply, she caught the scents of joy, playfulness, and contentment of the people on the beach.

She rubbed her nose to clear the unusual smells from it, then reached for the door handle, jerking her hand back from Lorgandy's heat. She hadn't seen the salamander for days.

"Are you going to let me in, Lorgandy?"

The salamander blinked, then raised her head. She crawled to the edge of the handle and stretched her twitching nose toward Catlyn.

"Oh, you must sense my new friend, Maak." Catlyn reached out her hand to let Lorgandy smell it. As she did, a huge, transparent white paw appeared above her hand. The salamander pulled back slightly, turning her head to look into Catlyn's eyes. After a few moments, Lorgandy flicked her tail, slithered off the door, and into the pot Catlyn surmised was her home.

The shop bustled with customers when Catlyn entered the main area after putting away her purse.

Michelle gave her a frazzled smile. "Oh, great, you're here. We have several people waiting for readings." She leaned forward and whispered, "Any news of Amelia?"

Catlyn shook her head. "The police still haven't found her, or at least they haven't told me if they have or not."

"I'll keep praying for her. She was a good customer."

"Thanks." Catlyn quickly set up the table in the reading room assigned to her with her things and called in the first client. The woman came in, bringing with her the strident scents of frustration and anger. She sat stiffly on the chair across the table from Catlyn. Breathing shallowly through her mouth, Catlyn shuffled the cards, clearing her mind. This wasn't going to be a happy session. An hour later, the woman left, and Catlyn sagged back in her chair. The woman's life was a mess, and she'd argued with Catlyn's interpretation of every card. Catlyn wondered why she'd even bothered to go to someone for a reading if she wasn't prepared to listen to the guidance shared. She sighed, remembering October also brought out the crazies who received readings on a dare.

Her next client was an excited young girl. The scent of budding love filled the small room. The girl's question about a boy and if he was interested in her didn't surprise Catlyn.

As the day progressed, Catlyn grew more proficient in correctly identifying the emotions she smelled. They aided her in understanding her client's deeper desires, allowing her to discern beyond the words they spoke. She glanced at her overflowing tip jar. Her increased awareness had thrilled most of her clients, and they'd showed their appreciation more freely than usual. Her eyebrows furrowed. *Is this your doing?* She mentally asked her new totem animal.

Indignation thumped her chest painfully.

Sorry! Trust her to tick off her guide. She fingered her mother's necklace, asking for guidance on how to handle the prickly Maak. Before she received any answers, a gentleman sank into her guest chair. Worry and guilt flowed from him, so sharp it made her eyes water.

She cleared her mind and reached for her tarot deck.

Back at the office, Sean debated if he should call his grandmother. She'd be a perfect excuse to see Catlyn again. His phone buzzed. He glanced at the caller ID. "What do you have for me, Brian?"

"The medical examiner's office identified your victim."

"Already?"

"That ... that fucking bastard!" Brian exploded. "You have to catch him, Sean. This was awful. The worst yet. We found the woman's identification in her uterus."

Sean's mind stuttered, trying to process what he'd heard. "How could the victim's driver's license end up there, of all places?"

"The creep used a pear of anguish in her vagina to open it wide enough to deposit it." Brian paused, choking. It took him awhile to recompose himself, and when he continued, he sounded like he read from a report, "One Amelia Caldwell, age twenty-four. She went missing..."

Sean clenched his teeth. *Don't say a week ago, don't say seven...*

"Seven days ago."

Sean's hope came crashing down, and he slumped back in his chair.

"Her work filed a missing persons report," Brian continued. "Get this she works for Thomas Drogger—"

Sean sat straight up and switched his phone to his other ear. "*The* Thomas Drogger? As in our prime suspect's father?"

"That's the one."

Sean heard the rifling of papers on the other end.

"Ah," Brian said, "there's another report filed by a Miss Catlyn Hennessey, a friend. She filed it after Amelia missed her ... healing appointment?"

"Yeah, a healing appointment. Get me Catlyn's work address." Sean pulled out his notepad as his heart sank. The old saying, 'Be careful what you wish for, you might just get it,' rolled through his mind. He wished now he could see Catlyn again under more pleasant circumstances. He wrote the information in his notebook as Brian read it off. The tech would send it to his phone, but Sean liked to handwrite things. It helped him remember better.

It seemed odd that Catlyn's name would come up in connection to the Iron Maiden case, as well as one of the weird crimes. The DA had finally relented and only filed battery charges against the unlucky tourist. There'd been too many other cases of people seeing creatures before an outbreak of violence and death. Carol Holcomb was still in a coma from her infected injuries.

Sean logged into the police database and did a background check on Amelia. The photo showed a beautiful, curvaceous blond with blue eyes and a sultry smile. She looked nothing like the ruined body he'd viewed a few days ago. But he'd seen her before. He pulled up the files of the pictures he'd taken of Drogger last weekend at the restaurant. A thrill raced through him when he found the only clear photo—of Amelia Caldwell and Drogger's limousine. Michael may have made his first mistake!

He read the preliminary report and learned that Amelia had moved to Southern California from Iowa to be an actress. She looked like every other pretty blond who hoped to make it into the movies. After a few years of chasing the dream, she'd relocated to Orange County, where she worked in various office jobs. She'd only been with Drogger International for a few months. The poor girl seemed to be in the wrong place at the wrong time.

Sean flexed his fingers, then broke down and checked on Catlyn. He had an official excuse now that she may be a material witness in his murder case. He lifted his eyebrow in surprise when she turned up in the system. After the murder of her single mom in San Francisco, she'd been raised by her aunt and uncle in Anaheim. The murder case still languished in the cold-case files and had little hope of being solved after twenty-three years. The file had a picture of Catlyn at age five, right after her mother's death. She looked way too frightened for such a little girl. *Did she always move through life, scared, lost, and alone?* Other than that, her police record was clean. Not even a traffic ticket marred it.

He stood up to leave, saw the clock, and groaned. This time of day, it would take him a good hour to drive the ten miles from Anaheim to Costa Mesa.

A purple neon sign blinked in the window of the Mystical Enchantments metaphysical store. When he opened the door, a bell tinkled, alerting the woman in her early forties behind the cash register.

"Oh, hello." She brushed her long, light-brown hair back from her face. Her smile warmed her pale blue eyes. "Is there anything I can help you find?"

"Is Catlyn Hennessey here?" Sean looked around the bright shop with interest. To the left of the entryway, a tall glass cabinet showcased some nice crystal specimens. The register sat on top of a glass counter, revealing an artful display of jewelry. He thought he detected several pieces of Catlyn's work. In the center of the store stood rows of shelves filled with books, candles, and other ritual paraphernalia he recognized from his grandmother's house. Soft music, featuring drums and flutes, played in the background.

The woman glanced at a clock. "She should be done with her reading in a few minutes. She'll have time to do one for you afterward. So what's your name? I'll get you booked." She held a pen poised over an appointment book.

"Sorry, I'm not here for a reading." He showed her his badge. "Police business."

"Oh, my! She isn't in trouble, is she?" The woman's eyes darted toward the room with the closed door and back to him.

"No, I just have some questions for her." He turned around, shutting off any further comments from the woman. With his hands in his trouser pockets, he wandered through the store, picking up an item here and there, examining it, then replacing it. There were some nice things here. His grandmother would love the place if she didn't know about it already. He was paging through a book when the reading room door opened. He shut the book and put it back on the shelf.

Catlyn stood on the threshold, her mouth open, her eyes wide, the color drained from her face. She swallowed hard. "Detective McLarkin?"

She gripped her necklace with one hand, her knuckles white. "She's dead, isn't she?"

 # CHAPTER 15 

The man across from Catlyn peered at the cards laid out on the table. When he surreptitiously brushed at his eyes, she turned away. She hated when readings confirmed the client's worst expectations. His marriage was in shambles from bad decisions and lies. A spicy-warm scent seeped into the room, and she lifted her head, gazing at the door. The scent was familiar. She sniffed deeply, recognizing it as Detective McLarkin's.

Twice in one day! Is he off work? Does he want to see me? A thrill zinged through her. Then the sour scent of worry and unease burned her nose. Her excitement changed to dread.

It took all her professional skill to finish her reading for the gentleman, giving him what hope the cards offered. She accompanied him to the door, and as she stood on the threshold, she noticed Sean flipping through a book.

The bloody vision of Amelia washed over her.

The world tilted. Darkness pressed down on Catlyn.

Detective McLarkin rushed across the store and caught her before she fell. "Here, let's get you sitting down." He guided her back into the room, onto a chair, and eased the door closed. He grabbed a bottle of water from the side counter and handed it to her.

She took several long gulps and blinked away the image of Amelia sprawled in a pool of blood. "When?" She cleared her throat. "When did she die? How?"

"We found her body yesterday. It wasn't good. But then, no death is good." He sat in the other chair.

She dropped her head into her hands, covering her eyes. Hot tears pricked, threatening to overspill. She blinked them back. There would be time to mourn. Later.

Raising her head, she looked him in the eye. "I told her not to go out with him and that it would end badly. I couldn't ethically tell her she'd die if she did. But, Detective McLarkin, I saw it. I saw her death in the cards. I tried as hard as I could to change her mind. But then, after she told me she wouldn't continue dating him, they showed up together at the restaurant. The smug bastard." She put a hand over her mouth. She hadn't meant to say the last.

"You say she went out on a date?" He leaned forward. She found it ironic that he was sitting in the chair she sat in to do readings. "Do you know who her date was?" Excitement tinged his voice.

She shook her head, then stopped. Jade had told it to her when he'd shown up at the Mexican restaurant.

"Michael Drogger. She mentioned he was her boss's son, and she works for Thomas Drogger, so I assume that's his name."

He dug into a pocket and pulled out his phone. He swiped a few times, then held it out to her. "Is this him?"

A man dressed in a business suit, his blond hair slicked back, hard pale-blue eyes, peered at the camera. A smile, rather than his usual smirk, revealed a dimple in his left cheek. Amelia had been with him at the fancy restaurant in LA. He'd appeared again with her watcher at the Mexican restaurant with Jade. She'd been too scared at the time to notice, but Blond Guy had treated Michael as a superior. Michael was her true stalker!

She shakily nodded her head, fighting the queasiness in her stomach. She hadn't truly believed Jade when she'd said he was bad news. However, having the detective—the homicide detective—asking about him made her reevaluate Jade's warning.

Detective McLarkin's eyes narrowed. "You know him, don't you, Catlyn? Where have you seen him?"

"He's had his men stalking me." She told Sean about the first time she encountered Michael at the beach and the two men who'd become her constant tails afterward. She left out the fact no one else saw the black sedans. While she talked, the detective picked up her tarot cards and idly shuffled them.

"I've seen the car often enough over the past two weeks that I know the license plate number by heart. Do you want it?"

Sean set the tarot cards aside and withdrew a small notebook from a jacket packet. She smiled at his old-school habit. As she rattled it off to him, she wondered for the first time why an illusionary car would have a license plate.

"I called the police," she added, "but they said they couldn't do anything unless they harmed me. What good does that do, Detective? By then it's too late for me."

"We have to have proof they mean you ill. If they've stayed on public property and haven't approached you, I'm afraid it's just hearsay." He sat back and ran a hand through his short, sandy-blond hair. "Believe me, I wish we could do more."

"How helpful. *Not.*" She glared at him. Then relented. He was trying to find Amelia's killer. "Sorry about that. I know you're doing your best."

"Well, if you think of anything else, call me." He dug into his pocket again, pulled out a business card, and wrote down a number. He put it on the table next to the tarot cards. "That's my personal cell."

After he left, Catlyn cut the deck and turned over the stack in her right hand. The two of Cups—the card of lovers and relationships. Her forehead crinkled as she pondered it. Then she recalled her recurring dream about the man with blue eyes. The detective had blue eyes. He might be the one behind the kind, gentle ones. A flush of pleasure tightened her core. Erotic dreams, leaving her horny as hell, always followed those dreams.

She set the card to the side, then laid the rest of the cards down on the table, fanning them out. She pulled another one—the Tower. Chaos and change would soon come knocking—but for her or for him? Or for both of them? She decided this reading was for both her and Sean. Catlyn disliked seeing that card in a reading. Its change was never easy. The next card was the five of Wands, indicating a time of strife and conflict.

The Devil turned up next. Usually she read it as signifying lust or addiction, rarely as evil. Memory flashed of the reading she'd done the night she'd first seen Michael. She'd used the Lakota Sweat Lodge oracle cards. The image of the card, *Mahpia,* which meant addiction and compulsion, pushed its way forcefully to the forefront of her mind. A shiver of clear insight told her the two cards were linked.

She recalled the cold, pale-blue eyes of her dreams. They had to be Michael's. The two cards indicated Michael Drogger was evil personified. Following after the other cards, this didn't bode well for her and Sean.

Taking a deep breath, she drew another card—the nine of Swords. A struggle of mighty proportions was inevitable, but with strength of will and courage, they could get to the other side of it. The last card of the reading was the Star. Through it all, hope and light would guide them through their ordeals. It also gave the reading, as a whole, a sense of destiny.

Were the three of them—Sean, Michael, and herself—destined to dance this game together? What part did she have to play? And why her?

She considered the question and drew one more card.

Her hand trembled. Her heart stumbled.

The High Priestess.

Catlyn stared at the card for a long time. Even though she made a living as a healer and psychic, she knew she only played with her abilities.

Something held her back from fully accessing them. Something more than the constraints and beliefs of society that what she did was strange and terrifying. But now she was being asked to step into her destiny.

A faint memory teased her. Terror blazed under her skin like flames licking at a burning log. Trembling, she lowered the card to the table.

It would take all her courage to draw back the veil to her unconsciousness to reveal her true nature. Was she ready to accept the responsibility of the position of high priestess? An image flowed to her, showing her holding a glowing sword guarding the passageways between the worlds against dark shapes straining to pass. A whimper escaped her lips. She wasn't a fighter. How could she be that type of high priestess?

Sean leaned against his car, legs outstretched in front of him, arms crossed, as he studied the metaphysical shop. Something about Catlyn called to him, making him want to enfold her in his arms and keep her safe from the ugliness of life—among other things. He imagined how it would feel to run his hands over her soft curves. He liked curvy women. From there, it was easy to visualize how she'd look flushed with desire, moaning beneath him, as he tasted her lips and body.

He scowled at his wayward thoughts, subtly adjusting his now too tight trousers. He'd sworn off women after Ginny had worked him over. His heart still ached from her betrayal.

Since then, he'd thrown himself into his work, tracking down any leads on the Iron Maiden killings, and investigating his other cases. The large city of Anaheim had enough cases to keep the homicide detectives busy. Sean used his work to make sure he didn't have time or energy for relationships. And now, here he was thinking erotic thoughts about a witness, his only eye witness so far. He rubbed his face to clear away the thoughts.

Out of habit, he scanned the Mystical Enchantments' parking lot and noticed an odd empty parking space in the otherwise full lot. Sean squinted, and the air wavered in front of the spot, giving him a glimpse of a black sedan. It vanished when he blinked. Frowning, he walked toward the spot, but it remained empty. Brushing it aside as yet another strange thing in his life, he climbed into his car.

As he drove the few blocks to the Red Orchid, he called Brian to check the plate numbers of the black sedans following Catlyn. He flipped the top back on his Camaro, enjoying the afternoon sunshine. It was a long-shot he'd find Michael at the club this early.

He walked up to the manager's office and knocked on the door. Joshua's eyes clouded when Sean entered. "There's been another killing, hasn't there?"

Sean sighed heavily. He took his phone from his pocket and showed Joshua a picture of Amelia. "Have you seen her?"

"Yeah. She was Michael's latest fling. Although she hasn't been here for over a week." Joshua paused, leaning his elbows on his desk and holding his head. "She's dead, isn't she?"

"She is. A victim of the Iron Maiden killer."

Joshua groaned and lifted his head from his hands. "When will this stop, Sean? We both know Michael is the culprit."

"He never leaves any forensic evidence. And as powerful as his father is, the District Attorney won't file charges without ironclad proof. Circumstantial evidence won't cut it in this case. When was the last time you saw him with Amelia?"

"That was her name?" Joshua leaned back in his chair, staring at the ceiling in thought, then rocked forward to face Sean. "A week ago, Thursday. How about the rape cases from the women Michael has attacked in the club? Have you heard anything from the special victims' unit? Tell me they are at least pressing forward with those."

Sean grimaced, sliding his phone back in his pocket. "They aren't following up on your leads. They claim none of the women will testify against Michael. It's likely Thomas Drogger's money shushed them."

Sean knew of at least ten women Michael had raped inside the club. Joshua probably knew about more. But unless one of the victims was brave enough to file charges and testify, his colleagues couldn't do anything.

Joshua swore, slamming a fist into his desk.

"I know how you feel, Joshua. If Michael were behind bars for rape, then he couldn't kill anyone. But I'd much rather convict him of murder. I just need to find the evidence."

Joshua made a face at the big screens above his desk. "You'd think with as many security cameras as we have installed, we'd catch him in the act. But he knows where they all are and never catches a woman where it can be filmed. Speaking of the devil, he just arrived."

Sean glanced at the screens, noting Michael settle into his favorite booth. He thanked Joshua and walked downstairs to the club's main floor. It was early still, and the nightclub hadn't filled with patrons yet. They wouldn't have to shout over the music. Sean slid into the booth across from Michael and glared at him. "Do you know Amelia Caldwell?"

"No," Michael said. "No, the name doesn't ring a bell. But then, I fuck so many women, I rarely ask their names."

"A regular Don Juan." Sean squeezed his hands together hard, fighting the urge to knock the smugness off Michael's face. "She's one of your father's employees."

"Good hell! He has over a thousand employees. How am I supposed to know them all? I take it she's missing, and you think I did something to her."

"She worked in his office. And yes, she's dead. We have an eye witness who saw you with her at La Bouchiere in LA. You were the last person to see Amelia alive. You remember, young, pretty, blond." Sean showed Michael her picture and watched him closely.

Michael leaned in, licking his lips. "Oh, yeah, I remember now. A great fuck. I took her there, plying her with drinks and expensive food. Too bad you can't take a date there, but then you'd have to have money and class, which you don't."

Sean let the jibe slide. "And after dinner?"

"We took the yacht on a jaunt." Michael examined his fingernails. "She started whining and wanted a commitment, which I can't tolerate. I sailed to shore, threw her off my boat, and the boys and I went down the coast to Mexico."

"Where did you drop her off?"

Michael leaned back and crossed his arms. "Del Mar? Oceanside? I don't remember. I haven't seen her since and don't plan on ever seeing her again."

Sean stood, towering over Michael. "I'll be watching you."

"Good luck. You won't see anything."

The next day, Sean convinced his partner, Jerry, to take point on their other cases while Sean followed Michael. At first glance, Michael's movements were innocent enough, but something niggled at the back of Sean's mind.

That afternoon, Sean eased onto the freeway, letting a few vehicles slip between his car and Michael's, while still keeping his quarry in sight. Michael sat behind the wheel of his black Ferrari, sliding in and out of the traffic. In conservative Orange County, the sports car stuck out like a sore thumb. It would have fit better in LA. Michael swerved across three lanes of traffic to take the interchange from the 55 north onto the 5 north.

"Where are you going, Michael? And where are your bodyguards?" Over the last two years, Sean had come to know his suspect well, and Michael rarely traveled alone. This was the first time in six months Michael didn't have at least one of his big hired guns at his side.

Michael took the exit to Buena Park, and Sean stomped on the gas to reach the exit in time to note which direction Michael turned. A few minutes later, Michael pulled into the rutted parking lot of a large white building with Arabic writing on the filigreed signage. Sean waited out of sight on the street until Michael strode inside the building. He winced when the undercarriage of his Camaro hit a large pothole in the parking lot.

When he opened the building's door, thick sweet smoke drifted out, making Sean grimace in distaste. Orange County only allowed smoking inside a few places. Hookahs sat on each table, most of which were filled with people lounging and smoking tobacco and herbal mixtures. Brightly colored pendant lamps hung from the ceiling, casting a warm glow on the red painted walls. The decor had a distinct Moroccan flair, and the spicy scents of Middle Eastern food and the various tobacco mixtures made his nose itch. He slipped into the hookah lounge unnoticed, hidden behind a party of young people jabbering excitedly about trying the new experience.

Sean glanced around the room and spotted Michael in the rear, sitting in a private booth with an older, well-dressed gentleman. The man's thick black hair was smoothed back from his face and silver lined his temples and short beard. As Sean slipped into a nearby booth, the man turned his head. A ruby glinted from his earlobe. He locked eyes with Sean.

Warning bells clanged, and Sean's heart pounded in his throat. On instinct, his hand floated to the gun at his side. Sweat beaded his upper lip as primal fear swamped him. He narrowed his eyes, and a black dragon superimposed over the old man. Sean blinked in surprise and shook his head.

"No. There's no way I saw that!" Sean murmured, rubbing his eyes and face. "I'm just exhausted and seeing things. Dragons aren't real." Sean lowered his hands, took a deep breath, and returned his gaze to the man. He appeared normal again, but a smirk played over his lips as he winked at Sean.

Sean ordered a Moroccan mint tea, sipping it while he strained to catch snatches of Michael's and the gentleman's conversation. The laughter from the noisy party-goers made it difficult to hear. He stuck a finger in his ear and wiggled it, trying to dislodge the strange, low humming in his ears. The hookah smoke burned the back of his throat and made his eyes water. Finally, the two men shook hands, and Sean hurried from the lounge before Michael could spot him.

The sun had set while Sean had been in the hookah lounge. He wrinkled his nose at the dearth of lights in the parking lot. Although it made it easier for skulking.

Michael exited the lounge, but before he could open his car door, three thugs surrounded him. Michael threw his arms out wide, and with a laugh, greeted them. Sean gaped as the men bowed low to Michael and kissed the ring on his left hand. The group talked in earnest whispers for several minutes. The biggest thug nodded, then reached into his jacket and held out something to Michael. As he did, his hand shimmered into a black claw for a split-second. Red paper crisscrossed with gold braid covered the package. An avaricious gleam filled Michael's eyes as he took it from the henchman.

Sean ducked behind a car as Michael whirled in his direction. A car's headlights caught Michael's eyes, causing them to glow red. Sean sucked in a panicked breath, hoping Michael hadn't seen him.

As Sean trailed Michael back onto the freeway, he considered the frightening red glow in Michael's eyes and the exchange with the thugs. Somehow, Michael was connected with the strange crimes that had been striking the county for the last month, and not only the Iron Maiden killings.

 # CHAPTER 16 

Sean opened his fridge, scowling at the looming emptiness. It matched his stomach. Ketchup, mustard, and mayonnaise wouldn't do much to feed him. A search in his cupboards revealed them just as empty. Not even the peanut butter jar held enough dregs for more than a taste. The last time he recalled going grocery shopping or eating at home was over a month ago. He liked to cook and usually made time to eat healthy.

Yawning so wide his jaw cracked, he rubbed his burning eyes. He'd give anything for a full night's sleep. Even when he wasn't being called out at all hours of the night because of the increased strange homicides, Sean tossed and turned. His mind kept searching for the missing evidence to link Michael to the Iron Maiden killings. Staying out late on his self-assigned task of following Michael didn't help either.

Giving up on eating, Sean flopped down on his couch and flicked through the channels on TV, but nothing held his interest. Thoughts of the evil Michael could be committing while he lazed about pushed Sean to his feet to pace the room.

"I have to get out of here! I'm driving myself crazy." He glanced at his watch. "It's still early. Michael should be at the club. If I go there, I can keep tabs on him."

After his last encounter, and the subsequent chewing out he'd received from Captain Green, Sean better have a good reason to be there. His stomach grumbled a complaint. He picked up his cell phone and called Charlie.

"You available to hang out tonight?" Sean asked when Charlie answered. He heard Charlie huff.

"Where? No, don't tell me. The Red Orchid. Where else?"

"Ah, come on, man," Sean wheedled. "This Michael guy is a nasty dude. I could watch him by myself, but then I'd get in trouble with my Captain. Again. He might go through with his threat and fire me. If you're there with me, we're just a couple of guys out for drinks and snacks."

"It's Thursday night. I can't stay long."

"Thanks, Charlie!"

"You owe me."

"Of course I do. I'll buy the drinks. Meet you in thirty?"

After hanging up, Sean changed into a nice pair of black slacks and a green button-down shirt, then slid into his leather loafers. He grabbed his black leather jacket to hide his sidearm and to complete his undercover look of a regular guy out clubbing.

When they met up, Charlie had dark circles under his eyes and a haggard appearance. They sat at a table where Sean had a clear view of Michael without it being too obvious. Charlie ordered his usual microbrew while Sean requested a Scotch on the rocks and a burger with chili cheese fries.

"What's going on, buddy?" Sean asked, taking a sip of his drink.

"A bodyguard gig. A nasty gang is after a sweet girl. They're as bad as the guy you're after." Charlie's eyes flicked to the booth where Michael and his frat buddies lounged. "She has something they want, but she doesn't know it. We're doing all we can to keep her safe. But it's difficult."

Sean watched a girl shimmy up to Michael's table and slip into the seat next to him. She looked like everyone else until the overhead rotating lights hit her eyes. They glowed an eerie yellow and reminded Sean of reptile eyes. When a long tongue slithered out and licked Michael's cheek, Sean sputtered, spitting out the drink he'd just taken. He slammed his glass back down so hard he knocked it over.

"Oh, good God, that was sick!" Sean wiped the whisky off his face and mopped up the mess.

Charlie turned toward Michael. "What did you see, man?"

"Nothing." He pinched the bridge of his nose. "It couldn't be anything," he muttered. Sean waved the waitress over and ordered another drink.

"You look as beat as I feel. Work must be bad for you."

"It's awful. We're still being hammered by weird, violent homicides. Last night, two men were out eating dinner when one of them suddenly attacked and stabbed his partner multiple times. A few minutes later, he crumbled, crying over the dead body, swearing a grotesque creature sat beside him, not his lover.

"In all these cases, there aren't any drugs in the perps' system to cause hallucinations. On top of it all, I'm no closer to stopping the Iron Maiden killer than I was three years ago when the killings started. This last murder was brutal."

Sean rubbed his chin, noting the scruff of his beard was longer than he liked it. He glanced at the waitress as she dropped off his fresh drink and his food. He fought to rub his eyes, instead blinked furiously. Small, twisty horns peeked from her black curls.

"I feel sorry for the victim's friend. Even though she witnessed Michael with her friend, and so did I, Michael has an alibi and an excuse."

Charlie stuffed a cheesy fry into his mouth. "That's the psychic chick you told me about, right? She seems like the real deal. Did you ask her to do a card reading? It might point you to something you're overlooking."

Sean shook his head, then levered his elbows on the table, leaning forward. "I'm afraid to have her read my cards. She might pick up on things ... emotions ... I'm not ready to face. I'm staying away from her. She brings up too many emotions I don't want. Not after Ginny."

Charlie rubbed the rim of his glass. "When are you going to get over that bitch, Sean? Not every woman is as cold or mean as she was. To sleep with someone else in your own bed, that's cruel. To tell you the truth, I never liked her." He grimaced before taking another drink. "So who is this psychic chick and where does she work? It's time I got a reading. And it would give me a reason to check her out and see if she's good enough for my buddy."

Sean laughed. It seemed like he hadn't for a long time. His gaze flicked over at Michael, who fondled the strange woman now sitting on his lap. He wasn't going anywhere for a while.

Sean took a bite of his burger. "Her name is Catlyn, Catlyn Hennessey." He noticed Charlie's eyebrows tick up before he schooled his face. *What was that about?* He doubted Charlie would know Catlyn. After telling Charlie about her, they discussed the latest football game. He enjoyed the normalcy of arguing with Charlie over the chances of the various teams to reach the super bowl.

As Sean wove his way through the crowded dance floor to the door, an inebriated couple bumbled into him. The woman murmured an apology, but the man glared at him, baleful green light shone in his eyes. He snarled, flashing sharpened teeth in a dark purple mouth. He spat out words in a language Sean didn't recognize. Charlie bumped into him from behind hard enough to make him stumble to the side. Out of the corner of his eye, Sean caught Charlie's hands moving in a complicated pattern and a red light burst from them. The man grunted, and when Sean regained his balance, the couple had disappeared into the crowd.

"Sorry about that, buddy." Charlie patted his shoulder. "I didn't notice you stopped."

Sean tried brushing it off as a simple accident. But as he drove home, he replayed the incident. He was beginning to accept seeing weird shit around Michael. But to catch his best friend doing what he could only think of as magic, Sean worried he was going crazy.

He needed to go visit his Granny. She could tell him what was happening to him.

Catlyn moved through her morning yoga routine. She slipped into the postures with more grace and ease than she remembered. Feeling courageous, she tried a pose she'd admired but didn't think she had the strength, balance, or flexibility to accomplish: the flying pigeon. With her hands on the floor, she wrapped her left foot around her right triceps. She only had to extend her right leg behind her to finish the pose. She hadn't reached this stage before. Taking a deep breath, she slowly extended her leg. *I did it!* Surprise made her fall. "This is awesome! If I can do things like this, it's worth it to have Maak share my body."

Later that morning, Catlyn leaned back to rest her eyes from the detailed work on a jewelry piece to find her cats staring at her. They'd cocked their heads as if they were listening to something. "Great, she'll talk to you, but not to me," Catlyn complained.

In the week since Maak had merged with her, Catlyn hadn't received any further insights why Maak choose to share Catlyn's body. Although she found being able to smell emotions helped her with her healing work and tarot readings. Some were easy to identify. Fear, a musty, sour scent, smelled vastly different from the sweet, alluring scent of love. The scent of similar emotions, like happiness, pleasure, and joy, was harder to distinguish between their subtle differences.

Smell wasn't the only sense that had heightened after Maak joined with her. A few days ago, she'd nearly jumped out of her skin when she clearly heard her client's heartbeat. Her improved hearing allowed her to hear the customers in the store while still back in her healing room. She scowled at the ceiling. Her upstairs neighbors were at it again. She'd have to learn how to tune out and ignore unwanted sounds, such as her neighbor's sexual exploits.

Catlyn stood up, stretching after the intense concentration of wire wrapping another crystal into a pendant. Her stomach growled, and she wandered into the kitchen for a snack before she left for her self-defense session with Jade. Mittens and Boots followed her, hoping she'd give them a treat too.

After opening and shutting several cupboard doors and not finding anything appetizing, Catlyn stood staring out her kitchen window. Ivy covered the wall separating her apartment complex with the one next door. Catlyn wished she could afford a house or condo where she could have a small garden. Her window garden provided a few fresh herbs, but she longed to dig in the earth and plant vegetables and flowers.

The sound of Mittens and Boots meowing broke into her reverie. They were both circling her legs, and Mittens reached up to snag something out of Catlyn's hand.

"Mittens! What are you doing?" Catlyn looked at what she'd been absently nibbling on. Her eyebrows rose. "Catnip! Really? At least it's in the mint family and won't kill me." She snipped a few leaves to give to her cats while stuffing more into her mouth.

When she arrived at Jade's house, Catlyn paused on the threshold of Jade's garage. She'd converted half of it into a dojo. Jade wore a gi, the traditional white karate uniform, tied closed with a black belt. She stretched both hands to the ceiling, then lowered to touch the floor with her palms.

"You're better!" Catlyn strode into the dojo, putting on her gi top and snugging a white belt around her waist.

Jade hooked her thumbs in her belt. "I heal fast. I need to get back into shape, so we're going to spar."

Catlyn groaned. She'd been sparring with Jade's newest recruit for her bodyguard business, Ariana Lambert. Ariana had been easy on Catlyn. Jade wouldn't be so kind. The young woman waited in a corner, lifting weights, and gave Catlyn a nod in greeting.

The three moved to the center of the room and warmed up, practicing the various punches, kicks, and blocks. Then Jade led them in several katas, or forms, that taught combinations for fighting. Catlyn liked doing katas. When she was in the groove, they provided a type of moving meditation. Today, she was hyperaware of the tensing and relaxing of her muscles as she performed the movements. Joy coursed through her at the newfound strength and power of her body. She threw a sidekick and her gi pant leg snapped.

Jade's eyebrows rose. "Nicely done, Catlyn. I don't think you've ever been that precise before."

"I haven't." Catlyn grinned, excited at her achievement.

"Let's spar." Jade motioned to Ariana, who moved off the mats to stand by the side wall. "We'll start out easy."

Catlyn stood several paces away and bowed, then lightly bounced on the balls of her feet, her hands held up in a ready position. Jade rushed forward with a backhand strike toward Catlyn's nose, following up with a thrusting front kick. Catlyn swung her arm in a downward block, knocking Jade's foot aside, immediately throwing a punch to Jade's face.

Jade scooted to the side, barely blocking with an upper block. She gave Catlyn an appraising look. "Your speed has improved considerably."

They continued to spar, trading punches and kicks. Catlyn saw an opening and threw a round house kick. Her eyes widened when her foot connected with Jade's ribs. Jade grunted from the impact. She eyed Catlyn. "You're much stronger, too. Care to explain?"

Catlyn opened her mouth to tell Jade about Maak, but Maak's voice stopped her. *"No, don't tell her about me yet. She won't understand our bond."*

"I've been practicing," Catlyn said instead. "Being scared and stalked is great motivation. Your guys might not be there when Smoker Dude or Blond Guy decides to do something to me besides watching and following me. Or worse, if Michael takes a more active role."

Jade narrowed her eyes. "He hasn't done anything to you, has he?"

"No." Catlyn shook her head, then a shiver ran down her spine. "He's just shown up at the oddest places, then seems to disappear. Monday I was at the grocery store, and he stood at the end of the aisle I was walking down, leering at me. As soon as he knew I saw him, he vanished. When I reached the end—which only took a few seconds—he wasn't anywhere to be found."

"Where was Dilan? Wasn't he your guard that day?"

Catlyn shrugged. "I don't know. Your guys are good. They mostly stay out of sight."

"I'll have to have a talk with them." Concern crossed Jade's face. "Has Michael done anything else?"

"No, I've only seen him a couple times."

"If Michael ever makes a move toward you or does anything, let my people know immediately. Don't try to fight him on your own. Even with your recent improvements, you're no match for him."

"Don't worry, that guy freaks me out. He oozes evil. Every tarot reading I've done where he's even in the periphery of the situation, the Devil card shows up for him. In his case, I think it's quite literal."

"It is."

Jade's ready agreement about Michael being a demon elicited a low growl from Catlyn's throat. Maak agreed.

Jade studied Catlyn.

Catlyn held her breath, waiting for Jade to comment on the sound. Instead, she glanced at the clock on the wall. "I have a meeting. Continue to spar with Ariana for another half hour, then you can leave." Jade strode to the doorway leading into her house. Opening the door, she paused and turned around. "Keep vigilant, Catlyn. And do your protection rituals every day. I want you to stay safe."

"Yes, ma'am." Catlyn promised. It was unusual for Jade to leave before their session was over. Catlyn suspected Jade would assign more people to her safety detail from now on. Apparently, Dilan or Charlie hadn't seen Michael stalking her, or they hadn't reported it to Jade.

CHAPTER 17

The next day after work, Sean braved the heavy Friday night, going home traffic to go visit his grandmother. He merged onto the 91 freeway and came to a halt as the cars crept forward.

Two-and-a-half hours later, he pulled into his grandmother's driveway in Temecula. Before he even turned off the engine, the front door opened. He gave a wry grin. His Granny had the "sight," as she called it, and knew things before they happened. He'd long since accepted that his unannounced visits wouldn't surprise her.

"Sean, my darling boy," Granny Eileen said, standing on the porch with her arms wide. "So good to see you. Ye havin' a bit of trouble, now, are ye?" Her Irish brogue slipped out when she talked about anything otherworldly or strange. She wore a long, purple flowery, tiered skirt and a sleeveless teal button-down shirt, which showed off her toned and muscular arms. A matching purple ribbon held back her short, curly hair, which she kept dyed a beautiful shade of red, even at seventy-three. Her bare feet poked out from under her skirt. She hated to wear shoes in the house.

"Hey, Granny." Sean stepped into her embrace. "Can't I just come to visit you?"

"On a Friday night when you could be out having fun? Driving through that awful traffic? Come inside and tell me what has you in a twist."

The aroma of Irish Breakfast tea wafted from the pot waiting on the coffee table. A plate of snickerdoodles, his favorite cookies, sat next to it, still warm from the oven. He bit into one, savoring the burst of cinnamon. His grandmother's enormous cat, Dahlyah, jumped onto his lap, demanding attention. Her purr sounded like a roar when he petted her. The pure black cat had a single white spot on her chest and intelligent gold eyes.

It seemed wrong to talk about evil while drinking tea and eating cookies, but he needed his grandmother's insights.

"Granny, something is happening to me." He stared at his tea mug. "It's this case I'm working on."

"The one you've tried so hard not to tell me about?"

Sean nodded, then sipped his tea again, stalling, afraid she'd think he was going mad. "Since the last murder, I've been seeing strange things. They are always connected to my suspect." He told her about all the weird incidents that had occurred over the past month. "Am I going crazy?"

Eileen patted his hand. "No, Sean, darling, you aren't crazy. Your gifts are reawakening. About time, too! 'Tis your calling to fight evil, and these gifts will help you. If your witch-sight is reasserting itself, you must need it."

"Witch-sight?" His eyes widened. His dad had taught him anything to do with witches was evil. "It isn't evil is it?"

"Hardly," Granny Eileen scoffed. "That would be your father talking. It's used to perceive magic and all things supernatural."

"But magic isn't real!" Sean protested. His teacup clattered to the table.

"There is more to this world than what your eyes see and your brain comprehends. Magic is one of those things." She paused, tilting her head as she studied him. "You saw this fellow's aura, and a nasty one, at that. If he isn't involved in your murders, he's enmeshed in something else wicked. I'll reteach you how to consciously access your witch-sight."

"Reteach me?" Sean frowned.

"Yes. I taught you once before when you were, oh, about eleven. You and Charlie when you visited me in San Francisco. It was shortly after that your father withdrew from the family. He wouldn't let me near you for three years." Sadness filled her face as she looked down at her tightly clenched hands.

"He told me you were out of the country. But I don't remember you teaching me anything. Just vague memories of the stories you told me."

Her lips pursed. "That blimey bloke! I love my son, but sometimes he makes me so angry. He erased your memories. I taught you this and so much more. Well, you've come to me now, and I have time to teach you what you need to know." She took a sip of tea, then leaned forward, her eyes narrowed with intensity. "There is great evil in the world, Sean. More than even you've seen. It's your duty to stop it when you have the gifts to do so. Now, let's get to work."

Dahlyah moved to sit on the couch's arm with her tail curled around her feet. Her gold eyes bored into him, making him nervous. He turned his back to her. His grandmother explained the mechanics of shifting his sight; a narrowing and softening of his eyes, relaxing, and not trying. The last part tripped him up. After half an hour of attempting to turn it on, he still hadn't slipped into his other sight. It'd come so naturally at the gym and nightclub.

"No, no, no!" Eileen exploded with exasperation. "In the words of wise Yoda, 'there is no try, only do.' Perhaps you need something to focus on. Look at Dahlyah using your witch-sight."

Sean scowled. He didn't understand how looking at the cat would make a difference.

Dahlyah tilted her head, then reached out a paw and dug her claws into his arm. Sean swore and slapped her away. Her loud meow sounded indignant. Without thinking, he shifted his vision. Dahlyah blinked at him, spreading wide, dark purple wings, and then she resettled them along her back.

He jumped to his feet with a yelp.

"Your cat ..." He swallowed. "Your cat has wings!"

His grandmother grinned. "Why yes, yes she does. She's a *Cait Sidhe*, one of the fae, or fair folk. We know them as Dih'nea. Show him, Dahlyah."

Dahlyah yawned, showing him her large teeth. She lifted her wings from her back. Her body expanded, growing to the size of a small pony. Sean shook his head and looked again. Dahlyah leaped, and with a strong down stroke, rose from the couch and flew straight toward the sliding glass door. The glass seemed to shimmer, then the winged cat appeared outside, where she curled up on a patio chair, her back to them, done with show-and-tell.

Sean returned his attention to his grandmother and gasped. Beautiful gold and purple light surrounded her. When he examined the plant by the window, it emitted a soft, green glow. He blinked a few times, and his vision returned to normal. Outside, the cat was once again a regular, albeit an abnormally large, cat.

His legs wobbled. He slumped onto the couch.

His grandmother patted his leg. "I know, 'tis a bit much to absorb all at once. While immense evil abounds, there is also great good. But remember, not all things that appear beautiful are good."

Sean thought of Michael, who most would consider handsome. He nodded. "The opposite is true, I assume."

"Yes. You can never take anything at face value. Use your witch-sight. It shows the truth. What did you see and sense when you looked at me or Dahlyah?"

He lowered his head, considering. "Peaceful... A beautiful, golden light surrounded you. After getting over being startled, Dahlyah had good energy, good vibes. I know it sounds hokey."

"Not to me." She laughed.

Sean joined her.

She stopped laughing. "And how about your suspect?"

Sean made a face. "Slimy and nasty. Too bad I can't use that in a court of law or even to get a search warrant."

"Don't worry about that. You'll catch him. Soon. Help is coming."

"Did you have a vision?"

Granny shook her head and looked away. "No, just a feeling."

He had a strong suspicion she knew more, but he refused to interrogate his grandmother.

She turned back to him. "Keep practicing shifting into and out of your witch-sight. But, like texting and drinking, don't do it while driving. Enough work." Granny Eileen stood and shook her skirt. "I'm starving. Take me out to dinner, my boy."

"Sure thing, Granny." He held out his arm for her. "I'd be happy to. We don't get together often enough."

Eileen wrapped her hand around the crook of his arm. "That will change, Sean darling, that will change. Now, where should we go?"

He took her to an upscale steakhouse he'd heard a lot about. They lingered a long time over steak, lobster, and wine, talking. When he dropped her back off at her home, the way he thought of her had changed. She was no longer the weird grandmother the family talked about in hushed voices. She'd returned to his beloved Granny and became his mentor in the strange world he found himself in.

"I don't like you living out here alone, Granny," Sean said as he turned onto her street.

"Don't worry, I'm fine." Eileen patted his knee.

He pulled into the driveway.

"Use your witch-sight, boy."

Dahlyah sat on the porch, looking like a Chinese temple guardian lion. He narrowed his eyes and shifted into his witch-sight. The word still made him uncomfortable. Her wings formed a hump above her back and she glowed. A shimmering light extended from her to surround the house. He blinked to return his sight to normal.

"There is some sort of energy field behind Dahlyah. What is it?"

"Her job. She's my guard-kitty. Nothing evil can pass through her protections. See? I'm fine."

She exited the car and shut the door. Instead of going inside, she stood on the sidewalk. She took something out of her pocket and looked at it for a long moment before turning back and coming around to his window. He rolled it down, and she held out her hand.

"Here, take this. It was your grandfather's. It's time you had it."

A gold amulet with strange symbols engraved on it lay on her palm. He gently took it from her. His hand tingled with its vibration. When he used his witch-sight, a warm, golden aura surrounded it that set his mind and heart at ease. He slipped the chain over his head. The amulet's warmth seeped into his chest.

"Tuck it under your shirt," she told him, "and don't let anyone see it, especially your father." She patted his cheek and sighed heavily with relief. "I feel better. Now you have some measure of protection until we can find you your own guard-kitty." Eileen leaned in and kissed him, then walked to the house.

Dahlyah resettled her wings, then licked a paw. He didn't know exactly how the cat—what did his granny call her?—the *Cait Sidhe* protected his grandmother, but he felt better now he knew she did. He waved at the cat and backed onto the street. He'd come to his grandmother hoping she'd have answers, and learned there was more to the world than he thought.

The drive back to Tustin took less than half the time; the roads had cleared of heavy traffic. After arriving home, he tried watching television, but nothing grabbed his attention. He flipped through a magazine, then picked up a book and, after reading only a paragraph, set it aside. Too keyed up after all the revelations, he went for a walk, wandering around his condo complex. Every few minutes he practiced shifting to his witch-sight, but didn't see anything—until he looked up.

A gasp of disbelief escaped him. "No fucking way!" Sean shifted back to his witch-sight. High above him flew a winged creature with a long, sinewy neck and a forked tail. *A dragon!* From this distance, he couldn't get any sense what side, good or evil, it belonged to. Freaked out, he hurried home and crawled into bed. It took all his will power to not revert to his childhood habit of pulling the blankets over his head to hide.

The world was vastly different tonight than the one he'd awakened to that morning. He wasn't sure whether he liked it or not.

Sunday morning, Catlyn stepped lightly down her apartment steps. She threw a jaunty wave at Charlie, then growled at Blond Guy as she passed his car.

On her way to the Jupiter Moon to meet her friend Lisa, Catlyn stopped at the pet store. She wandered toward the front to check out after selecting her cat's favorite food and a box of litter. A dog's low rumbling growl nearby stopped her in her tracks. Fear spiked daggers into her stomach. A boxer in the aisle of dog toys strained at his leash in her direction. His owner fought to hold him back. Poised to run, Catlyn noticed the boxer's attention wasn't focused on her, but behind her.

The stink of sulfur filled her nose. The dog tucked its tail and scampered the other direction, dragging his owner behind him. Dreading what she would find, Catlyn slowly turned around.

"People should leave their animals at home," Michael growled. A red gleam sparked in his eyes as he glowered at the retreating dog.

"Well, this is a pet store," Catlyn said. "Dogs like to come and choose their own toys."

He peered down his nose at her. "How would you know? You don't own a dog, just cats."

For a moment, Catlyn's mind froze. *He's been in my house!* Her gaze dropped to her cart filled with cat food and laughed at herself. He reached out a hand and ran a fingertip over her bare arm. She jerked it away, rubbing at the burning sensation.

Michael leaned closer. "You're very beautiful. It's a shame your beauty will be ruined when I'm finished with you. But don't worry, you still have time to spend with your wimp of a boyfriend before I take you."

"What?"

He made a kissing sound, then strode down the aisle after the dog.

Catlyn pulled her phone out of her purse. Her hands trembled so badly she dropped it. She hurriedly scooped it from the floor. When she stood up, Michael had vanished. She watched the front door as she called Charlie.

"Michael ..." Catlyn stuttered. She licked her lips and tried again. "Michael is here."

Charlie swore, and she heard running feet. Charlie skidded to a halt next to her. "Damn it! I was watching you and didn't see anything! Where did he go?"

She pointed at the aisle. "I haven't seen him leave the store."

"Stay here!" Charlie ordered. He talked rapidly on his phone as he raced down the dog toy aisle. A few moments later, he walked up the next aisle, shaking his head. "No sign of him."

Catlyn's heart pounded. "I've been watching the entrance, and no one has left."

"Todd didn't see him in the parking lot either." Charlie's lips thinned. "He couldn't have disappeared ..." He trailed off. "What did he say to you?"

His eyes hardened, and his fist clenched around his phone as Catlyn told him.

"You're in serious trouble, Catlyn. It would be easier to guard you if you stayed home, or better yet, stayed at Jade's house. It's like a fortress. No one can harm you there."

"I'm not going to let some asshole scare me from my home! Besides, I have to go to work, otherwise I can't pay my rent or buy groceries."

"Please, Catlyn," Charlie implored, "call in sick today and come with me to Jade's." Worry creased his forehead.

"I can't let fear run my life. I have faith you can protect me. Now, move out of my way, please. I need to pay for this. Lisa is waiting for me." She pushed her cart and Charlie stepped aside.

As she drove to the coffee shop, the fear Catlyn had been stifling bubbled to the surface and tears rolled down her face. *What have I done to deserve this unwanted attention?*

The image of her curled up in front of a fire, cuddling a white tiger flashed in her mind. Well-being suffused her. "*I am here,*" Maak said.

Catlyn's fears fled. Logically, she doubted a spirit tiger could protect her. But a deep certainty filled Catlyn's heart that Maak would keep her safe.

A few minutes later, she parked and hurried into the Jupiter Moon.

Lisa waited for her at the entrance. "You're late. Is everything okay?"

"Yes. It took longer at the pet store than I expected. Have you ordered yet?"

"Nah, I was waiting for you." Lisa moved into line.

Catlyn tapped her chin as she contemplated the menu board, deciding if she wanted breakfast or lunch. The scent of bacon wafted from the kitchen, and her mouth watered. "Breakfast it is."

After they ordered, they found a table and chatted. Catlyn's neck hairs rose, chilling her, and she looked over her shoulder. A tall man with close-cropped dark hair sat at a nearby table, staring at them. He reminded her of her watchers. As she scooted her chair to the side to keep him in sight, she noticed he wasn't watching her, but Lisa. The faint scent of an obnoxious incense tickled her nose. She'd smelled it before at the metaphysical shop. Narrowing her eyes, she concentrated on the man. She drew in a shocked breath. *He doesn't have an aura! I've only experienced that once, and the person had been following Lisa then, too.*

Catlyn crossed her arms over her chest and leaned back in her seat. "That guy gives me the creeps." She tipped her cup to indicate the man. "Let's go sit outside."

Lisa turned in her seat and looked around. "What man? Do you mean the guy with the three kids?"

"Come on, stop teasing me. Don't tell me you can't see the creepy dark-haired guy. He's staring at you."

Lisa tilted her head to the side and frowned. "The only man in here is the family dude." She sighed. "It's nice outside. We can go if you want."

Lisa stood, gathering her purse, coffee cup, and the table marker. She walked to the door ahead of Catlyn, and as she reached it, the man brushed past her, leaving ahead of her. Lisa shivered and rubbed her arm. She took two steps, then clutched her stomach. "Oh, I don't feel good." She put a hand over her mouth, shoved her cup at Catlyn, and rushed to the restroom.

Catlyn's forehead furrowed as she thought about the strange man's behavior. She whirled around, scanning the empty parking lot. Perplexed, she sank onto a patio chair. Her heart fluttered as menace crawled up her spine. He'd done something to cause Lisa's sudden illness. When the server arrived with their food, she asked for containers.

Several minutes later, Lisa came out of the restroom, her face pale. "I don't know what came over me. I felt fine, then suddenly I was nauseous. My stomach's still queasy. I'm going to go home."

"I thought that might be the case." Catlyn tapped the takeout boxes. "Do you need me to drive you?"

Lisa shook her head. "No, I think I'm good enough to drive the few blocks home."

Catlyn stood to hug her friend.

Lisa backed up a step. "Are you sure you want to hug me? I might be contagious."

Catlyn rolled her eyes. "You don't get the flu that fast." She put her arms around Lisa. Her stomach roiled as she caught the rotten egg stench of sulfur. She remembered Lisa rubbing her arm. Catlyn stepped back, grabbed Lisa's arm, and examined it. The faint outlines of a rune-like symbol marked her upper arm.

"This isn't a natural illness. Evil touched you. Can't you smell the sulfur?"

Lisa's eyes widened. "Oh, is that what it is? It's awful." She covered her mouth. "I think I'm going to throw up again."

"Wash your arm off. It might help," Catlyn suggested as Lisa hurried back to the restroom.

Lisa returned, her face still pale. "Washing helped get rid of the obnoxious odor, and I'm not as queasy. Thanks."

Catlyn smiled. It faded as she noticed the mark was even more pronounced. "It didn't remove the mark, though."

"What mark?" Lisa craned her neck, and her mouth dropped open, aghast. "What the hell? Do you know what it is?"

Catlyn shook her head. "Nothing good. Come to the store with me, and I'll try healing it. I have time."

Lisa agreed and followed Catlyn to her healing studio at Mystical Enchantments.

Once there, Lisa laid down on the massage table, rubbing her arm. "There's a burning sensation under the skin."

"I can't promise this will help," Catlyn warned. "I don't have experience clearing this type of evil."

"I trust you." Lisa's eyes drifted shut, but her breath didn't deepen. Instead, it came in shallow pants.

Standing next to Lisa, Catlyn bowed her head and closed her eyes. She prayed to Hecate to help her. The powerful presence of the Goddess filled the room and guided Catlyn in placing the crystals around and on Lisa's body. She ran her hand above Lisa, sensing her friend's aura through her fingertips. When she reached the spot where the symbol was etched on Lisa's skin, the energy became dense and made Catlyn's skin crawl.

She chanted under her breath in an unknown, ancient sounding language. Her conscious mind balked, but she told it to shut up, and allowed the song to continue to flow. The energy within her built. Unexpectedly, a green light streamed from her hands. Stunned, Catlyn watched the light wrap around Lisa's arm.

Lisa flinched, her face tightening with pain.

"*Barra, utuk xul!*" Catlyn commanded, when the green light darkened to almost black. The mark vanished, and Lisa relaxed. A few moments later, the light dissolved. Catlyn spent a while longer doing her normal energy work.

Lisa blinked her eyes open and stretched. "Thanks, Catlyn. I'm feeling much better now. I don't know what happened."

"That evil guy marked you."

Lisa grimaced. "I can't disbelieve you after being so sick. But I swear, I didn't see anyone."

"I did. I don't know why you couldn't."

Lisa shrugged.

After Lisa left, Catlyn stood behind the counter in the empty store. She idly shuffled her tarot cards, thinking about the mark on Lisa's arm. Two cards fell from the deck and plopped onto the counter. With a feeling of dread, Catlyn hesitantly turned them over.

The Devil and Death card glared up at her.

A vision filled her mind of Lisa trapped in a strange metal cage, blood dripping from numerous wounds.

"No, no, no! Not another friend!" She cried out, her knees buckling. She huddled on the floor, her hands shaking as she called Jade. "You have to help my friend, Lisa," she sobbed when her godmother answered. "Michael is after her."

 # Chapter 18 

Catlyn tossed and turned throughout the night, worrying about Lisa, even though Jade promised to protect her. After all, Michael had threatened her at the pet store without Charlie or her other guards seeing him. Why couldn't he do the same with Lisa? How could she warn her friend she was in danger without unnecessarily frightening her?

Daylight didn't bring with it any solutions to Catlyn's problem. Needing a distraction, she drove to her favorite Jupiter Moon in Tustin. The October morning was unusually warm. As she walked across the parking lot, she decided spending time in the sun with a good book would take her mind off her problems for a while.

She carried her iced chai and gooey pecan-cinnamon roll outside. She ignored Smoker Dude, sitting in his car in the parking lot. With Dilan's truck parked next to it, she doubted her stalker would do anything. So far, he and Blond Guy only watched her, keeping tabs on her for their boss, Michael.

The scar on her palm tingled as she sat down, and a wave of terror swamped her. Catlyn's eyes darted all around, finally catching sight of a green bushy tail disappearing into the bushes. She didn't know why the creature made her so afraid. She watched the area for several minutes, but didn't see the creature again.

Relieved, Catlyn propped her book up to read while she ate and settled more comfortably into her chair. As she popped the last bite of pastry into her mouth, she sensed someone approach her table.

"Mind if I join you?" a man with a sexy voice asked.

She looked up and smiled at the cute detective McLarkin. "Sure." Catlyn indicated the empty seat.

Since the night at the La Boucherie, she hadn't spoken to Karl. As Sean sat, Catlyn studied him over the rim of her cup. He wore black pants, with a button-down teal shirt opened at the collar. Every other time she'd seen him, he'd been wearing a tie. She liked the more casual style on him better. His short sleeves revealed muscular, tanned arms that weren't too muscle-bound. His dark blue eyes had crinkles at the corners, and as he smiled, she decided they enhanced his rugged charm. She wished his sandy-blond hair was longer. The buzz-cut reminded her too much of her watcher, Blond Guy.

"I showed your jewelry to my grandmother," Sean said. "I saw her Friday night. She likes your work. She's intrigued by your sound healing, but she lives out in Temecula. It's difficult for her to come this way. She hates to drive."

"The traffic is worse in Orange County than in Riverside. Although there is the toll road now that helps somewhat."

"She'd never pay to drive on a highway! She argues that we pay enough in taxes that we should have good roads."

"I agree with her." Catlyn wished his grandmother would book a healing appointment. She sounded like someone Catlyn would enjoy meeting.

They chatted about inconsequential things, such as the weather and the latest Hollywood couple. The more they talked, the more she liked him and wanted to spend time with him. A purr rumbled in her mind. Maak approved of him as well. Their talk turned to movies, and Sean seemed pleased when he found out she adored action-adventure and futuristic science fiction movies. He, in turn, surprised her by being interested in the new musical coming out.

He grinned at her. "Once you're no longer part of my case, I'd like to take you out on a date. Maybe go see that musical."

Catlyn's heart raced and heat flushed her face. "I'd like that." Then she thought about his case—Amy's murder—and her chest tightened. "Have you had any luck on your case?"

Sean grimaced. "I have a suspect. The guy she was dating. But he has an alibi."

"You know he did it."

"Yeah, I do. And many others. But I can't prove it." He pressed his lips together, perhaps thinking he'd told her—an outsider—too much.

Catlyn ducked her head and clenched her hands in her lap. Could Sean help keep Lisa safe? Or would he believe she was a crackpot? She liked him and didn't want to jeopardize their budding friendship.

"I know this is going to sound crazy," she said quietly, then lifted her eyes to stare into his. "But I think my friend Lisa is in trouble. I think..." Catlyn looked to the side. Blond Guy leaned nonchalantly against his car. Lisa's life was worth more than the hope of going on a date with Sean— no matter how handsome he was. She took a deep, calming breath. "I think Michael is after her."

She told him about the incident yesterday and the strange mark on Lisa's arm. Instead of looking at her with disgust or like she should be locked up in the looney-bin, Sean listened attentively to her.

"My godmother, Jade Lowery, put a protective detail on her," Catlyn added.

Sean's eyebrows knitted together. "Doesn't she own the Sentinel Guard Company?"

Catlyn nodded.

"My best buddy, Charlie MacNamara, works for her. I know they do good work, but after the things I've seen this killer do, I'm not sure any private firm can protect a potential victim." He slumped back in his chair and rubbed his eyes. "Unfortunately, I don't have enough evidence to warrant putting your friend into protective custody. I wouldn't want to arrest her and have her spend days in jail. As long as I've chased this guy, I can't figure out his routine. There has to be a pattern to when he kills, but it eludes me."

Sean leaned forward and patted Catlyn's hand. His hand lingered over hers, and tiny electrical pulses passed between their hands. They didn't hurt, quite the opposite. She felt a tingle respond in her core. Sean's eyes widened at the zipping energy, and he pulled his hand away from hers.

"I think your friend will be safe for a little while longer. If Michael is the Iron Maiden killer, he made a kill last week. It's usually about a month between murders. I'll do what I can, but I'm afraid it won't be much."

"It was worth a try to tell you about it."

"Here." Sean reached into his shirt pocket and handed her a small notebook. "Write down her name, address, and phone number, and I'll look into it."

Catlyn smirked at the old-fashioned notebook. "You don't have a smart phone?"

Sean grimaced. "Yeah, I do. I prefer things I can touch."

Catlyn scrawled the information on the paper, then gave it back. "What's your phone number? I'll text you a picture of Lisa." This way, he'd have her number when—if—he called her for that movie date.

He smiled at her as he gave her his number, perhaps thinking the same thing. When his phone dinged, telling him he had a text message, his smile grew wider. It fell when he picked up his phone. "Damn! I'm going to be late for work. I've really enjoyed talking with you, Catlyn."

"Same here."

Sean gathered their empty coffee cups and plates, tossing them into the trash as he left the coffee shop.

Catlyn's sensitive ears heard him whistling a jaunty tune as he sauntered to his car. She hoped he'd call her soon. Nice guys were hard to find.

Wednesday evening, Catlyn set up the store's classroom for the monthly crystal class she taught. Her friends, Bri and Lydia, strolled in together, pulling Catlyn into their conversation. Fifteen minutes into the class, Lisa hadn't arrived yet. Catlyn's heart hammered in her chest. Lisa usually called if she wasn't going to make it. Come to think about it, Catlyn hadn't heard from her since the incident on Sunday afternoon. Fear trampled through her thoughts, making it difficult to concentrate. She ended the class early, rushing from the room to dig her phone from her purse.

She glared at the blank screen. No messages had come in while she'd been teaching. Pacing the small kitchen, Catlyn dialed her godmother's number.

"Jade, she's gone! Lisa didn't show up for the crystal class tonight. She never misses."

"I know." A tremble in Jade's voice betrayed her worry. "Ariana and Caleb were watching her. They followed her home from work and waited for her to leave for the shop. When she didn't come out, Ariana went to investigate. She found Lisa's apartment in shambles and drops of blood on the floor. We're trying to track her down now. We'll find her, Catlyn, I promise."

"I'm going to call my new homicide detective friend, Sean McLarkin. Maybe he can help you search for her."

"If he's a homicide detective, there isn't much he'll be able to do until Lisa's body turns up."

"Don't say that, Jade. I can't lose another friend."

"I know, honey. We'll do everything we can to find her. I have good people on it."

"But not your best."

"No, they are watching you."

Catlyn clicked off the phone and slid against the wall until her butt bumped the floor. She hugged her bent knees, tears streaming down her face. Her illusion of safety crumbled. She'd been a fool to think Charlie, Dilan, Todd, and the others from Jade's company could protect her. Because of them, she'd been confident Michael wouldn't be able to touch her. Someone had abducted Lisa while under their protection. Doubts assailed Catlyn. What could they do to stop him from attacking her?

Perhaps she should pack her bags and go stay with Jade. Between her gated community and her fenced-in yard, anyone would have a difficult time taking her. But the only way she'd be safe there is if she never left the house's confines. She'd be in prison. A very nice one, but a prison just the same. She couldn't live like that.

Catlyn felt a hand on her shoulder, and she looked up into Bri's brown eyes, full of concern.

"What's wrong, Catlyn?" Bri crouched down.

"Lisa's missing. Someone took her."

Bri's eyes widened. "That's horrible! The others haven't left yet. They were waiting for you to go out to dinner together. Let's do a ritual for Lisa's safe return."

Catlyn eased onto her feet. A ritual might help Jade's team find Lisa before Michael could do whatever terrible things he planned for her. The image of Lisa in a cage with metal spikes piercing her body flashed into Catlyn's mind. She shuddered, hoping she wasn't seeing Lisa's future, but she was afraid she was.

Sean sat in his comfy recliner and flicked on the TV to watch his favorite show while eating dinner. He glared at his phone as it rang. "What now?" he groused. "It's already been a long day." The creepy creatures were still causing problems for the police department. He was tempted to let the call go to voicemail, but duty made him answer it.

"Sean! Sean, she's gone. Lisa's gone."

"Catlyn?" He bolted upright as he recognized the voice.

"Yeah, sorry. My friend I told you about is missing."

"Wasn't the Sentinel Guard Company watching her?"

"She disappeared from right under their noses. Sean, you have to do something. I don't want another friend murdered."

Sean's stomach clenched. It couldn't be time for another gruesome Iron Maiden crime scene so soon. His unease grew as he elicited more information about Lisa's disappearance from Catlyn. He promised he'd do everything he could to find Lisa. Hope flared momentarily. This was the first time he'd known a potential victim was missing so early.

He needed to know the details of the girl's disappearance. "What happened, Charlie?" he asked when his friend answered the phone. "I thought your company was protecting Lisa."

"We were! We had a team watching her outside her apartment. She was only inside for ten minutes before we realized there was a problem. We had eyes on the only egress. She didn't come out the front door."

"Maybe they were just slacking."

Charlie snorted. "We're professionals and good at what we do. We're working on tracking her down now."

Sean rubbed his forehead, unsure how a bodyguard company could help with the investigation. "I want to talk to the team watching her."

Even though Sean didn't work on missing person's cases, he knew in his bones the Iron Maiden killer had taken Lisa. He wanted to save her from a gruesome death. He grabbed his car keys and drove to Lisa's apartment. On the way, he called his partner, asking him to check the traffic cameras and other electronic surveillance in the area.

When he arrived, a muscular woman with short strawberry-blond hair waited in front of the door. The logo on her t-shirt proclaimed her to be from the Sentinel Guard Company. He flashed his badge and introduced himself.

"Ariana Lambert," the woman said. "Charlie asked me to wait for you and tell you what we know. It isn't much."

Sean held up a finger. "Give me a moment to examine the crime scene and then I'll talk to you."

Ariana nodded and moved to let him through the door.

A chair lay on its side. Crystal and flowers from a shattered vase covered the small breakfast bar, water dripping on the floor. There were other signs of a struggle, suggesting Lisa didn't go without a fight. Sean narrowed his eyes and shifted into his witch-sight.

So far, he'd only been able to see the auras of people as well as the strange beings and creatures that appeared human. Yesterday morning, he'd jumped when his neighbor had turned into someone seven-feet tall, with blue and orange skin, pointed ears, and gold eyes. Since having his witch-sight activated, he'd seen several dragons of various sorts. Some were the Western winged reptiles and others were the sinuous Eastern types. Good vibes radiated from most of the beings he saw, and it gave him a thrill to see mythical creatures hiding under the illusion of humanity.

Then there were the beasts that made his flesh crawl. At the Red Orchid, he'd seen numerous ones that had horns, forked tails, long faces, talon-like fingers, and various shades of red skin. A frequent comrade of Michael had short, curly, black fur, and two heads; one normal and the other goat-like with sharp, carnivorous teeth. Michael and his buddies remained human when he looked at them with his witch-sight, except their auras were black, nasty, slimy, and gave off a sickening stench.

As he gazed around Lisa's apartment, the same black, slimy energy slithered on the ground and gathered in the corners. When he walked into the bedroom, the slime concentrated into a blob in front of the closet. The mirrored doors hung off kilter, and one had a crack and smudge about the height of Lisa's head. Sean stepped closer to peer at it. Blood. Most likely it'd be Lisa's. A faint buzzing caught his attention. He groaned when he knelt beside the bed and pulled out Lisa's phone. They wouldn't be able to track her using it. He studied the disarray. It gave him a ray of hope that it might hold clues or evidence he could use.

Sean called the crime tech department and went outside to talk to Ariana. After the crime technicians arrived, Sean drove to the station to see what, if anything, his partner had learned.

"I found the footage of the missing vic's apartment." Jerry opened the traffic camera videos on his computer. "There isn't much to go on."

"Just show it to me."

Sean watched Lisa arriving at her apartment with a silver truck parked in front.

"That belongs to Dilan McGowan, an employee of the Sentinel Guard," Jerry commented.

A few minutes later, a muscular woman in jeans and biker boots exited the truck and ran up the stairs. Sean recognized Ariana. She frantically knocked and when there wasn't an answer, leaned over the doorknob. Sean blinked at the flash of light before the woman opened the door. When he glanced over at Jerry, he acted like he hadn't seen anything. So far, the video confirmed Ariana's story.

A few minutes later, she bolted from the apartment, waving and gesturing at the waiting man. They pulled something from the truck. The image blurred, then cleared. The two guards were leaning over the truck's bed again, then they walked up the stairs and stood guard in front of the door. He paused and replayed the last few seconds of the video.

"What are they taking out of the truck?" he mused.

Jerry looked at him askance. "What are you talking about, man? They didn't pull anything out."

Sean stopped the video where it clearly showed Ariana and Dilan leaning over the truck bed and removing something. He pointed at what appeared to be a small duffel bag. "That."

Jerry shook his head. "They're just leaning on the truck bed."

Sean pressed his lips together. Suspicion niggled that someone had altered the video. He watched the other footage Jerry had queued up, but Sean couldn't see any unusual activity on them. Except in one angle he glimpsed the blurry outline of a black sedan, but when he rewound the video and paused it, nothing was there.

He wanted to talk to Ariana and Dilan about what they'd pulled from the truck. But more importantly, his gut told him his favorite suspect was involved. Excitement griped him; this might be the break he needed. He glanced at the wall clock. It was after one in the morning. The club didn't close until two, and therefore, Michael should still be holding court there with his cronies.

"I'm going to check the Red Orchid and see if Michael has been there all night," Sean told Jerry. "Why don't you head home to your family. There isn't much more we can do tonight."

Sean stalked through the club and to Michael's reserved booth. He frowned at the empty space, then turned to scan the dance floor. A scowl furrowed his forehead when he didn't see any of the men usually hanging around Michael. He found Joshua at the end of the bar, taking away the keys of a woman so sloshed that she tumbled from her barstool. He passed her to a bouncer and hung her keys on the wall with several other sets.

"Detective McLarkin," Joshua said, leaning against the bar, "it's a bit late for you to be here in the middle of the week." His face paled, and he put a hand over his chest. "There hasn't been another murder already, has there?"

Sean shook his head. "No. But a woman is missing, forcibly taken from her home. Has Michael been here tonight?"

Joshua ducked his chin as he thought. His frown deepened. "No. I don't believe so. We had a huge crowd. It was karaoke night."

"Let me know if Michael doesn't show up for the next few days, okay?"

Joshua agreed. Sean declined the drink Joshua offered. He had more work to do. He drove to Michael's house on Balboa Island. The mansion's lights were off, and it seemed deserted. Sean checked the marina where Michael berthed his yacht, but it was dark and empty.

Defeated, Sean returned home. He spent a sleepless night. His worry about Lisa led to nightmares about being skinned alive and the other tortures the Iron Maiden killer had used on his victims.

 # CHAPTER 19 

Leaning against the jewelry display cabinet at Mystical Enchantments, Catlyn picked up her phone for the umpteenth time. She sighed in frustration when the screen showed she hadn't received any new text or voice messages. She kept hoping—praying—for a call from Sean or Jade, letting her know they'd found Lisa safe and unharmed. It had been two days since she'd disappeared. From what Catlyn knew based on television shows, the likelihood of finding Lisa alive was nearly gone. Her hand went to her mother's pendant as she squeezed her eyes shut, fighting back the sobs that threatened to drown her.

"Anything yet?" Michelle asked, leaning her arms on the counter.

Catlyn shook her head. "I'm scared she'll be hurt like Amelia. I've stopped by her place several times, hoping this is all a mistake, and we can laugh about it."

Michelle moved around the counter and squeezed Catlyn's shoulder. "It's difficult to think she's been abducted. She's such a sweet person. I don't know why someone would do such a thing."

"I don't know either." Catlyn's gaze swept the shop, taking in the candles, crystals, and other ritual paraphernalia they sold. None of it had stopped Michael from snatching her friend. What good was magic if it couldn't protect her or the people she loved? "There has to be something we can do."

"We can pray for her. We'll include her in our full moon ritual. Why don't you go set up the room for it? It will help take your mind off your worry for a few minutes."

Catlyn agreed. But first she pulled up a photo on her phone of Lisa laughing. She seemed so happy and carefree in it. Catlyn sent the picture to the printer.

Going into the back room used for classes, Catlyn vacuumed the floor, then scattered pillows in a circle. Using tall jar candles, pictures, and flowers, she created an altar in the center of the room. A crystal grid of rose quartz went down next. Lastly, she lovingly set the picture of Lisa in the middle.

Lighting the bundle of sage leaves, she walked around the room, smudging it and clearing it of negative energy. The sharp, clean scent washed over her, and she took a moment to clear her own energy. She stood in the center, breathing deeply and letting the serenity she'd created to seep into her mind and soul. By the time the first participant arrived, Catlyn had regained a measure of inner peace.

Bri came in, saw the photo of Lisa, and cried. "Have they found her?"

"Sadly, no." Catlyn dipped her head, wiping away the tears threatening to fall. "We're dedicating this ritual to her and her safety."

"Good." Bri pulled a tissue from the box, wiped her eyes, and blew her nose. Then she sat on a pillow to wait.

Catlyn sunk on a cushion next to her friend, silently praying as the room filled.

When Michelle led them in a guided meditation, Catlyn focused on Lisa, hoping for one of her new and unexpected flashes of pre-cognizance to appear. Something that would help the police find Lisa. Instead, the vision she'd had for the past week resurfaced.

She walked on a dirt road, the darkness making it difficult to see much past it. Her feet hurt and were swollen from walking so long. A crossroads of three roads appeared ahead of her. An old woman, wearing a dark cloak and holding a torch, stood in the center of the crossroads. A three-headed dog sat beside her.

"It is time you choose," the Goddess Hecate said, "which path you will take. Only one leads to your destiny, will you take it?"

"What is my destiny? Which path is the right one for me?"

"Look within, dear child. The answer you seek is there. But choose quickly, for the time has come for you to accept your calling or let it slip away forever."

Catlyn searched for Maak. Surely, her new spirit guide would show her the path to take. The white tiger was conspicuously absent.

"This must be your choice," Hecate admonished. "The Shi'naik can't help you choose, but if you accept your calling, she will help you fulfill your destiny."

Catlyn studied the three roads. The one on the left grew brighter, as if it was lit by the noon sun. Butterflies flitted across it, and roses bloomed on the edge of the path. That way would be easy. As tempting as it was to have a life of smooth sailing, that couldn't be her destiny.

The center path was rocky and marked by potholes. It felt like her current life, a struggle to survive. When she turned her attention to the right-hand path, a dark mist covered it. She shivered, rubbing her arms for warmth.

A woman wearing pale armor and carrying a glowing blade strode confidently into the mist. It parted before her. She looked over her shoulder, and Catlyn recognized her own face, slightly older and care worn. That woman had seen and experienced much, but there was also an air of serenity about her. That path would be hard in a different way than the center road.

Catlyn looked longingly at the brightly lit road on the left. Would it be wrong to choose the easy way? Then she considered all the recent weird events, including Amelia's murder and Lisa's disappearance. Whatever her destiny held, she knew deep in her heart it had something to do with Michael. If it meant stopping him and his evil, she would do what she must. Her older self smiled and nodded, then disappeared into the mist.

Taking a fortifying breath, Catlyn pointed to the road to Hecate's right. "That one. I choose my destiny."

Joy lit the Goddess' face, and her torch grew brighter, almost blinding Catlyn. "Then I will show you the way." The Goddess stepped onto the path Catlyn had selected, the black mist parting before her. Catlyn trailed behind her.

The sound of the gong and Michelle's voice brought Catlyn back to reality. Before she could open her eyes, Maak filled her vision. Maak's eyes danced with delight, and she licked the side of Catlyn's face. *"Now we can begin,"* Maak said, then faded from Catlyn's awareness.

The strange vision of Hecate played over and over in Catlyn's mind as she drove home. She had chosen her destiny, but she didn't understand exactly what it meant. She wasn't a warrior. Why would the Goddess show her in armor?

"Maak?" Catlyn called to her spirit animal. *"What does it all mean?"*

Silence answered her. Trust a cat to reveal a mystery and then refuse to divulge anything else. Exhausted from worrying about Lisa, Catlyn changed into her pajamas and crawled into bed. Mittens curled up next to her. Still thinking about the vision with Hecate, Catlyn slid into sleep. She dreamed she walked through a temple.

White and black marble tiles covered the temple's floor in a complicated pattern. Sconces shaped like old-fashioned torches lined the wall, giving off a soft, pale lavender light. The corridor led to the open doors of a vast room. Inside, the High Priestess card came to life.

The priestess, wearing a translucent gown, danced with abandon between the pillars of light and dark. Moving between the physical world and the non-physical with ease as she whirled and spun. She leaped, head thrown back, arms outstretched, and joy lit her face. She landed, balancing on one toe as if she wore pointe shoes in an arabesque. The priestess gazed through the columns and into the vastness of the universe.

As if sensing Catlyn's presence, the priestess stepped lightly onto the ground and turned around. Catlyn gasped. She recognized the face; she saw it every day in the mirror. This woman, though, was sure and confident, with strength radiating from her. The same strength Catlyn had seen in the woman in armor in her vision with Hecate. The priestess moved gracefully across the floor and took Catlyn's hands in hers, gazing into Catlyn's eyes.

Catlyn's third-eye buzzed, vibrating almost painfully. Her heart beat a frantic pace in her chest.

"I'm glad you have made the choice," the priestess said. "Come, it is time."

Before Catlyn could ask time for what, the priestess embraced Catlyn and merged with her. Her body sizzled with intense energy, unlike any she'd experienced before. The tidal wave of energy built and washed over her. The intensity was almost orgasmic. Light and vast knowledge filled her mind.

A shimmering golden-rainbow hued curtain spread between the two pillars. Catlyn stepped through it. On the other side of the portal, at her feet lay a giant white tiger, proud and powerful: Maak.

"Do not be afraid to look beyond the veil of your mind," Maak said. Even in her dream—or was this a vision?—Maak's voice had an otherworldly quality to it. *"It is time you accepted who you are and your purpose in life. You have a great work to do, Catlyn. You are a High Priestess. The Goddess calls you to Her service."*

"She does?" Catlyn gasped. "How can I serve Her? I'm nothing important." She recalled her earlier vision of following Hecate down her chosen path. Chills covered her body, bringing with them a deep knowing and reassurance that this was her destiny.

"But you are," Maak said. *"You are called to guard the portals between this world and those beyond. There are many who wish to bring evil to your world. We cannot let them. I am here to help you stop the daemons from crossing the portal. But first you must quit being frightened of your power. Now! Remember the truth of who and what you are."* The tiger surged to her feet and lashed Catlyn with her tail.

Catlyn stumbled forward from the force of the blow. Her hands landed on a clear, crystal ball. Sparks of electricity sizzled across its surface, bouncing between her palms and the sphere. Her hands tingled, and the sensation ran up her arms and into her head. She tried to pull her hands off the globe, but they wouldn't budge.

Visions, like a movie, passed before her eyes. Terrible beasts and nightmarish creatures crowded in front of a door. Only a thin, translucent barrier kept them from bursting through. Evil wreathed them like smoke. Catlyn could sense their overriding desires were to conquer, to kill, and to wreak havoc and chaos. A being of impossible beauty, only vaguely humanoid, waded through the crowd and at his passing, the creatures stilled and bowed in deep obeisance. He radiated an immense, dark power.

"That is a daemon opening the portal from his dimension into this one," Maak explained, standing next to Catlyn. She pronounced the word as 'day-mons.' *"His minions are evil incarnate and their influence pollutes your world. This is but one portal, one daemon. There are many more. Look what happens on the other side of a portal where a Sentinel stands guard."*

The scene changed. A woman dressed in shining armor, a winged helmet covered her head, faced a similar portal. She held a long sword aloft behind her, at the ready. She reminded Catlyn of the knight of swords, prepared for anything that came her way. Emblazoned on her chest was a heptacle, a seven-pointed star surrounded by a circle. She stood in the center of a huge heptacle drawn on the floor. Sacred symbols, painted in gold, shone in each point and at each cardinal direction.

The warrior-priestess gripped her sword tighter as a tear appeared in the barrier, and an ugly denim-blue beast squirmed through. Catlyn had seen its type before. One like it had caused the incident in front of the amusement park. The creature hit the edge of the circle and screeched. Chanting, the woman swung her sword, neatly cleaving the demon in two. Its bits sizzled before melting into a putrid puddle. She barked a sharp command and drew a different sigil with a crystal dagger. Pure white fire blossomed over the puddle, consuming it within moments. The woman stepped back into position. Another demon wriggled through the hole.

She fought them all with the same precision until three small rat-like creatures slipped through on the heels of a large beast. The larger one attacked the priestess, distracting her while the little ones escaped. The woman glimpsed their tails disappearing and swore. She took a step, as if to chase them down, but stopped and turned her attention back to the portal where another hole formed.

"Wait, she can't let them get away," Catlyn cried. "Maak, you have to do something!"

Maak flicked the tip of her tail and licked a paw. "*There are others who will hunt them down. The portal Sentinels are only the first defense. Many fight this war of good versus evil. The Gods do not simply watch the evil invading your world dispassionately. They call warriors to their service to fight for the survival of all that is good in this world and beyond. They have called you.*"

Catlyn's heart lurched. She'd never deliberately killed anything in her life. She didn't think she could, even if it meant saving the world from demons. "I can't fight and kill like the portal priestess did. Besides, I don't know how."

"*You will fight in a different way.*" Maak sat back, her head nearly level with Catlyn's. Her gaze snared Catlyn's and held it. "*It is why I am here. I, too, have been called into service. I have sacrificed much to come to this world and meld with you. The demons are not ours to fight, but their masters, the daemons.*"

Catlyn's legs shook, and the world swirled around her. She thought she'd faint. How could she fight one of those powerful beings? She raised her hands to cover her face. The globe had freed her hands once she'd seen what it wanted her to see. The faces of many people, including Amelia and Lisa, paraded across her mind's eye. She knew, with a clarity that surprised her, they had been sacrificed in service of a daemon, the one Michael served. How many others would die because she let her fear of her own power rule? She couldn't allow even one more.

She took a deep breath, lowered her hands, and as the High Priestess had done, gazed within and saw her infinite possibilities and capabilities. In the light of truth, she couldn't deny she had the power and courage to protect the world, starting with those she loved.

"Yes," Catlyn said. "Yes, I accept the calling."

A deep purr erupted from Maak, and she licked Catlyn's cheek once. Catlyn felt the High Priestess separate from her. She guided Catlyn back through the portal, but rather than returning to the temple, they were in Catlyn's bedroom. Catlyn expected the priestess to fade. Instead, she smiled encouragingly at Catlyn before zooming into Catlyn's body.

Catlyn jerked awake, still feeling the presence of the High Priestess in her heart and mind. The choice she'd made would irrevocably alter her life. She groaned at the image of the Tower card. The change it brought was never easy or comfortable.

A purr vibrated in her mind. Maak. Catlyn wouldn't face the daemons alone.

Chapter 20

By Saturday afternoon, Sean and Jerry had gathered and exhausted all the leads they'd unearthed to find Lisa. They hadn't had any luck, even with help from the Sentinel Guards. She had vanished.

"We can't do anymore today." Sean tossed his notebook onto his desk, drained and frustrated. "I need a break. I promised my grandmother I'd visit her."

"A break will do us both good," Jerry agreed. "My wife wants to take the kids to the beach while the weather is still nice. She'll be happy if I go with them. And a happy wife is an 'attentive' wife." Jerry wiggled his eyebrows and grinned. He whistled as he tossed his keys in the air and caught them while he walked to his car.

Sean envied Jerry's happy relationship. He and his wife had been married for twenty years, and had four kids. Sean wished he would find someone to love. Catlyn's freckled face popped into his mind. He growled with frustration. Ethically, he couldn't date her until he solved her murdered friend's case. It gave him a new motivation to catch the Iron Maiden Killer.

The drive to Temecula took less time for a Saturday afternoon than he expected. As he approached his grandmother's house, he frowned, piqued at the unknown motorcycle parked in the driveway. They'd made arrangements for him to come today for more training. *Why would someone else be here?* Dahlyah waited on the front porch. As soon as he turned off the engine, she shifted into her large, winged form and flew through the window. A moment later, Granny Eileen opened the door for him.

When he entered the house, a woman with super short, light brown hair and brown eyes rose from the couch. Her body looked toned and athletic. She smiled at him, and wrinkles crinkled at the corners of her eyes and mouth, making him revise his first estimate of her age upward to late forties.

"Sean, this is my good friend, Jade Lowery," Eileen said.

"It's so nice to meet you." As Sean shook Jade's hand, he noticed she stood only a couple inches shorter than his 5 foot 11 inches. He'd heard of her through Charlie and various cases, but he hadn't met her. "Charlie speaks highly of you. He enjoys working with you. Thank you for your help in trying to locate Lisa Moon."

"Have you found her yet?"

Sean shook his head. He raised a questioning eyebrow at his grandmother.

Granny Eileen grinned, a twinkle in her eye. "She's here to help with your lessons, my boy." Before he could question her further, she led them to her back patio, where she poured them each a glass of iced tea.

A fountain murmured in one corner, and the wind chimes sang in the breeze, providing a serene setting. Sean leaned back in his chair and tried to relax. *How can a woman involved in personal security help me learn magical skills?*

"Eileen tells me your witch-sight has opened." Jade put her glass on the table. She sat at the edge of her seat, looking ready to leap up and fight at a moment's notice. Her eyes roved the yard as if she were searching for enemies. "What have you seen?"

Sean told them about the people transmuting in the club, the various dragons, and how his neighbor had morphed. "I've also seen light orbs that resolved into what I imagine are pixies."

"Your neighbor is a fae," Jade said. "They aren't to be confused with fairies, who tend to be mischievous brats. The fae could be good or bad, just like humans. I suspect your neighbor is on our side. The people in the club are demons, who are all evil. They originate in the lower dimensions, and they are soldiers for their daemon masters."

Sean frowned. She'd pronounced the second word as day-mons. "Aren't demons and daemons the same thing?"

Jade shook her head. "No. Although they come from the same world, demons are lower-level beings. They are capable of easily crossing the portals between our dimension and theirs. Most people can't see them for what they are. Some species are able to appear to be human when they choose. Their only job and desire is to cause mayhem and trouble. They can't possess humans. But they can manipulate a person's mind, causing them to do stupid things they'd never do otherwise."

"What about causing people to riot, push someone in front of semi-trucks, or kill their loved ones?"

Both Eileen and Jade gave him sharp looks.

"We've had an epidemic of those types of crimes lately." He shuddered as he remembered the bite on the Holcomb baby's arm. The poor child hadn't survived. "People are seeing strange creatures immediately before committing the crime. You mean they could be telling the truth, and demons had coerced them?"

Jade and Eileen shared a look before Jade nodded to him. She resettled in her chair, curling one leg under her. Even then, she appeared more ready for action than relaxed. "It's likely, especially with what you describe. Although humans are quite capable of doing evil and making bad decisions on their own without help from demons.

"Now daemons, on the other hand, are the royalty and leaders of the demon world. They can, and do, possess humans. It's the only way possible for them to survive in this dimension. The higher ranking they are, the more problems they have crossing the boundary into our world—thank the Goddess. Otherwise, we'd be their slaves.

"We would consider their world a hell, but to them, it's home. Like warlords and greedy people here, they want more than they have. Their objective is to conquer and control this world. If they do, their next step is to reach for the worlds in the next higher dimension. They will never be satisfied, and it's why we have to keep them from overtaking our world."

Sean made another notation in his notepad. "Right, got it. Demons: soldiers, daemons: generals. How do we kill them? Do I need to go see Father Burcher and get some holy water?"

Both Jade and Eileen broke into a fit a laughter. Sean looked between them, confused.

"Doesn't that stop them? How about reciting the Lord's prayer or Christ's name?"

Eileen wiped the tears from her eyes. "You've been watching too many television shows, Sean. This isn't '*Supernatural*' or '*Charmed*'. The beings from the lower dimensions, commonly called demons, predate the Judeo-Christian-Islam religions by thousands of years, if not hundreds of thousands of years. Holy water and prayers just pisses them off. Although, *Supernatural* did get one thing right. Salt does create a boundary evil can't cross. It also eliminates negative energy."

"Your witch-sight allows you to differentiate friend from foe." Jade leaned forward and removed a dagger from the sheath she wore behind her back on her belt. Symbols covered the bone handle, and creamy white moonstones adorned the cross-guard and pommel. She eased the blade from the case, revealing not metal, but a clear-crystal blade.

"This," she said, "will kill a demon. The blade is specially created with magic, making it super strong and unbreakable. It has been dipped in an herbal solution toxic to demons. The moonstones hold moonlight, which banishes the demons back to their dimension. This one is mine."

His grandmother rummaged in a bag by her side he hadn't noticed and pulled out a similar knife. She laid it on the table in front of him. "This was your grandfather's. I want you to have it."

As Sean examined it, her meaning sank in. "Wait, if this was my grandfather's, does that mean he fought demons? You want me to fight demons?"

"Yes, to both." Sadness flitted across her face. "You might say it's the family business. One your father has tried to forget he was once part of. When a demon killed your grandfather, it devastated your dad. He refused to continue the fight. He left our organization and wouldn't let me teach you. Magic flows in your veins, Grandson, just like it does mine, and Jade's. The Gods have called us to fight a holy battle that has been going on for tens of thousands of years."

The light glinted off the moonstone settings and seemed to wink at him. He used his witch-sight to look at it. A dazzling white light shone from the dagger. It called to him. His fingers itched to pick it up.

"Take it," his grandmother urged. "You don't have to decide on anything else today. But now you can see the world as it truly is, you'll need protection beyond what your amulet can provide. The supernatural beings will sense you can see them, and those who are evil won't like it. They'll try to kill you. Your gun won't harm them. Please, Sean, for my sake, take the dagger."

Sean reached out and touched the knife. Energy zinged from it up his fingertips and through his body. It didn't hurt. It made him feel alive. "I'll take it, just for you, Granny. But I have to think about the other stuff. It's a lot to process." He looped the sheath onto his belt and adjusted it behind his back. He slid his shirt over it. Warmth seeped into his skin.

When he left a while later, his grandmother patted his cheek. "I know you'll do the right thing, Sean. Call me if you have any questions."

Sean promised he would. Warmth crept up his back, reminding him of the unusual weapon he now wore.

When he arrived home, he pulled out his grandfather's dagger. As he examined it, moonlight fell on it, and pulses of electricity tugged at him. He wondered how it worked against a demon, and if it was sharp. Pulling a blank sheet of paper from his notebook, he sliced down. The paper parted like butter, and Sean gaped at the blade's sharpness. He thought of Michael and the missing girl and growled with suppressed anger. He glanced down and squeezed his eyes shut against the dazzling white light shining from the crystal blade. It seemed the blade didn't like Michael either.

He wasn't sure what he'd decide to do, but he'd become a cop to protect people. Wouldn't fighting demons protect them even more?

Sean's knuckles whitened from his tight grip on the steering wheel. The only reason the captain would call him to investigate a murder on his day off was if it was another Iron Maiden killing.

Sean drove north on the 91-freeway out of Orange County and into San Bernardino County. Instead of going surfing on his rare Monday off, he'd searched the internet for information about demons. The little he could find on demons was completely different from what he'd learned from his Granny and Jade. Now that he knew about daemons, his instincts were telling him the Iron Maiden Killer was somehow connected to a daemon. A shudder rolled through him. It took a special kind of monster to willingly summon a daemon. As far as he was concerned, Michael Drogger fit that description.

"Do you think the victim is our missing person?" Jerry asked from the passenger seat.

Sean shrugged. "I hope not, but it's probable. Drogger disappeared the same night Lisa did."

Jerry gaped at him. "You haven't been following Michael Drogger again, have you? The chief warned you to stay away from him after the last murder. Do you want a restraining order placed against you?"

"He's our prime suspect," Sean grumbled as he switched lanes to move around a car poking along in the fast lane. "I'm going to do my job regardless of what Thomas Drogger says or how rich he is. Money shouldn't determine how we do our jobs."

"If you piss off the Drogger family, they have the power to get you fired." Jerry glanced over and grinned. "I've finally trained you to be a good partner. I don't want to deal with another newbie."

"Old man, you and I are equals," Sean sputtered. "We're the same rank. The only seniority you have over me is your advanced age. In fact, I do most of the work in this team."

"See, I've trained you well."

Sean rolled his eyes and focused on the traffic. Lourdes had only been working on this case with him for the last year. Captain Green had assigned him a new partner after his old one had blown his knee, chasing a suspect.

They rode in silence. Sean hoped and prayed the victim wouldn't turn out to be Catlyn's friend Lisa. If this murder was the work of the Iron

Maiden killer, it didn't bode well. The only other times there had been more than one killing in a month had been the initial killing spree and another a year later. Then, they'd discovered three victims.

Guilt and regret filled him as images from the first gruesome crime scenes assailed him. After nearly three years, Sean wasn't any closer to catching the killer. He was sure Michael was behind it, but he simply hadn't found the evidence to prove it. Now he knew more about his heritage, he wondered if his certainty was related to his Granny Eileen's "sight." Sean's chest tightened. Heat washed his face. Michael had been paying far too much attention to Catlyn lately. He cringed at the thought of one day finding her mutilated body.

Sean turned into the parking lot of the dilapidated warehouse, two hours shy of leaving Anaheim. The rundown industrial area, far from residences, seemed a perfect place to torture someone for days without anyone noticing.

Brian met Sean and Jerry at the warehouse door, plastic booties and face masks in hand. "I don't know how it could get any worse, but it is. You haven't eaten recently, have you?"

Sean scowled and shook his head. After putting on the protective clothing, he followed Brian through the maze of trash and machinery of the abandoned manufacturing plant. Yet another business lost to the constant outflow of products produced overseas. They passed several places where homeless people had squatted. The stench of death grew as they traversed deeper into the building.

Brian pushed past the plastic sheets hanging over a wide doorway. Sean stepped through, and even though he thought he'd prepared himself, he gagged. Brian's question about eating now made sense.

All the bodies they'd found before had been intact, albeit, gruesome. Like the others, this corpse had been skinned and hung from two meat hooks piercing its shoulder blades. Unlike the others, this one lacked a right arm and left leg. The little skin remaining was blackened as if it had been burned. A terrified scream froze the features in what remained of the mutilated face. A hank of long, black hair stuck to the skull.

Another woman.

He closed his eyes. Catlyn's friend Lisa had long, black hair. Perhaps, if the Gods were kind, this wouldn't be her.

"What's that?" Sean pointed to the mess lying on the floor, along the line of the circle and beside one of the star points.

"The victim's arm." Brian's face screwed up in disgust. "Well, what's left of it. It's been gnawed on. Something ate the flesh off of it. Same thing with the leg." He gestured to where it lay directly opposite the arm.

"I told you it was worse. We need to catch the sick bastards before they do this again."

"No argument here." Sean paced the outside of the circle, sensing ghostly figures marching around it, swinging smoking censors, and chanting.

He stopped in front of the leg and switched on his witch-sight. He grimaced at the phantom image of a beast—unlike any seen on this earth—crouched over the leg, ripping off the flesh and devouring it. It had a dog-like head, except for the four eyes and knobby horns on top. The squat, muscled body sported six legs and two barbed tails. He gazed across the circle to the arm and saw the ghostly image of a similar creature.

Demons.

Sean walked to the edge of the circle, and the crystal blade he wore all the time now warmed his back. He suspected it did that when in the presence of demons or their ilk. He'd lay odds the unknown substance in the blood was demon blood.

"Hey, Sean!" Brian called. "You need to see this." He stood in the corner over a pile of rags.

Dread crept up Sean's spine as he hurried over. "What is it?"

Brian crouched and picked up a woman's blouse. "Clothes. The victims, I'm betting." He dug in the pile and pulled out a wallet, frowning. The perpetrators had never left clues or evidence before. He opened the wallet and read the identification. "Lisa Moon, she lived in the city of Orange."

Sean bowed his head and groaned. They'd been too late to save her.

"Wait a minute," Brian continued. "I recognize the name. I saw a missing persons report on her a few days ago."

Jerry examined the driver's license and the wallet's other contents. His eyes held a haunted look before his professional mask dropped into place. Jerry put the wallet into an evidence bag while Brian tapped furiously on his tablet.

"What are you doing reading missing persons reports?" Sean asked.

"Trying to get a head start. It was getting close to the time for another murder. Ah, here it is. You won't believe who filed the report. Catlyn Hennessey. She seems involved in this."

"Not in the way you think."

Brian looked up at Sean. "Your name is on this, too. Why?"

"Michael Drogger has been taking a special interest in Catlyn, stalking her, in fact. Lisa was her friend, and Catlyn reported her missing."

Brian's gaze shifted between Sean and Jerry, perplexed. "That's two of her friends and clients we've found murdered by this guy, and you don't think she's involved."

"I've talked to her at length." Sean waved at the gore. "She isn't capable of this violence. She's being taunted. And so are we. I don't know why she's caught the attention of Michael Drogger, but she has."

Jerry's lips pursed as he studied the crime scene. "I'll dig into the other victim's background again and see if there's any connection to her. It seems odd the last two victims knew her, but the others didn't, especially if Drogger is taking an interest in her. Maybe they went to the same coffee shop or grocery store. This may be the break we've been looking for. Brian, check Lisa's movements over the past few weeks. Pay attention if she crossed paths with Michael Drogger."

"Will do." Brian bagged the clothes.

Sean walked the perimeter of the circle. Using his witch-sight, he tried sensing who had been in the circle with the victim besides the beastly demons. Nothing registered on his psychic alarm system. As he turned to leave, a deep, nasty laugh filled his mind. *"Too late. You'll be too late. I am almost here."* The voice dripped with evil.

The amulet his grandmother gave him blazed on his chest, and the voice disappeared. His body shook like an earthquake. If the voice had been a daemon's, then he needed to do everything he could to stop it from entering his world. He'd start by visiting the person he'd bet his life—and his career—was responsible for summoning it.

"I'm going to visit our prime suspect," he told Jerry. "Do you want to come with me or ride back with Brian?"

Jerry wrinkled his nose. "I hate the Red Orchid. I'll go back with Brian and go over the background checks again with this new focus."

 # CHAPTER 21 

As soon as Sean hit the Anaheim Hills area on his drive back, traffic slowed to a crawl. Worry gnawed at him as he crept forward. *Why is Michael so interested in Catlyn?* Sean thought she was pretty special, but most people wouldn't. Did her being a psychic target her? But then, why weren't other psychics, who were more prominent than Catlyn, Michael's focus? By the time he reached Newport Beach, his anxiety had transformed into fury. He'd do everything in his power to ensure Michael wouldn't hurt Catlyn!

Sean stalked into the Red Orchid and toward his quarry ensconced in his regular booth, several of his buddies with him. Sean pushed through the crowd and stood over Michael's table, trembling with rage.

"Oh, let me guess," Michael said with a sneer, "there's been another murder. Let's save time, Detective. Me and the boys here took the yacht out and had a poker tournament." Michael leaned back, rolling his tumbler between his hands. "It started Wednesday evening and went on all weekend. We didn't finish until last night. The prizes were Cuban cigars, a bottle of Dalmore 40-Year-Old Single Highland Malt Scotch Whisky—that's expensive scotch, by the way, $2,600 a bottle—and first pick of the girls. I won the scotch and the girl. I had a great time with her."

Sean's stomach clenched, thinking about what Lisa had endured before she'd died. He glared at Michael. "I'm sure you did. You'll make a mistake soon, Michael, if you haven't already. I'll be there to catch you when you fall." He turned on his heel, not bothering to ask Michael's friends for corroboration—they'd only lie—and stomped out of the club.

Outside, the cool, crisp air of late autumn cleared Sean's head. Too many mutilated bodies filled his mind. When it was quiet, he heard their screams and entreaties for help. If he believed in ghosts, he'd swear the victims were haunting him, begging him to give them rest. When he talked to his granny again, he'd ask her about ghosts. He now knew demons, dragons, fae, and pixies were real. Why not ghosts?

Sean sat in his car, staring blankly at the parking lot, dreading his next stop. Over the years, he'd told many people their loved ones were gone, but he hadn't personally known any of them. He didn't want to watch Catlyn's eyes well up with grief and sorrow. He'd much rather see them twinkle with laughter—and maybe love, if he were lucky.

Sitting here wouldn't help him find the right words to tell Catlyn another friend had been murdered. He hated this part of his job. Finally, he started his car and drove to the Mystical Enchantments store.

His breath caught as he watched Catlyn through the window, helping a customer at the register. Every time he saw her, she seemed more confident, more graceful, and more beautiful. He shook his head as if that would negate the feelings blooming within him. It would be wrong for him to fall in love with her while investigating her friend's murder. He waited until the customer left before going inside.

Catlyn saw him and gave him a welcoming smile. Her smile faltered, and the color drained from her face. "She's dead, isn't she? Lisa's dead."

He nodded and scooted across the counter. "We found her body today."

She covered her face with her hands. Sean tentatively touched her shoulder. She lowered her hands, revealing tears brimming in her eyes.

"Why are my friends being targeted, Detective?"

"I don't know, Catlyn, but I'm doing my best to find out. Are you going to be okay?"

"Yeah, I'll be fine..." The tears she'd held back flowed down her face.

Sean's protective instincts kicked in, and before he could think better of it, he hopped over the counter and pulled her into an embrace. Her quiet sobs filled the space between them. He wished he could do more for her. His thoughts flirted with bending down and kissing her tears away. Instead, he rested his chin gently on her head, regretting his ethics prevented him from following his desire.

After several minutes, Catlyn sniffed, wiped her face, and stepped back from him. With her eyes lowered, she murmured, "Thanks. I'm sorry if I messed up your shirt."

He glanced down at the darker blue spots on his shirt. Already he missed holding her. "It will dry."

"If there isn't anything else, I need to lockup." She pulled her shoulders back, and when she looked at him, she'd hidden her emotions behind a mask of professionalism.

"I'll wait and walk you to your car." He wanted to spend more time with her.

She didn't object, and he stood off to the side, out of her way. Her quiet movements of turning off lamps, blowing out candles, and straightening up relaxed him and made him feel peaceful. It helped to squash the memory of her mutilated friend hanging by meat hooks from his mind.

Another friend dead—murdered. Catlyn had been wrong to think the *Tower* card hadn't come into play yet. How many more friends would she lose before the struggle of the *Nine of Swords* was through? She remembered the *Star* card and held onto the hope everything would work out in the end.

Catlyn sneaked glances at Sean as she worked her way around the store, shutting it down for the night. He'd startled her when he'd scrambled over the counter, but it had been so nice to have someone hold her while she cried. Her tears still darkened his blue silk shirt. As she thought about it, none of her previous boyfriends had shown her such compassion. She and Sean weren't even dating.

A smile curved her lips. She hoped they would. An image of Catlyn and Sean cuddling—naked—in bed floated through her mind. A purr rumbled in her throat. Maak apparently approved of Sean.

"I'm finished," she said. "We can go out the back way."

Sean followed her, frowning at the dimly lit parking lot. "You should be more careful, especially if Michael is targeting you and your friends."

"I have protection." She pointed to the big white Chevy truck parked next to her tiny Honda Civic and grimaced. Even though she understood the necessity of it, she still hated having a guard babysit her. "My godmother has assigned a detail to watch me."

Sean stiffened beside her, then let out a relieved laugh. "Charlie? Charlie MacNamara is one of your bodyguards?"

Catlyn's eyes widened. "You know him?"

"He's my best buddy. We grew up together." Sean made a beeline for Charlie's truck, pulling her with him.

Charlie exited the truck wearing a sheepish grin. "Sorry, I couldn't tell you, bro. You know, client privacy and all."

"You're keeping a good watch on her, aren't you?"

Charlie gave an offended huff. "Why are you here?"

"They found Lisa's body." Catlyn sniffed, trying to staunch the tears that threatened to flow again. Sean patted her back, and she longed to sink into his embrace. But she wouldn't in front of Charlie. He'd tell her godmother, and that would be the end of any burgeoning romance between her and Sean. Jade never thought anyone was good enough for her goddaughter. She was worse than Catlyn's Aunt Lucy.

"I'm so sorry, Catlyn." Charlie's eyes filled with sympathy. "We tried to protect her. I don't know how she disappeared from her apartment. Are you sure you won't go live at Jade's house until this blows over?"

Catlyn shook her head.

"At least let Ariana stay with you."

"No. I'll be fine." Catlyn doubted Michael could take on Maak.

"It's late," Sean said, glancing at his watch.

Catlyn's shoulders slumped. She didn't want to be alone. And she wanted to spend more time with Sean.

"Have you eaten dinner yet?" he added.

She straightened and gave him a shy smile. "No, I haven't. There's a Tres Toros close by that is still open."

"Perfect! I love Mexican food. Why don't you join us, Charlie? No need for you to sit out in your truck while we eat."

Charlie considered for a moment. "Sure, why not? For a hole-in-the-wall, Tres Toros has excellent fish tacos, and I'm hungry."

"Catlyn, would you like to ride with me?" Sean asked, then grinned at Charlie. "There won't be much room to park. Charlie's monster will take up half the space."

"You're just jealous you don't have a truck." Charlie laughed as he punched Sean on his bicep.

Sean made a face, acting as if the punch had knocked him over. Catlyn chuckled at their antics. Their playfulness helped lighten her mood. She didn't have any siblings, but she'd grown up with her cousins and had seen Tommy joke around with his friends the same way.

Sean opened the car door for her, and she slid inside. While he walked to the driver's side, she studied his car. Unlike hers, no fast-food wrappers, empty water bottles, or unopened junk mail littered the interior. The air freshener smelled new and there weren't any smudges on the leather seats or windows. It looked like he'd recently washed it. A holder for a notebook was attached to the dash, as well as other paraphernalia she assumed was related to his job.

During the short drive to the restaurant, they talked the entire way. Catlyn thought about her last date with Karl and the long, uncomfortable, silent drive into LA. She found Sean easy to talk to, and he didn't look down on her for her "weird" occupation or style of dress. He had her laughing so hard when they walked to the restaurant's entrance that she had to stop to catch her breath.

When they were seated, Catlyn fiddled with her fork, worried she'd be left out of the conversation because Sean and Charlie were such close friends. But within moments, they included her. She'd spent some time with Charlie simply because he worked with her godmother—and he'd attended a number of Sabbat rituals Jade facilitated. It had surprised her the first time he showed up. She wouldn't have pegged him as a pagan.

"Jade is doing a healing ritual at the shop on Thursday," Catlyn said, in between bites of her cheese enchilada. "Charlie, you can come in and join us. You don't have to wait outside."

"I just might. It's been a bad month." Charlie filled a tortilla chip with beans, rice, and salsa, then stuffed it in his mouth. He looked over at Sean. "Hey, you should come. How long has it been since you've been to a ritual?"

Sean grimaced. "I haven't been to one since Dad forbade me to go see Granny Eileen. That's been a long time now. He became a devout Catholic and turned his back on anything Granny or Grandpappy had taught us."

"It's a simple ritual," Catlyn explained, "more of a healing circle, with crystal bowls, a gong, and meditation."

"After all the shit you've seen lately, Sean, you could use it," Charlie said.

Sean put down his fork and rubbed his face. When he lowered his hands, despair filled his eyes. "You're right, Charlie. This last one was the most gruesome yet." He cast a horrified look at Catlyn. "I'm so sorry. Please forgive me. I forgot the victim was your friend."

The abject sorrow on Sean's face moved Catlyn. He seemed to care deeply about the murdered people he investigated. She reached across the table and patted his hand. "You don't have to apologize. I understand. You must see so much hurt in your job."

Sean squeezed his eyes shut. "Most of the time, I can handle it. But this Iron Maiden Killer is a sick psychopath."

"You should ask Eileen to come with us," Charlie suggested. "I bet she'd love it."

"She would." Sean's face lit up. "She'd enjoy meeting Catlyn, too. Maybe you could give her a sound healing the same day?"

"I'd love to!" Catlyn longed to meet Sean's grandmother. She sounded like a fascinating lady.

"There's a problem. I'd have to drive to Temecula and pick her up. She doesn't drive much these days. And it would depend on my work schedule. With everything that's been happening, I might not even be able to go."

"Well, it's at the Mystical Enchantments at seven, in case you can," Catlyn told him. One of the things she yearned for in a relationship—that she hadn't found yet—was to share her spirituality with her partner.

They finished eating and Sean drove her back to her car.

"I'll try going to the healing ritual." He laid his hand over hers. "I had a great time tonight with you, even if Charlie hogged most of the conversation."

Catlyn grinned, her heart expanding. "He did, didn't he? Thank you for taking my mind off of Lisa and Amelia for a while." She waited a moment, hoping Sean would lean over and kiss her. She let out a sigh of disappointment when he exited the car and went around it to open her door.

Wednesday evening, only three days after the police found Lisa's body, Catlyn slipped into a dark gray dress. The only black dress in her closet was the one Lisa loaned her, and she couldn't bring herself to wear it to Lisa's funeral. Catlyn settled her mother's pendant around her neck. The diamond in the center of the seven-pointed star sparkled, a bright point in all the darkness in Catlyn's life.

Her phone beeped, letting her know Bri had pulled into the parking lot. Catlyn threw on a black shawl and trudged down the stairs, the tears already threatening to flow. She hadn't bothered putting on any mascara; her tears would wash it away in a few minutes. Out of habit, she scanned the area around her apartment. The scent of Smoker Dude's awful cigarettes made her gag. Todd, her bodyguard for the day, waved at her, reassuring her she was safe.

Lydia sat in the backseat of Bri's car and gave Catlyn a sad smile. The three women, including Lisa, had become friends through the classes held at Mystical Enchantments. The unusual quiet as Bri drove to the funeral home nagged at Catlyn. She recalled the many trips the girlfriends had taken. Laughter and music had filled the car then. Never again would Lisa cackle like a witch, scrunch up her nose, and wiggle her fingers while saying, "I'll get you, my pretty," in response to Lydia's teasing.

"I can't believe she's gone," Catlyn said, to fill the empty silence.

"I remember when we met her," Bri said, switching lanes. "It was the first crystal class she took at the store..."

"Her first witchy class, ever," Lydia added. "She was so scared, but that didn't stop her."

"Yeah." Catlyn smiled at the memory. "She never let anything stop her. She was always so brave."

They continued to reminisce about the good times they'd had together with Lisa until they walked into the funeral home. The sight of the casket sitting at the front, surrounded by flowers, sobered Catlyn. She didn't want to know what atrocities the damned serial killer had committed before Lisa had succumbed to death. It had to be awful for her family to insist on a closed casket.

When she walked up to the casket to pay her respects, an overwhelming stench made Catlyn's eyes water. No one else seemed to notice it, but it reminded her of Smoker's Dude's nasty cigarettes. *What does Michael want from me? Will this be my fate?* Tears rolled down Catlyn's face.

"Not if I have anything to say about it," Maak whispered. *"It will be that weasel who will lie in a casket and not you."*

Catlyn shivered at the vehemence in Maak's voice. Bri noticed and reached over to pat Catlyn's hand. Catlyn gripped her best friend's hand. She couldn't live if another friend was killed. *Why me? Why my friends?*

After the funeral, Bri drove to the Applebee's restaurant by the metaphysical store for dinner. It had been one of Lisa's favorite places to eat at after classes. This would be their own memorial for their lost friend.

Catlyn ordered her steak rare, rather than barely seared she truly craved. Her mouth salivated when the waitress set the huge plate of meat in front of her, bloody juice pooling around the mashed potatoes.

Bri glanced over, did a double-take, then frowned. "Since when do you eat your steak rare? As long as I've known you, you've always asked for it well-done. If there's any blood on the plate, you send it back."

Catlyn picked up her utensils. "Tastes change. I discovered I like it better this way. It has more flavor." She took another bite, savoring the warmed blood and juices running down her throat. She growled in pleasure.

"Was that a growl?" Bri laughed.

Catlyn threw a hand over her mouth to cover her embarrassment. "No. It was a moan. This just tastes so good. The chef did an excellent job cooking it."

"Whatever floats your boat." Bri cut into her chicken breast.

Quiet ruled as the group dug into their food, but once they had assuaged their hunger, they shared stories about Lisa. As the laughter and wine flowed, the conversation shifted to talking about their lives, and hopes and dreams, in an affirmation they still lived. Lydia regaled them about her new boyfriend. The scent of lust wafted off her, stinging Catlyn's nose. She sniffed deeply to get a better whiff and detected an underpinning of love.

"You're falling in love with him," Catlyn blurted.

Lydia's eyes widened, and she dropped her fork. "No, I'm not! Well, maybe a little. But how did you know? You didn't do a reading, did you?"

Catlyn shook her head. "No. I can sense it in the way you talk about him." She refused to tell her friends she could smell emotions. Even the most open-minded ones, like Bri, wouldn't understand.

 # CHAPTER 22 

Sean entered the Mystical Enchantments, trepidation making his stomach churn. His last pagan ritual had been when he was eleven. Michelle pointed him to the back room. Soft music drifted from it. Shoes clustered with abandon outside the door. He slipped his off and put them neatly to one side. He stopped on the door's threshold, his mouth dropping open in surprise.

Jade bent over the gold cloth spread in the center of the floor. She placed flowers on it around the beautiful pattern formed by various crystals. He recognized the rose quartz hearts, and the apache tear obsidian stones. He wasn't sure what the rough, creamy pink stones or the blue and green ones were. Eight people sat on the pillows arranged in a circle on the outside of the cloth. There was space for about another half-dozen people. Lit candles set around the room provided a warm glow. An assortment of large white bowls and a huge gong waited behind the circle.

Jade wore a white chiffon tunic over black, flowing pants. She glanced up, beamed at him, and hurried to greet him.

"Sean, so glad to see you." She gave him a hug. "I knew you'd find your way to us. Although, I thought it wouldn't be so soon. How did you know about this?"

"That would be because of me." Catlyn came up and stood next to him, her hand finding his elbow. "I invited him. But how do you two know each other?"

"I met her last weekend at my grandmother's. Apparently they are old friends."

"We are," Jade said. "Catlyn, help him get settled, please. It's his first time. I need to welcome our other guests."

Catlyn guided him to a pillow on the floor. "Don't bother sitting. We'll just have to stand again in a minute for the cleansing."

She introduced the brown-haired, brown-eyed woman standing next to her as her friend Bri. Well-defined biceps popped from her arm as she shook Sean's hand. She smiled warmly at him as she welcomed him to the circle. "Now, I see why you like him," he overhead her whisper to Catlyn.

Catlyn shushed her, then turned to Sean. "I'm glad you made it. Your grandmother wasn't able to come?"

"She wanted to, but I couldn't leave work early enough to drive to Temecula and get back here in time."

"I hope to meet her soon." She paused as Jade shut the door.

Catlyn scanned the room, smiling at the dozen people standing in front of the pillows. Sean raised an eyebrow in question to Catlyn.

"The ritual is about to begin. Follow my lead. There's nothing to be worried about."

Jade held two small cymbals joined by a leather strap and stood behind the first person to the right of the door. She struck the cymbals together; they created a high-pitched ringing. She continued to walk around the circle, ringing the tingsha over each person.

Sean slipped into his witch-sight, watching in wonder as the tones jumbled the person's aura, like television static. When it cleared, their aura appeared stronger and cleaner to him. The light of Catlyn's already blazing aura leaped higher. He wished he could see his own aura, curious how it had changed because of the cleansing. After completing the circuit around the circle, Jade settled on the pillow nearest the gong.

"The purpose of this healing circle," Jade explained, "is to let go of the stress you hold and that we suffer through every day. Once the stress is released, your body's own healing power can work more efficiently. The vibrations of the crystal bowls will realign your energy to be in full health and vitality. Let their sounds and that of the gong take you deep into the guided meditation. Allow your body to relax."

Jade picked up a wooden mallet covered in white suede, then lightly hit the biggest bowl. Sean jumped at the bell-tone. Jade ran the mallet around the edge of the bowl, and the sound changed to a thrumming note, repeating over and over. The deep tones vibrated in Sean's chest. Jade struck the various sized bowls, each one ringing with a different note. The waves traveled through him, growing with intensity. Jade's voice rose over the sounds, urging them to close their eyes.

Sean relaxed as he followed Jade's words deeper into a meditative state. Catlyn's soothing energy next to him allowed him to let his mind float. The scenes behind his eyes took on a dream-like quality. He knew he wasn't asleep since the crystal bowls sang in the distant background. His grandfather's amulet that he hadn't taken off since his Granny had given it to him warmed his chest.

Sean mentally frowned as the images in his mind cleared. The city's lights glowed below him. The sound of the crystal bowls and gong receded.

Flashes of gunfire caught his attention, and he zoomed toward it. A riot of people milled in a plaza. Banners fluttered, depicting German mugs, were strung between the plaza's street lights. An Oktoberfest. Probably at Old World Huntington Beach. Shots ricocheted off shop walls and into the crowd. The screams of the injured and dying filled the air. A dozen men armed with rifles and AK-45's hid behind the overturned tables that guarded all the egress points from the plaza, firing into the packed throng of people. Sirens wailed. A jumble of cars blocked the police's access to the fenced-in shopping plaza. Several shooters turned and fired on the police.

Anger boiled in Sean.

Four beasts ran from the bloody scene and down an alley. They had the long legs of a greyhound, the sleek body of a black cat, and a thick crocodile-like tail. Their heads looked like an owl—if that owl had a beak filled with needle-sharp fangs. Behind them scampered a small, thin, naked man with pumpkin-orange skin, pointed ears, short goat-like horns on its furred head, and long, clawed feet. It carried an old-fashioned bellows. It turned, puffed out its cheeks, and blew hard, using the bellows to carry its breath back to the mob. Fresh fighting broke out, even as the gunmen continued to shoot.

Demons!

These creatures had to be lower-ranking demons his Granny Eileen and Jade had told him about. As if to confirm his suspicion, the amulet on his chest flared with heat.

The beasts were running away after causing the chaos playing out below him. He couldn't let them escape to harm more people. He had to stop them.

He reached for his gun to find empty air. He'd taken it off to attend the peaceful meditation. Warmth spread along his back, reminding him of the crystal knife sheathed on his belt. He reached behind him and withdrew it. The blade glowed sapphire-blue, and he gripped the handle tight. He wished he could wield it against the demons.

He landed on the ground, crouching in front of the demon with the bellows. It screeched. The foul odor of its breath made Sean's eyes water.

He blinked, clearing his eyes as he lunged at the creature, knocking away the bellows and driving his dagger into its chest.

The blade slid through the skin, smoking as it liquefied tissue. The shrieking creature lifted a leg to kick at him. Sean sucked in his belly and narrowly missed being clawed. He drove the blade in deeper and twisted. Something gave, and he wrenched the knife—and his hand—from the demon's chest. It burst into flame and burned to ash in seconds.

His amulet warmed, and Sean heard hissing behind him. He turned in time to dodge the leap of an owl-headed beast. It flew past him. Its mates circled Sean, and he wished he had more protection than a thin shirt and a crystal knife.

One of the beasts lunged at him, snapping its fangs at his face. Its weight hit him in the chest, knocking him down, tearing at him with its claws. He tensed. The lack of pain surprised him. He thrust the blade into the beast's side and ripped it open. It also burst into flames.

Sean glanced down at his chest. "Nice!" He now wore a flexible silver chain mail shirt over his button-down.

He rolled to his feet and charged at the first beast. It howled. The unearthly noise rattled Sean's brain, giving him a headache. He ignored it as he swung his blade. It connected with the creature's throat. Thick blood spurted from the gaping hole. *Two down, two to go.*

The surviving demons attacked him in tandem. One raked his cheek with its claws while the other bit down on his forearm—the one holding his weapon. Pain flared up his arm, and he switched the dagger to his left hand, driving the blade into the belly of the creature hanging onto his arm. The bottom half of it lit up as it burned. He swung it around, slamming it into the remaining demon. The fire leaped between them, consuming them both.

Sean bent over, hands on his knees, gasping for breath. He thought he was in shape, but this had taken a lot out of him, especially for being a dream.

"It isn't a dream, Sean my boy."

The voice of his grandmother startled him, and he jerked around to face her. She was riding—riding!—Dahlyah and wore silver armor complete with a winged helmet. A black cape flapped in the breeze behind her back, and a crystal sword hung off her hip.

"Granny?" he stammered.

"It's time you know who you really are, what I am. Sean, you're a Sentinel, from a long line of witches. We protect the world from the encroaching demons, who want to enslave humanity."

"How is this possible? How did I get here?"

"The usual way. You see, when two people who love each other..." The dimple in her right cheek peeked out from her grin. "I'm thinking you know that part. So, how did you get in this alley? Magic."

"Magic!" His eyes bugged out. "That just isn't possible."

"Of course it is, deary. It's the only way we can fight the demons." Eileen swung a leg over Dahlyah's back and slid off. She closed the distance between them. "Our family has been Sentinel Witches for eons, Sean. In the dark ages, people called us witches, because we use magic in our fight. They accused us of consorting with the very creatures we'd sworn to defeat. We were killed by the thousands, almost to extinction. It's in your blood to fight demons. It's why it was so easy for you to kill them. You can't hide from your heritage, Sean. We need you. We need your strength in this war. Have you made your decision yet?"

Sean considered what he'd learned in the past few weeks. If he doubted his calling to fight demons before this, he didn't any longer. For some reason, Catlyn was at the center of it all. He *knew* she wasn't evil. As a Sentinel, he could protect her better. He hoped.

"Yes, Granny. My answer is yes."

She beamed at him.

"Granny, there's this girl, Catlyn. She seems to be involved in this demon stuff somehow, but she isn't a demon. Do you know what's going on?"

"I do. But I can't tell you yet. All in good time, my boy, all in good time."

"But—"

"And slowly come back to your body," Jade's voice intruded into his vision. "Take a deep breath ... and another one."

Sean opened his eyes, stunned to find he was back in the Mystical Enchantments, sitting next to Catlyn. It had simply been a dream brought on by the meditation. But it had seemed so real. As he took another deep breath, expanding his chest, his muscles ached. He frowned and felt something trickle down his cheek. He raised his hand to it, and his fingers came away bloody. "What the hell!"

Catlyn turned to him, her admonishment dying on her lips as her eyes widened. She reached out and touched his cheek. "You're bleeding. What happened? It looks like something with claws scratched you."

"I don't know." He caught Jade's eye. She had a smile playing across her lips. She nodded as she mouthed, "Welcome, Sean."

Somehow, what he'd experienced in his vision had been real. Which meant everything was real. He was a witch. He was a Sentinel. Now he had to figure out what it all meant.

 # CHAPTER 23 

The cell phone's insistent ringing jolted Catlyn awake. She fumbled, searching for it on the nightstand, finally grasping it. Without looking at the caller ID, she answered it with a mumbled, "Yeah?"

"Rise and shine!"

Catlyn groaned at Bri's chirpy voice and peered blearily at the clock that read eight a.m. After the healing circle last night, everyone had gone out to dinner, staying out way past midnight. She glared at the phone, irritated Bri had woken her up so early.

"It's my birthday today," Bri said. "Don't tell me you forgot! You have to help me celebrate! It isn't every day I turn the big three-oh."

"Most people don't think that's a celebratory milestone," Catlyn grumbled and sat up, displacing her cats. Mittens gave her an affronted look as she jumped off the bed.

"But you're only thirty once. Hurry up and dress. I'll be there in forty-five minutes to pick you up. Pack your swimsuit. We're going to the beach first."

Catlyn rolled her eyes. "You can't be serious! It's the end of October. It will be freezing."

"It's the only time I can get you out to the beach. You always complain about your pale skin burning so easily. Besides, it's supposed to be in the high 70s today. So no excuses."

"But—"

"Up and at 'em! See you in a bit." Bri hung up.

Grumbling, Catlyn tossed her phone on the nightstand. After having two friends murdered, she worried about all her friends. She wanted to protect Bri by staying away from her. The thought of losing her best friend terrified her. Bri loved her birthday and probably had the whole day planned on how to celebrate it with Catlyn. If she didn't get her butt up and dressed, Bri would be deeply hurt—and mad. Could she justify hurting her friend because she was afraid of some nebulous threat?

Reluctantly, Catlyn threw off the covers and climbed out of bed.

Forty minutes later, she'd showered and dressed. Although she didn't plan on playing in the cold water, she slathered on waterproof, heavy-duty sunscreen. Bri could be persuasive. Catlyn packed a big bag with a beach towel, blanket, and book. Digging in the back of her hall closet, she found her beach umbrella and put it by the door. A brightly wrapped package containing the necklace, earrings, and bracelet set Catlyn had made for Bri sat on the table.

Catlyn dished out food for her cats, then pulled out a steak from the fridge, devouring it raw. Maak gave a satisfied purr while Catlyn washed her hands.

Bri knocked, and without waiting for Catlyn, used her key to open the door. "Happy birthday to me!" she sang.

"Happy birthday, Bri!" Catlyn hurried over and hugged her friend.

Bri's eyes lit up when she saw the package on the table. "Is that for me?"

"Who else? It isn't my birthday. Go ahead, open it."

Bri did, and "oohed," at the wrapped flourite cabochon with a chain of apatite, moonstone, aventurine, and amethyst beads. She immediately put the jewelry on. "This is beautiful, Catlyn. Now, go grab something to wear to a nightclub tonight—something that shows off your legs, not your usual long skirts. Oh, and heels, bring high heels. We're going to the Red Orchid."

Catlyn rolled her eyes and returned to her bedroom to rummage in her closet. She didn't like going to nightclubs. Her psychic abilities went haywire from too many people and so much noise. She pulled out the little black dress and heels Lisa had loaned her. Catlyn hadn't had a chance to return them, and now she would never be able to.

A stab of loss punched her insides, making her curl over the clothes as she gasped. Tears spilled, blotching the silky fabric. It took her several minutes to regain her composure. When she returned to the living room, Bri had already taken her beach things out to the car and stood by the couch, petting the attention-loving Mittens. Boots eyed her from the other end of the couch.

"So what's the plan?" Catlyn asked as she grabbed her purse. "I should be the one planning your party."

"Ha! I'd rather do it and know I'm going to have fun. Your idea of a party is sitting around listening to trance music."

"Hey! I have fun doing that—so do you."

"But not for my birthday." Bri's face fell, and she lost her exuberance. "Just before Amelia died, she gave me coupons for discounted drinks at the Red Orchid. It was the last time I talked to her." She plastered on a bright smile. "So we're going tonight both for my birthday and to remember her—and Lisa."

"They would like that." Catlyn smiled. A frisson of fear slid down her spine at the mention of the Red Orchid. But it was Bri's birthday, and she wouldn't rain on it by refusing to go to the club. She prayed Michael wouldn't be there. "Well then, let's get your party day started. Beach first?"

"Yes." Bri hustled out the door with Catlyn close on her heels.

Bri drove them down to Laguna Beach. They walked along the shoreline. Out of the corner of her eye, Catlyn glimpsed Ariana keeping watch. She breathed a bit better. The last time she'd been at the beach was the first time she'd seen Michael.

Catlyn stopped, lifting a hand to her forehead, blocking out the sun while she watched Bri skip in the waves lapping the sand. Catlyn let out a screech when cold water washed over her toes. Bri laughed as Catlyn lifted her skirt and ran away from the encroaching wave. Arm-in-arm, they strolled back to Bri's car.

They ate a leisurely lunch at a funky little burger place on the beach. People drove miles for their ice cream shakes. They sat on the shaded patio watching the die-hard surfers, runners, and beach goers, making up stories about the interesting ones. By the time they drove to Bri's to wash off the salt and sand, Catlyn's melancholy had subsided.

Bri made a big production out of styling Catlyn's hair into an elegant updo. Catlyn usually wore it down with as little effort as possible. When Bri finished, Catlyn gazed into the mirror. Her mouth dropped open, stunned. She grudgingly had to admit she looked beautiful.

Bri wore her own dark-brown hair in a loose French-braid. Her low-cut navy blue sheath set off her blue eyes. She fastened on the jewelry Catlyn had made her. The pendant hung above her cleavage, drawing the eye to her ample assets.

"Where are we going to dinner?" Catlyn asked. "Pick wherever you want to go. My treat."

"Amelia covered it." Sadness darkened Bri's eyes. "The coupons she gave me included dinner and two cocktails each. The Red Orchid is rumored to have amazing cocktails and pretty good food. Lydia, Michelle, and some of the gang are meeting us there, so we'll have a great party."

Cars filled the parking lot of the popular club. Bri pulled into the valet station and beamed at the attendant. "It's my birthday. We're here for a party."

The attendant wished them a good time as he helped them from the car. As Catlyn and Bri waited in the foyer to be seated—apparently Amelia had reserved a table for them—Catlyn took in the scenery. It was the first time she'd been here. Clubs like this weren't her thing. She'd much rather have gone to a drum circle.

A DJ stood on a small stage with a spotlight lighting him up. Colored lights flashed and flowed over the crowd on the dance floor. Catlyn's hips moved to the beat of the music, and a smile spread over her face. Lydia and Michelle came in, both carrying gift bags, much to Bri's delight. The others in the group weren't far behind, and the hostess led them through the maze of tables.

Their drinks arrived, and as they sipped them, waiting for their food, they watched a tall, well-built man doing magic tricks at another table. The occupants laughed as the cards turned into a dove that shot toward the ceiling, disappearing into the dark depths of the club.

"Ooh, do you think he'll come over here?" Bri asked, avidly watching the entertainer. "I love magic tricks."

As if he heard her, the man bowed to the table and spun around to face theirs. Catlyn gasped. Nothing she knew about Michael Drogger indicated he was an entertainer. The light must be playing tricks on her eyes. She blinked. Much to her consternation, he was still there. Her stomach dropped, and she wished she could leave. But Bri was having such a good time, Catlyn couldn't ruin it for her.

"Man, he is cute!" Bri waved a hand in front of her, as if fanning herself. "Be still my beating heart."

"No, he isn't." Catlyn countered, fear and anger in her voice. Catlyn scanned the room, hoping to catch Charlie's attention. She'd spotted his truck pulling into the parking lot as they entered the club. An image of teeth tearing into Michael's throat, claws ripping open his belly flashed into her mind. Maak didn't like him much either. "I find him quite loathsome."

"Come on, Catlyn. You never think anyone is good-looking or good enough. You need to get past how Karl treated you."

"Can't you see something is wrong with him?"

Bri stared at him, her eyes narrowed. Her forehead creased. "That's strange. I'm not seeing his aura." She laughed and held up her nearly empty glass. "Must be because of this lovely drink."

Catlyn leaned close and whispered into Bri's ear. "He's the one who is stalking me."

Bri's eyes widened. "No way."

Catlyn nodded.

Michael sauntered toward them, his smile bringing out the dimple in his cheek. With both hands, he swept back his longish, blond hair, the movement opening his shirt wider, revealing his muscled chest. He appraised all the women at the table, his eyes stopping on Bri for a long moment. His predatory glance made Catlyn fist her hand under the table and the hackles on the back of her neck rise.

As he stopped at their table, a low growl vibrated her throat. Bri turned to her with wide eyes, and she coughed to cover it up.

"You okay, doll?" His voice was a practiced, smooth-as-honey-make-women-melt tone.

She heard Lydia sigh and smelled her lust. Catlyn held up her glass. "Yeah, just swallowed wrong."

"That seems to happen here all the time." He smiled, rubbing his chest, and winked at the girls, who giggled like they were part of an inside joke.

Catlyn rolled her eyes and turned in her chair to watch the DJ. She toyed with her phone. *Should I call Charlie? I haven't seen him inside the club. He has to be here.* She sniffed deeply, then snarled with frustration at her inability to make out his scent with all the people in the crowd.

While Michael entertained her friends with his illusions, Catlyn sent a text to Charlie: *Michael's here, taunting me! Help!* The longer Michael stayed at their table, the more uncomfortable she became. Even over the myriad emotions clogging her nose, his evil smell swamped her. His craving for power overshadowed his lust for women. She kept looking at her phone and searching the crowd for Charlie. *Where is Charlie?*

When the others clapped, she whipped her attention back to Michael. Her relief that he was leaving was short-lived. As he bowed, playing the charade of graciously receiving her friend's accolades, his gaze snagged hers. "I'll get you. Soon," he mouthed. A malicious grin darkened his face and his eyes glinted red. When he stood, he wore a charming smile.

She shivered. She'd seen his evil under his mask of a handsome playboy. Catlyn tried to forget the threat and stay in the spirit of celebrating Bri's birthday. But Michael hovered in her peripheral vision. She continued to search the crowd for Charlie, but the dim lighting and mass of writhing bodies made it difficult to see people distinctly.

After a while, she'd had enough drinks that her bladder felt like it would explode. She glanced around, sighing in relief when she couldn't spot Michael anywhere.

"Bri, I'm going to the bathroom."

"Do you want me to go with you?"

"No, I should be okay. He wouldn't do anything with all these people here."

Catlyn slipped through the crowd. She caught sight of Charlie standing by the long, narrow hall leading to the ladies' room. She let out a pent up breath. She was safe. He inclined his head at her. *Why didn't he return my texts?* As she approached the restroom, her nose twitched and uneasiness flooded her. *Why couldn't I see him before? Is it actually Charlie, or is it one of Michael's illusions?* She shook her head to clear it of her silly thoughts. *Maak, am I being paranoid? Is it Charlie?*

A sense of frustration rose from Maak. There were too many people to pick out an individual.

Once in the ladies' room, her uneasiness passed. She headed back toward her friends. Two steps from the restroom, the sharp scent of danger hit her. Before she could react, someone grabbed her and dragged her into a dark closet. Her face slammed into the wall. Stars swam before her eyes.

"I told you I'd get you soon," Michael crooned into her ear, while he pressed against her back. One hand held a knife to her throat while the other groped and fondled her breasts.

Catlyn struggled, stamping her heel hard toward his instep, but missed. She managed to jab her elbow into his abdomen. She smirked with satisfaction when his breath whooshed out.

"Stay still," he warned.

The knife bit into her skin. A sharp pain cut through her, and as he drew the blade slowly down her neck, she felt something warm trickle on it.

Blood.

"Maak, help!" she screamed silently. She waited for the great cat to do something. Maak snarled in frustration. Anything Maak could do would jeopardize Catlyn's life. Michael wouldn't hesitate in slitting her throat. She stopped struggling, but couldn't help the growl that escaped.

His hand moved further down her body, his touch making her skin crawl. He lifted the skirt of her dress, found her panties, and pulled them aside. Catlyn struggled to pull away, and when that didn't work, she tried crossing her legs to stop him. She gasped when he thrust his finger inside her.

"Oh, I knew you'd like it. You've been waiting weeks for this."

He licked the blood trickling down her neck. Terror gripped her. *Will he kill me like he did my two friends?* She squeezed her eyes shut, crying as he finger-fucked her.

"This is just the beginning, Catlyn," Michael's voice oozed. "Oh, the fun we'll have. Soon. But not yet. The timing isn't right. He isn't quite ready for you."

The pressure from the knife lifted. Michael disappeared.

She crumbled to the floor, sobbing and shaking. She wanted to shower and wash the stink of his violation off her. Finally, she stopped shaking. Her neck throbbed where the knife had bitten into her. Her mind skittered from thinking about what else he'd done to her. To be raped like that was almost worse than Michael using his penis. No one would believe he'd raped her. Wearing Lisa's mini dress had been a mistake. They'd say she'd been "asking for it." No woman ever asked to be raped!

Even with all of Jade's security precautions, Michael had found a way to get to her. None of her magical protections had worked. She'd thought having a giant tiger as her spirit guide would keep her safe. But it hadn't.

"I'm sorry," Maak said, her voice soft and contrite. *"There wasn't anything I could do to help you."*

"You're not to blame. Nothing could have stopped him." Catlyn scrubbed at her face, wishing it would be as easy to wipe away the incident as her tears. She sniffed deeply. Her questing fingers found the light switch. Michael had taken her into a supply closet. She opened a package of toilet paper and blew her nose, leaning against the door for support.

"The bastard will receive the reward he deserves, I promise."

Maak's promise settled Catlyn's racing heart. Never again would she be so complacent. As much as she hated it, she'd devote more time to her martial arts training with Jade. When Michael tried again—and she didn't doubt his threat that he would—she wanted to be able to put up a fight. She vowed she wouldn't go down like a cowardly mouse.

Catlyn sat up, resolved to make Michael pay. She refused to be the rape victim who wouldn't press charges. Even as she made her way back to her friends to get her phone, she replayed Michael's last words to her.

What the hell did Michael mean that he wasn't ready for me?

CHAPTER 24

Sean waved his hand in front of him, wishing he could clear the cars blocking his way from the road. His lights and siren weren't making them move fast enough to suit him.

"Why in the hell wasn't I at the club tonight? I knew Michael would be there." He slammed his palm on the steering wheel. Terror and panic had taken residence in his stomach since the phone call from Joshua. *But why was Catlyn there?* She'd never been there in the months he'd been haunting the place.

His instincts screamed that Catlyn was the ultimate target of the Iron Maiden Killer. Jerry's research discovered over two-thirds of the people killed had some type of association with Catlyn. Most of the connections were innocent. They'd received a tarot reading, or bought her jewelry and left a review, or took a class she'd attended or taught. Nothing his team had found so far indicated why the killer—why Michael—had singled her out.

And now he'd attacked her. At his father's club, no less. *Why did Michael let her go?* Sean shied away from those implications. His unhelpful mind served him an image of her hanging by hooks, her body flayed. He swallowed the acrid taste of bile. Instead, he tried to wrap his brain around Michael's sudden stupidity.

He finally slid into the Red Orchid's mostly empty parking lot, his tires flinging pebbles and dirt. He parked at the valet station, jumped out before the engine cut off, and sprinted into the club. It was blissfully quiet without the DJ's blaring music. The bright lights ruined the club's normal sultry, sexual ambiance.

A knot of women sat at a table strewn with empty glasses. Birthday gift bags on the floor surrounded Catlyn's friend, Bri, whom he met last night at the healing circle. Mascara ran down her face. The party explained Catlyn's uncharacteristic attendance at the club.

Narrowing his eyes, Sean slipped into his witch-sight. At the absence of demons, the tension in his shoulders relaxed slightly.

Joshua, the club manager, saw Sean and angled to cut him off before he reached the women.

"Detective, you arrived quickly," Joshua said, holding out his hand. "Catlyn's in my office. She wouldn't go with the paramedics until she talked to you."

"The bastard hurt her?" Rage burned like fire under his skin.

"Not too badly, scared more than anything. Come this way."

When Joshua opened the office door, Sean found Catlyn reclining on the leather sofa. She turned her head toward him and grimaced. Sean's fist clenched as he took in the bandage affixed to her neck and her paler than normal face. He strode across the room and knelt next to her. He put a hand on her thigh, pulling it off when she flinched at his touch. *What the hell did Michael do to her?*

"Tell me what happened."

"That asshole attacked me!" Catlyn sat up and clenched the side of the couch, swaying.

Shock or blood loss. I'll kill the bastard.

"I have proof, see!" She ripped off the bandage to reveal a long, shallow cut on her neck from her jawline to the base of her throat. "I wouldn't let the paramedics clean it off because the bastard licked me. He licked me! Just like a fucking vampire, he licked off my blood. He liked it too." She choked on the last sentence.

"We should be able to get some DNA evidence. Is that all he did?"

She curled into a ball, wrapped her arms around her knees, and dropped her head. "No. He ... he ... raped me," she stuttered, so low he barely heard her. She swallowed hard, tears streamed down her face. She avoided looking into his eyes. "Sean, he held a knife to my throat, cut me, and then that fucking monster raped me. I swear I tried to get away, but he was too strong."

"You are the victim here and did nothing wrong. You need to go to the hospital for a rape kit." He dropped his shaking hands between his knees to hide them. They should find enough evidence to at least hold Michael. He'd finally made a big mistake attacking Catlyn.

"It won't do any good." Catlyn's jaw muscles tightened, and she squeezed her eyes shut. "He used his hand, not his dick. That's almost worse."

"All isn't lost. We can get DNA from his fingers up to twelve hours after the incident. We may be able to gather other evidence too."

"I don't want to go in an ambulance. I can't afford it. Can I have my friend, Bri, take me?"

"When we're done here, I could take you." Sean stood and glanced around the room. He dragged a chair over to sit next to her, then pulled out his notebook and pen. "Tell me what happened and everything Michael said to you or did."

The routine of asking questions helped settle him. His fury reached new heights as he listened to Catlyn recount the incident. He hadn't ever interviewed a rape victim he cared about.

Afterward he went downstairs and took the statements of her girlfriends, but none of them had seen the attack. A familiar face loitered by the bar. Sean stormed over.

"What the hell, Charlie!" Sean grabbed Charlie's shirtfront, nearly lifting him off his feet. "You were supposed to protect her."

"I followed her toward the bathroom. Some demon prick jumped me." Charlie knocked Sean's hands away, whirled around, and pointed at the gash on the back of his head. The paramedics had cleaned it, but blood still trickled. When he turned around, anguish filled his face. "When I came to, she was staggering out of the cleaning closet with blood dripping down her neck. I searched the club for Michael, but he'd already disappeared."

"After this, I'm insisting we place her in protective custody."

"After this, Jade will compel Catlyn to stay at her home. She has protections that no one, not even Michael, can breach."

The door to the club banged open, and Jade stormed inside.

Charlie groaned. "She's going to kill me! Jade loves Catlyn like a daughter, and I was entrusted to keep her safe. I failed."

For the second time, a hand wrapped around Charlie's throat and slammed him into the bar. "What the fuck, Charlie!"

"I tried, Jade," Charlie wailed.

Sean put a restraining hand on Jade's shoulder. "Michael's goons knew he was protecting her and jumped him."

"Where is she?" Jade growled. She released Charlie and fastened her gaze on Sean.

His stomach flopped at her intensity.

"Is she all right?"

"She's upstairs." He pointed to the stair's entrance. "She won't let the paramedics take her to the hospital."

"Damn stubborn girl." Jade shot a glare at Charlie before she stomped up the stairs.

With Catlyn's godmother here to look after her, Sean convinced Catlyn's friends to go home. Bri insisted on staying and when Catlyn came down, leaning heavily on Jade, Bri ran to her other side. Together, they helped Catlyn into Jade's SUV, then drove to the hospital.

Sean watched them leave, wishing Catlyn would turn to him for help, or at least give him one last glance over her shoulder. He mentally slapped his face for acting like a lovesick teenager. He could help her more by keeping Michael away from her.

This time, Sean had enough cause to warrant questioning Michael at the police station. Even though he was a homicide detective, Catlyn's connection—and Michael's—to the Iron Maiden Killer allowed him to investigate it as germane to his case. He'd turn whatever he discovered over to the Special Victims Unit.

Several hours later, Michael lounged in the interview chair, one arm thrown over the back and his legs outstretched. The creep acted as though he didn't have a care in the world.

"Yeah, I was at the Red Orchid tonight." Michael glanced at the clock. "Well, last night. I'm there most nights, as you're aware, Detective. You're there watching me. Do you get off on it? Are you a voyeur who gets his rocks off watching other people? Because you know, man, I certainly get my rocks off there."

"Did you sexually assault Ms. Hennessey?" Sean gritted his teeth against the overwhelming desire to plant his fist in Michael's face and wipe off his sneer. Now that would excite him.

"I was with several women, all of them wanting what I gave them." Michael sat forward. "Let me see her picture, and I can tell you if I remember her."

Sean opened the folder in front of him and slid a photo across the table.

Michael peered at it, not touching it. His bent head made it difficult for Sean to read his expression. Finally, using the tip of his index finger, he pushed it back. "This little mouse? She's the bitch accusing me of raping her? In her dreams. She isn't my type—you know, tall, willowy, blond."

"What about long black hair?"

"If the girl's pretty enough, possibly."

Sean passed Michael a picture of Lisa. "How about her? Does she fit your profile?"

"Now, she's someone I would have gone after. But I'd have fucked her, not killed her. I assume she's dead. Go find someone else to harass."

A knock sounded on the door.

Michael smiled, leaning back in his chair. "Ah, that must be my lawyer. It's been fun talking to you, Detective. While he is here, I should file a complaint against you."

"This time, we have evidence. DNA evidence," Sean snarled. "You won't be able to weasel out of this one."

Michael crossed an ankle over his knee and draped a hand over it. "What are you going to test your evidence against? My father has more money than god. That usually takes care of nasty business like this."

The door opened and Michael's lawyer entered.

Sean surged to his feet. "Don't go far. We should have a warrant for your DNA soon."

"Oh, I wouldn't count on that," the lawyer said. "No judge is going to go against Thomas Drogger. Come on, Michael, you're free to leave."

Sean fumed as Michael followed his lawyer from the interrogation room. The lawyer was probably right. But there had to be one uncorrupted judge in the county. Sean only had to find out who. Until the lab processed the evidence from Catlyn's attack, he had nothing to hold Michael on or obtain a search warrant. With the rash of violence lately, the lab was overworked. It would be weeks, if not months, before they worked on this case.

By then, Catlyn could be dead.

Since following Michael seemed useless, Sean would keep tabs on Catlyn. Sean's instincts told him Michael was the Iron Maiden Killer, and sooner or later he'd go after Catlyn. The gruesome murder scenes flashed through Sean's mind. He wiped his clammy hands on his thighs. He'd do everything in his power to make sure that didn't happen to Catlyn.

Catlyn stood in the shower, scrubbing her skin until it nearly bled, but she still felt unclean. The stench of Michael's lust and sickness continued to ooze from her pores. She'd tried not to show it, but the attack terrified her.

Michael thought of her as prey. A predator lived under her skin now, and like recognized like. As a predator, he'd be coming after her soon. She doubted it would be today or tomorrow. He'd want her to live with the fear of never knowing when he'd attack her again.

What did he mean by me 'not being quite ripe'? Ripe for what?

When they'd left the hospital, she'd been in too much shock to argue with Jade when she'd insisted Catlyn stay in her home in Newport Beach. Now she'd had time to process the incident, Catlyn admitted to herself she didn't want to be home alone tonight.

Finally, the cold water propelled Catlyn from the shower. She breathed in the comfort of her old bedroom. Whenever her uptight, conservative, and ultra-religious aunt and uncle had become too much for her, she'd escape to her godmother's house. By the time she was a senior in high school, she'd lived with Jade. The sleigh bed beckoned to her exhausted body.

She pulled out a pair of pajamas from a drawer in the matching dresser. It also contained several pairs of underwear, a couple of bras, and a few dresses hung in the closet. There might even be jeans and t-shirts from her younger days tucked in another drawer. Catlyn curled up in the bed, wishing her cats were there to lend her their comfort.

She awoke to sunshine streaming through the lace curtains. She stretched. The movement pulled the bandage on her neck, bringing back the terror of the night before. Catlyn huddled under the covers, wanting nothing more than to hide from the world, and the horror her life had become. But the thought of her cats left home without anyone to feed them goaded her out of hiding.

Another shower, and scouring her body with lavender scented soap, washed the last residue of Michael's stench from her. She put on a long-sleeved dress and leggings. When she padded down the stairs, voices drifted from the formal living room. She paused on the bottom stair, surprised to hear Sean's voice. Curious, she entered the living room.

Sean and Jade stopped talking as soon as they saw her.

"Darling, how are you feeling?" Jade asked.

"Okay. Tired. Sore. Ready to go home."

"You can't go home." Sean rose to his feet. "It isn't safe. Michael is on the loose."

"What? You have his DNA. Shouldn't he be in jail?"

"He has an excellent lawyer," Sean grimaced. "The lab won't have the results of the DNA test for days, possibly months, considering how backed up they are. I can't hold him or charge him until it comes back." Sean crossed to her and placed his hands on her shoulders. Concern filled his eyes. "I need you to stay here," he implored. "Don't go to work. Don't leave the house."

Catlyn pulled away from him and rolled her eyes. "Great. I'm the victim, and I'm the one put under house arrest."

He lifted a shoulder. "Essentially, yes."

"What if I refuse? I have bills to pay. If I don't work, I don't get paid."

"Let me take care of that for you," Jade said. "I can cover your expenses for you."

Jade's business did well, and she could afford to help Catlyn out for weeks, or even months. Catlyn hoped she didn't have to depend on Jade for more than a few days.

Catlyn slouched, dejected. "Can't you at least come to my place?"

"No. One, you don't have enough space. Two, your apartment doesn't have the right protections installed, and three, it's too hard to defend." Jade lifted a finger with each point. A sympathetic smile tugged her lips. "Come on. I'll even let you bring your cats here."

Catlyn's shoulders slumped, and she lowered her eyes. They made sense, but she didn't like being bullied. She recognized how much of a concession Jade was making to keep her safe. Jade didn't care for cats. *Wait until she sees Maak!* Catlyn pulled her lips tight, hiding her delight at the thought.

"I'll drive you home to pick them up." Sean offered with a shy smile. "I can protect you in case anything happens."

Catlyn's spirits lifted. Maybe he'd agree to stop for breakfast on the way. Her stomach growled loudly. She glanced at the clock, surprised to see it was nearly noon. Brunch then. The Jupiter Moon still served breakfast this late on Saturday.

"I'll even take you to get something to eat," Sean added. He had to have heard her stomach. "The city of Anaheim's treat."

Jade studied them for a moment, her hands on her hips. She snorted, giving a little shake of her head. "Dilan will trail you. The more protection you have, the better."

Catlyn bristled. She'd wanted time alone with Sean.

Sean opened the passenger door to his black Camaro for her. As she stepped into it, he stared at her, his mouth slightly agape.

She frowned, puzzled. "What's wrong? Do I have something on me? I swear it was clean when I put it on." She glanced down at her dress.

"No, no. You're ... you're just beautiful," he whispered, then hurried to his side of the car. As it roared to life, he looked over at her. "I'd like to get to know you better, if that's all right with you?"

Her stomach fluttered, and her cheeks warmed. "Yes, I'd like that very much."

"How does the Jupiter Moon sound?"

"Perfect."

When Sean shifted gears, his fingertips brushed her thigh. She involuntarily jerked away. Biting her lip, she refused to allow the incident with Michael to mar the day with Sean.

When they arrived at the Jupiter Moon, Catlyn automatically scanned the parking lot. She let out a breath of relief when for the first time in over a month she didn't see a black sedan lurking in the lot. Her hand drifted to the bandage on her neck.

"Do you have to go into the store today?" Sean asked as they waited for their order.

Catlyn shook her head. "No. I knew we'd celebrate Bri's birthday until late, so I didn't schedule any healing appointments. I also requested the day off."

His eyes lit up, and a mischievous grin flitted across his lips. He jumped up to get their food when their number was called.

Catlyn's stomach rumbled again as he set her plate in front of her, echoed by Maak's growl of hunger. She glanced up, but he didn't act like he'd heard it. She dug into her eggs and sausage.

After brunch, Sean turned left out of the café's parking lot, instead of turning right in the direction of the freeway toward Anaheim. A few minutes later, he drove south on Pacific Coast Highway.

"Where are we going?" Catlyn asked.

"I have a surprise for you. After what you've been through, you could use some relaxation."

"Don't you have work?"

"My only active case right now is the Iron Maiden killer." His knuckles whitened from his hard grip on the steering wheel. He stretched out his hands. "There isn't anything else to investigate until he makes his move again. So, I'm enjoying a day off, too."

She caught the scent of a half-truth, but she wasn't sure what he'd be lying about.

They entered the town of Corona Del Mar, and her stomach clenched. Only a few miles further lay Crystal Cove—the first place she'd seen Michael. A soothing purr from Maak comforted her.

Sean turned into the parking lot of Sherman Library and Gardens, the botanical gardens above the ocean. A breeze ruffled the hem of her long skirt. Even in late autumn, the gardens took her breath away. As they walked through the cactus garden, the sun warmed her shoulders, and her breathing eased.

Sean held open the hothouse door for her. Steam rushed out. The path followed an artificial stream leading to a koi pond. They sat on the bench, watching the fish and talking. Sean's hand drifted toward hers. Disappointment swamped her when he returned it to his lap. She inhaled deeply, and his uncertainty flooded her senses. She remembered her early flinch when he'd touched her. Catlyn casually placed her hand in his. When he looked at her in surprise, she smiled.

"You aren't Michael. You'd never hurt me."

"I could never hurt you." Sean gently squeezed her hand, then lifted it to his lips.

A thrill went through her at the gallant gesture. The knot in her stomach that had been a constant companion since seeing Michael at the club eased from her.

When they left the hothouse to continue to explore the gardens, she linked her hand over his elbow. They stayed until the sun dipped low on the horizon, talking about everything—and nothing.

While Sean drove toward her apartment, Catlyn decided it was the best first date she'd ever had, even though it technically wasn't a date.

She pushed open her apartment door to find Mittens and Boots waiting for her, their tails swishing in agitation. As soon as she walked in, they yowled and twisted around her ankles. "Sorry, babies! You must be starving." She hurried into the kitchen, opened a can of cat food, and divided it into two portions.

Catlyn turned back to Sean where he waited, leaning against the tiny breakfast bar of her kitchen counter. "Do you want any tea or water while I pack?"

He shook his head. "No. I'm fine."

She packed her bags, including several bins of jewelry making supplies. If she had to be cooped up for the next few days, she'd use the time to make some jewelry to sell. The cats didn't like it when she put them in the cat carriers, and they squalled the whole ride to Jade's house.

Sean was helping her carry in her things when Charlie arrived.

"I have food," Charlie announced, holding up two large bags of takeout from Tres Toros. "There's enough here for you too, Sean. I got your favorite, chili relleno, shredded beef taco, and a beef enchilada." He set the bags on the kitchen counter.

Catlyn grabbed one of the fresh, crispy-fried tortillas, breaking off a piece and popping it in her mouth. "What did you get me?"

"The same, except a chicken enchilada instead of beef."

"Green sauce?"

"Of course." Charlie pulled out the food, divvying it between them.

They carried their food downstairs to the family room, Jade joining them. After they ate, Catlyn convinced Sean to stay and play cards with them. Sean let his guard down as they played, and she again glimpsed the funny guy he hid behind his mask of being the serious cop.

She wished they could actually date. She was starting to like him a lot, perhaps even falling in love with him. But he wouldn't date her as long as he was investigating the murder of her friends.

As she waved to him from the door, Maak whispered, *"Soon. It will be over soon."*

Catlyn shuddered at the warning. She had a strong suspicion the only way it would be over was when Michael came after her, for real this time.

 # CHAPTER 25 

It had been quite a while since Catlyn had been so lazy, even for a Sunday. After sleeping in late, she put on a sundress, then went outside and reclined on a lounge chair by the pool, reading. If there hadn't been a cloud of fear hanging over her, it would have been a mini vacation. Alarms and closed-circuit cameras protected Jade's house, along with magical spells. Fort Knox might not be as secure.

Catlyn jerked from her doze, sitting straight up. Her eyes wide, she searched for the danger. She finally identified the buzz of a lawn mower in a neighbor's yard. She settled back on her lounge chair. Shrill cries made her heart leap. A moment later, she heard a loud splash, then laughter. The kids next door were playing in the pool.

Mittens wandered out and jumped on her lap. "I don't how I'm going to do this. I can't handle days—or weeks—living in terror." She lifted the cat to her face and rubbed her cheek in the soft fur. "In some ways, kitty," she whispered, "I hope Michael will hurry and do whatever he has in mind for me. This waiting is driving me crazy."

"You shouldn't have to wait too long," Maak said. *"I can sense a disturbance in the portals."*

A daemon must be ready to cross. Catlyn leaped to her feet, pacing the concrete in front of the pool. A shiver went through her. She felt exposed being outside, and she hurried into the safety of the house. The thought of sitting, waiting for Michael to snatch her, made her skin crawl.

Gathering her jewelry making supplies, she carried them into the family room. She dragged the pub table closer to the patio door for more light. At least she could continue crafting inventory for her Etsy shop. That part of her life hadn't changed. She selected rose quartz heart-shaped beads and silver balls to make a necklace and earring set. The motions—and the quiet energy of the rose quartz—soon soothed her jangled nerves.

A tail thumped on her shoulder as she worked. She twisted around and glared at Boots, where he sat on the back of her chair. He didn't like being in the strange place. Mittens sprawled in a patch of sunshine. The tip of her tail twitched as she dozed. Catlyn leaned her head back, petting Boots. Her eyes soon drooped closed in the quiet.

The sound of the patio door opening disturbed her nap. As she sat up, she rubbed the grogginess from her face. Sean's normally olive complexion was ashen, and his feet dragged. Catlyn's stomach dropped to her toes.

"Something awful has happened, hasn't it?"

"I have bad news." Sean pulled out a tall chair across the pub table from Catlyn. He wouldn't look at her, but kept his eyes locked on his clenched hands. "We've been doing research, trying to find out why Michael is targeting you."

"And why he hasn't killed me yet like the others?" Catlyn had wondered the same thing. It had to do with her not being "ripe", but she still didn't have a clue what that meant.

Sean looked up, his face bleak. "These murders started two-and-a-half years ago. From what we've recently discovered, you seem to be in the center of this mess. Of the thirty-three people killed, twenty-six had contact with you in some way. Do you know why he's targeting people close to you?"

Catlyn gaped and her muscles stiffened. "No! There's no way." How had she not known so many people she knew had died?

Sean reached over, lightly stroking her forearm. "We just made the connection. Why do they want you?"

"I don't know!" Catlyn leaned away from Sean, her eyes wide. "I ... No, this can't be..."

"*You know it's true,*" Maak whispered to her. "*There is power deep within you the daemons can sense and want to use.*"

Catlyn resisted the urge to squirm. She watched Sean's face to see if he had heard Maak. He didn't act like he had.

"*A daemon prince is being summoned.*" Maak showed Catlyn an image of a large, muscled male with smooth, hairless ice-blue skin, electric blue eyes, and blood-red lips. He had an allure about him that made Catlyn suspect people would do whatever he wanted.

Catlyn rubbed her eyes to wipe away the vision. She couldn't blurt out to Sean that a daemon was preparing to cross into their realm. He'd never believe her. How could she help him without him thinking she was a weirdo? She thought back to the visions she'd had of her friend's death. Both of them had the flavor of human sacrifice about them.

"Sean, do the killings look like they're part of a ritual, or is there something strange about them? Weird symbols? Anything?"

"Everything about them is weird and strange." He gave her a sidelong glance and shifted in his chair. "In every single instance, we find the victims hanging in various ways in the center of a pentacle. There are symbols drawn in it and an eight foot circle drawn around it. We haven't found any indication the murderer killed his victims elsewhere and moved their bodies. Based on the killing methods, blood should drench the room. But not even a drop mars the outside of the circle. It's as if some kind of force-field or barrier trapped it inside."

"Do you have pictures?"

"Yes." He pursed his lips and rubbed his upper arm. "You really don't want to see them."

"No, I don't want to see them. But I need to see them. I need to see the symbols."

Sean pulled out his phone, sliding through the pictures, then reluctantly handed it to her.

Catlyn steeled herself and looked at the first picture. It wasn't too bad, only concrete walls painted with arcane symbols. Then she clicked to the next one and gagged at the mass of exposed muscle and sinew hanging inside a metal frame. Gore dripped from the wicked-looking spikes. She recognized the medieval torture device—an iron maiden. Catlyn quickly swiped to the next picture, which, thankfully, focused on the pentacle. She studied the symbols.

"Those are of the first murder," Sean said. He'd moved to stand behind her, looking over her shoulder. "We found the body on May third, two years ago. Her name was Francine Miller..."

Catlyn frowned. The name sounded familiar, but she couldn't place it. "I don't know a Francine Miller."

"She attended a few of Jade's classes that April, and you gave her a tarot reading two weeks before her murder. She cut your hair once."

"Oh, I remember her now. It was a terrible haircut and I had to have it redone by someone else."

"She'd been dead at least two or three days when we found her. We estimate the killer tortures his victims for three days before they're killed. We usually find them within a few days of their death."

Catlyn tapped the back of the phone. "That means the first ritual was completed on Beltane. It's a sacred day for Wiccans and pagans to celebrate the fertility of the earth. How often are the murders?"

"Usually one every four to six weeks. I haven't been able to figure out any type of pattern or timing."

"Besides the current string of deaths, has there been any other instance when more than one murder occurred?"

Sean paced behind her. "Yes, the first time there were three victims, then a little over a year ago, three more over several days. All the others have been a single victim. Do you have any idea what it means?"

She shook her head. "Not yet. But in the occult world, everything has meaning. And for certain rituals, the timing, such as the moon phase or planetary alignments, are very important." She clicked through more pictures. By the tenth one, she couldn't look at any more gruesome deaths.

She stopped on one with a clear shot of the symbols. Something about them niggled the back of her mind. They were similar to the ones Jade had taught her, but different enough they weren't from the same system. Although, she was certain she'd seen this set somewhere. She wracked her memory. Finally, she recalled seeing it in a book—an extremely old book.

"Sean, I need to go to my place." She stood and handed his phone back to him. "I have a book there that might have the answers. I also need the dates of every murder."

He tapped on his phone. "I'm emailing them to you."

She grabbed her laptop, opened her email program, and printed the file. On the drive to her apartment, she compared the dates to a lunar calendar. The majority of murders corresponded to a dark moon; the time when the moon couldn't be seen in the sky. Astrology called it new moon.

In the magical system she followed, new moon occurred three days later, when the first sliver of the moon shone in the evening sky. The only time there had been a killing on a full moon had been on the last blue moon. It also corresponded to the three-victim killing spree. While Sean drove, she mulled over what the original three killings meant. But until she looked it up on the internet at home, she didn't have a clue.

When they reached her apartment, Catlyn rushed up the stairs and threw open the door. It seemed so empty and forlorn without her cats greeting her at the threshold. She searched her bookcase for the book she wanted. The ancient tome dated to the middle ages and was written as journal entries, with references even farther back into prehistory. She carefully carried it to the coffee table and laid it down.

"It's about the efforts of a secret society called, 'The Sentinel Witches', who hunted down and stopped demons and other malevolent beings," she told Sean. He jerked at the society's name, but he didn't say anything. Now that she had the book in hand, she remembered more about it.

"There's a daemon prince. What was his name?" —she opened the book and carefully flipped the pages— "Oh, yeah, Bho-Ahp. He's manifested in our world several times, and humankind suffered terribly while he ruled. He possessed Caligula, Attila the Hun, and Pope Innocent IV, the one who legalized inquisitors to use torture in 1252. As well as King Ferdinand II of Aragon in 1480, who established the Spanish Inquisition. His latest possession was Adolf Hitler. Each time Bho-Ahp has crossed the portal onto Earth, the Sentinels have managed to send him back to his own dimension. But they haven't been able to destroy him."

She finally found the entries she remembered. When she'd first seen the illustration, it had sent shocks of terror through her, and it still did. Now, though, she had a full-color photograph to match it.

"I've seen that." Sean's hand trembled as he pointed to the page. "Thirty-three times, I've stared at that scene. What is it?"

"It's a ritual to make the host ready for inhabitation by Bho-Ahp. Since he's a high-ranking daemon, he can't just waltz into our world and possess a person. First, he has to have the consent of the person. Second, they have to summon them, and third, the human body can't hold the power of the lower dimensions without preparation. Long, exacting preparation." She leaned over the book and read. "It says here the ritual can only be conducted on the dark moon. I'd already figured that out. And oh, it must commence and end on a black moon."

"I've heard of a blue moon, but what is a black moon?"

Catlyn put up her hands up, palms facing up, then searched the internet. "A blue moon is two full moons in a single month, while a black moon is when there are two dark moons. It only occurs every two-and-a-half years. The next one will be..." A wave of dizziness washed over Catlyn, and she gulped. "The next one is this Friday."

"Fuck!" Sean swore. "That isn't very much time. How do we stop it?" Sean leaned forward, turned the page, and blanched. If the other rituals had been gruesome, they were nothing compared to the last one.

The sensation of Michael's tongue licking the blood from Catlyn's neck returned. Along with it came the stench of his hunger, and his thoughts crept back into her memory. *'So sweet, so strong. I want you ... Bho-Ahp wants you. You are the one to release him!'*

Tremors shook Catlyn's body.

"Catlyn, what's wrong?" Sean pulled her into his shoulder. "What has you so terrified?"

"That ... that's what Michael has in store for me. I just remembered what else he said to me when he attacked me. I'm to be the final sacrifice that brings Bho-Ahp across the portal and into this world."

Sean stiffened, pulling her closer. "I won't let that happen."

"Wait!" She stepped back from him. "You believe me? You believe all of this?" She waved at the book about witches who fought demons.

"I do." She couldn't quite fathom the emotion that filled his face. "There's no way he'll get his hands on you. We'll keep you hidden, and Jade's protections will keep you safe."

Realization struck Catlyn, and she raised her hand to her neck where the cut from Michael's knife had scabbed over. "No. No, it won't. Nothing will. He has the power of a daemon prince helping him. He'll find me no matter where I am. Sean, I'm scared."

Sean's strong arms enveloped her, and she clung tighter to him. His solid presence reassuring and offering safety. She would gladly stay there forever.

"I'll keep you safe. He won't get you," Sean promised. His confident voice had the ring of a vow to it.

 # CHAPTER 26 

Sean closed his eyes against the ancient illustrations of the final sacrifice to raise Bho-Ahp, still lying open on the coffee table. He didn't want that to happen to Catlyn. Spending time with her over the past few days, he found he was falling in love with her against his better judgment.

The memory floated to the surface of their day at the botanical gardens. As she sat on the edge of a pond, watching the koi, her contentment had struck him. He'd switched on his witch-sight and gasped at her beautiful aura. The gold and silver of it had extended several feet from her. A definite feline energy surrounded her, but he couldn't see anything beyond her blazing aura. He'd wanted to bask in that beauty.

Taking her to the gardens had been a sudden impulse as an early birthday gift to himself, especially since he'd had a rare day off from work on Saturday.

The soft thump of Catlyn closing the book drove away the pleasant memory. Sean gazed into her beautiful green eyes, and a smile curved his lips at the blush blooming on her face. An unfamiliar sensation of warmth seeped from his heart—one he hadn't ever expected to feel after Ginny. As he stood, adjusting his trousers, it hit him like a sledgehammer. His feelings were more than lust.

As Sean drove Catlyn back to Jade's home, he kept glancing at the old tome on her lap. The images of the last ritual sacrifice replayed in his mind. He would do everything in his power to stop it from happening to Catlyn, including tying her up or tossing her in a jail cell. The book intrigued him. If his grandmother had told him the truth—and he didn't doubt it—it seemed to be a history of his people.

"Where did you get that?" He indicated the book with his chin. "It's ancient."

"It was weird, even for me," Catlyn said with a laugh. "A few years ago, I was in an old, used bookstore in Eureka. I was minding my own business, browsing the fantasy romance novels, when a book fell off a shelf and bonged me on the head. I looked around, thinking someone had pulled it out and dropped it by mistake, but no one was nearby. When I picked it up, I felt a tingling sensation pass from the book, into my hands, and spread throughout my body. I knew I had to have it. The shop owner didn't remember he had it in stock and charged me a ridiculously low price for it." She shook her head and gazed out the window. "I've always wondered why it made its way into my possession. I'm not part of any secret society. If these Sentinel Witches still exist, I haven't met any of them."

Sean snorted, and when she gave him a confused frown, he changed it into a cough. Her godmother, Jade, was a Sentinel. It was her secret to share with Catlyn. If she hadn't, she must have good reason. Although, he doubted her secret would remain hidden much longer.

"Does it tell us how to stop the ritual and keep Bho-Ahp from coming into our world and wreaking havoc? If Hitler was his last incarnation, and it was bad then, can you imagine how much worse it will be now? Especially in today's age of computers, nuclear bombs, and global media."

"I've been trying not to think of that. It's terrifying." She picked up the book and dropped it back onto her lap. "I'll have to read it again, but I don't recall there being any magical solution. These Sentinels have attempted to destroy Bho-Ahp for centuries—perhaps even eons. Yet, here he is again, pushing his way into our world. So, I doubt we'll find an answer in here."

Sean made sure she safely entered Jade's house, then he checked in with the guards stationed around the property.

As he drove toward his parent's home, Sean ruminated about Catlyn's book and wanted to get his hands on it and read it. He might learn more about his heritage from it. *Why does she have it? Is she a Sentinel, and like me, just doesn't know it?* A shudder passed through him. From what they'd learned, Michael would attempt to abduct Catlyn soon. According to the book, her torture would be more horrible than the previous ones, if that were even possible. Sean vowed to stop it.

His drive took him past the Red Orchid. A sudden urge pressed on him to find Michael and bash in his brains. He had time to stop and still arrive at his mother's for his birthday dinner. Flipping a U-turn, Sean drove to the club. A slow drive through the club's parking lot revealed a distinct lack of Michael's or his cronies' cars. Sean checked with the club manager, and Joshua hadn't seen Michael since he'd attacked Catlyn.

Sean pulled into his parent's driveway and sat there, thinking about what his grandmother had told him his father had done to him. *How could he have stolen my memories and lied about my heritage? I'm out of my depth and putting an innocent woman's life in danger because of my ignorance. All because he was scared!* His sister, Rachael, finally came out and dragged him inside. Sean struggled to have a civil conversation with his dad. He felt obligated to stay through dessert, since his mom had made him a German chocolate cake for his birthday.

The next morning, Sean's guts writhed with anxiety about Michael not being at the club since his attack on Catlyn. Sean drove by Michael's house, knowing he risked a reprimand. But no one was there, not even the housekeeper. He drove to each of Michael's friend's houses and found the same thing. All of Sean's innate warning bells screamed at him. If this ritual sacrifice was the last big one, Michael and his cronies would have more preparation to do for it.

When Jerry tried to call them, their cell phones went directly to voice mail. The GPS on the phones showed they were at their homes, so did the lo-jack on their cars.

Throughout the day, Sean called Catlyn to ensure Michael hadn't abducted her. He called so frequently that finally, her phone would ring once and she'd answer with, "Yes, Sean, I'm here and alive," before he even said hello.

That evening, he stopped at her favorite Mexican place and picked up food before heading to Jade's.

"I have a peace offering." He gave her a timid smile and held up the bag when she answered the door.

She smiled and grabbed the bag from him. "Awesome, I'm starving! I'm not upset, Sean. I know you're worried."

She led him down the stairs and into the cozy family room. A giant flat-screen television dominated one wall with surround-sound speakers in each corner. A pub table sat in one corner with a good view of the TV over the couch. She placed a couple of place mats on the table, then opened the bag and divvied up the food.

After a few bites, he asked, "Have you found out anything yet?"

She shook her head and loaded a tortilla chip with beans, rice, and salsa. "Only that I'm screwed. These daemons are difficult to kill. It takes a special knife, made from quartz crystals, dipped in an herbal solution, and charged in the full moon. I don't have any of those things. Besides, I'm not a fighter. I don't even like to kill bugs."

"Maybe I can look through it?" He raised an eyebrow and tried to keep his voice calm. He had such a knife. At the thought, his back where it rode next to his skin warmed. "I might notice something you missed."

She considered it a moment before nodding once. "Sure. I'm too close. All I can see when I read it is me hanging over a pentacle, and being horribly tortured, while I'm still alive and screaming. The more the sacrifice screams in pain, apparently the more Bho-Ahp likes it. Sick bastard."

Sean shuddered. He'd seen the aftereffects of that torture. The pictures didn't show the horror of the real thing. "Michael has disappeared and so have his cronies."

"That can't be good." Catlyn put down her fork.

"My thoughts too. Promise me you'll stay here and inside? We can at least make it more difficult for him to get to you."

She pursed her lips, her face paler than normal. "I will. But I doubt it will matter."

Sean glanced at the immense TV with rows of DVDs lining the shelves on either side of it. "Let's watch a movie," Sean suggested. "It'll take your mind off things."

"Sure, what do you like to watch? Jade has a wide variety to choose from." Catlyn slid off the tall chair and gathered the trash.

"You choose. I'm up for almost anything." He wandered over and glanced at the titles. "But not horror, okay? We have enough of that in real life to contend with."

She shuddered. "I agree."

He settled onto the comfy couch and watched as she searched the movies, then plucked one out.

"How's this?" she asked, holding it up with a raise of her eyebrows.

Sean chuckled at the light romantic comedy she'd picked. "That will do. I could use a laugh."

Catlyn put the movie on and sat on the opposite end of the couch. Before long, both her cats wandered into the room. The orange tabby curled up in her lap, while the gray one perched behind Sean. He reached up and petted her. A few moments later, the cat eased onto his lap, purring.

"Huh. Mittens usually doesn't like strange men," Catlyn said, glancing over. "You must have good energy, Sean."

Ducking his head and smiling, he continued to pet the cat. It reminded him of his grandmother's *Cait Sidhe*. He switched into his witch-sight and sighed with disappointment. Mittens was simply a cat.

When he left that night, he had the book tucked under his arm and a smile on his face. Even with all the terrible shit in the world and surrounding them, he'd had a good time watching the movie with Catlyn.

The heavy tome weighed on his mind. It excited him to learn about his history as a Sentinel Witch. He had to stop the gruesome ritual Michael had planned. Bho-Ahp's evil couldn't be allowed into the world again. In the morning, he'd call his Granny Eileen. She had to know more about it than she'd let on so far. He grimaced. Of course she did. The old woman loved her secrets.

After Sean left, Catlyn lay on her bed, her cats curled up next to her. She put aside the novel she'd been attempting to read. The gruesome images of the final ritual for Bho-Ahp to cross into their world kept intruding on the story. She wished she hadn't read about it in the Sentinel's journal.

Dropping her face into her hands, she considered what she'd learned. Bho-Ahp materializing on this plane of existence would plunge the world into chaos and violence. Millions of people would die, while the Daemon King would enslave the rest. She couldn't allow that to happen.

Maak's presence pushed closer to the surface.

"Is there a way to stop Bho-Ahp?" Catlyn asked, hopeful, but not expecting an answer from the being who shared her body.

"Yes, it's one reason why I am in this dimension."

Catlyn jumped when the massive white tiger appeared before her and sat on her haunches. Maak's head was level with her own.

"The Goddess chose you for this task, and I agreed to help. Together we will do more than stop Bho-Ahp. The daemon believes you are the key to bring him across the portal. But with me here, we can destroy him." Maak's intense hatred burned through Catlyn.

Catlyn remembered her vision of being a High Priestess, protecting the world's portals. "Why me?"

"You have faced Bho-Ahp before, in other lifetimes. Your encounters always ended in failure. However, this time you will succeed because now I am here to help you."

Her chest tightened and her stomach knotted at Maak's words. While Catlyn had read the Sentinel's tome, she'd experienced several incidences of déjà vu. Maak only confirmed what Catlyn had sensed.

"Not to be rude or anything, but how will it be different with you here? The Sentinels have tried to destroy him for centuries, and they've failed every time."

"We will succeed precisely because I am with you." Maak flexed her front paws, her long claws extending a moment before retracting. *"I am not fully in either the physical or the non-physical plane. We must attack Bho-Ahp simultaneously from both realms. While I fight the daemon in the non-physical, you will fight his physical host."*

"Why now? What's changed? Why haven't you come to help before this?"

"I was not ready." Maak shared an image of her as a young cub. *"Nor were you."*

"I'm not ready now," Catlyn protested. She stood and paced around the room. The space limited by the presence of the tiger. "I'm not a fighter. I don't have a clue how to fight Michael or Bho-Ahp."

"That isn't true. You have training. You know what to do."

Doubt assailed Catlyn. Most of her magical training focused on healing people, not to fight or harm them. Her minuscule martial arts training she'd done with Jade might help, but she hadn't ever been in a real fight. Just because she'd fought Bho-Ahp in a previous life didn't mean she could fight him—and win—in this one.

"I don't know what to do!" Catlyn wailed. "I can't do this."

"You must!" Maak stalked toward her, her tail flicking in agitation. *"Remember your vision of becoming the High Priestess. That power, and more, is within you. I will help you access it. You can do this, otherwise, I would not be here. The Goddess has called us to fight this evil, and She will provide the way for our success. But we must hurry. There is not much time to prepare before the final ritual."*

Maak paused and when she spoke again, regret filled her voice, and her cerulean-blue eyes held something akin to pity. *"You need to be part of the ritual for us to destroy Bho-Ahp. It will be our only chance. He is weakest when transferring into a new host."*

Maak's implication slammed into Catlyn. She broke out into a cold sweat. The room swirled around her, and she stumbled, leaning heavily on the bed's footboard. Maak was suggesting she place herself in mortal danger in an attempt to kill a monster, a daemon. One no one had managed to kill in centuries—perhaps eons. Catlyn had always believed she had a specific reason, a purpose, for her life. Was this it? To protect the Earth from Bho-Ahp's evil?

"I'm to be bait." Catlyn's heart raced as cold fear slid down her spine. The scenes from Sean's crime photos zipped through her head. She could only imagine the agony and terror they'd endured while Michael tortured them. The final ritual promised to be much, much worse. Her stomach lurched, and she ran to the bathroom and retched, emptying her stomach until only bile came up.

After cleaning up, she returned to the bedroom where Maak waited. Boots cautiously peered at her from over the edge of the footboard, while Mittens curled up between the tiger's massive paws.

"Do ... do you have a plan?"

Maak dipped her huge head, not meeting Catlyn's eyes. *"Indeed. I do."*

As Maak detailed her plan, Catlyn bit her lip to keep from screaming in terror. Her part in it would test her strength of will to the limit, physically, emotionally, and spiritually.

Even as she trembled in fear, she changed into workout clothes to begin her intense training with Maak. Relieved to discover her fight with Bho-Ahp would be magical instead of physical, Catlyn dove wholeheartedly into her lessons. For them to succeed, she needed to learn so much from her past lives. All before the black moon on Friday. Her training built upon the magical foundations she'd learned from Jade and involved sigils, chants, and her personal magic.

It would be just her—and Maak—against the daemon prince.

 # CHAPTER 27 

Sean stayed up all night reading, and by the time he finished, despair pressed down on him. He had hoped the Sentinel book would detail how to stop Bho-Ahp from manifesting. Instead, it dealt with how to banish him back to his world once he'd crossed over to theirs. And it hadn't been his family's journal, but a McConner and MacGreggor family.

He needed to talk to a Sentinel who lived in this century. He called his granny.

"I'll be there as soon as I can," she said when he mentioned Bho-Ahp's name.

He had enough time to shower, shave, dress, and make coffee before his grandmother knocked on the door.

"Sean, my dear boy, you look awful." Eileen kissed his cheek. As she entered the house, her black cat, Dahlyah, slipped in at her side.

He raised his eyebrows. Dahlyah yawned at him, then leaped onto the back of the couch.

"I didn't sleep at all last night. I was reading that." He pointed to the book lying on the coffee table.

Her eyes widened. "Where on earth did ye get this? We thought it lost forever."

"It's Catlyn's. It dropped on her head in some used bookstore."

Eileen laughed. "They usually have a way of doing that when they find their owners." She sat on the couch and reverently picked up the book. "This book disappeared many years ago. Does Jade know Catlyn has it?"

Sean shook his head, frowning. "I haven't seen Jade since Saturday. For someone so concerned over Catlyn's welfare, she's been absent an awful lot."

"Now, don't be too hard on her, Sean. Jade's doing all she can to protect Catlyn."

"Like what?"

Before Eileen could answer, the doorbell rang. When he opened the door, Jade slumped in apparent fatigue, dark circles under her eyes.

Next to her stood his best friend, Charlie. His cop senses tingled, and he suspected why Jade was on his doorstep. But Charlie? Was he a Sentinel Witch too?

"Close your mouth and let us in." Charlie pushed past Sean to enter the house. "Eileen! It's so good to see you again." Charlie pulled Eileen into a hug. "You look as beautiful as ever."

Sean gaped as his grandmother blushed.

"Do I smell coffee?" Jade asked. "I sure could use a cup. I'm beat. I've been up seventy-two hours straight, searching for that bastard."

"Yeah, I just brewed a fresh pot." Sean felt better knowing Catlyn's godmother had been doing something. He walked into the kitchen, fixed a tray with mugs, sugar, cream, and heated water for tea for his grandmother. She abhorred coffee. When he came out, Charlie and Jade were staring at the book, awe on their faces. Sean handed out mugs.

"So, Charlie," he said, glaring at his friend. "Does this mean you're a Sentinel, too? Why didn't you tell me?"

Charlie ducked his head and grinned. "I've been dying to tell you. But after the fit your dad pitched, I wasn't about to let him know I'd chosen to become a Sentinel. He would've banned me from your house. I didn't want to lose your friendship, bro."

"Don't be faulting, Charlie, boy," Eileen rebuked Sean. "It be your father to blame. But that's over and done with now. We can initiate you more fully once we've taken care of this mess."

"Where did you get this book, Sean?" Jade asked, holding it to her chest. Her eyes glistened with moisture.

"Catlyn had it."

Jade lowered her head, and her voice quivered when she spoke. "That makes sense. These books have a way of finding their own. It's her family's history. It vanished when her father, Ian, was killed. I've searched for years to find it."

"Her father?" Sean leaned back. "She never talks about him. Was he a Sentinel?"

"Yes. But she doesn't know it." Jade took a deep breath, her voice steadier. "He died when she was little. Due to the circumstances at the time, we felt it would be safer for her if she was unaware of us. I've been her godmother, mentor, and protector ever since his death. Have you read the book?"

Sean nodded and sank into his recliner. "Have you?"

Jade and Eileen shook their heads.

"Each Sentinel family keeps their own journals," Eileen explained. "And we detail different aspects of fighting demons and our magic in case the books fall into the wrong hands. We learned that the hard way during the Inquisitions. The McConner family kept the secret of the summoning rituals. Is it in there? Does it describe what rituals are necessary for summoning Bho-Ahp?"

"It does." Sean held out his hand for the book. Jade reluctantly gave it to him. He opened it to the now familiar pages. "This is the ritual, and it's nearly complete." He showed them the picture.

"Damn, damn, damn." Jade swore. "We hoped it was another daemon being summoned."

"You know about the murders?" Sean glared at Charlie. "You told them about them? I shared it with you in confidence."

"Hey, man," Charlie held up his hands. "Calm down. I didn't tell them anything. We've been to all the ritual sites." He paused, looking away before mumbling, "Before you saw them."

Sean surged to his feet and towered over Charlie. "What? You've known about this and haven't stopped it?"

"Sean, Sean," his grandmother pulled on his pant leg, "sit down. 'Tisn't Charlie's fault."

"Sean, we've tried." Charlie ran his hand through his hair. "We've been doing our damnedest to stop this. We'd sense the ritual starting, and by the time we found where it was being held, it would be too late. The victims were beyond saving. You can't imagine what it was like to hear their pleas for help and their rattled last breaths as we fought the demon spawn to get to them. The leader always escaped, using a translocation spell to pop out as soon as we entered the building. Do you know who it is?"

"Michael Drogger." Sean spat. "I've suspected him all along, but now I have proof. He's already chosen the final sacrifice, the one to finish the summoning." He looked significantly at Jade.

Her face drained of color, and she threw a hand over her mouth. "No, not Catlyn." She exchanged a significant look with Eileen that Sean couldn't quite understand.

"He marked her when he attacked her," Sean growled. He turned the page to the illustration of the last sacrifice and pointed to it. Although he averted his eyes, he could still see it. The gruesome scene had been burned into his brain. Sean hadn't thought there could be any worse torture than what the previous victims had experienced. He'd been wrong.

"We can't allow him to take her. She'd never survive having that done to her."

Eileen leaned over and gasped at the picture, before covering her mouth with her hand and squeezing her eyes shut. After a brief struggle, she regathered her composure. "You said he marked her? How?"

"He cut her neck, then licked the blood."

"Shite!" Eileen stared at her cat. After a few moments, she turned back to them. "Dahlyah says there isn't any way to remove the mark. With Bho-Ahp's power, he'll be able to find her no matter where we hide her."

"She's staying at my place," Jade said. "She should be safe there with all the protective spells and sigils I've laid on it."

Eileen shook her head. "That won't work. Those will help make it more difficult for him, but eventually, he'll locate her."

"So why don't we kill Michael?" Charlie tightened his hands into fists.

"Yeah, why haven't you?" Sean snapped.

Jade crossed her arms. "Yes, we've known a daemon was being called since the first sacrifice, but we couldn't determine who was doing the summoning. Bho-Ahp protects his own, cloaking their identities from us. Our organization has been hunting the culprit as long as you have. Believe me, we wanted to catch him even more than you did. We *knew* what he was doing and how bad it would be if he completed the ritual. There will be thousands, no millions, killed if Bho-Ahp manages to materialize on our plane."

"But Charlie told you who I suspected." Sean glared in accusation at Charlie. "Didn't that help you?"

"I wish it had." Jade sighed, placing her coffee mug with a clink on the glass table. "He has strong protective spells we can't break. We can't get near him. Until now, there wasn't any proof of his involvement. We don't go half-cocked and take out civilians. We have to have evidence, like you do, to put down any humans."

"Do you know where he is, Sean?" Eileen asked.

"No, dammit, I don't, Granny. The bastard has disappeared. He isn't at any of his usual haunts, and neither are his friends."

"I wasn't able to find him either," Jade admitted, slumping back on the couch.

Sean glanced back at the open book, then slammed it shut. There had to be a way to save Catlyn. He couldn't let her suffer through that horror.

"Any idea when the final ritual needs to take place?" Charlie asked.

Sean nodded bleakly. "Catlyn figured it out. Black moon, which is this Friday."

"Then we do everything in our power to protect Catlyn." Jade fisted her hands. Determination filled her eyes. "To stop Bho-Ahp from crossing the portal, all we have to do is prevent Michael from taking her. It's only for the next four days. That should be doable."

"I don't think it's going to be that easy," Eileen replied. "We are dealing with a daemon prince. He is only slightly less powerful than the Daemon King. Let's assume he can break through any protection spells we put in place."

Jade's eyes hardened. "Then we prepare as much as we can."

"What do you propose?" Sean asked, sinking onto the arm of the couch next to his grandmother.

"We cast a tracking spell on her, and you give her a mundane device."

"That's it? Tracking devices?" Sean threw his hands into the air. "You can't be serious!"

"The tracking will give us the means to follow them to the ritual site in the event Michael somehow breeches our spells. We'll get there before Michael starts the ritual, and kill him. That will prevent Bho-Ahp from entering our world."

"You'd use her as bait?"

"I don't like it any better than you do," Jade snapped. "She's my goddaughter!"

His grandmother reached over and placed her hand over his. "Sean, my boy, believe me, if there were any other way, we'd do it. We don't like putting innocents in harm's way. We'll do all we can to protect Catlyn. But more innocent lives will be destroyed if Bho-Ahp completes the crossing into this world. The violence and wars that plague the world now will be nothing compared to what he will bring. He's a daemon prince and commands armies of demons."

Sean ducked his head to hide the moisture in his eyes. The woman he was falling in love with was going to be put into a horrible situation. Sharp pains stabbed his heart at the thought. But his grandmother was correct. They had to stop Bho-Ahp, even if it meant placing Catlyn in danger.

"Okay," he said quietly, not looking up. "What do we need to do?"

Throughout the night, Catlyn worked with Maak. She finally stopped in the afternoon, hungry and exhausted. Peering into the fridge for something to eat, she pushed back her sweat-soaked hair. She pulled out sandwich makings, and as she slathered mayonnaise on bread slices, Jade walked into the kitchen. Behind her trailed Sean, Charlie, and an elderly woman she didn't know. Catlyn gulped, embarrassed by her unkempt appearance.

"This is my grandmother, Eileen." Sean introduced the older woman, who wore a royal purple top over a brightly patterned skirt.

Smiling at the audacity of the older woman's bright red hair, Catlyn instantly liked Sean's grandmother with her quick smile and kind energy. Catlyn hoped when she was old, she'd have some of the same flair.

"Catlyn, we need to talk." Jade folded her arms across her chest.

"Let her finish making her lunch, Jade," Eileen admonished. "Can't you see the girl is famished?"

Catlyn gave Eileen a grateful smile. She could manage being sleep deprived for a day or two, which seemed likely with as hard as Maak was pushing her. But she couldn't survive without food. Her stomach grumbled a loud protest.

Jade wrinkled her nose at Catlyn. "What on earth have you been doing?"

"Working out." She glanced at Sean, dreading the coming conversation. She wished she could sprint upstairs and take a quick shower before the confrontation with Jade—and Sean. Neither her godmother nor Sean would like what she needed to tell them.

While the others went into the living room to wait for her, Catlyn finished constructing her sandwiches and bit deeply into one. She fought against the urge to stuff the whole thing in her mouth. As it was, she was glad she'd made two. The intense magical training with Maak drained her. Catlyn carried her second sandwich to join the others, curling up on the couch.

Jade looked between the three other people, then took a deep breath. "We need to talk about this thing with Michael."

"Yes, we do. You won't like—"

"—You need ... sorry." Jade pursed her lips, her hands clamped tightly together between her knees. "Why don't you go first."

Catlyn gulped and closed her eyes. Maak's warm energy wrapped around her, supporting her. She could do this. "I have to let Michael find me."

Jade's eyes widened. "While it's possible, highly unlikely, but possible, for him to get past my protection, we won't just 'let' Michael find you! But in case he does, we'll put both magical and mundane trackers on you so we can locate you and stop the ritual before it starts—"

"—And kill Michael," Sean added, a hard gleam in his eye.

"No, *you* aren't capable of killing him." Catlyn rubbed her arms. "And you can't stop the ritual. I have to participate in the final ritual in order to stop Bho-Ahp. There is no other way."

"No!" Sean exploded onto his feet. He thrust a hand through his hair. Haggardness pulled at his face like he hadn't slept much last night.

"You can't be part of it. Catlyn, you've seen the pictures and read the descriptions. You know what it involves. *It will kill you.* There has to be another way."

"There isn't." Catlyn reached for Sean. He looked down at her with such concern, her throat tightened. Even with Maak's help and the training Catlyn was doing, she still might not survive the encounter with Bho-Ahp. She wanted to live through it, to see the budding romance with Sean bloom.

Swallowing hard, she pushed the words through her uncooperative throat. "If you kill Michael, it will only stop Bho-Ahp from manifesting now. In a few years, he'll try again and again until he succeeds. But there is a way to destroy Bho-Ahp once and for all. And to do that, we must let the ritual begin." Catlyn paused.

Maak insisted Sean had an important role, too. Somehow, he fit into the energy stream that needed to form to annihilate Bho-Ahp. Catlyn frowned at Sean. He didn't do any magic. With a name like Sean McLarkin, she had taken him to be a good Catholic boy who would stay away from such things. Then she remembered he had attended the full moon ritual with her. Perhaps he was more open to magic than she expected.

"Um ... Sean ... you need to be there too."

"She's right, my boy," Eileen added, rubbing her chin. "Dahlyah says for it to work—whatever 'it' is—you must be there." She cocked her head and studied Catlyn. "You just might be the one to pull this off. There is great power in you, sweet girl. Sean, I know you don't like it, but we've been trying to destroy Bho-Ahp for a very, very long time. We have to take the opportunity she's willing to give us."

"We?" Catlyn's eyebrows furrowed.

"Yes, we." Eileen smiled and motioned to include all of them. "The Sentinel Witches."

Catlyn slumped into the couch cushions. "They still exist? I didn't think they did."

A wide smile crossed Jade's face. She patted Catlyn's hand. "We've been around for many millennia. You're also a Sentinel, at least, you can be. Your father was one. It's his family's book you've been reading."

"My father was a Sentinel? Tell me about him, please Jade." Catlyn had only a name, not even a picture of her father. It had never bothered her before; you can't miss what you don't have. But now, a pang of longing pierced her heart.

"I will. After this is all over," Jade promised.

"Now, darlin'," Eileen said, leaning forward, "what do you need from us? How can we help you?"

Catlyn looked around at the faces watching her. She wouldn't be doing this alone. Gratitude eased her anxiety. She focused on Sean's face. He was becoming more than a friend. It soothed her soul to know he would be at her side through her ordeal. She took a deep breath and outlined Maak's plan.

 # Chapter 28 

The next morning, the marine layer coming off the Pacific was more dense than usual. The clouds held a hint of rain, making the day dark and gloomy. It seemed fitting for what could be Catlyn's last day of freedom—or life.

Sean and Jade joined her for breakfast. Catlyn didn't want to eat, but Jade insisted. In too short a time, she'd leave the safety of Jade's protection to become bait for a monster. Her stomach roiled. It was an effort to take each tasteless bite. They didn't know exactly when Michael would find her; no one had seen him since the night he'd attacked her. They ate what could be her last meal in silence.

Finished with breakfast, Catlyn found her cats and gave them what could be their last loves from her. Tears trickled down her face and wet their fur. They'd be safe here—or so she hoped. Terror washed over her at the thought of Michael doing something to her pets to draw her out—and make her more afraid. Bho-Ahp thrived on human fear. He kept coming back to this plane because there was so much of it here. Once here, it was easy for him to generate even more terror to feed off.

Jade came into Catlyn's room and sat on the edge of the bed. "Don't worry. I'll take care of your cats. You remember how to activate the tracking spell?"

Catlyn nodded.

"Good. I'll be there, right behind you, keeping watch over you. I can't tell you how proud I am of you. Not only for doing this, but for the amazing woman you've become. Your dad would be proud, too." Moisture glinted in her eyes, and she pulled Catlyn into a tight hug. "I love you like my own daughter, Catlyn."

The two women sat there hugging and crying for a long time, until Jade finally pulled away, wiping her eyes. It took all of Catlyn's meager courage to pick up her bag and go down the stairs.

Sean waited in the living room for her. He walked to the door and stopped, his hand on the doorknob. "Are you sure you want to do this?"

"No, I don't want to, but I have to." Catlyn placed a hand on his cheek. "You'll be there, watching over me, so I know I'll be okay. Thank you."

He nodded tersely and opened the door.

They drove in silence. The drive from Newport Beach to Anaheim seemed to take hours instead of the half hour. Before getting out of the car, Catlyn glanced around, surprised when no black sedans skulked. Her fingers traced the scab on her neck. Her stalkers had disappeared after Michael "marked" her. He must not need them any longer to keep tabs on her.

Sean stayed in his car while she trudged up the stairs. She threw open the door and stopped on the threshold.

Home...

Her apartment wasn't much, but it was all she had to call home. It felt different, empty and sad without her cats. She took a deep breath and blinked back the tears; she'd cried enough already with Jade. Dropping her bag on the floor, Catlyn curled up in a ball on the couch to wait.

She waited for death to come and claim her.

The images of the grisly photos Sean had shown her of Michael's previous victims paraded before her. Those were just a prelude to this last ritual—her ritual—which would be much worse. After quite a while, Catlyn rubbed her face. If she kept thinking about it, she'd be a hysterical mess whenever Michael showed up. Then she wouldn't be able to do her part in destroying the beast.

Catlyn pushed off the couch and paced the living room—then stopped. It would be a dead give away to Michael that she expected him. What did people do when they were waiting for death to come knocking on their door?

First, she cleaned her apartment. When she reached her bedroom, dirty clothes spilled from the hamper. She hadn't done her laundry before being whisked to Jade's place. Filling a laundry basket, she headed to the laundry room in the next building. She paused at the top of the steps, surprised at the darkness blanketing the apartment complex. As she turned on the washer, she considered fixing some soup for dinner, but her stomach balked at the thought of food.

Later, Catlyn pulled her first load from the dryer and trudged up the stairs with her filled laundry basket. As soon as she pushed open her front door, she sensed something was wrong. She peered over the pile of clean towels.

"You!" she shouted, hoping Sean heard her over the wire. "How did you get in here?"

"I have my ways," Michael practically purred. "I told you I'd be seeing you again. When you were ripe." He breathed in deeply through his nose. "And my, you are so ripe."

Catlyn froze in fear, the basket shaking in her hands. Maak prodded her, reminding her she couldn't let Michael take her without a struggle. They didn't want him knowing she wanted to go with him. Catlyn tossed the basket at him, towels flying everywhere, and ran past him.

Michael threw back his head and laughed. "Oh good! I love playing cat and mouse. Run, little mousy, run."

Catlyn stumbled over the broom propped next to the kitchen doorway. She grabbed it, remembering her Uncle Robert telling her the best weapon a woman could use in her home was a broom—both ends were effective.

Sprinting through her bedroom door, she slammed it shut and locked it. She kicked away a pile of clothes waiting to be washed and stood facing the door, the broom held across her body like a staff. It trembled, and she prayed she'd remember her martial arts training.

The air pressure in the room built, pressing down on her, and clogging her ears. She heard a "pop" as the pressure released. Michael appeared, standing in front of the still closed door.

"Oh, ho, a mouse with a stick," Michael snickered. "But, see here, little mousy, this cat has claws." A long, wickedly sharp dagger appeared in his hand.

He swung at Catlyn over-handed. She raised the broom and blocked it. Surprise flitted across his face before he sneered and struck again. She brought the broom handle across her body, blocking his knife, then whirled the broom around, thrusting the bristle end at his face. He jumped back and she followed up with an overhand strike. Catlyn tried to keep the shock from her face; her fighting ability and speed were more than even she expected.

Michael attacked with a flurry of strikes, which she blocked with ease. Maak's assistance was making her fight too well. She didn't want to give away Maak's presence. Michael's smugness changed to frustration, anger flickered in his eyes. Frustration she wanted, anger not so much. He might forget what he wanted her for and do some serious damage to her. A quick death would be better for her, but not for the world.

She deliberately slowed her speed and began breathing hard, as if she was out of breath. Michael's dagger swung toward her, and she purposely missed blocking it, hissing in pain as it sliced across her forearm. She glanced down. It didn't seem too deep, but it stung like hell.

"You son-of-a-bitch," Catlyn spat. She hadn't heard anything from Sean yet. *Is the wire working?*

"I told you this cat has claws, little mousy." Michael snickered and swung again, this time nicking the back of her hand. "This is just the appetizer. There is much, much more waiting for you. Don't worry, our cop friend won't even realize you're missing—that is, until it's too late to save you. Poor Sean, always too late, always too stupid, to see what's in front of him."

"So, how are you going to get me out of here? You 'popped' in. I can't imagine your little appearing trick is real or that you can take someone with you."

"Oh, it's real. Compliments of my master, who you'll meet shortly." Michael lunged at her.

Her slightly off block resulted in a slice across her left bicep, adding to her numerous cuts. She grimaced against the searing pain. Doubts seeped into her mind, and she regretted agreeing to this mad plan. How could she go through with this? The pain was too much already, and it was only the beginning of what she'd have to endure. She drew in a deep breath to scream for Sean, for Jade, for anyone to stop this madness.

Michael glanced at the bedside clock. "Enough of this game. Time to go." The dagger disappeared. Michael raised his hand, forming a ball of energy. He flung it toward her.

"Oh, shit!" Catlyn tossed up the magical shield she'd been practicing. It wouldn't stop the magical attack, just weaken it. The ball hit her.

It hurt like hell. She screamed.

She vaguely heard Michael laughing as he picked her up and tossed her over his shoulder. Layered beneath his voice was a deeper, more sinister laugh.

Bho-Ahp.

Sean watched Catlyn bravely walk up the stairs to her apartment, her head and shoulders thrown back, and her back rigid. He didn't know if he could be so courageous to be the bait for a madman. When she shut the door, he wondered if he'd ever see her again alive and healthy. It took all his willpower to stay in the car and not run after her.

He parked in an empty parking spot and joined Jade and Charlie in the back of the Sentinel's black panel van. They had a good view of Catlyn's apartment. The door slid shut and Sean blinked. All the gear and gadgets inside would make a police surveillance van weep with envy. Then the passenger captain's seat swiveled around, and he swore.

"Granny Eileen, what are you doing here? This isn't safe for you."

His grandmother wore the same tight-fitting black cargo pants and long-sleeved shirt as the other Sentinels. She'd strapped a crystal dagger to one leg and a sword to the other. The numerous pockets of her pants bulged.

"Ach, Sean, my boy," she said, "I've been fighting these nasties since before you were born. I can handle myself better than you can. You're the untrained one here. If I had my way, *you'd* be the one not included in our little party. But Catlyn insists on having you here, so behave."

Sean ducked his head. "Yes, Granny."

Jade, Charlie, Eileen, and three men he didn't know occupied the van. Charlie introduced him to Catlyn's other bodyguards. Todd Fleming was a tall, well-built man who wore his brunette hair in a long ponytail. Dilan McGowan had red hair and green eyes.

A man with close-cut dark-blond hair had his back to them, his focus on the computer and monitors. He turned around long enough to nod at Sean. "Collin Drennan, here. The computer wizard."

He swiveled his chair back around, and Sean leaned forward. The Sentinels had set up surveillance cameras inside Catlyn's apartment. A split screen showed the living room and kitchen area on one side and her bedroom on the other.

His heart went out when Catlyn curled up on the couch, looking helpless and scared. He wished he could be with her. Eileen passed around mugs of coffee from a thermos carafe and the team settled in to wait. No one knew when Michael would show up.

Catlyn spent the first hours laying forlornly on her couch. He imagined her mentally shaking herself as she stood, then paced. Then she cleaned her home. She sorted her laundry, stuffed a large load of towels into a basket, and headed for the front door.

"No, no, no!" Jade slammed a fist on her thigh. "She's supposed to stay inside. We don't have any cameras outside of her apartment."

"I'll go watch her." Charlie levered off his chair.

Sean put up a hand to stop him. "Michael has seen you with me. You'll tip him off." He glanced at the others sitting tensely in the van before his eyes fell on his Granny Eileen, then frowned. In her current getup, she looked like a commando, not a harmless grandmother.

"I'll go." Eileen twirled her seat around and rummaged on the floor. Then she stepped out of the van and slipped on a long, animal print raincoat. It covered her commando outfit, making her appear like an eccentric old lady. It worked until you noticed her hard eyes that were all business.

She hurried toward the laundry room. As she neared it, her strong steps slowed to a shuffle, and she leaned forward, immediately looking like a frail, harmless old woman. Her pace slow enough that before she reached the laundry room, Catlyn had come out and retreated up the stairs. As soon as she shut her door again, Eileen straightened up and strode back to the van.

"I didn't see or sense anything." Eileen slid the door shut. "It's quiet out there, almost too quiet."

"I'll go make sure we have eyes in the laundry room." Collin gathered some equipment, then hurried outside. A few minutes later, another screen came online showing the added video feed.

They continued to wait with Catlyn. Everything indicated Michael had to begin the final ritual today in order for it to be finished by the black moon. They needed to ensure that it didn't. Normally, it would take three days to do the ritual. The first two consisted of torturing the victim. Somehow, this completed preparing Michael's body to accept the daemon's possession and integrate with it. The third day opened the portal and allowed the daemon to cross into this world.

Sean watched Catlyn carry the load of towels up the stairs. When she stopped on the threshold, he knew something was wrong. He leaned forward and searched the other screens. Michael stood in her living room.

"How did he get in there?" Sean shouted at the same time Catlyn asked Michael the same thing.

Jade swore. "He just appeared! It's that damned translocation spell he uses. It allows him to pop in and out of places."

Sean leaped to his feet, fully intending to run in and stop Michael.

"No, Sean!" Charlie stood in front of him, blocking the van door. "You can't go in there yet. You know what has to happen. None of us like it anymore than you do. Catlyn *will* survive this."

"Good girl." Pride filled Eileen's voice.

Sean whirled around in time to see Catlyn grab a broom, run into her bedroom, and slam the door shut. Michael strode down the hall. In one moment to the next, he disappeared, then reappeared on the other side of the door with a long, wavy dagger in his hand. Sean watched, transfixed, as the two fought. Catlyn moving with a speed and agility he hadn't thought she possessed. She faltered and a bright line of blood appeared on her forearm. Michael continued to attack her until he glanced at the clock. Then he flung a ball of light at Catlyn. She screamed when it hit her, then dropped to the floor, unconsciousness.

Michael laughed as he picked her up, and a moment later, they vanished.

Sean stared at the screen, unable to believe what he'd seen. He had expected Michael to use some kind of vehicle they could follow, not some fucking magic spell.

"Where are they?" Sean demanded. "Where are they?" He turned to the computer tech. "Is the tracking device working?"

Collin shook his head. "That damned translocation spell wiped out the signal. It isn't transmitting."

"What about your tracking spell?" Sean asked Jade.

Her eyes were closed, and she mumbled some words, drawing symbols in the air. Her eyes flew open. "No. She didn't have time to activate it before he knocked her out. Or they've gone beyond my reach."

"We have to find her!" Sean banged on the side of the van. "Come on people, find a way to locate her."

They tried both magical and mundane means, to no avail. The night deepened and Eileen pressed a cup of coffee and a sandwich into Sean's hands. He looked at them, perplexed. His stomach was too tied up in knots to eat. After a moment, he placed them on the counter by the computer.

He wandered up to Catlyn's apartment, walking carefully to avoid stepping on her scattered clean towels. His feet took him to her bedroom. Standing in the doorway, he tried to assess the scene dispassionately as a police detective. The broom she'd used to defend herself lay in pieces. Drops of blood spattered the carpet, her bedspread, and the walls. She'd fought well until the end.

Sean switched to his witch-sight, hoping it would offer clues of where Michael had disappeared. When nothing appeared, Sean swore and slammed a fist into the wall. He stood there for a long time, his head against the wall, fighting the despair threatening to overwhelm him. They'd all believed they could track her, either mundanely or magically. That she would be safe if she allowed Michael to abduct her.

They'd failed her.

He failed her.

 # CHAPTER 29 

Catlyn either passed out or the translocation spell blocked all sensory input. The next thing she knew, Michael dropped her on a hard, concrete floor. Biting her lip, she stifled her groan to keep from alerting Michael that she was awake. She mumbled the incantation to activate the tracking spell, hoping it or Sean's tracking device would lead them to her in time. She surreptitiously looked around where Michael had dumped her.

In the dim lighting, she could barely make out the confines of the room. It seemed to be a basement of some sorts. But that didn't make any sense because there were few basements in Southern California—something to do with the water table and earthquakes. Had Michael taken her out of state? The thought terrified her. If so, there wouldn't be any rescue from Sean or Jade.

"Maak," Catlyn asked in her mind, "can they find us?"

"Yes. Both trackers are working. We are far from your home, though. It will take several hours for them to arrive. I'll help you hang on until it is time."

Michael moved around the room, humming as he gathered tools and implements that Catlyn didn't want to think about what they were for. It seemed even sadistic bastards could find joy in their work.

While he was otherwise occupied, Catlyn chanted, singing under her breath, the spell that would block most of the pain to come. It wouldn't prevent all of it; she still had to react to it.

Her pain and terror added to the energy that would open the portal for Bho-Ahp to materialize into this world. He had to cross the threshold in order for her and Maak to defeat him. His weakest point would be after he crossed and before he possessed Michael. Even with the spell, she didn't look forward to the next few hours. When the time came, she hoped she'd be strong enough to do her part.

She soon heard the sound of chains being lowered. Her body trembled. Her self-preservation instinct overrode her logic, and she couldn't stop struggling to move, to get out of there.

Catlyn pushed off the floor and onto her feet, swaying as a wave of dizziness assailed her. She blinked it away and staggered toward the door she'd seen, hoping it led to the stairs and out of this place.

Michael laughed. "Oh, good, you're awake. I had expected you to sleep a bit longer. But no matter. I would have woken you soon, anyway. It is much more effective, not to mention more fun, when the victim is aware of what is happening to them."

A robed figure materialized out of the dark and blocked her path to the door. She turned, searching for another escape route.

"Good, little mousy," Michael cackled. "Run, mousy, run. It gets the blood moving."

Her growl at him held more than a little of Maak's voice in it. She hated it when he called her a mouse. A tiger shared her body. He'd soon find out who was the larger cat. Both Catlyn and Maak fought the urge to shred his belly and snap his neck between their jaws. Now wasn't the time. She debated about whether to oblige him and run, or conserve her energy. Her eyes fell on the instruments he had laid out.

She obliged him and ran.

The chase didn't last long. More robed figures stepped out of the dark, blocking her way, herding her back to where Michael stood waiting. When she dashed past him, he whipped out his hand and grabbed her arm in a vise-like grip. Even though she knew it was useless, she struggled against him, her survival instinct still working overtime.

"Such a good, obedient, little mouse." Michael slapped a manacle on her wrist.

She slammed her other fist in his face and smiled at the satisfying crunch of his nose breaking.

He roared in pain. "Bitch!"

Before she could attack him again, one of the large, robed figures punched her in the kidney. Another monk clapped on the other manacle. The chain clinked, raising her arms above her head. It continued to clink until she was high enough for Michael to have clear access to all of her body. She grinned at the blood pouring from his nose.

He wiped it with the back of his hand, and without thinking, flicked the blood to the floor. It spattered across the circle, mixing his blood with that which had been used to draw the protective ring. From what she knew of magic, he'd created a weak point in the circle.

Bad move on his part. He just made his first mistake. Or is it his second?

While he was in range, she kicked out with her still free legs with all her strength. She caught him square in the chest. He doubled over gasping for breath; the wind knocked out of him.

Catlyn laughed. "I guess you're not used to mice with teeth." She bared her teeth at him, wishing for Maak's more impressive set.

"Get ... that ... fucking ... bitch ... secured," Michael gasped.

His robed followers swarmed Catlyn, grabbing her legs and attaching shackles to her ankles, forcing her legs open, spread-eagled. Glaring at her, Michael stalked toward her with a large knife.

Maybe I pissed him off enough to end this fast.

The first slash of his knife dashed her hope. The cold blade brushed against her skin, nicking it as it sliced her bodice from neck to waist. She closed her eyes against the sound of shredding fabric as Michael cut off her clothes. He didn't notice the small tracker hidden in her skirt pocket.

Hanging naked, completely exposed and vulnerable, she fought back the burning tears of shame. She refused to give him the satisfaction of breaking so early in the game. By the time Michael had divested her of clothing, she had small cuts all over her body.

I hope I'll still be in one piece when this is finished.

"You will be," Maak assured her, fiercely. *"This ritual will be much shorter than what either Michael or Bho-Ahp expects."*

"Let the ritual begin," Michael intoned.

A dark priest lit foul smelling incense in a brazier at the end of a chain. He walked around the circle, swinging the brazier and scattering the sulfur and rotting flesh scented smoke throughout the room. The other priests followed him, chanting in a language Catlyn didn't recognize. They were careful to stay on the outside of the circle and not mar the blood marking the boundaries. She counted twelve men. Michael would make the proverbial thirteen needed for magical work.

After thirteen revolutions, the blood drawn circle glowed a sickly green. The chanting priests' spell formed a dome within the circle. It would contain all the energy Michael created during her torture and focus it on opening the portal.

It would also keep any unwanted energy, spells, or people from entering.

The darkness of night eventually gave way to the soft glow of dawn. Sean paced outside the van, unable to stay cooped up in it any longer. His pacing took him to the outside of Catlyn's door. The gruesome images of Michael's other victims flooded Sean's mind. All of them wore Catlyn's face.

He glanced down at his watch. "Fuck! She's been gone for fourteen hours. I can't imagine what she's going through." He slammed his hands on the door frame. "Fuck!" *She must believe I abandoned her.*

"Think, think!" Sean leaned his head against the door, hitting his temples with his palms. "Come on, you've been chasing this guy for a long time. You know where he goes." He slumped down on the top stair, pulled out his phone, and thumbed through his files, paying attention to locations. A pattern he hadn't noticed before emerged.

He ran back to the van and threw open the sliding door, startling those inside. "I think I have an idea about the general direction where Michael has taken her. He likes the San Bernardino desert, toward Joshua Tree. If he's out there, it would explain why we can't find her. It's well out of range for my tracking device."

"It would be out of my magical range, too," Jade confirmed. She climbed to the front of the van, Eileen on her heels. Eileen took the wheel while Jade rode shotgun. She turned back. "Are you coming?"

Sean shook his head. "No, I'll take my car. Charlie, ride with me?"

Charlie tossed his gear into the trunk and climbed into the passenger seat. Sean gunned the engine and sped out, his tires squealing and leaving a trail of rubber. The van, along with another one, fell in behind him. Sean hit his flashing lights, and they made decent time getting to the 55 northbound freeway and to the 91 east.

When they reached the 60 east, he flipped them off, swearing in frustration as they came to a crawl in the heavy traffic through Riverside and Moreno Valley. His lights didn't do any good; the cars had no place to move over. When they turned onto the 117 toward Yucca Valley and Joshua Tree, the faint beep of his tracking device popped up on his laptop. At the same time, Charlie's phone rang.

"Yeah, ours just came online, too." Charlie disconnected. "Jade's tracking spell kicked in. It's weak, but enough to tell we're headed in the right direction."

Sean stepped on the accelerator. The area surrounding Joshua Tree held many small roads heading into the wilderness. He stopped for gas when they reached the town of Joshua Tree. As the tank filled, he took in the vast desert of rocks and the Joshua tree cacti marching for miles in every direction. The tracker indicated Catlyn wasn't anywhere near any towns. How would they ever find her in the unmarked territory where one cactus looked the same as the next one? He much preferred a city street with street signs as landmarks.

Charlie sauntered back to the car loaded down with a couple of sodas and a plastic bag. He handed Sean a hot dog and a soda. "You haven't eaten since last night and it's several hours past lunch. You need to eat."

Sean glared at the food and considered tossing it in the garbage, but his rumbling stomach protested. He dug in, bolting it down without tasting it, then started his car again. He studied the display on his laptop, and getting his bearings, drove east, away from town.

Away from the tether of civilization.

# CHAPTER 30 

The priests continued their dizzying walk around the circle, chanting in a dark monotone. Michael swayed as he entered into a trance. Catlyn kept her eyes averted from the tray of grisly implements standing nearby.

The Goddess Hecate floated into her consciousness. Hecate touched the center of Catlyn's forehead and whispered into her ear. As the priest's chant grew louder, Catlyn began singing a counterpoint to it under her breath. Her chant was in the same language Hecate had spoken. Catlyn didn't consciously know what the murmured words and sounds meant; but she knew on a deep, subconscious level that she had cast a spell of protection—and something more. Maak added her power to the spell.

Catlyn glanced to the circle where Michael's blood had crossed it. A small crack weakened the energy of the dome at that point. She thanked Hecate for the opportunity, then concentrated on opening it even more. Sean needed to get in when the time came.

The air became thicker, making it harder to breathe. More than the smoke from the incense created the noisome fug in the room.

"They are creating a denser atmosphere, more like Bho-Ahp's plane of existence," Maak explained. *"If we are unsuccessful, it will give him time to acclimate to the lighter gravity and higher vibrations of Earth."*

It made sense. Catlyn hoped she hadn't put herself into this position just to fail. She bent her head and focused on her chant. The pricking of a knife on her skin startled her. Michael slit open her forearm and held a chalice under the cut to catch the blood. When it was about half-full, he turned to the altar.

He lifted the cup high in offering. "Great Bho-Ahp! I bring to you an offering of blood. May it give you strength to walk on this plane." He brought it to his lips.

"May you choke on it!" Catlyn glared at the chalice.

Michael stalked to her and backhand her. Her head flew back, and her lip split.

"How dare you," he raged. "You will not mock this ceremony!"

He returned to the altar.

As he lifted the chalice to his lips, Catlyn whispered, "May it bring about your destruction!"

Michael took a drink, a large gulp, and choked. As he sputtered and coughed, Catlyn couldn't help a smug smile from creeping onto her face. He tried drinking her blood again, only to gag on it. After the third time, he gave up and poured it out in the center of the circle, mumbling under his breath. He made a circling motion with his hand; the blood followed his movement to form a smaller circle within the larger one.

"The portal will open inside the inner circle," Maak said.

Catlyn stifled a groan. She would be the main course when Bho-Ahp crossed. Michael turned back to her. His evil grin spoke of unimaginable torture. She quickly chanted the pain blocking spell Maak had taught her. Her agony was about to begin.

He picked up something from his tray, leaned down, and grasped her left foot. She screamed as he broke first one toe, then another, until he broke all of them. Heat assailed the bottom of her foot, and the horrible stink of charring flesh filled her nose. She closed her eyes and escaped into her mind, continuing to chant as Michael assaulted her body.

After leaving the town of Joshua Tree, Sean drove through an alien countryside filled with nothing but sand, sagebrush, and Joshua trees. They'd left all signs of civilization behind them, and Sean shuddered at the eerie emptiness. As a city boy, he rarely ventured into the rural areas.

They drove for miles on bumpy, dirt roads. As his undercarriage rubbed on yet another rut, Sean wished they'd brought Charlie's big Chevy truck rather than his low-to-the-ground Camaro. The beeping of his tracking device growing louder kept him going. Catlyn definitely was in this area.

Then it went silent.

"What the hell happened?" he screamed at Charlie.

"I don't know. It just stopped working." Charlie picked up his cellphone, tried to call Jade, then put it back in his shirt pocket. "No service. There isn't any cellphone service out here in the boonies. That must be what's wrong."

"Great. How are we going to find her?" Sean stopped, lowering his head to the steering wheel, trying to breathe through the tightness in his throat. A tidal wave of fear crashed over him. What horrendous torture was Catlyn enduring while they searched? Would they arrive in time to save her? At this point, he wasn't concerned about stopping the daemon; he only wanted to discover Catlyn alive.

The van behind them honked, drove off the road, and pulled up beside them. Sean rolled down his window, coughing at the cloud of dust. He peered at Jade. "My signal died. Do you have her?"

Jade gave him a thumbs up. "A surge of energy hit me at the same time. She can't be too far. We're on the right road, if you can call it that."

"I'll follow you, since your spell is working."

"Are you sure you want to continue driving that thing on this road?" Jade contemptuously sneered at his Camaro. "You can leave your car here and ride with us. It should be okay. This road doesn't get much, if any, traffic."

Sean shook his head. He'd go crazy if he didn't have his hands on the wheel and focusing on driving. Otherwise, his mind kept conjuring all manner of torture Catlyn could be—probably was—going through.

They continued on, the sun dropping lower on the horizon. Finally, a tiny house appeared ahead of them.

"This can't be it." Sean frowned as they stopped in the yard where the dirt road ended in front of the shack. He climbed out of the car and stretched, tired from sitting so long. Jade, Eileen, and the others clambered from the vans.

"This is it," Jade assured them. "This is where Catlyn and Michael are. They must be underground."

Sean switched on his witch-sight. Strange symbols appeared, glowing a sickly green. They covered the walls and several feet of the ground surrounding the house.

"This is definitely it." Eileen settled her sword harness over her hips. "There are demon sigils and spells protecting this place." She flung a hand out to stop Sean. "Not yet. Let me take these down or you'll be fried—literally."

His grandmother held out her hands, and a mist of golden light formed around them. She drew several symbols in the air, the golden light swirling like the afterglow of sparklers, but these were so bright they hurt his eyes.

"*Barra!*" Eileen commanded in a language Sean didn't know. "*Me peta babka. Me salamu tebu.*" The golden sigils zoomed to the house, blanketing it with their light. The sickly green ones blinked once, then vanished.

Eileen dusted off her hands. "Now it's safe. It shouldn't have warned those inside, but be ready in case it did." She drew her crystal sword from its sheath.

The other Sentinels had also drawn crystal daggers or swords in a rainbow of colors. The tall cactus surrounding them took on eerie shapes from the setting blood-red sun. Sean shuddered as evil seemed to crawl in the shadows.

Jade led the way to the shack, her crystal dagger glowing a pale lavender. Carefully easing the door open, she peered inside, then motioned for the others to follow her. Sean slipped in behind her, frowning at the odd room which only contained a staircase leading below ground. The Sentinels quietly crept down the steep concrete stairs.

After a few steps, Sean caught the faint sound of men chanting in a strange language. The air stank of the same noxious incense he'd smelled many times before. His heart fluttered with hope. If the ritual was still in progress, they weren't too late.

Jade held up her hand and Sean froze. She drew a sigil in the air, her magic making it glow a dark indigo. "*Masku*," she intoned, quietly. She turned to Sean and whispered, "Now we're concealed. They shouldn't see or sense us until we're ready for them."

Sean nodded and slunk down the remaining stairs, trying not to make any noise, still unsure how magic worked. He paused at the bottom to take in the large chamber. A pentagram painted in red filled the center, and symbols blanketed the walls.

Two figures inside the circle held his attention. Catlyn hung limply from a chain holding her shackled hands over her head. Blood covered her from head to toe. Her eyes were swollen shut from the beatings she'd endured. Michael stood in front of her, carving something into her skin with a long, flexible blade.

Sean gritted his teeth, clamping down on the urge to rush Michael and stop Catlyn's torture. If he did, she'd have suffered for nothing. They were here for more than rescuing Catlyn.

Sean felt a gentle push, and he moved aside to let Charlie and the other Sentinels enter. Sean inched toward the circle as the Sentinels silently filed into the room. They surrounded the twelve robed men, who looked like monks and paced around the circle, chanting. Madness— and passionate fervor—gleamed in Michael's eyes. Evil rolled off him in putrid waves, filling the space with its repugnance.

 # CHAPTER 31 

Catlyn didn't know how long the torment lasted. It could have been hours or days. The only break from the agony came in the brief moments when Michael chose a different method to torture her.

And still she chanted.

It was that or be consumed by the evil spilling from Michael. Hecate's spell kept the vileness from penetrating her soul through the various cuts and wounds in her body.

When her mouth became too swollen and bloody from his blows, she mentally chanted. Without the focus on the pain blocking spell, she doubted her mind could survive the unrelenting waves of excruciating agony.

She refused to consider what Michael was doing to her. Once she destroyed Bho-Ahp, her work would be finished and she could escape into the death Michael skillfully held at bay. Sadness seeped through the physical pain, intensifying it. She wished she'd had a chance to explore the growing romance with Sean. Now, it would die on the vine. It had shriveled up the moment she agreed to this madness. Even if she somehow survived her present nightmare, their relationship could never bloom. No one would ever look at her again and think her beautiful or want to be intimate with her mangled, disfigured body.

Much later, lost between reality and the edge of unconsciousness, she dimly became aware of Maak feeding her energy and power. Even as her blood dripped to the floor, and she screamed in pain, she grew stronger.

"Sean and the others are here," Maak's voice broke through her haze. *"It's time."*

Time for what? She asked, confused.

Deep within her, Catlyn sensed something stir. Power bloomed in her root chakra and wove up her spine. A fresh burst of strength rushed through her, clearing her mind and extinguishing her misery. It was like a shot of adrenaline, but much stronger. The pain encompassing her body receded.

Catlyn began a new chant. At first, no sound slipped through her lips. She licked them, tasting the salty copper of her blood, and tried again. This time, the chant came out in a whisper. Heartened, she raised her head and recited the words, loud and strong.

The monks stopped their own chanting. They paused in their procession around the circle and turned as one to stare at her.

"Stop! What are you doing?" Michael screamed at her. He slammed his fist into her mouth.

She grinned through the fresh flow of blood and continued the spell.

"No, no, no!" He gaped at the small circle of blood, the doorway meant for the daemon's emergence. "It isn't time! You're not ready for Bho-Ahp. He can't come yet."

The inner circle glowed. Flames shot up from it, forming a large oval in the air. The portal was opening. The thick, opaque center grew translucent and thinned as Catlyn chanted.

Michael whipped back to her. "Stop! I'm not ready!"

Catlyn continued to call Bho-Ahp through the gate. Movement behind the still staring monks drew her attention. She shook the blood from her eyes. Shadowy forms quietly surrounded the monks. She heard another quiet chant under her own, sounding close by her. Her eyes widened.

Jade stood by the crack in the protective dome, unnoticed by Michael's followers. She winked at Catlyn and drew a sigil in the air.

Intense heat flared around Catlyn's ankles, and she squirmed before realizing it hadn't burned her. She almost lost the thread of her chant when she saw the shackles melting away. Real magic did exist in the world! The heavy iron clanked to the floor.

Michael blinked at it as if dumbfounded at the interruption. The monks whirled around as they finally noticed they weren't alone in the room.

Chaos bloomed.

Jade continued to burn through the wrist manacles. Catlyn fell as the manacles lost their unrelenting grip on her. New agony erupted when she hit the concrete floor. She crammed the pain behind her block and ignored it. What was one more hurt among the myriad of others?

The rising magic within Catlyn wrapped her in a cocoon of strength. It didn't heal her body of the terrible wounds inflicted during Michael's torture, but it allowed her to move as if she were whole. She stood, turning her attention to the portal.

Catlyn took up the chant again to open the portal. Maak's voice added her power. A sliver tore in the membrane, and an immense form appeared behind the veil.

Pandemonium filled the room as fighting broke out. The monks, suddenly able to see the Sentinel Witches, whipped out long knives from under their robes. They were exactly like the one Michael had when he abducted Catlyn. Heat warmed Sean's back, reminding him of the crystal dagger he wore.

He jerked it from its sheath. Its pure white light pushed aside the murk. He let his pent-up rage overtake him. A knife swung toward his face.

He blocked it, sparks flying as the blades met. His dagger glowed brighter and seemed to eat into the black metal. Horror filled the monk's eyes as his blade melted. Sean slammed a fist into his opponent's face. He fell back, blood spurting from his broken nose. The monk's fingers twisted, forming dark sigils in the air. Sean's senses told him he didn't want those malignant spells hitting him. He plunged his dagger into the monk's chest. The sigils broke apart and as they fizzled out, a few motes landed on his arm. His flesh sizzled and bubbled, and he whipped his arm behind him, wiping the corrosive ash from the surface of his skin.

A loud pop drew his attention toward the stairway. Two monks conjured a hellish opening. A pack of a dozen of the strange greyhound-cat demons with crocodile tails and owl-like heads burst through. Their master followed, a dark blue-gray hairless creature with an elongated face and tall domed skull. It flicked a whip at its pack of demons. One yelped, letting out a tremendous screech, showing the needle-sharp fangs filling its beak.

A three-foot tall denim blue demon scurried from the opening. It ran-hopped in an ungainly gait due to its one leg hoofed like a goat and the other a skinny crow's foot. The bells tied across its squat barrel-shaped body jingled. It raced to a witch, prodding him with a two-pronged stick held in its lobster-claw appendage. The witch jerked as if hit by a Taser. Sean blinked at the creature, remembering the incident last month where a man had been pushed into a semi-truck. The veterinarian—and Catlyn—hadn't lied when they said a demon caused the accident.

More demons scrambled through the hellish opening and attacked the now outnumbered Sentinels.

Sean ignored the demons and fought the monks on his way to the circle. He had to save Catlyn.

His mind gibbered when he saw what was coming through the portal.

Sean truly hadn't understood the difference between demons and daemons until that moment. Immense power rolled off the creature, who stepped from the gateway. The daemon turned his baleful eyes on Sean. He took an unintentional step toward the daemon, reaching for him as he would a lover. The darkness called to him, beckoning him to drown in its depths. All the other demons Sean had glimpsed were mere puppies compared to this monster.

The daemon laughed, and Sean recognized it as the same one he'd heard at the Iron Maiden Killings.

Michael reached for the daemon.

Horror froze Sean in place. *What were we thinking? There's no way the Sentinel Witches can stop Bho-Ahp. He's too powerful!*

Sean's grandfather's medallion warmed against his chest, and at the same time, his crystal knife flared. Its brilliance, and the amulet's power, broke the daemon's spell.

Sean gaped.

Catlyn is in the circle with the daemon!

 # CHAPTER 32 

An ice-blue hand with long claws reached through the tear in the veil. Michael's eyes widened, and he chanted with Catlyn, his voice filled with righteous fervor. He'd been working toward bringing Bho-Ahp into this world for the last thirty months. He knelt in homage in front of the portal.

The shape resolved into a muscled creature, obviously male, with smooth, hairless ice-blue skin and electric blue eyes. Catlyn recognized him as the same daemon she'd seen in her vision. This time, she noticed he had four arms. The long claws on his four-fingered hands had inspired the knives Michael and his acolytes used. The daemon stepped across the threshold, bringing with him a sickening stench.

Bho-Ahp had arrived.

"You look more delicious in person," the daemon crooned, his voice running over her skin like rough velvet made her shiver.

He licked his blood-red lips as his gaze roved over Catlyn from head to foot, suddenly reminding her of her nakedness. His phallus hardened, and the symbols carved into his skin and the horns on his forehead glowed, giving him an unearthly beauty. Even though she knew he was evil incarnate, lust gripped her, and she took an involuntary step toward him.

"No, Catlyn!" Maak cried. *"Don't succumb to his allure."*

Power burst within Catlyn, releasing her from Bho-Ahp's spell. At the same time, Maak initiated the spell that would allow her to manifest in this plane through Catlyn. Tingles crept over Catlyn's body, and her fingers became transparent. Maak's presence rose to the fore.

Adoration shone on Michael's face as he stood and reached for Bho-Ahp.

"They can't make contact or they will merge," Maak warned her.

Horrified, Catlyn stared at the tableau. If they touched, all the pain she'd suffered would be for nothing. But in the middle of her metamorphosis, Catlyn couldn't stop them. She glanced around and saw Sean. He stood mesmerized a few feet away.

"Sean!" Catlyn yelled over the tumult. "Stop Michael! Don't let him touch Bho-Ahp."

Sean shook his head as if clearing it. His blue eyes locked on hers, then he ran toward her. He didn't seem to notice as energy crackled and sizzled around him as he vaulted over the circle, tackling Michael before his fingers met Bho-Ahp's.

"Now!" Maak yelled.

Catlyn joined the spell Maak chanted. As the words spewed from her mouth, somehow, Catlyn and Maak merged. They existed simultaneously in the physical and non-physical worlds. Catlyn's human body faded, along with all her wounds, as the huge white tiger materialized.

Catlyn-Maak shook her body, ridding it of the last tingles of her change. She roared. A monk saw her, now a great white tiger instead of a bloody, broken woman. He ran screaming, right into Jade's sword.

Catlyn-Maak leaped, and her claws raked Michael's back as they sailed over him. She grinned at his scream of pain. She landed in the middle of the closing portal, bowling over Bho-Ahp.

He flipped to his feet with his hands stretched out. He threw back his head and let loose a roar of his own. It echoed on the concrete walls. The fighting outside the circle momentarily halted at the sound before resuming.

Catlyn-Maak whirled and slashed her claws across his calves. Bho-Ahp thrust one of his arms out toward them. The edge of his claw sliced into her hide. She flipped and sank her fangs into his arm, gagging at the foul, rotten-egg taste.

The symbols on Bho-Ahp's skin shone brighter, and he spat a string of words. A wave of black magic swept from him and slammed into Catlyn-Maak. They gritted their teeth as thousands of tiny pests bit into them. Maak mumbled a spell in her language. Magic pulsed off her, eliminating the pests. Another pulse and a blast of fire flew at Bho-Ahp.

He spun away, but the edge caught one of his arms. He howled as flames engulfed it. The stink of charred skin added to the reek in the enclosed space. Bho-Ahp spat another spell as he slid a hand over the flame. It gathered into a ball, which he tossed back at them. Catlyn-Maak twisted out of the way. The ball of fire whizzed past them, heating the tips of their fur. It hit the energy dome of the circle and fizzled out.

Bho-Ahp leaped at the same time as Catlyn-Maak. They crashed into each other. Catlyn-Maak sank her teeth into the juncture where his neck met his shoulder. She roared when he bit her. His teeth were nearly as sharp as hers. Warm blood trickled from the wound. He wrapped his arms around her and squeezed. The air whooshed from her lungs. His talon tips dug into her side. Desperate for breath, she scrabbled her back claws against his legs.

She finally twisted out of his grasp, away from his talons, and swiped his chest, digging deep gouges with her claws. Seeing an opening, Catlyn-Maak sank her fangs into his flesh, tearing out great chunks. Snarling, she spat out the nasty taste. Green slime from his many wounds made the floor slick. She slid as she ducked from the sharp horns protruding from his forehead. The tip of one caught her flank and ripped it open.

Anger and hate filled Sean as he dove for Michael. He slammed into his opponent, knocking him away from the daemon, away from Catlyn. They rolled across the floor. Power flared as they hit the side of the energy dome and knocked them apart.

As Sean leaped to his feet, the many murder scenes he'd witnessed at Michael's hands flashed before his eyes. Now was his chance to give the victims vengeance. They'd never receive justice. Michael's father's wealth assured he'd never face trial for the murders.

"You'll pay for all the hurt you've caused," Sean ground out through clenched teeth. He crouched in a ready-stance, holding his crystal dagger in front of him.

Michael laughed. His eyes glinted, flashing a red sheen. "You wish. Now that my master is here, I'll be unstoppable. And more powerful than even my father. Bho-Ahp chose me," —he pointed his dagger at his chest— "not him! You've been a thorn in my side long enough." Michael swung his blade at Sean.

Sean stumbled back, raising his dagger. The blades hit, sending a shock wave down Sean's arm. He slashed. Appalled that it was a bit wild.

Michael threw back his head, laughing as he easily evaded Sean's clumsy strike. "Is that the best you can do? This fight won't last long. Pity."

Sean's police training had included some knife fighting, but that had been years ago. He felt awkward and out of his depth. In the enclosed space, he didn't dare use his gun, afraid he'd hit Catlyn or one of the Sentinel Witches. He touched his grandfather's amulet. It buzzed under his hand and a burst of energy filled him.

Sean slashed again. This time, it seemed as if someone guided his movement. His crystal dagger slid across Michael's face, laying his check open. Michael bellowed. His eyes flared with red light, and he swore in a language Sean didn't know. A bolt of electricity slammed into Sean's chest. His amulet blazed, and instead of killing him, Michael's magic only knocked the wind out of him. He bared his teeth as he struggled to regain his breath.

Michael ran toward Sean. Their blades flashed. Sean's shone with a bright light. Michael's oozed darkness.

Sean hissed. Blood welled on his bicep from a lucky slash. He blocked another swipe, then swung at Michael. They clashed and sparks flew from their blades as they traded blows. Sean's knuckles bled from the various nicks he received.

A ball of fire zipped toward them. Sean swore, then twisted. The hair on his arm sizzled. Michael took advantage of his inattention and slashed at Sean's chest. Sean leaped back, but not enough to stop the blow entirely. His shirt split, and he gasped at searing pain. Blood gushed from the deep gash on his chest.

Sean saw an opening and thrust his knife at his opponent. The tip slid across Michael's forearm. Their fight took them close to Bho-Ahp and a great white tiger. Sean gaped, not sure if he was hallucinating. *Where did Catlyn go? Or is that her?* Michael reached toward the daemon, and Sean remembered Catlyn's admonishment to not let the two touch. He dove, tackling Michael, and knocking him away from Bho-Ahp. Both Michael and Bho-Ahp growled in frustration.

Michael attacked, his teeth bared. He drove his blade deep into Sean's thigh, ripping through muscle. Sean screamed, but he wouldn't allow the wound to stop him. He had to keep Michael away from Bho-Ahp.

Sean and Michael circled each other, blood dripping from their wounds. Michael lunged, and Sean twisted to the side. Michael recovered, quickly switching his hold on his dagger and slammed it into Sean's scapula. The blade hit bone. Sean's hand went numb. Luckily, it was his left hand. He hunched over, nearly vomiting at the sick squelch as Michael withdrew his knife. He reversed his grip and thrust backwards. His blade sunk into Michael's thigh.

Michael spun away, flinging blood. His spin took him close to Bho-Ahp. He reached out his hand. Sean slashed his dagger across Michael's hand, severing two fingers. Michael cursed, moving away from Bho-Ahp. His eyes no longer held the haughty confidence. Worry—or was that fear?—scrunched his face. He swung again at Sean.

Sean ducked, then buried his knife into Michael's side and was rewarded by Michael's scream.

Bho-Ahp lunged to the side, attempting to touch Michael's hand. The two had to make physical contact for Bho-Ahp to assimilate into Michael. With a roar, Catlyn-Maak swatted Bho-Ahp's arm aside, her claws digging deep furrows.

Bho-Ahp retaliated, spitting a spell. The black dust glittered like a million diamonds. Catlyn-Maak moaned as the sharp motes burrowed beneath their protecting fur and burned their skin. She uttered a counter-spell, sighing when coolness replaced the burning sensation.

Using her strong tail, she slammed it into Bho-Ahp, knocking him away from Michael. She leaped, jaws wide open, aiming for Bho-Ahp's neck. He backpedaled, but his foot slid on the slick, blood covered surface. He fell to his knees and Catlyn-Maak sailed over his head. She twisted in midair, raking her claws along his back.

Over and over, Bho-Ahp attempted to reach Michael, but Catlyn-Maak never allowed him to get near his vessel. Sean did his part to keep the two separate. Bho-Ahp growled in frustration. He swiped at her again. His long claws raking along her arm. It stung.

Michael screamed as Sean slammed his crystal dagger into Michael's side.

Catlyn-Maak backed up and gave the shallow wounds on her arm a quick lick. A glance around the bunker showed Jade and the Sentinel Witches stood victorious over Bho-Ahp and Michael's defeated monks. Piles of black goo or ash were all that remained of the demons she'd glimpsed earlier. The only clashes remaining were the ones between Sean and Michael and her battle with the daemon.

She took stock of her wounds in this combined form, relieved to discover none were life threatening. The worst one was the gash in her right hindquarters. Whereas blood poured from numerous slashes or gouges from both Michael and Bho-Ahp. Michael was missing two fingers, a flap of skin from his cheek, and held a hand to his side in a vain effort to staunch the blood flooding from his side.

They'd torn off one of Bho-Ahp's four arms, and chewed through a second. His right eye was missing. The slash that took it also laid open Bho-Ahp's cheek. He'd lost great chunks of flesh to their teeth. Given time, his magic might heal his wounds. But Catlyn-Maak wouldn't allow that to happen.

"It is time," Maak said.

"Sean, get out of the circle now!" Catlyn yelled. "The rest is up to us."

Sean nodded, casting a wary glance at the being she'd become. He scurried out, trailing blood from the gash in his thigh.

As soon as he crossed the circle's boundary, Catlyn-Maak closed the break in the energy dome. Now, it was only the four of them. Only one symbiotic pair would leave the circle, and she was determined to be the one who did. In their merged form, Catlyn and Maak were neither fully physical or non-physical. They were part of both dimensions. It was the only reason they'd been able to cause so much damage to Bho-Ahp.

With a roar, Catlyn-Maak drove Bho-Ahp toward Michael. A flash of light filled the room as Bho-Ahp and Michael made contact and the assimilation of daemon and host began.

Michael screamed.

Bho-Ahp laughed.

Catlyn-Maak pounced.

Already weakened from the fight, and weaker still from the transformation in progress, the daemon and human collapsed under her weight. She landed on top of him, wrapped her teeth around his throat, and raked his belly with her rear claws. Shredded guts spilled out, adding to the malodorous stink in the air. A shake of her massive head broke Michael's neck.

Bho-Ahp tried to escape his dying host. When he couldn't leave, his struggles turned frantic. Catlyn-Maak raised an enormous paw and tore out Bho-Ahp's throat. He fell limp. Fire bathed the daemon's body, burning it to ash, leaving behind Michael's battered corpse.

Bho-Ahp was finally destroyed and would never threaten the world again with his evil.

The energy dome collapsed.

"Well done. We fought well together to destroy the daemon," Maak said smugly. She initiated the shift back to their separate forms.

Catlyn returned to her human form, screaming in agony. The pain from the injuries she'd suffered during torture flared all at once and hit her full-blast. Barely conscious, she crumpled next to Michael's ravaged body.

"Catlyn! Catlyn! Please don't be dead." Sean's concerned voice broke through her fog.

His gentle touch caused the fire in her nerve endings to flare anew. "I'm still here," she croaked, and her eyes fluttered open. "I wish I wasn't. I hurt."

"I know, sweetheart. We'll get you to the hospital. You're a mess."

Did he say 'sweetheart?' Catlyn smiled at the thought and allowed oblivion to take her.

She was safe and so was the world.

 # CHAPTER 33 

Sean swiped blood from the cut above his eye, unsure when he'd received it. He ignored the other knife wounds on his chest, left thigh, left scapula, and right bicep. They could wait. He limped to the crumpled form lying next to Michael's, leaving a trail of blood behind him. Sean fell to his knees.

"Catlyn! Catlyn! Please don't be dead." He blinked away the sudden tears blinding him when he heard her moan. *She's alive!*

Exhaustion from his fight with Michael and no sleep for thirty-six hours had made him hallucinate. He couldn't have seen Catlyn transform into a giant, white tiger. After sensing the daemon's incredible power, Sean had doubted they would be able to destroy it. But surprisingly, the creature—Catlyn?—had killed the merged being of Michael and Bho-Ahp.

Even after seeing the daemon and experiencing the magic of Jade's tracking spell, he still disbelieved the reality of magic. But it was the only thing that would explain what he'd seen Catlyn become.

The carnage in the underground bunker left blood spattering the walls. Bodies littered the floor from the fierce battle between the Sentinel Witches and Bho-Ahp's followers. Since they hadn't used any guns—only knives and swords—Sean imagined it looked like the aftermath of a medieval battlefield. Sean's own fight with Michael had been bloody and nasty. Blood still gushed from his leg. He pulled off his belt and made a quick tourniquet.

Sean gazed at Catlyn and decided it didn't matter to him if magic was real or not, or what she'd become. He ran a gentle finger over her forehead, one of the few places on her body not damaged. At his touch, she thrashed and tried to pull away from him.

"Easy, Cat, easy. You're safe," he whispered to her. "I thought I'd lost you."

"I'm still here," she croaked, and her eyes fluttered open.

"It's all right, sweetheart. We'll get you to the hospital soon. You're a mess."

She struggled to smile, but the wound on her cheek wouldn't allow her to do more than lift the corner of her lips. "You called me sweetheart." Her eyes drifted closed, and she fell into unconsciousness. With the many injuries covering her, it was better for her to be unaware of them.

A moment later, Jade and Eileen knelt at Catlyn's side.

"Is she alive?" Jade asked, her throat husky and moisture filled her eyes.

"Barely." Sean's voice cracked. "Is ... is there anything you can do for her? In her condition, she might not survive the trip to the hospital."

"I don't have any healing skills. Those are Catlyn's gifts." Jade's cheeks blazed, and she dropped her chin to her chest.

"Dahlyah and I can help." Eileen's voice was thick with unshed tears.

Sean glanced at her side and did a double take. Somehow her *Cait Sidhe* had found them. Sean didn't remember the large black cat being in the van with them earlier. Dahlyah winked at him. She padded to Catlyn and gently laid a big paw on her chest. The soft pink light glowing from Dahlyah extended into Catlyn.

"Sean, my boy, go call an ambulance," Eileen said, pulling his attention away from the cat. "Better yet, a helicopter. We can stabilize her, but she needs the type of medical treatment we can't give her."

Sean hesitated. He didn't want to leave Catlyn's side.

"Go." His grandmother's sharp voice struck him like a slap. "She needs that helicopter. Now, Sean."

He leaned over, kissed Catlyn's forehead, then struggled to his feet. A groan escaped him as his own wounds protested the sudden movement. Pulling out his phone, he grimaced—no signal. He limped up the stairs leading above ground. Sean pushed his car as fast as he dared on the rutted dirt track until he finally found a cellphone signal.

When he came back down, Charlie and several other Sentinels walked around the room, checking the monks for survivors. Other witches were helping wounded comrades. A pair pulled unknown paraphernalia from a duffel bag similar to what he'd seen Ariana and Dilan use at Lisa's. They walked to the first pile of demon goo, pointing a device at it. It slurped up the goo, leaving nothing behind.

Bile burned Sean's throat as he caught sight of Michael's guts spilling from the long rips in his abdomen. His head lolled at an awkward angle from a broken neck, and only a gaping hole remained where his throat had once been.

Charlie joined him. "You don't look like a man who just saved the world. What's wrong, bro?"

"I'm in so much trouble," Sean huffed. He gazed at the ceiling and shook his head. "How am I going to explain Michael's wounds? They are obviously from a large animal. What excuse can I give for why I didn't call for back up, but instead used a shadow organization of witches? Captain Green will never believe we stopped a daemon incursion."

"No worries. We've been cleaning up these types of messes for ages. We'll leave Michael's body here for you. You need it to close your Iron Maiden Killer case, but we'll take everyone else with us. Then you won't have so much to explain." He scanned the mop-up efforts. "There's only one or two of Bho-Ahp's followers left alive, and we have questions for them."

"But, they're my—"

"Face it, Sean, the police don't know how to deal with this type of criminal. We do. We have someplace that will hold them that daemons can't reach. If you take them into custody, you risk the lives of every cop in the station. Do you want that on your conscious?"

"No. But what about the forensic evidence? Even though I have Michael's body to show them, they'll do a full investigation of the scene."

Charlie snorted. "Have you found any evidence at the other Iron Maiden crime scenes?"

Sean's mouth dropped open, and his face burned as fury rushed through him. "What! You've been cleaning my crime scenes? What the fuck, Charlie. You knew I was searching for the killer. There might have been clues we could have used to stop this sooner. Stopped it before there were over thirty murders. Before Catlyn—"

"Trust me, we wanted to catch him as badly as you did. There's no way," —Charlie's voice cracked, and he rubbed his eyes as he looked over at Catlyn— "there's no way we wanted Catlyn to go through that. The world isn't ready for real witches. And we're not ready for the world to know about us. You'll soon become a Sentinel, Sean. We'll require you to swear an oath to not reveal our presence. You'll have to hide what you are, what we are, from your colleagues and supervisors. If you can't do that, tell me now, and you'll forget any of this happened." He waved a hand at the scene.

The swing of the chain hanging from the ceiling caught Sean's attention. Again, he saw Catlyn hanging on it when he'd entered the room. Phantom images of the other victims he'd discovered dangling from a similar chain flashed with her face superimposed on them. He sucked in a breath and blinked to clear the image.

"You know all those strange cases you couldn't solve?" Charlie asked. "Even before the Iron Maiden Killer?"

Sean raised an eyebrow at him.

"Demons and their ilk caused every one of those. You can do a lot of good as a Sentinel, Sean. Maybe even more good than as a cop."

Sean thought about it, then gave a sharp jerk of his head. "Yes, I can keep the Sentinels' secret."

Charlie beamed. "Excellent! I didn't want to wipe your memory. Our people are almost finished."

The witches had carried out the injured and dead, except Catlyn and Michael, while Sean and Charlie had talked. Jade and the pair of Sentinels he'd seen earlier slowly walked from one end of the room to the other. Sean shifted into his witch-sight and saw magic flow from them and zap away any traces of the fight. Blood, body fluids, and flesh sizzled into nothingness as their magic touched it. He wrinkled his nose. The magic had obliterated most of the symbols on the walls and floor. The forensic team wouldn't find anything, not even a hair. Although the stink of the monk's incense still lingered.

Sean glanced down at his watch. "The helicopter should be here soon."

Charlie toed Michael's mangled body, then whistled. "Catlyn did a number on him, didn't she? I'll do what I can to hide it." Charlie held his hands over the corpse and chanted. The gaping holes closed until they could pass for knife wounds. After a few moments, he dropped his hands and wiped the sweat from his forehead. "That's the best I can do. I can't do anything about the broken neck. If you can keep them from doing an autopsy, that would be best. My repairs won't stand up to close scrutiny."

Dilan ran down the stairs. "The helicopter is approaching. We need to leave."

Charlie helped Eileen off the floor. In a few minutes, the only occupants left in the room were Sean, Catlyn, and Michael's corpse. Sean knelt by Catlyn and touched a finger to her pulse. He lifted his eyes up to the ceiling in gratitude when he felt the strong beat.

Thumping sounds alerted him of the helicopter's arrival. The door upstairs banged, and Sean looked toward the stairs. He grimaced at the sight of his captain's face scrunched in fury as he led the charge into the room.

Sean rose to his feet. There would be serious repercussions because of his actions. He glanced down at Michael's body. Whatever punishment he received would be worth it to have stopped the Iron Maiden Killer— and to save Catlyn.

Sean slumped in the chair, rubbing his face, grimacing at the stubble coating his chin. He winced as the movement pulled on the deep knife wound across his right bicep. Thursday night he'd been in the fight of his life, stopping the Iron Maiden Killer he'd tracked for nearly three years. Instead of being hailed as a hero, his captain had locked him in a tiny interrogation room and grilled him. The stuffy air made it hard to breathe and the stink of disinfectant burned his nose.

His Captain sensed Sean wasn't telling the whole truth about the incident or why he'd gone so far out of his jurisdiction in Orange County. Now he knew how a suspect felt, endlessly being asked the same questions over and over.

"Why didn't you just shoot him, McLarkin?" Captain Green leaned on the table, his eyes boring into Sean, searching for any indication he was lying.

Sean gritted his teeth. "I told you, Captain, at least ten times. There was so much smoke from the nasty incense Michael burned, I could barely see the victim. I didn't want to fire my weapon and risk hitting Ms. Hennessey. She'd already suffered enough.

"I don't know how she survived the brutal torture Michael put her through. When I arrived, she hung limp in chains suspended from the ceiling. Blood covered her from head to toe from multiple injuries. Her eyes were swollen shut from being badly beaten. Michael stood in front of her, carving into her with a long, flexible blade. I grabbed one of the knives spread out on a nearby surgeon's tray, and we fought."

He hadn't come away from the fight unscathed.

"In case you hadn't noticed, I barely survived." Sean carefully rubbed his chest, where Michael's knife had gouged him, drawing Captain's Green attention to his wounds. Sean leaned back, hissing as the deep gash in his shoulder came into contact with the hard surface of the uncomfortable chair. As he stretched out his left leg, his eyes watered from the searing pain from the wound in his thigh. It had taken nearly fifty stitches to close it.

Anger burned through the pain. He should be home recuperating from his injuries, not sitting for days being interrogated. He hadn't even been able to send a message to Catlyn or visit her in the hospital. She must think he abandoned her.

"At first, I just tried to save Ms. Hennessey from being hurt anymore," Sean continued, "but it quickly turned into a fight for survival. Michael must have been on some sort of drug. He was out of his mind, faster and stronger than he'd be under normal circumstances. The only way I could stop him was to kill him."

But Sean hadn't struck the blow that killed Michael. He still couldn't believe what had happened.

Sean truly hadn't understood the difference between demons and daemons until he'd seen the creature stepping through the portal and experienced the power rolling off it. He'd encountered other demons during his investigation of Michael, but they had been like naughty children compared to the monster that Catlyn faced.

Sean's stomach clenched as he recalled the moment when the daemon turned his baleful eyes on Sean. He'd taken a step toward Bho-Ahp, reaching for it as he would a lover. The only thing that stopped him had been his crystal knife flaring and breaking the daemon's spell.

Sean was taking the credit for the killing to protect Catlyn. All everyone not involved would know was that she was the victim of a vicious serial killer. No one would believe she'd turned into a giant, white tiger, and in that form, killed Michael and the daemon, Bho-Ahp.

Captain Green flicked his pen back and forth. "Tell me again why you violated your jurisdiction, didn't call for backup, and landed forty miles outside of Joshua Tree."

"There wasn't time, Captain. That lunatic Michael abducted Ms. Hennessey. After he threatened to kill her, I'd put a tracer on her, in case he was the Iron Maiden Killer—which I was right, and he was. Once he took her, it was a race to locate her."

"How in the hell did you find that place? It's out in the middle of nowhere and without any substantial structures to mark it."

Sean huffed. "Pure luck and detective work. I followed the tracker's signal, continuing on the same road when I lost cell service. Eventually, I stumbled on that ramshackle hut. As it was the only thing in the area, I deduced it was the place." He shifted on the hard seat again, grimacing as pain flared. Luckily, the Sentinel Witches didn't rely solely on magic.

"Ms Hennessey's godmother installed surveillance equipment on her apartment. You've seen the video footage of Ms Hennessey's abduction, right?"

Captain Green reluctantly nodded.

"That shows irrefutable proof Michael Drogger kidnapped her. The rape kit will show he raped her first." Sean leaned forward, his gazing snagging his boss's. "I discovered her mangled body in the same type of scene as the other Iron Maiden murders. I'm sure forensics has found Michael's fingerprints all over the tools he used to torture her."

Again, Captain Green gave a grudging nod.

"Then what's the problem, Captain? Why am I being interrogated? We have proof Michael was the Iron Maiden Killer." Sean would've been lauded as a hero if Michael wasn't the son of the wealthiest man in the state, perhaps the country.

"There's something strange going on here. There's more you're not telling me. I can smell it." Captain Green tapped the side of his nose as he squinted at Sean. "But you've stuck to your story. Go write your report. I want it in my inbox by 7:00 tonight." He gathered the papers strewn across the table, stuffing them in a folder, then left.

Sean leaned forward and laid his head on his forearms. His mind was foggy from the constant barrage of questions, lack of sleep, and pain. He'd need massive amounts of coffee to write a coherent report. Maybe that was what Green wanted, to find inconsistencies between his written report and his statements.

Sean couldn't afford to make any mistakes. He had to ensure nothing pointed to Catlyn's involvement. Her fight with Bho-Ahp and Michael's torture had nearly killed her. At some time during the ordeal of finding Catlyn, he realized he'd fallen in love with the pretty psychic.

Sean slowly pushed to his feet, groaning with pain. As he shuffled out of the interrogation room, he glanced at the clock. He only had three hours to write his report. He gazed longingly at the coffeepot. The way he hurt, the distance between it and his desk, was an impossible chasm to cross.

He eased into his chair, grateful for its plush softness, at least compared to the torture device he'd been sitting in for the last—what? Sean had lost track of time during his ordeal with Green. The date on his computer made him shake with fury. Five days. He'd spent five days in intense questioning.

A mug of coffee appeared in front of him. "Here, you look like you need it." His partner eyed him, then whistled. "Man, that was some fight! No wonder Drogger's body is mangled, so are you. By the way, your girl, Catlyn, is still unconscious, but the doctors are sure she'll pull through."

Sean sipped his coffee, wishing it had a shot of whiskey to dull the pain. A dose of codeine would be nice. Green had rushed him from the hospital to the precinct before he had the opportunity to fill the prescription.

Jerry pushed a bottle of pills toward him. "I filled this for you. I knew you'd need it." He scowled at Captain Green's closed door. "He wouldn't let me give it to you while he questioned you. Why are you here instead of going home?"

"He insists I write my report before I can leave." Sean dumped two of the strong painkillers from the bottle, swallowing them quickly, followed by a shot of coffee.

"That's plain mean and cruel." Jerry shook his head. He patted Sean's shoulder before sitting at his own desk. "Let me know if you need more coffee or want me to grab you something to eat."

"Thanks, partner. I'm good for now." The codeine and caffeine were starting to work their magic. Sean no longer felt like he'd keel over from pain and exhaustion.

He opened up the program and started typing. With some creative spin doctoring, he managed to explain Michael's death, reminding himself to keep to the facts he'd reported—repeatedly—to Captain Green.

Two hours later, he leaned forward, placing his elbows on his desk, and scrubbing his face with his hands. He only had one more loose end to wrap up in his report.

Why did he chase Michael alone, without his partner, and out of his jurisdiction of Anaheim City into San Bernardino County? Sean did have backup, but it had been the magical kind. Not only had his friend Charlie been there, but also his Granny Eileen, Jade, and several other Sentinel Witches. The ancient organization of witches had been fighting demons for thousands of years. The Anaheim Police Department—or any police department, for that matter—didn't have the necessary weapons to fight demons. The Sentinels did. They were the best support team to have at his side.

Pulling up the video of Catlyn's abduction, Sean noted the time stamp, and let out a whoosh of relief. *Bless Jade and her magic!* They'd changed it, giving him just enough time to discover Catlyn missing, then follow his hunch about Michael's lair in Joshua Tree. His fingers flew over the keyboard, weaving truth in with the subterfuge, while remembering what he'd told his captain.

"Is your report done yet, Detective?"

Sean jumped at Captain Green's voice booming through the intercom.

"Yes, sir. Just finished, sir." He hit the key to file the report. With it, he could finally put the Iron Maiden Killer behind him. After working the case for nearly three years and seeing the gruesome murders of over thirty victims, he was more than ready to move on. He'd be able to focus on the future. Whatever that may be. He wasn't sure what he'd agreed to when he told Charlie he'd join the Sentinel Witches or what it would entail.

He glowered at his captain's door, anger pulsing in time with his heartbeat. After his interrogation, he might have to ask Jade for a job in her security company. He loved being a cop and helping people. But if they were going to continue treating him like dirt, perhaps he could help people more by being a Sentinel Witch.

He straightened up his desk and shut down his computer. He stood and snagged his jacket from the back of his chair, pausing when his boss stalked toward him.

"I've read your report, and some of the events are questionable. But there is little doubt Michael Drogger was the Iron Maiden Killer. Even his father, Thomas Drogger, can't fault the evidence. Enjoy the notoriety while it lasts. I'll be watching you closely."

"Yes, sir." Sean dipped his head, then straightened stiffly and looked Captain Green in the eye. "Sir, I was simply doing my job. I'm a good detective. The fame means nothing to me. Only stopping that psychopathic killer was important to me, and finally saving one of his victims. I understand she's still unconscious, but I'm sure she'll answer any of your questions when she wakes up."

"Are you involved with her?"

Sean shook his head. *Not yet.* "Now, if you'll excuse me, sir, I'd like to go home and get some rest."

Captain Green glared at him for another moment, then moved to let Sean pass by him.

Finally home, Sean sprawled on his bed, too tired to even take off his stinking clothes.

Why is Green suddenly out for my blood? Is he under the influence of a daemon? Or more likely, has Michael's father, a rich and powerful man, paid him off to get rid of me?

The questions looped endlessly until exhaustion finally shut down his brain.

 Chapter 34 

Catlyn slowly became aware of beeping and humming machinery nearby. She breathed deeply to clear her fuzzy head. The white room and machines told her she laid in a hospital bed.

She couldn't move her left leg or feel her foot. Pain swamped her at the memory of the methodical way Michael had broken each bone in it. She attempted to sit up, afraid she'd lost it. A gentle pressure pushed her back down.

"Shh ... it's okay." Jade's face came into view over her. "You're okay."

Catlyn tried to talk, but her mouth was desert dry. She swallowed, choking on the tube shoved down her throat. A nurse hurried in, removed the tube, and gave her a sip of water.

"How ... long ..." Her swollen tongue and sore throat made it difficult to speak.

"Five days." Jade took her hand gently, careful not to mess with the IV needles. "It was pretty touch and go for a while. The first day, the doctors didn't think you'd survive. But you did. And you're healing."

"My foot? I can't feel my foot. Is it gone?"

Jade's eyes widened. "No, honey. They did surgery on it and put in several pins. Whatever he did to it was bad. It's a miracle you survived."

"Thankfully, I blacked out for most of it."

"I'm sorry. I shouldn't have let Michael abduct you."

"It isn't your fault. I chose to allow Michael to take me. It was the only way to destroy Bho-Ahp."

Jade shuddered. "I've read stories of him and his evil. Whatever you did worked. He's gone."

A doctor came in to examine her, pushing Jade aside. Catlyn submitted to his poking and prodding. Listening to the catalog of her injuries, it amazed her she was still alive. If it hadn't been for Maak's help,—and the Goddess Hecate's—she wouldn't be.

The doctor's eyebrows knit in confusion. "It's amazing. You're healing extremely well. You'll be able to go home in a few days. When I first saw you, I'd have said you'd be in here for months. Before I release you, I want to make sure all your internal injuries are healed."

After he left, Jade returned to her bedside.

"I'm so relieved you're getting better." Jade stared at her feet. "I'm so sorry it took so long to find you. We didn't expect him to take you so far into the desert."

"Where was it?"

"San Bernardino County, past Joshua Tree. It was beyond my range. Even Sean's technology failed."

"Where is he? Is he okay? I remember him fighting with Michael."

"He's fine, we think. No one has seen him since his captain hauled him from the hospital. We assume he's filling out reports and dealing with the legal repercussions. Sean's keeping your part of killing Michael out of it. All anyone else knows, including your aunt and uncle, is that you were an unfortunate victim Sean rescued. We're helping as much as we can. Very impressive, by the way, shapeshifting into a tiger. You'll have to tell me sometime how you did it."

Catlyn considered her helper. Maak hadn't wanted anyone to know about her before, and Catlyn doubted the sentiment had changed.

"Someday, Jade, I will. Once I figure out how I did it. I think I just reacted to all the torture and evil magic Michael subjected me to for ... how long was it? I lost track of time."

Jade gulped and turned away. "Over twenty-six hours. It took us twenty-six hours to find you."

Catlyn shuddered. The nightmares of it would plague her for years. She lifted her hand to reach out to Jade, but stopped with a moan. The painkillers were wearing off, and the numerous cuts, stabs, and other abuses to her body clamored for attention.

Jade looked back at her, moisture in her eyes. "Do you need more painkillers? I'll get the nurse."

Catlyn didn't want her mind dulled with the drugs and shook her head. "Jade, you did the best you could. We stopped Bho-Ahp, and I'm alive. It's all good." She smiled, and the bandages on her cheek pulled. Based on the list the doctor had rattled off, there wasn't much of her that Michael hadn't damaged.

Jade gave her a tentative smile. For the first time in Catlyn's memory, Jade appeared fragile.

Catlyn's eyes grew heavy.

Jade stood, patted her hand, and to Catlyn's surprise, leaned over and kissed her forehead. "Rest easy."

Now that the painkillers weren't dulling her senses, Catlyn checked inwardly for Maak's presence. Her lips quirked into a small smile when she sensed Maak still within her. She'd expected her body mate to leave once they destroyed Bho-Ahp.

Catlyn shifted in the bed, yipping with a flash of pain when she put weight on her hip. Bho-Ahp had slashed her—or was it Maak's?—flank during their battle.

"How are you Maak," Catlyn asked, "after our fight with Bho-Ahp? Are you healing from your wounds?"

"*I am,*" Maak sighed. "*I heal fast. The wound in my flank was the worst. By the time they release you from this awful place, I will be fully recovered. It stinks here.*" Maak shared an image of her nose crinkled in disgust.

That evening, Catlyn grimaced in distaste at the hospital's antiseptic scent. The sharp scent couldn't quite hide the other, less savory smells of death and illness. She rubbed her nose. Times like this, she wished she didn't have the enhanced senses that came with sharing her body with a four-hundred-pound white tiger.

Catlyn was becoming used to being able to smell and differentiate emotions and to see much better, especially at night. The biggest change she was still coming to grips with was the craving for raw meat—and catnip. Maak loved catnip, and Catlyn had found herself more than a few times munching on the mint.

A low growl of displeasure rumbled through her mind. "*Please, do not think of meat or treats,*" Maak complained. "*The food they feed you isn't fit for consumption by rats, let alone humans, and sick humans at that. No wonder the people on your planet stay ill for so long.*"

Catlyn agreed. Her dinner hadn't been substantial or tasty. "Can't you leave me to find food more to your liking?"

"*No. Once we merged, I must stay with you until our work is completed. I'm sorry you are in this awful place. I did not protect you well enough.*"

"It isn't your fault. I made the choice to stop Bho-Ahp."

A shudder shook her as she recalled the terrifying creature stepping out of the portal. His electric-blue eyes had held the power to compel her to allow him to have his way with her, which meant eating her alive. Luckily, Maak stopped his spell by initiating the transformation to merge Catlyn and Maak into one being. Together, they'd killed Michael and destroyed Bho-Ahp, for good this time. The daemon would never again plague this world with his evil.

Catlyn jerked as her left foot began to itch furiously. During her torture, Michael had broken every bone in it. She was fortunate the doctors could mend it and hadn't amputated it. Maak was responsible for that miracle, along with her healing as quickly as she was doing.

"Maybe I can ask Jade to sneak in a raw steak for me." Catlyn chuckled. Before joining with Maak, she rarely ate red meat, and when she did, she preferred it cooked well-done. Jade sneered at her preference and had tried to convince Catlyn how much more flavorful a rare steak was. "But that will probably make her suspicious. Do you want me to?"

"No," Maak grumbled. *"It is not time for Jade or the others to know about me. I can survive another day or two until you leave this place."*

Catlyn sensed Maak's presence fade. A few moments later, footsteps approached her room.

A nurse bustled in and brusquely took Catlyn's vital signs and noted them on her chart. She pulled off the bandage on Catlyn's forearm and frowned. "I don't know how you're doing it, but this is healing super fast. I've never seen anything like it. We can take out the stitches in the morning."

She lifted the sheet to examine Catlyn's abdomen. Her eyebrows rose. She gently ran her finger over Catlyn's skin where that morning symbols had been etched in it. "The wounds are gone! The scarring is even faint. It's unbelievable." The nurse shook her head. "Anyone else with your injuries would be here for at least two months. Too bad we don't know why you're healing so fast. We could patent it and help so many people."

"I just heal quickly." Catlyn shrugged. *And I have a supernatural being inside of me.*

The nurse checked the deep gouge in her hip where Bho-Ahp had slashed her while merged with Maak. She tsked. "This one isn't healing as quickly as the others, but even it looks like it's been weeks, not days, since you received it. Your doctor should be here in—oh, hello, doctor."

The doctor strolled into the room. He nodded at Catlyn and took the chart from the nurse. His eyebrows crawling upward as he perused it.

"So, can I go home tomorrow?" Catlyn heard the desperate hope in her voice. "I haven't coughed up any blood since this morning, nor passed any in my urine. Doesn't that mean my lungs and kidney are healed?"

"Let me examine you first before I promise you anything. But, yes, it does indicate you are healing." He warmed his stethoscope as he talked before putting it on her chest.

Even she was surprised by how little she winced with pain as he poked and prodded her. Although her three cracked ribs still hurt when she took a deep breath. "So, what's your verdict? Can I go home?"

"If I hadn't seen you with my own eyes when you came in, I wouldn't believe how badly injured you were. If you don't have any more bleeding throughout the night, then yes, I'll release you in the morning."

"Yes!" Catlyn pumped her fist in the air, then hissed as the movement jarred her sore ribs.

After the nurse and doctor left her room, Catlyn called her godmother. "I can leave the hospital tomorrow morning," she said as soon as Jade answered. "Will you come and take me home?"

"That's marvelous news!" Jade's voice brimmed with excitement. "Of course, I'll pick you up."

On the way home, Catlyn vowed to grill her godmother about the Sentinel Witches. Who were they? Was she one of them, and how?

Jade stepped into Catlyn's room, passing the nurse on her way out from removing the IV's and other medical equipment. Catlyn stretched, grimacing at the twinge from her broken ribs. A boot encased her left foot and leg. Even with Maak's miracle magic, it would be weeks before her shattered foot healed.

"I'm so glad to be going home!" Catlyn crowed, sliding on her dress.

"Hm, sweetie, you can't return to your apartment. You'll have to stay with me until you've recovered."

"But—"

"Unless you'd like to go to your Aunt Lucy's and Uncle Robert's."

Catlyn grimaced. "No, that's okay. Your place is fine. Robert will make my life miserable. I'd rather just go home."

"You can't live alone right now, and not just because you're hurt. Truthfully, you can't stay with your aunt either. It isn't safe." Jade snapped her mouth closed when the nurse returned and helped Catlyn into a wheelchair.

Once they were in Jade's big SUV and pulling away from the hospital, Catlyn asked the question she'd been dying to ask since she regained consciousness.

"So, Jade, the Sentinel Witches. Tell me about them. How long have you been one?"

Jade tilted her head and studied her for a moment, drumming her fingers on the steering wheel. "We are an ancient organization dedicated to protecting humanity from the monsters, demons, and other evil that goes bump in the night. I've been a Sentinel my whole life. It's hereditary."

"Does that mean Sean is too, because his grandmother is one?"

"Well, sort of." Jade merged onto the 405, slowing with the heavy traffic. "Although the magic runs in family lines, each individual has the choice whether to be active in the organization or not. Sean's father left when Sean was still a boy, and he didn't know anything about us until recently. But after this mess with Michael and Bho-Ahp is cleared up, Sean will be joining our organization shortly."

She paused and tapped her chin for a long moment. Then she took a deep breath. "You're a hereditary Sentinel, too. Your father was one of us. He was my partner, and I've been protecting you since you were born."

"Why can't I go home? Bho-Ahp is gone, completely. He'll never trouble earth again."

"We don't know what the other daemons will do when they discover who killed Bho-Ahp. The last time we managed to kill a high-ranking daemon was over 150 years ago. The civil war began a few days later, and we're fairly certain a daemon was behind the attack on Fort Sumter."

"Jade! You can't be serious." Catlyn sucked in fast breaths as anxiety threatened to overwhelm her. "I stopped a creature who probably would have pushed the world into World War III, and now you're saying I might have started another war?"

"We're always at war with the demons, Catlyn. Most people are kept in the dark about what really goes on in this world. I wanted to keep you from this dangerous life. But if you'd like to fight evil and protect humanity, we're offering you a position in the Sentinels."

Catlyn considered it, watching the business district buildings in Irvine slide by. The tallest tower caught her eye and drew her gaze upward. A huge sign blazed across the top: Drogger International. If the richest man in Orange County found out about her part in his son's death, she doubted he'd let it go. It wasn't only daemons she had to worry about. Maybe it was a good thing she was going to Jade's house.

Jade pulled into her driveway and helped Catlyn hobble into the house. Her cats jumped onto her lap. Their loud purrs vibrated her chest. She petted them for a few moments.

"I'll let you rest," Jade said.

"When do I have to decide about becoming a Sentinel?"

"Not today, certainly," Jade laughed. "But once you're healthy and back on your feet. If you join us, we need to put you into training quickly for your own protection."

"I'll think about it."

After Jade left, Catlyn closed her eyes. The Sentinel Witches had intrigued her from the first time she'd read that book she'd found.

"What do you think, Maak? Should I join the Sentinels?"

"*Of course.*" Maak's voice sounded affronted. "*You're one already. We still have work to do together. The war with the demons isn't over yet. The Daemon King has other nobility he can send to soften and ready this world for his rule. He is our ultimate target.*"

Catlyn recalled her vision of the High Priestess. If she must guard the portal to Earth,—and beyond—she would need Maak's help. She thought of Sean and Jade, as well as Eileen and Charlie. She could rely on them for assistance. They, too, were part of this war. There was no question of whether or not to accept Jade's offer.

But that didn't mean she had to tell Jade immediately. She'd make her wait. It might be petty, but she wanted Jade to fret that she wouldn't join the Sentinels. She hadn't forgotten the little bomb Jade let slip about Catlyn's father. Just before Michael kidnapped Catlyn, Jade mentioned her father had died fighting demons.

Catlyn had never known her father and had always assumed he'd abandoned her and her mother. *Why hasn't Jade ever told me about him? Who was he? Do I take after him at all?* The questions she hadn't dared even consider about him crowded her mind now the answers were available. One thought prevailed over the others.

She was a Sentinel Witch—just like her father.

WHAT TO READ NEXT

Thank you for reading Crossroads to Destiny! I hope you enjoyed it. The second book in the series, Descent into Darkness, continues the story of Catlyn and Sean.

They are initiated into the Sentinel Witches and a surprise, no one expects, makes their ceremony extra memorable. Their training immerses them into the world of magic, as they learn the spells to fight the demons. Amid the trials of navigating their new life, a new daemon crosses a portal and kidnaps Sean.

With the Goddess Inanna's help, Catlyn descends into the depths of the daemon's realm to rescue Sean. But the spells that opened the gates are failing. Can she reach him and return home in time, before they are trapped in hell forever?

Get the second book in the series to continue the Sentinel Witches' ongoing battle with the demons. Due out in August 2022.

You can purchase this, and all my books, on my website at ToraMoon.com or at your favorite retailer.

Also By Tora Moon

Legends of Lairheim (Epic Science-Fantasy)

Ancient Enemies
Ancient Allies
The Scourge Incursion
Exile's Vengeance
Redemption

The Sentinel Witches (Urban Fantasy)

Crossroads to Destiny
Descent Into Darkness
Well of Sorrows

Indie Author Guides

Business & Accounting for Authors
Author Business Plan Workbook (forthcoming)

To get an up-to-date listing of all my books or to purchase visit
www.ToraMoon.com

Thank You!

I hope you're enjoying discovering the world of the Sentinel Witches and Catlyn and Sean's story. There's more planned in this series.

If you have a moment, please help others enjoy these books too by leaving a review on the retail site where you purchased this book, review it on a blog, share it on your social media, or even just tell your friends about it. Reviews help other readers choose what to read and authors depend on reviews to get the word out on good books. Honest reviews and genuine word-of-mouth recommendations make all the difference. I'm not asking for one of those awful book reports we did at school. Leaving a review will only take a minute: it doesn't have to be long or involved, just a sentence or two that tells people what you liked about the book. This will help other readers know why they might like it, too, and help me write more of what you love. But please, no spoilers!

The truth is, VERY few readers leave reviews. Please help me by being the exception.

I love hearing from my readers!

Visit my website (www.toramoon.com)

Join my Readers Club to receive the latest news and updates about new releases, bonus stories, and more! Sign up at toramoon.com

About the Author

Tora Moon writes genre-bending fantasy and science fiction. She loves blending elements from various genres. Common elements that seem to show up in all her stories is a Goddess, shapeshifters, and magic. There is also usually a romantic sub-plot because love is an important part of life.

Besides reading, some of her hobbies are sewing, crocheting, and making wire wrapped jewelry. Human Design fascinates her, and she's using it to help her create more rounded characters—and to understand herself and those around her better. Her love of travel has taken her to several countries and saw her living in an RV for several years. She makes her home in the southwestern desert with her feline companion and caring for her elderly parents. Oh, yes ... she loves and practices Goddess spirituality.

You can find out more about her and her work at www.toramoon.com